Praise for *Outside the Ordinary World*

"Dori Ostermiller is one of those rare novelists
who can touch both the hearts *and* the minds of her readers."
—Diane Chamberlain, author of *The Lies We Told*

"The deep maturity of plot,
gorgeous use of language and deft stacking of three generations
of women dealing with life-altering secrets make this book's
label of 'debut novel' look like an error."
—Suzanne Strempek Shea, New England Book Award winner
and author of *Sundays in America*

"Ostermiller has written one of those rare books
that is simultaneously gripping and deeply felt.
Outside the Ordinary World will make you think,
it will make you feel, it will make you want to
grab those you love and hold them close."
—Alison Smith, author of *Name All the Animals*

"Ostermiller's lyric prose illuminates the grace
and resonance present in our everyday lives.
Outside the Ordinary World [makes us] realize our
broken families are families nonetheless, that
the distances created by time and by sorrow can be bridged."
—David Lovelace, author of *Scattershot: My Bipolar Family*

OUTSIDE
THE
ORDINARY
WORLD

Dori Ostermiller

MIRA®

Recycling programs
for this product may
not exist in your area.

ISBN-13: 978-0-7783-2889-6

OUTSIDE THE ORDINARY WORLD

For questions and comments about the quality of this book please contact us
at Customer_eCare@Harlequin.ca.

www.MIRABooks.com

Printed in U.S.A.

First Printing: August 2010
10 9 8 7 6 5 4 3 2 1

Dedicated to my family—then and now

Was there whiskey in the garden—

heat to cool
the blood that calls
to the blue wing at the edge of the sky?

There is that apple.
They don't say
how long Eve dreamed
of reaching

—her belly taut with the tang of it—
before she took.
—SARAH BROWNING

The way of love is not
a subtle argument.

The door there
is devastation.
—RUMI

PROLOGUE

I'M PACING CIRCLES IN THE FAMILY THERAPIST'S waiting room, trying to discern what my daughter is saying on the other side of that door. Hannah hasn't spoken to me in days, but she seems to have plenty to say to a stranger: I can hear the muffled inflection of her voice, rising and falling with some thick emotion, her footsteps beating the length of the wood floor. I time my own gait to match hers—step for step across the narrow, windowless room. Though I've never been taught to believe in purgatory, it must be a place like this, where we hold our breath while the stories converge. A land where we linger, mourning our nature like obstinate children whose parents warned them about the crack in the sidewalk, the fissure in the glass, the lethal fork in the trail.

The night my father died, a Santa Ana wind sent tumbleweeds as big as these waiting-room chairs across our yard. Lying on my bedroom floor, I heard the dry clapping of palm fronds, people's trash barrels bumping down the street.

dnight, the electricity sputtered out. They say we
w the exact moment of a loved one's passing: I
sirens, and in the blackness felt my body expand
as though it would fill the house. The weight of my guilt
pressed down like water—massive, immovable.

I got up then, stood on tiptoe to reach the secret boxes in
the upper corner of my closet and brought them, bulging
with contraband, into the night. It was almost impossible to
light the fire pit in that swirling wind, but I kept at it, lighting
match after match, holding each illicit letter firm until it
caught, curled and blackened in the flame, until the boxes
were finally empty and bits of ash scattered and danced across
our patio. Then I hopped the fence, joined with the wind. I
walked until an orange dawn bled over the San Gabriel
Mountains, until I could no longer feel my feet, until my
mother finally drove up beside me and told me to get in.

Until two days ago, I hadn't spoken to anyone of that
night.

Thirty years and three thousand miles from that history, I
can't believe it's come to this—pacing past the stacks of
Parenting and *Family Circle* while my thirteen-year-old, on the
other side of that door, makes her case against me. Don't we
all assume we'll do it differently, not repeat the past? We
believe with all our hearts that we can rise above the things
they couldn't. Sometimes, our beliefs blind us.

1968

WE'D BEEN RIDING WEST IN THE GREEN-PANELED station wagon for the better part of three days when our cargo trailer came unhinged. We saw it overtaking us in the right-hand lane.

"Look, that car's passing on the wrong side of the road," announced my big sister, Alison, who at eight was old enough to know. "And look—no one's driving, and it's going all wild!" We gawked, openmouthed, at the trailer shimmying beside us, swaying like a drunk. Fiery sparks kicked up where the metal hinge scraped hard over asphalt.

"Holy cow—our *things!*" my mother gasped. "Our whole life, Don. It's getting away!" Her hands fluttered to the half-open window, as if she might be able to reach out and stop the runaway trailer with her bare fingers.

We were driving on Interstate 80, well into Nebraska. A few miles back, my father had swerved left, to avoid three enormous hay bales bouncing off a truck. Apparently our trailer had come loose from the jolt, passed us on a decline.

Now it was a good bit ahead of us, threatening to rear-end a blue VW bus. My father veered into the right-hand lane behind the trailer and blared his horn until the bus jerked out of the way—just in time, before the trailer would have smashed into it. After that, there was nothing to do but tail it and wait for the worst.

"Keep your distance, Don." My mother's voice was as taut as a telephone wire. "The darn thing's going to crash. It's going straight into that cornfield!"

"Cut the hysteria," muttered Dad. Mom fell silent then, clenching her eyes and knitting her fingers together while Ali and I, perched on the edge of the backseat, vied for the best view between our parents' headrests. We hadn't had this much fun since we'd left our apartment in Chicago. I slid my hot pink Calamity Jane hat back on my forehead and held tight to my sister's knee.

We jostled onto the shoulder of the road, about twenty feet behind the trailer. Dust swirled around us, obscuring our view, and our father suddenly threw back his head and let out a high-pitched cowboy *whoop,* so unlike him that Ali and I burst into giggles.

As we watched the highway bend ever so slightly to the left, the trailer broke free from the asphalt and bounded over the shoulder of the road. It smashed clean through the corner of an old wooden shed before careening into a cornfield, disappearing from sight.

"My new bike's in there," Ali wailed.

"The wedding china," whispered Mom, placing her hand on Dad's thigh.

"Yep—everything." He slowed to a stop, the cloud of dust rising around us and filtering through the windows. Some of it landed on the skin of my bare arm, coating the thin blond hairs. Midday sun glared through the windows and we were quiet, each of us staring at the gap in the cornfield that had just swallowed our possessions. There wasn't much: my wagon with the peeling red paint, our bulky winter clothes and photo albums, some treasures from Mom's wealthy parents, Dad's fishing gear and medical books. We'd left all the ratty, secondhand furniture behind, since it had come with the apartment. The idea was we'd buy all new stuff when we got West. We were starting over with a better house, better furniture, better climate, better schools. We were going back to California, where we came from—like the song said—in search of the good life, just as the pioneers and our grandparents before us had done. At least that's what Dad kept saying. But this didn't seem to comfort Alison any; she burst into tears at the thought of losing her new bike.

"It's all right." Dad draped his arms over the steering wheel, the wild cowboy spooked out of him. "If we're going to be pioneers, then we gotta be tough, right?"

I loved the idea of being a pioneer, or better yet, a cowgirl. I could imagine ditching the old trailer *and* the station wagon, donning a pair of chaps and riding a wild palomino filly across every wide-open acre between here and Los Angeles. I didn't remember much about California, being only two when we left, but I knew plenty about Annie Oakley and Dale Evans, and I figured a girl should be able to get her start in one of the westernmost states of the country.

"Well, we'd best get out and see what damage there is," said my father, opening the car door. And then we heard the sirens.

Half an hour later, Ali and I sat on the bumper of the Ford watching as the tow truck hauled our trailer from the cornfield, as the police lights flashed and spun, as the brick-faced farmer, flanked by officers, barked words I couldn't understand. He wanted *collateral*. There'd better be *reparation*. And why in hell hadn't the chain been fastened on the goddamn hitch? His hands dove like angry crows around my parents' faces until one of the policemen placed a restraining paw on his forearm. I couldn't quite fathom all this fuss over a rickety old shed, a few dozen rows of corn. But clearly we were in trouble.

Dad gripped Mom's bare shoulder. He stood weirdly erect in his blue plaid shirt; even so, he was scarcely two inches taller than her. We were fully insured, he insisted, squinting into the glare. He was terribly sorry. In their hurry to get on the road, he must have overlooked the chain. The tall officer wrote things down while the other just stared at Mom, his gaze sliding over her green sleeveless sweater, down the slim length of her khaki pedal pushers. I could have sworn he even winked, after which Dad tightened his hold on her, the dark circles expanding beneath his armpits. I was pretty sure I'd never heard my father apologize before, and I elbowed Ali in the ribs, wanting her to take notice.

"At least they're not arguing anymore," she noted then sighed, nudging me back. "Move over, Sylvie—you're hogging the whole car." She was in a better mood now, having discovered that her new bike was still intact, little pink basket and all. Our things had been spared, in fact, except for a few glasses and the wedding china. When Mom picked up one of the boxes, heard the faint tinkling inside, she'd bit her lip, eyelids fluttering, while Dad patted her wrist bone.

Now Ali hoisted herself onto the hood for a better view, and I wondered if she was right—if the accident had put an end to our parents' bickering. Perhaps this was why God allowed it. I was six, and still believed God was in charge, directing the show like some capricious old ringmaster—allowing this disaster but not that one. This was God's Plan, I decided while Dad explained to the officers, pointedly massaging the back of Mom's neck.

"It won't happen again," he was telling them. "I assure you."

Still, it didn't take long for the bickering to resume once we were finally back on the highway, our dented trailer secured behind us. My mother argued, in her clipped, quiet way, that we needed a break, that we girls had been traumatized. The accident was a reminder to slow things down, she said, rethink our priorities. We ought to stop for some lunch, maybe end the day early and find a Travel Lodge with a little pool.

"It's hot, honey. You're expecting too much of them," she continued.

"We'll stop at supper time," Dad said, reminding her the accident had just cost money we didn't have, that we were now two hours off schedule, our budget blown to hell.

"There's no need for *language*. The girls will pick it up."

"And what are they picking up from you? That there's money to burn? You know we can't afford fancy motels—not yet."

"What about the park? You did promise." She was whispering, as if she actually believed we couldn't hear. Ali and I had started our own silent war in the back, over where the imaginary line between us was supposed to be. We'd moved on from gentle shoving and were grinding our knuckles, hard, into each other's bare thighs. In the course of our short stint as "pioneers," we'd learned how to practically kill each other without making a sound—stomping each other's defenseless toes, suffocating one another with our blue bears. We knew if we got wild, made too much noise, we were asking for it. Usually, it was me who got it. Maybe because I was easier to yank out of the back, throw against the hot metal side of the car. Two days back, in Iowa, I'd gotten a mouthful of roadside dirt for calling Ali a farty old pig's ass. So now I relented, slipping out of the game as it got too rowdy. But Mom wouldn't relent.

"It was all this rushing that got us into a fix." Her shoulders were creeping up around her ears. "Besides, you promised them."

"That was before we had to buy a damn *shed*."

"For heaven's sake, don't curse."

"Why didn't you use some of that feminine charm to get us out of a ticket?"

"I haven't a clue what you're referring to."

"I mean, if you're gonna flirt, may as well make it useful."

They ended by falling into a bulky silence, Dad drumming his fingers on the steering wheel, Mom heaving exhausted little sighs and turning her face to the window. After a while, she doled out stale peanut butter sandwiches and dill pickles without saying a word.

For the past four years we'd been living in the damp three rooms of an apartment in one of Chicago's shabbier suburbs. We'd been sleeping on someone else's mattresses, eating at someone else's green Formica table, watching someone else's black-and-white TV on their ratty polyester sofa with the stuffing spilling out one seam. Mostly, my mother and sister and I had been doing these things while Dad worked, completing his medical internship, taking most of his meals at the hospital, because he could. Sometimes, he didn't come home for three nights running. When he finally appeared, Ali and I were usually in bed. I'd hear bits of his talk as my mother poured him a drink, asked about his day as if she were entertaining an important stranger. I knew I wasn't allowed to go to them, no matter how many dark blue bats startled through my nightmares. I feared and longed for that prohibited after-bedtime world, ice clinking in his drink, his voice—as strange and ubiquitous as the moon.

I often wonder if her restlessness took root there, shut into three rooms during those Midwestern winters, caring for us by day, typing medical reports by night. She was new to the city and didn't have a car. She loved Dad, but how lonely it must have been in that apartment when we were tiny and whiny and underfoot, clinging to her knees. How relentless it must have seemed, one baby crying on her hip, the other running wild, tossing Tupperware into the toilet and trying to cut her bangs with the nail scissors, no husband in sight.

What else to lean into but the secret, infrequent lunches with her "special friend"?

A few days before we left Chicago, we had the last of those lunches, my mother, Mr. Robert and I, at a Big Bob's on University Ave. I wasn't supposed to mention Mr. Robert, with his gap-toothed smile, his Broadway songs and wavy, silver-streaked hair. During that last lunch, he bought us ice cream sodas, as usual, and we ate them with the heavy, long-handled spoons I loved. Then I colored on the place mat while they talked in somber tones.

"So you're really going next Sunday?" Mr. Robert asked.

"Sunday, that's right." My mother stared into her lap.

"Well, I have to admit, I won't be sorry not to make this trip every few months."

"I thought these trips were all about *business,* Robert."

"Now let's just quit being silly, Lainie. Just tell me the town, for God's sake."

"You *know* I'm not telling you this time. I'm just not." They were quiet for a while. My mother's breathing reminded me of the ocean at Goat Rock, when we'd last visited Gram and Poppy. Finally looking up, I was startled to see a single tear glittering along the side of her nose. She glanced at the people in the next booth, the bluish office buildings outside, traffic lurching past in the summer afternoon—she was looking everywhere but at Mr. Robert, who suddenly reached out and wrapped his meaty fingers around her wrist, as if to take her pulse.

"Is this your friend Sammy's silly advice? Why don't you just quit this game?"

"We need to let it go. Don't you *see?* This is a chance to—" She faltered, hugging herself as if she were cold, though the afternoon was humid as a gym sock.

"What? A chance to be foolish? Miserable?" Mr. Robert's voice seemed thin and stretched now, a balloon ready to burst. I wondered why Mom was being so difficult. I wondered why she didn't want Mr. Robert to find us, when he was so nice, and bought us ice cream sodas, and made her laugh like a man—mouth wide, head tossed back. I'd never seen her laugh that way for anyone else.

"You know I'll find you," he whispered.

"We need to let it go," she repeated after the waitress brought our check on the little red tray. Mom extracted her dark glasses from her handbag, slipped them on. I loved her in those glasses, which were huge and round, and made her look like Jackie Kennedy.

"I will *never* let it go," Mr. Robert said in a thick, radio-announcer's voice, as if he wanted the whole restaurant to hear. Into the startled silence that followed, he hummed a tune, his fingers beating out a cheerful rhythm on the linoleum tabletop. "Lainie, Lainie, 'give me your answer, do. I'm half crazy all for the love of you,'" he sang. Then he winked at me, as if somehow, we were in this together.

1974

THE NEXT TIME I SAW MY MOTHER'S SECRET FRIEND, I
was nearly twelve, and had just learned that Jesus would come
on a cloud shaped like a man's fist. I learned this from the
Sabbath School teacher at our Seventh-day Adventist Church,
Mrs. Sullivan, who kept her black hair wrapped around her
head helmet-style. My sister and I called her *Iguana Woman*—
she seemed that scaly and cool, skin pale as plaster behind her
bright makeup. Her voice was reptilian, too, as she whispered
about the Last Days, about fire and falling boulders as if these
things were secrets she wasn't supposed to tell. In the car on
the way home, Ali and I would sometimes roll our eyes and
snicker at Mrs. Sullivan's grim predictions. But I never forgot
the image of that cloud, its silent, impossible fury, the way
endings could surprise you like that—with a crack and a
flash when you least expected it.

I learned about the cloud on a dry June morning in 1974.
Fires burned in the Santa Ana foothills, turning the air milky-
brown and bringing the occasional distant wail of a siren. My

mother woke us with her morning song, her high heels clicking against the Mexican tiles as she sang, "Good morning, merry sunshine, how did you wake so soon, you scared the little stars away and shone away the moon." Her voice was clear and intrusive as a shard of glass, and it worked. By the third or fourth time she clicked by my door I was awake, anticipating the Sabbath morning hustle. My father would be sitting at the dining room table in his dress shirt and slacks, sipping his coffee, finishing the *Los Angeles Times*. Already, at 7:00 a.m., he'd have committed several sins against the church: the coffee, the newspaper on a Sabbath, the fact that he was not attending church with the rest of us but heading off to work. My mother never verbally chided him for his transgressions, but each time she swished by him in her buttery-yellow church dress, she heaved a small sigh, pressing her lips into a crease. He took no notice.

It was a Saturday like any other, except for the pungent smell of ash as we emerged from the church sanctuary, made our way across the blistering pavement. Today was potluck day, and Mom had decided, against our will, to participate. As she rummaged in the car for paper plates and cups, Ali and I stood staring at the sky, the brown columns of smoke rising on the horizon.

"Maybe it really *is* the end of the world," I said, elbowing Ali in the side. "Maybe Mrs. Sullivan was right."

"I bet our whole neighborhood is on fire," Ali murmured in the direction of our mother's bent back. "And our mother thinks this is a good time for a picnic."

"All right, girls, all right." Mom emerged from the backseat with her paper grocery bags, her red handbag dangling from one elbow. "Do you think you can *manage* being pleasant this afternoon?" She thrust the bags at us, smoothed her sleeve-less dress over her hips.

"It's a hundred million degrees," Ali whined. "And the food here—"

"Now listen." Mom looked hard at us. "There's someone meeting us today. A dear old friend, okay?" And before we could ask, she was strutting toward the meeting room, hoisting her pocketbook up her shoulder. She was the only person who didn't cower in the heat, didn't glance toward the blazing hills. There was nothing we could do but follow.

Mom's friend didn't appear until the end of the potluck, as people were gathering their empty casserole dishes, mopping damp necks and noses. Ali and I were lobbing pieces of veggie dog from the baked beans at each other when suddenly he was standing close beside us, crooning our names.

Though he'd lost most of his gray curls, he still had the same mischievous eyes and gap-toothed smile. He spread his fingers over Mom's bare shoulder, just as he used to. He wore plaid knickers—he'd been golfing, he explained—and she introduced him as her dear old friend, *Mr. Robert*. I started to say I remembered him, that we'd met before, but she narrowed her eyes and shook her head slightly. I took my cue and fell silent.

"So these are the infamous Sandon girls I've heard so much about," Mr. Robert said in his thrumming voice, dimples flexing. Ali gnawed on a thumbnail.

"What have you heard?" I pushed the sticky beans across my plate.

"Oh, secrets." He sat beside me, his cotton-clad thigh pressed slightly against my own. "Only your darkest, most dreadful secrets. But don't worry," he added, winking at Mom, "my lips are sealed. Isn't that right, Elaine?"

"Don't chew your fingernails, honey." Mom reached to tap Alison's wrist. Then she took my sister's hand and examined the well-chewed fingertips, tsk-tsking, as if to demonstrate what a conscientious mother she was. Ali whipped her hand away. Had she noticed the way our mother's name slid off Mr. Robert's tongue like heated syrup? Or the way Mrs. Dixon and Mrs. Alexander were gawking from the next table over? Mom loaded up a plate for her tall stranger, as if she expected him to stay for a good, long time.

"You don't come to this church," Alison announced just as Mr. Robert stuffed a forkful of casserole into his mouth.

"Why, no," he garbled, wiping his big lips. He used his own monogrammed handkerchief rather than the paper napkin Mom handed him. "I really only come for the bean casserole, which is, uh—exquisite." He elevated his fork and let a pasty mound plop to his plate. "I'm afraid they won't win many converts through the *cuisine*."

"Oh, Robert." Mom waved her hand round Mr. Robert's face as if to scare off a troublesome fly.

"You're not even Adventist, are you?" Ali pursed her lips, and I pressed her foot with my own. I felt sudden sympathy for our old friend, who had done nothing, as far as I knew, to deserve Ali's grilling.

"As a matter of fact, I'm not, my dear. But I grew up surrounded by them." He lapsed into a story about growing up in Walla Walla, Washington, where everyone was Seventh-day Adventist, except him and his nutty old mother. "It took me a while to figure out that the whole world wasn't filled with bean eaters—that's what we called them back then. But you girls don't look like bean eaters to me," he added quickly. "You girls look more like, let's see, butter-and-Karo-syrup sandwich eaters, maybe? Chocolate-chip cookie dough straight from the bowl? Or do you still prefer ice cream sodas?" He raised his bristly eyebrows as Alison rose from her seat and stalked off to join her friend Veronica at the next table.

Mr. Robert shrugged. "I have a teenage daughter of my own, you see, Sylvia," he said. "So I'm used to being snubbed."

"What grade's your daughter in?" I was hoping to atone for my sister's rudeness. But Mr. Robert didn't seem to hear; he was now watching fiercely as Mom gathered up paper plates and bowls, frosted hair sweeping the tops of her freckled shoulders. I would have thought him angry, but for the sly smile tugging his cheeks. My insides lurched. *Why did he come back? What did he want with us?* I suddenly remembered what he'd said the last time I'd seen him, about tracking us down, whether or not she wanted him to.

Since then, we'd had four different addresses, traversing the boundaries of the Greater Los Angeles Basin as my father completed his residency, went to work as a surgeon and began his own practice. During those six years, we'd gone from renting a two-bedroom, roach-infested duplex beside the Riverside Freeway to creating our own five-bedroom, Mexican-style dream house near the Santa Ana foothills, complete with inground pool and Jacuzzi.

"We're coming into our own, girls," Mom had declared during the weeks after our move, and I knew she meant more than those wallpaper samples she'd been itching to get her hands on. She meant quitting her job as a medical tran-scriber after tiresome years of night work. She meant the end of my father's residencies. Maybe now he'd tell stories again, chase us across the lawn and dig in the vegetable garden. Maybe we'd even go for drives up to the mountains, or down to Tijuana—just the four of us. And we'd never again have to load our things into boxes and shove them into a U-Haul.

As always, my mother's faith worked inside me and grew there like a sweet disease. And for a while, it *was* sweet.

"We actually should be getting home soon," Mom said now as she crammed her potluck things into paper bags.

"Your hair looks great long, Lainie," Mr. Robert observed. "It's the only thing different, you know."

At this she paused, biting the inside of her cheek. She had a canker sore just there—she'd been worrying it with her tongue all morning. "And *your* hair—"

"I know, I know." He ran his fingers over his sparse waves, the perfect pink oval of skin at the back. "Time hasn't been quite so kind to me, I dare say. But I'm hoping—"

"We really do need to get going." She resumed her gathering and packing.

Mr. Robert placed his boxy hand over my mother's. He wore a thick gold band on his ring finger, adorned with a single ruby. "I've only just gotten here."

"But it's late, Robert. And the fires. I know they're saying everything's under control, but the whole thing makes me nervous."

"All the more reason to go somewhere else. Let the firemen do their jobs." He stood, snatching the bags from her. "I know—I'll take you all to Disneyland. How 'bout it? I haven't been there myself since I moved north."

"Disneyland on a *Sabbath?*" I asked, my eyes popping.

"It's not what we do on Saturdays," my mother explained. "You *know* that."

"Ah yes, the Sabbath ritual. Let's see if I can remember… Sabbath School, then potluck or lunch at the club, then, let's see, home for the weekly call to Gram and Poppy, a few hymns around the piano… 'We gather together to whatsa-majigger?'" He boomed out a tremulous tenor, winking at me. "Am I missing anything?"

"You make it all sound so tedious." She slapped his arm.

"It does sound a bit dull, doesn't it? In any case, this isn't a *usual* Saturday. How often do I get to come to town for the weekend?"

My mother, sighing, pressed her hand to her forehead, as if to take her temperature. I held my breath. My father would soon finish his rounds at the hospital. He'd probably go to the club to practice his shooting and arrive home by early evening. He hadn't been to church with us in years—I wasn't sure if this was a question of faith or just scheduling—but he always made it home for the end-of-Sabbath hymns sung around my mother's Steinway. Saturday night was *family* night (after sundown hymns, we watched *All in the Family* and *The Carol Burnett Show,* sprawled on the orange sofa, eating take-out Chinese straight from the cartons) and I was certain he'd miss us if we were absent when he arrived. At the same time, I must have harbored a small, secret wish for revenge. *Let him be the one, for once, who waits and wonders,* I must have thought, for I felt an awful, deep thrill when my mother said yes to Mr. Robert, then broke into a girlish grin. "I guess it wouldn't be so very terrible, just this once," she said.

Mr. Robert beamed. Surely the good Lord couldn't disapprove of a little harmless fun on a Saturday afternoon. He even invited us to bring some of our friends. I didn't have any friends at the potluck that day, but Ali invited Veronica, and the two of them whispered and giggled all the way to Anaheim in the back of Mr. Robert's cavernous rented Buick. I sat on the front bench seat, sandwiched between the two adults, listening for clues; they spoke of Southern California golf courses, the impeachment hearings, the SLA and Patty Hearst—things any two old acquaintances might discuss. My mind sprang to what I'd learned in Sabbath School that day: Jesus would come on a cloud in the eastern sky when we all least expected it. We had to be vigilant every minute of every day. *He might even come today,* I thought, glancing at the mirrored buildings along the highway, the blurred brown horizon. What would He do with us if He found us like this, going to Disneyland on a Sabbath with a mysterious friend of Mom's—an old friend who had now draped his arm across the seat behind me and was brushing his fingertips against the nape of her neck?

That my mother might have a *boyfriend* seemed as plausible as the sun turning to blood. She was the kind of mother who took Ali and me to the fabric store every Tuesday, wallpapered the insides of her silverware drawers, ironed our father's dress shirts and had the house scoured on Fridays, in preparation for the Sabbath. She was the kind of wife who kept my father's dinner warm on the stove all the nights he stayed late at the hospital, who endured his absences and outbursts with a sigh.

Alison and I always teased her about being so perfect. The most heinous crime she could remember committing as a girl was cutting through Mr. Snyder's forbidden peach orchard on her way home from school one rainy afternoon. The one time we'd heard her swear—when she locked herself out of the house on a Sabbath before church, then stomped around the courtyard breathing, "Damn, damn, damn"—we could hardly contain our delighted shock. Even our father, whose piousness had turned to worldliness over the years, teased

Mom by pouring her a drink now and then, insisting it would
do her good. She always refused.

It wasn't that she didn't want things. I knew she'd once
dreamed of being a professional singer, and had the voice to
prove it. Each year, she was chosen as the lead soprano in the
Christmas and Easter cantatas at church. For weeks leading
up to these events, Mom's piercing, bright melodies floated
from the shower and the laundry room, even the produce aisle
at the grocery store. I could have recognized that voice anywhere. I knew it as intimately as I knew the lemony smell
behind her ears, the five moles hovering on her left shoulder
like a tiny constellation, her clean, bony fingers and the four
rings that adorned them—one for every five years she and
Dad had been together. I'd thought I knew everything about
her by heart, even the contents of her cosmetics cases, her
girlhood photos and retired longings.

But watching her at Disneyland that afternoon—she was
sucking sticky sheets of cotton candy from her fingers, trying
on every hat in the Mad Hatter's shop, laughing openmouthed as we rounded the Matterhorn—I had the sickening feeling that my mother was a stranger, that if I were to
walk up behind her and press my nose into her back, as I was
longing to do, she'd turn with a start as if I were some other
woman's child, mistaking her for my own.

As we were standing in line for the Haunted Mansion, Mr.
Robert sidled up beside me, looping his heavy arm through
mine. "Hey, twerp, bet you haven't had this much fun on a
Sabbath before?"

I flinched, resisting the desire to yank myself away. It
wasn't exactly that I didn't like him. I just didn't like how hard
it was to *dislike* him. He was silly and buoyant, two things I

could never have accused my father of. Despite my edginess and my sister's complete rudeness—rolling her eyes at his jokes, whispering behind her hand to Veronica—Mr. Robert was trying. He asked about our favorite radio stations. He bought us souvenirs, candy and Cokes, which Mom never let us have. And he didn't mind making a fool of himself—donning a French-fry mustache, performing a jig to Tinker-bell's ballet or impersonating W.C. Fields—just to make her laugh. I'd never seen my mother so giggly and flushed.

"Your mother tells me you still love horses." Mr. Robert's arm tightened around mine as he leaned down to whisper in my ear. I caught a whiff of spicy mustard on his breath, and my stomach curled into a hard ball, like a pill bug. "I'm an old cowboy myself," he said. "I'll take you riding sometime—how 'bout it?"

"Sounds great." I loved riding above all else, and was ob-sessed with the wish to own a horse, which my parents had failed to grant. Too dangerous, said my mother. Too costly and time-consuming, said my father, and besides, they were sure it was a passing whim—a typical little-girl fancy I would tire of soon enough. It felt eerie and enticing to have my dream acknowledged now, by this familiar stranger. I dropped my bag of fudge so that I could extricate myself from his meaty grip. He seemed to get the message and took a step sideways, but during the ride, I occasionally felt his hand resting on my shoulder, or on the small of my back, in a gesture that was comforting, and too intimate.

My own father, whose hands were small, precise and knuckly, rarely touched me this way. My own father needled and tickled, or slapped and spanked, depending on the occasion. Just that morning, I'd been blowing bubbles in my milk after he'd told me not to, and I felt the customary, sudden sting of his backhand, his ring scraping my cheek-bone as the glass toppled, drenching my dress. After I'd sopped up the mess, Dad placed his hand on top of my head, ruffled my hair—his way to say *sorry*—but never this strange, open-handed caress in the center of my back, as if he wanted to calm me, or claim me as his own.

By the time Mr. Robert left us at the church parking lot, the sun was going down, smoldering red through layers of haze from the nearby fires. Helicopters circled the pillars of smoke, their percussive beat filling the sky. Ali and Veronica had stopped talking about ninth-grade boys and were oddly silent as we rode home in Mom's Jaguar. In Veronica's drive-way, Ali begged Mom to let her friend spend the night. She clung to Veronica's arm until our mother said, "Not tonight, Alison! For the hundredth time, *no!*"

I couldn't have named my own dread about returning home until Mom stopped the car at the top of our street and peered at us in the back, a fierce, unfamiliar thrust to her jaw. Backlit by the setting sun, evening shadows sharpening her cheekbones, she reminded me of Pocahontas in my fifth-grade history reader.

"Please, girls, do not mention Mr. Robert, or Disneyland, to your father."

"What? You want us to lie?" Ali's eyes gleamed in the dusky orange light.

"No. I don't want you to lie, exactly. I just— Dad wouldn't understand, that's all. It might upset him to know that Mr. Robert and I are still friends."

Ali and I cast each other a glance.

"So, what have we been, like, *doing* all day, Mom?" my sister demanded, hooking her golden hair behind her ears, licking her lips. My own lips felt as dry and rubbery as erasers.

"Well," our mother offered after a pause, "we can say that the potluck went late, which is true. Maybe I had choir practice and you girls played with your friends in the meeting room." Her gaze darted to the side windows, like a fly feeling for an opening, battering itself on the glass. "Or we could say we had some errands to run."

I glanced at the souvenirs on the seat beside me—a Minnie Mouse hat, Ali's glass Cinderella figurine, a box of fudge with the Matterhorn on the front.

"We don't run errands on Sabbath," I said.

"Sometimes we do," my mother insisted.

"Like, when?" asked Alison.

"And besides, your *father* certainly does. He's always running errands on Sabbath these days. Actually, I really don't think he'll be home." Here she nodded. "We'll order Chinese, or a pizza. How does that sound? Hmm? Maybe we can catch an old movie on channel 7."

Neither of us answered. She turned toward the road again, hands braced evenly on the wheel, as if this last thought had given her the necessary courage to drive down our long street, pull into the driveway. She even hummed a few lines from one of the hymns we'd sung at church, as if this were an ordinary Sabbath afternoon, as if we weren't six hours late and the world wasn't on fire.

2004

WE WERE PLAYING ANOTHER ROUND OF "THIS OR THAT"
as we drove up the mountain, Nathan's sunburned arm braced
in the open window. Emmie was sucking on a pickle and
Hannah's hair billowed in the breeze, like warm auburn
snakes thrashing about her head.

"Okay. Would you rather spend school vacation week
shoveling horse shit, or eat three cans of sardines in a row?"
asked Hannah, stealing a bite of Emmie's kosher dill, then
beating out a familiar rift on the back of my headrest.

"Can you please say horse *manure*, Han?" I tried in my best
parental scold. "And ease up on the Phil Collins thing?" I
sometimes had trouble believing I was the mother of an
almost-teenager with ADD, though I'd had plenty of time
to get used to it.

"I'll go with the sardines," Nathan muttered, steering us
through Haydenville.

"I'd shovel, gladly," I said. "I happen to like the smell of
manure."

"Okay, how about this." It was Nathan's turn. "Would you rather spend a week touring the London theater scene with your buddies, or have one lunch date in Hollywood with Orlando Bloom?" This one, clearly, was directed at Hannah.

"Hmm. That's brutal, Dad. But I'll have to say Orlando—he's *so* hot." She shrugged as Nathan's mouth gaped in mock-horror.

"What's an Orlando?" asked Emmie.

"Ask one that Em can answer," I said.

"Here's one for your princess self." Hannah squeezed her sister's chubby thigh. "Marry the prince and live happily ever after in the castle, or eat hot fudge sundaes all you want."

"Why can't I eat sundaes in the castle?" Emmie demanded.

Nathan shook his head. "Just like her mom."

"You can't have both, little dude," Hannah explained. "Not how the game works." But Emmie, smothering her face with Pink Bunny, refused to choose.

"Your turn, bean." Nathan used our old, shared nickname—perhaps trying to release us from the morning's redundant quarreling.

"Okay." I sighed. "Would you rather live in a tiny rented duplex for the rest of your life, or own a lovely old five-bedroom dream house with a view?"

"Don't start," muttered Nathan.

"Anyway, that's too easy," Hannah objected. "It has to be a difficult choice."

"Well, here's the catch." I smirked at my husband. "The beautiful farmhouse is never going to be finished. You can own it, and you might get to live there someday, but you're going to have to spend every weekend for the rest of your life working on it. Replacing shingles and scraping—"

"That's *our* house!" squeaked Emmie. "You're talking 'bout our house, Mommy!"

"All right, Sylv, cut it out." Nathan snapped on his AM station, rolled his eyes. "You're supposed to keep it in the realm of fantasy, remember? It's supposed to be fun."

We were on our way to the paradise of Ashfield, where Nathan is renovating our own "dream house" on a picturesque hillside, only a short walk from the pond. When I tell people about the place, when I see the envy or curiosity steal over their features, I always add that they shouldn't get too excited. "We've been working on it for seven years," I tell them. "We might never actually live there."

We bought the property at auction. An antique farmhouse on twenty acres intersected by a stream, a fourteen-acre wood bordering a meadow and several neglected gardens that were once, no doubt, spectacular. There's a two-story barn that Nathan hopes someday to convert to a double studio. At first, friends came up to marvel at our fortune—how could we get this place at such a price? All we had to do was shore up some plaster, replace a few cabinets, rebuild the porch. Nathan estimated the work would take six months, a year tops. We took out a loan. We hired some friends.

Over the months, as the work got deeper and more involved, as Nathan uncovered the insufficient framing, the knob-and-tube wiring, the stream that ran beneath the basement floor, we started to wonder what we'd gotten into. What we'd envisioned as a simple face-lift quickly became major reconstructive surgery, then morphed into what Nathan called a "total gut." The money ran out, friends went back to their lives and Nathan had to return to his hateful government job.

Now he works on the house during those precious chinks

of time between parenting and full-time city planning. He goes on Wednesdays and weekends, and sometimes the girls and I tag along. For the first few years, it was fun meandering through hardware stores, dreaming over paint chips, learning to run trim. Hannah could wield a hammer by age six and was adept at using a cordless drill and level by eight. After she turned ten and realized that her dad might never finish the house—that she might never inhabit the cozy dormered room with its secret stairway to the attic—she became disinterested in carpentry altogether, and she and I would come up just to roam through our woods or walk to the pond for a swim. By then, we had Emmie, who is four now, and still too young to don a tool belt.

Still, we make the forty-minute drive every Sunday, except in the foulest weather, hauling ice chests and picnic blankets, our swimsuits in summer and fleece vests in fall, our blueprints and sandwiches and all the other accoutrements of hope. We go to give Nathan moral support, to experience the thrill of walking on our own acreage, of standing inside the shell of what could, someday, be our home. We go despite Nathan's and my ongoing battles—my desire to borrow more money, hire out the work and be *done,* always losing to Nathan's exacting pride, his refusal to let anyone tamper with his masterpiece. "How would you feel if I hired someone to finish one of your paintings?" he always asks. I've finally stopped pointing out that we don't someday hope to *live* inside one of my paintings, because I've realized that the house is Nathan's only creative outlet.

The foundation is repaired now, the framing shored up and the house rewired. We can't use the stairs to our bedrooms yet, but we can stand inside the vacant, whitewashed kitchen, pretending to warm our hands at the imaginary woodstove, gazing through the bay window at the view—a view that reminds me, each time, of the one from my grandparents' house in California; a view I want to breathe and bathe in, almost worth the frustration of endless waiting, the growing divide, the slow unraveling of expectation that is our family life.

That July Sunday, the girls and I, sick to death of waiting for Nathan to conclude his struggle with the sliding glass doors, decided to walk to the market. Nathan had requested a coffee, and Hannah needed balm for her peeling lips. Emmie craved a chocolate doughnut and I wanted nothing more than to be done with the whole damn thing—the blueprints and the bickering, the Dumpsters and even the fourteen-acre wood, which was full of blackflies and mosquitoes that morning.

Tai was sitting at the counter in the Ashfield Market, sipping black coffee and reading the paper, and if Emmie hadn't careened into his stool, spattering his coffee all over herself and him, we might not have said a word to each other. Isn't that the way these things often go—an accident, a chance encounter? You might call it a turn of fate—the architecture of destiny—if you're inclined toward the romantic. Either way, it's the oldest story I know.

At the time, it just felt like another irritation: Emmie, careening around like a tiny water buffalo, slipped on the newly washed floor and crashed into his stool as he was bringing the mug to his lips. He sprang to his feet, cursing. Coffee streamed down his fingers, the leg of his jeans, splashed across Emmie's bare arm. She plopped on the floor, mouth gaping, silent for a good thirty seconds before the wail erupted. I watched as if in a dream, noticing for a split second her perfectly white teeth, the gums as smooth and pink as a salmon, the tongue a small amphibian.

Then the scream came. I thought the glass in the windows might splinter. No one can scream like Emmie; not even Hannah as a baby could have held a candle to that scream. Finally jolted into action, I snatched her up, kissed the frizzy head, plopped her on a stool and started rummaging in my backpack for Band-Aids. But he was ahead of me, ready with a blue handkerchief soaked in ice water. He applied it to the reddened skin of her arm and she allowed it, this child who for six months had clung tenaciously to Nathan's and my legs, refusing anyone else's touch. She'd stopped screaming and was just whimpering now—the pathetic whine of a newborn pup. Hannah inspected the jewelry boxes in the corner, oblivious or embarrassed. There is nothing so mortifying as being almost thirteen with a noisy, obtrusive family.

"I'm so sorry," I apologized, indicating his soaked jeans, the soggy *New York Times*.

"Yeah—luckily the coffee here isn't that hot." Without looking up, he tended to the burn, dipping the blue cloth back in his water, pressing it to my daughter's skin. She watched him obediently, as if she were his patient, so I watched, too—the dark curls swarming over striking, olive-skinned features. He looked distinctly familiar, the close-cropped beard edged with silver, sinewy hands that matched a compact frame. Finally he met my eyes. His, behind wire-rimmed glasses, were fiercely green, unsmiling.

"I'm terribly sorry." I was starting to feel annoyed at his seeming refusal to absolve us. Hadn't he been around pre-schoolers before? Didn't he know these things happened? "She's always a bit wound up in the mornings, and—"

"How do I know you?" he interrupted. It might have

sounded like a line, had he not said it so crossly and had I not felt so incapable of being hit on. My frizzy reddish hair was clamped in a haphazard ponytail, I was dressed in ten-year-old jeans, muddy clogs and Hannah's purple tank top—the kind with the built-in shelf-bra that threatens to squeeze you in two. Also, I was exhausted, and knew I had dark circles the size of portabella mushrooms.

Eveline, the proprietor, shuffled over with a mop in one hand, a pink lollipop in the other. "Is she okay? I've got ointment in the back."

"She'll be fine, thanks." I accepted the lollipop. "*This* will be the best medicine."

"I have the lolly now, Mommy," Emmie demanded, her plump, violent fingers curling around the white cardboard stem.

"And I heard what you said about my coffee, Tai. So next time it will be *extra* scalding—you better not go spilling it down your pants."

"Ev, you know I love your coffee," Tai muttered with flushed cheeks. "Otherwise, why would I sit here drinking too much of it every damn Sunday?"

"Don't curse the Lord's day." Eveline shot him a scolding glance, mopping up the mess.

"I guess I'm in trouble," he whispered, taking the damp rag from Emmie's arm, patting the top of her head. "And there's no other coffee joint in this town. You have to— Ah, I've just remembered." His features were transformed when he smiled. It was a huge smile, insanely joyful somehow, despite teeth that were pointed and small.

"Remembered what?" I asked as Hannah crept up behind me. She tugged on the strap of my tank, then snapped it rudely against my skin. "Han, cut it out."

"You're an artist. My son Eli took your printmaking class. Vacation week, last year?"

"Oh, right—of course." I remembered Eli, with his sullen good looks and his insistence on too much red. And now I remembered Tai, too, who came only once to pick up his son and lingered awhile, examining my watercolors, talking about Paul Klee and California scrub oaks. I remembered that afternoon—how prematurely warm it was, how I had to open a window as we talked, how the icicles dripped onto the tin roof below—because it had a kind of thick, surreal quality, like this one. Even as I lifted Emmie onto my hip, unwrapped her lollipop, I felt outside my body, watching from a safe distance across the room. "You bought one of my landscapes," I said, ignoring Hannah, who was now tugging on my belt loops. "The one with the water tower—what *is* it, Han?"

"Can I get one of those jewelry boxes, since you do owe me, like, forty-five dollars."

"I owe you twenty-five, for your information, and I don't have it. Go find your lip balm."

"But it's only fifteen, and it would be perfect in my collection, and anyway, you said—"

"I don't *have* it, okay? I just brought a ten, so save your breath!" My daughter, who is normally charming in front of strangers, rolled her eyes, sighed with histrionic exasperation and stomped off. "She used to be sweet," I said under my breath.

"I know. It's almost criminal, the way they turn on you. Like bunnies with rabies. My son is almost seventeen—well, you remember."

"The sullen type."

"Yeah. A bit more than sullen."

"Has talent, though."

"Well, he loved your class," said Tai, toweling off the leg of his jeans with his kerchief. "I think he's planning to take your watercolor workshop this fall."

"Okay, I'd better get more red paint." I laughed.

"I still stare at that painting of yours. Scrub oaks in the fog—and that amazing old water tower. It's got this ghostly light—people are always commenting."

"I'm glad it's found a good home." The heat moved up my throat, spreading quietly as a curse. I've always blushed like a burning bush at the slightest provocation, giving myself away. "I can't tell you how many times I changed that painting—it was my last landscape." I shifted Emmie's weight on my hip, swept a spiral of unwashed hair from my eyes.

"Now *that* seems criminal." There was that searing smile again, and I found myself wishing I'd shampooed or at least put on some lipstick before leaving. But of course, I never would have. It's always such a feat just mobilizing the four of us on Sundays. And now I remembered Nathan back at the site, waiting. I could picture him on the other side of his newly installed slider, hands on his swimmer's hips, ready for a break. I could almost feel his impatience, his need for caffeine itching through those thick veins. It's a precarious thing, sometimes, knowing someone so well.

"I have to bring my husband a coffee. Let me get you one, too, since, well—" I indicated his stained jeans, the ruined *Times*.

"No, no. You're sweet, but..." He tossed the kerchief on the counter, nudged his glasses up the ridge of his nose. I was intrigued and repelled by his New York accent, the slow deliberation of his gestures. "Save your money for that jewelry box." He winked. "I've had way too much coffee anyway. Look, my hands are shaking."

"It's true, they are. At least let me buy you a new paper. I mean, look at it!"

"Tell you what." He tucked his lower lip into his mouth— a generous mouth, shapely as a woman's. "You can treat me to coffee sometime."

"Sometime?" I giggled like a girl, despising myself.

"There's that new café by your studio, the earthy-crunchy place. I think it's called The Wild Rose."

"Uh, it's just…"

"How about a Tuesday morning?" His right hand grazed the skin of my wrist—the same wrist gripping my forty-pound girl—his fingertips as weightless as the eyelash kisses my mother used to give. I felt a corresponding tug behind my navel. It could have just been a friendly gesture. He was a New Yorker, I told myself. People touched each other all the time in casual ways.

"You must have really liked that painting." I took a small step sideways.

"I'm nuts about the painting." He grinned, eyes creasing. "I'd like to see what else you've been painting, if not gothic water towers." I dropped my gaze to his left hand, resting on the counter, unadorned save the tan.

"The thing is," I stammered, "you mean this Tuesday? I'm pretty sure I'm booked." Emmie squirmed like a trapped gerbil, so I placed her on the wood floor. She instantly asked to be picked up again. "Go now, Mommy?" she said, as if sensing my apprehension.

"Any Tuesday's good for me," Tai pronounced, running a hand over his beard. "Maybe I'll buy another painting." He wore a faded black T-shirt, snug over well-strung shoulders.

We stood inches apart. I felt a chill creep along my arm, though the day was already sultry.

The world seemed to pause and swell. My tongue tasted sweet and slightly charred, and I glanced around the market. I wasn't sure what I expected to see, but it had occurred to me that the whole town might be watching, enraptured, to see what I'd do. Of course, no one was paying the slightest attention, not even the child on my hip, immersed again in her lollipop. It *was* a business opportunity, I told myself, a chance to make several hundred dollars, which we needed.

And besides, I was not my mother.

It must have been this last thought—of not allowing the residue of her mistakes to coat and complicate my every interaction—which brought me to the two simple phrases that would open a fissure. "Sure, let's have coffee," I said to Tai. "That sounds lovely."

1974

A FEW DAYS AFTER THE FIRES DIED DOWN, I GOT MY FIRST letter from Mr. Robert. Coming in from skateboarding one afternoon, I opened the mailbox and spied it atop a pile of junk mail and bills. It was addressed to Ms. Sylvie Sandon, Esq., in a bold, looping script. It began,

> Dear Little Twerp. I can't tell you how great it was to see you again, the apple of your mother's eye, after all these years. Remember how we used to eat chocolate ice cream sodas, after your mom picked you up from kindergarten? But Elaine doesn't want us to talk about that time, so we'll pretend we met just the other day, at Disneyland, how does that sound? Hope you enjoyed all the fudge! You seem like real cowgirl material to me, Sylvie, and I was thinking maybe we can take a trip to my log cabin up in Horse Country and go riding. A real trail ride into the mountains. We could even ride to one

of the glacier lakes where the Nez Perce Indians used
to make their camps…

Here he'd drawn quite a good caricature of himself—I
could tell it was him by the deep dimples and gap-toothed
smile. He signed the letter, "Love Love, Kiss Kiss, Big Twerp."

I took the letter to my parents' bathroom, where Mom was
preparing for a hospital fundraiser. I adored watching her
prepare for these functions with my father, loved to stare at
her slim, clean body as she picked out her dress, slipped on
bright, scented underthings. Sometimes she'd let me watch
her bathe, telling me stories while she soaped her stomach and
small breasts.

Then I'd perch on the bathroom counter as Mom opened
her mouth, applying eyeliner and mascara with the sketchy
strokes of an artist. "You never want to apply blush right
below your eyes," she'd say, "and never on the chin! Just on
the cheekbone…."

She'd been talking about beauty lately, selling Mary Kay
cosmetics in their pink plastic containers to Dad's partners'
wives, or women from church and PTO functions—anyone
who gave her the time of day ended up with a pink carton
of Mary Kay. Many of these women got recruited to sales
positions themselves. Mom's best friend Sammy had convinced her to sell the makeup, promising that if she sold
enough in a year, she could win a trip to Hawaii or Mexico,
a set of luggage, or the grand prize—a pink Mary Kay
Cadillac. "Sammy is unattached," she liked to say, "but she's
doing much better since Mary Kay."

A warm breeze pushed the scent of old fire and roses
through the open window. I was still clutching Mr. Robert's
letter as my mother struggled with her bra clasps.

"Give me a hand here, angel, would you?"

"Sure." I stood, slapping the letter on the bathroom counter. Her shoulders stiffened as she glanced at it.

"The mail came early."

"There was nothing else, just bills and—"

"What did he write?" she breathed.

"You can read it, if you want." She scanned the letter, her brows softening. Then she peered into my face.

"We need to hide this, Sylvia."

"Like the souvenirs?" The night of the fires, we'd come home from Disneyland to find the house empty but full of noises—television blaring, radio on—and the first thing we did was find a place to stash our souvenirs from Mr. Robert. It felt sinister and thrilling, hiding things from our very own father, like the spy games Ali and I used to play with our cousins. I had stashed my Minnie Mouse hat and glass castle on the top shelf of my closet, behind a stack of old *Highlights* magazines, but my sister refused to play. Before stomping off to her room, she handed her Cinderella figurine and box of fudge to Mom, who crushed them in the trash compacter, beneath a section of Dad's newspaper.

"No one but us can know about this letter. Okay, angel?" I nodded, holding my hand out for the letter, but she'd turned from me and was rummaging inside the bathroom cabinet, behind the Mary Kay boxes. I could see the naked outline of her spine through her skin. My own spine prickled uncomfortably.

"Where's this cabin he wants to take us?" I asked. She stood, clutching a tattered Kinney's shoe box as she moved to the bathroom door, quietly pushed in the lock. "He says it's in horse country. With Indians and glacier lakes."

"Listen to me, Sylvie, we're going to keep your letter here, in this box." She removed the lid, revealing dozens of other letters, bundled together with tight green rubber bands. I ran my finger across their tattered edges. She placed my letter on top, then shut the box and returned it to the darkest corner of the cabinet, arranging the makeup boxes before it like a pink wall.

"If you get any more of those, you just bring them straight to me, okay?"

I nodded, my mind burning with questions I feared she wouldn't answer: How long? I wanted to ask. Has he been writing to you all along? I wanted to know exactly when he'd found her again, and whether our trip to Disneyland was the first she'd seen of him since Chicago. I wondered if he would write to Alison, too, and what my sister would make of it. Would she be so willing to hand her letters over to Mom, or would she turn them in to our father, like a double agent? But I couldn't find a voice for any of this in my mother's blue bathroom, the muffled drone of Dad's news program seeping through the wall. Instead, I repeated my earlier question. "Where the heck is horse country?"

"He's probably referring to his place in Oregon. Why don't you write back and ask?"

"You think I should?" A gnawing heaviness started in the pit of my stomach, as if some small, famished animal had burrowed in to stay.

"I suppose, if you want to." She reached out and smoothed the hair from my eyes, her brow ruffled. "Now, why don't you keep me company while I fix this old face. Let's see what we can make of ourselves tonight." She patted the bathroom counter for me to hop up. We could hear Dad switch off the TV in the bedroom, clinking the ice in his drink, and Alison playing "I Am the Walrus" for the fifth time in her room.

Suddenly, it occurred to me that Mom's secret made us special—better than the other members of our family. Her love for me seemed as safe and contained, that evening, as if it were tucked inside the Kinney's shoe box.

The letters came every few days and after that first one, my mother always intercepted, handing them over in the silent afternoons, or placing them, barely visible, between stacks of my clean underwear. The envelopes were all postmarked "Orinda, CA." I knew Orinda because it was the next town over from my grandparents' house, where we vacationed each summer. Mr. Robert drew pictures of mountains and clown faces, cowboys and barns. He called me his "Little Twerp," and told me that he'd once been a cowhand, of sorts, before becoming a salesman. He wrote that he'd lived in London and had seen Elton John having tea. "I bet that would have given you a thrill, eh?" He said my mother reminded him of Audrey Hepburn, and promised that we'd take a real trip soon, someplace where I could ride a horse for hours. My mother repeated that I needed to hide these letters, along with hers. But I wanted to believe my letters were distinctive, so I began hoarding them in my own box—a carved pine jewelry box my father had given me—which I stuffed in the top of my bedroom closet. Once or twice, I sat down at my desk to compose an answer, but each time I felt utterly blank and exhausted.

I wondered if my mother's secret was making her tired, too. She began spending late afternoons curled on the carpet in the corner of the living room, a sweater bunched beneath her head. Sometimes she'd wake long enough to say hello, or ask about my school day, but before I could answer she'd close her eyes again, and soon her mouth would fall open crookedly.

I felt a little nauseous, seeing her twitch on the living room floor like a cat squeezed into the last patch of sunlight. It was warm as a greenhouse next to those corner windows, and the air was dense with particles of dust, like a swarm of sleepy gnats. My mother had forbidden Dad to put any of his things in that room, and except for her ebony grand piano, there was nothing but yellow carpeting and sun. More than once, I wanted to lie down next to her, but it seemed dangerous. I had a strange feeling that if I curled beside her, we might sleep for days. Instead, I'd crouch down to stare at the tiny rows of blond hairs on her upper lip, the freckles on her neck, below her right ear. Watching her like that, my cheeks and eyelids felt heavy with sadness.

Mom was usually fluttering about doing three things at once, filling out makeup orders or talking to Gram on the phone while stirring the red bean chili, laughing her high, musical laugh. Sitting in the Sabbath School room, listening to Mrs. Sullivan talk about the Last Days, Ali and I often heard Mom's clear soprano rise above the rest of the choir in the sanctuary overhead. We'd smile, then look away from each other to avoid laughing. Still, the sharp knowledge of her presence above kept me from becoming too frightened by Mrs. Sullivan's apocalyptic stories.

I tried not to look at Iguana Woman's face as she spoke about Jesus on the fisted cloud, focusing instead on her long middle toes hovering at the edges of her sandals, like drops of water about to spill. But no matter what I did, the stories sprang to life in my mind while Ali and I followed the other kids through the church lobby. By the time we reached the main sanctuary, slid into our second-row pew with Mom, my head would be bursting with pictures—mountains crumbling to crush the wicked, hair singeing and faces melting below hundreds of winged Mrs. Sullivans who circled the dark, holy cloud.

More and more often, during the summer of '74, I'd escape midsermon and sneak out through the huge front doors into a flood of smoggy sunshine. I'd take off shoes and stockings to walk barefoot between rows of empty cars in the parking lot, the bottoms of my feet scraping rough asphalt. Pastor Wilkins's words echoed down, sliding over hoods and windshields. The cars seemed to know some glittering truth about each person in church, and I'd run my finger over their paint, stare into vacant windows, discovering stacks of sweaters, empty soda cans, comic books.

One Saturday late in June, after fleeing a sermon about the Mark of the Beast, I peered into the tinted window of a black Jeep Cherokee and saw a girl I recognized from school—the freckled nose, the deep chestnut eyes—Theresa Chapman. Her legs were stretched across the back and she held a book with a half-nude woman on the cover. She made a face at me, then slid across the seat and opened the door, motioning for me to get in.

"Hurry up," she said.

"What for?"

"Get in. Hurry, before someone sees."

I hopped up, scooted in beside her. My bare legs stuck to the seat. She reached over me and grabbed the door handle, slamming it shut. The car's heat was stifling.

"Hi," I said feebly. "Can't we crack a window or something?"

"Nope—power windows."

"Oh." I nodded. "You look different for some reason."

"It's the dress," she suggested. "I never wear them at

school. Have to here, even though they know I sit in the car most of the time."

"I didn't even know you came here."

"We don't. My mom wants us to try—her friend Barbara comes. Part of the new Family Togetherness thing, I guess. Ever since Davey came back from the war."

"Oh. But you're not *together.* You're out here."

"Yeah, well." She licked her plump lips. "We support freedom of religious expression."

I dropped my shoes and stockings on the car floor, staring at Theresa's flushed cheeks and damp auburn bangs. She smelled of Dr. Pepper lip gloss and Suave shampoo.

"I'm not sure this church believes in *free expression,*" I said after a pause. "This church believes in the Second Coming, and Sabbath on Saturday, and not eating meat, or wearing jewelry or reading books like, like that—" I pointed to the Harlequin paperback on her lap.

"Oh, no one knows about this." She smiled primly. A cool trickle of sweat inched down my left side.

"Can't we at least crack the door a little?"

"What are you doing looking in people's cars anyway?"

"I just—nothing," I stammered, feeling foolish and caught. "I should probably go back." Cracking the door, I peeled my right thigh from the seat.

"Wait. The sermon's not over yet. You can't just stroll back in *now.*" She rolled her eyes, then began reading again as if she didn't care whether I stayed or left.

"Listen to this," she said. "'He parted her lips with his hot tongue, and she yielded, felt his calloused hands searching beneath the silk blouse—' I'm just getting to the good part. Should I keep on?"

I hesitated, thinking of Mom in church, fanning herself with the bulletin. *Our father who art in heaven…* I pictured her looking up, wide-eyed and grateful as I slipped back into our pew. Theresa smiled, exposing two large and shining front teeth.

"Okay. Read it, then." I hoped that being here together made us equals. We preferred the sticky backseat to a velvet pew, the warmth of our guilt to the air-conditioned church. I shut my eyes and slouched as Theresa began to read, trying to erase my mother's face from my mind, picturing instead the heroine stretched over some glowing bed. Theresa was a good reader—her words were pleasantly rough, like scoops of beach sand. I imagined the man's face as he undressed the golden-haired woman, his hands caressing her. Would his hands be gentle or cruel? Were his fingers soft and thick as babies' thighs, or knobby and crooked, like my father's? I pictured my father's fingers, quick and treacherous as they stung across my cheek, or suddenly tender, handing me a yellow rose from his garden, smoothing the hair from my eyes. Two nights ago, his hands had trembled as he stood examining the letters on Mom's desk, turning each one over, holding each up to the light.

I'd seen him searching her desk before, but never understood what he was seeking. Now I peeked through the wooden slats in the hallway door as he inspected each letter and bill, his hands beginning to shake in a way that made my stomach roll. Suddenly, I understood that he was looking for Mr. Robert's letters. How did he know? My heart bulged, and it occurred to me that I should interrupt him *now,* or at least call for my mother. She was in her bedroom, laughing on the phone to Sammy, saying, "Well, I snagged Mrs. Phelps from the school committee; she's already sold seven hundred dollars' worth of night cream…." My father began throwing open cabinets and drawers, tossing out phone books and cookbooks, growing frantic, then stopping as Ali banged through the back door. They greeted each other casually, Dad running his fingers through his dark hair. "I can't seem to find my reading glasses, sweet pea." He held my sister's shoulder, as if for support, and I ran to the bathroom, thinking I might vomit.

The next day, Mom hid her box of letters next to mine, in the top corner of my closet.

"You'd better go." Theresa had stopped reading and was staring out the back window. "They're out." She buried the book beneath her seat, smoothed her skirt along the edge of her knees. "I'll save it, if you want."

"Save what?"

"The book, dummy. You can come over later. My parents will be at an art show." She folded her hands in her lap, as if she'd just finished praying.

"Thanks." I gathered my shoes and stockings from the car floor, held them against the pain in my chest. *Something terrible is going to happen,* I wanted to say. "You live at the top of La Loma, right?"

"Last house on the left. Across from the orange grove."

"Okay. I'll call first."

People were coming out of the church now, drifting in nicely dressed clumps or wandering to their cars alone, shimmering in the heat. They seemed to move in slow motion, talking close to each other's faces, the women touching one another's arms before joining husbands, children. I wondered if they'd heard something in there to make them feel peaceful, or sad, if they'd hold it around them for a while or slip out of it as they drove home.

My mother always smelled nice after church, like warm, spiced tea. "What did you do with your good stockings?" She glanced at me in the rearview mirror.

"They're here, on the floor." I suddenly felt that taking off my stockings was the worst thing I'd ever done—worse than sneaking out of church, or hiding letters. "I was hot," I said.

Silence. Warm Saturday sun blasted through the car windows. She clicked on the turn signal, steered us onto Seventeenth Street.

"I didn't feel good."

"At least you got to hear Iguana Woman," said Ali. "It's important to know about the last plagues, because according to her, they might start up any second now."

I forced a laugh, wondering if Alison believed anything she heard in church. Did the stories unfurl in her mind, growing wings and scales? Ali was sitting in front, tearing pictures from a *Seventeen* magazine, searching for the perfect haircut.

"Hey, Mom, Shelly Freedman's going to ski camp next week," she said, gathering her hair in a thick gold knot with one hand, switching on the air conditioner. "God, it's roasting in here."

"Don't take the Lord's name in vain," clipped Mom.

"Shelly said they've got six really cool ski boats at the camp. Did you hear, Sylvie?"

"No. Sounds neat, though." I smiled at the back of her head, grateful she'd said my name. Beads of sweat dried on my upper lip, cooled by the stale air. Mom sighed as if she'd just been told she'd never win the Mary Kay Cadillac, not in a million years, and I knew I wouldn't get her back for a while. Outside, two women and a man walked arm in arm, their heads bent against the heat.

"It doesn't cost that much, Mom," said Ali.

"Hmm?"

"The camp. The *ski camp*. It'd only be for a week."

"No," she snapped, switching off the air. "We're going to Gram and Poppy's, like we always do." I wanted to push my nose into the downy hollow at the base of her neck.

"So how was church?" I asked as we pulled into the driveway.

"You've been sick three Saturdays in a row," my mother said. "Sick, *right?*" She jingled the keys in her lap.

"It's only a week, Mom," said Ali. "Shelly's mom's letting her go for two weeks."

"Maybe you should just stay home with your father, Sylvia. If you're going to get sick every week, or whatever you do, I just won't bring you, that's all." The pain in my chest crawled up to my throat and tightened.

"It's just camp," whined Alison. "It's not like I'm asking for a car or something."

"It's a shame, Sylvie. You could at least try to be good." Their dresses rustled as they got out of the car, slammed their doors, heels clicking against the concrete—*click click click* until they reached the grass, then silence.

I sat in the warm car for what seemed like hours, my mother's words ringing in my head—*you could at least try to be good....* I cried, hating her, vowing to be as hard as she was. I would punish her for this coldness. I'd run away, go live with Theresa and her family. Or, at the very least, I'd never speak to her again. I wondered how much this would inconvenience me, and I pictured the two of us walking past each other every day for six or seven years, turning our faces away, communicating occasionally with a terse note or hand signal. Still, I knew there was something different in her withdrawal this time. And I remembered how she had come into my room a few nights ago; I'd woken with a start to find her sitting on the edge of my bed, crying. Suddenly, the thought of her felt like a gloved hand over my mouth, a calm white suffocation. I gathered my shoes and stockings from the floor.

Inside, all the curtains were drawn except those in the living room—the bright, empty yellow room. The entryway tiles pressed smooth against my feet, and I heard my parents arguing in the kitchen, her voice quiet and even, his a straining whisper, now fading to almost nothing, now rising, breaking above hers.

"You know it's illegal to open other people's mail."

"Jesus, Elaine. She's my *daughter*. I have a right—"

"*Shh*. Please, listen to me. He's a dear old friend from work. You remember."

"I don't particularly like what I remember."

"I told you, we simply ran into him and now, I suppose he's just trying to be friendly."

"This is friendly? *'Love Love, Kiss Kiss'* is friendly?"

"*Shh*. It's a harmless little note. You'd understand if— I need to explain."

"Please do."

"I don't want to get into it now, with the girls here."

"Right. Everything on your schedule."

"That's not fair, honey."

"You mean *fair* like when you decide, at two in the goddamn morning—"

"How often are you even home before two?" She saw me

standing in the doorway, touched her forehead with one hand. "What is it, Sylvia?" Now they were both staring blankly as if trying to remember who I was.

"What do you want, angel?" Her hand dropped to the counter. Dad held a letter, which he slapped onto the tile. Then he pinched his nostrils together, turned his face away. He didn't look anything like the man in Theresa's book. My lips and tongue were too heavy to move.

"Christ." He snatched his car keys from the counter and left, rattling the glass shutters on the back door.

Neither Mom nor I turned to watch him go, but kept our eyes fixed on each other. She looked frozen, leaning against the counter like that, and I remembered how she'd woken me that morning, how she'd slid under my covers, warm and tickling.

"I just wanted the phone book," I answered, feeling the heaviness lift a bit. "My friend Theresa said I could come over."

"I thought you were sick."

"I told her I'd call, either way."

"Oh." She picked up the letter and handed it to me. I glanced at my name—*Sylvia Sandon, Esq.*—written in the familiar looping script. "Don't worry," she said. "There's really nothing in it. Just a silly old cowboy poem." She snatched her purse from the kitchen table, walked past me, then turned and smiled a little. "You'll have to wait, angel. Alison's on the phone." She walked down the hallway toward the living room—*click click click* until she reached the carpet. I knew without looking that she'd take off her shoes, pad across the yellow expanse and lie down in her silk dress.

I listened to the garage door creaking open, Dad's car backing out the driveway, moving down the street. After a while I followed my mother. She was all tucked in the corner, like a toy. I watched her for a moment, then went in and knelt beside her, curled into her curl, smaller than her. She draped her arm over me. We breathed together, fast and then more slowly, her warm tea smell in my dress, my hair. We disappeared, sunk right down into the yellow room, faded quietly like sunlight.

2004

THE SUMMER WAS THICK WITH PLANS AND HUMIDITY, and I pushed Tai's offer to the corner of my mind. Aside from my work and the perennial house project, there was Nathan's family reunion, summer camps and two complicated birthday parties. Emmie wanted a tropical pony theme with horseback rides and treasure hunts and fat slices of frozen pineapple. Then Hannah begged for a slumber party; her begging was insistent and rhythmic, every day for weeks, like water eroding rock. Nathan and I finally acquiesced, regretting it almost the moment her six girlfriends tumbled through the back door sporting nose rings and belly shirts emblazoned with the names of obscure indie-rock bands. They came loaded down, too, with sleeping bags, henna kits and iPods, teen magazines and nail polish, as if they were all planning to spend a week. They took over the entire first floor, camping out in the living room, scavenging through the kitchen for bowls of microwave popcorn and guacamole and extra slices of cake.

After a few failed attempts to organize them into a craft project, Nathan and I retreated upstairs, where, once Emmie was asleep, we lay side by side on the rough white quilt, our legs crossed over each other's, feet touching the pine foot-board. We listened to the girls giggling downstairs, talking, we were sure, about boys and crushes, and probably sex. Some of Hannah's friends were turning fifteen soon, and we speculated about which ones had been sexually active. Neither of us suspected our own daughter; she was still young, we told each other, occupied with girlfriends and music and dance.

"We could be fooling ourselves, you know," I said.

"It wouldn't be the first time." He glanced at me sideways through his dark almond eyes.

"I was nearly eighteen myself, but things are different these days."

"Yeah, and Hannah's not being raised in Adventist School."

"Right. But sometimes those repressive environments backfire."

"You know we're too permissive, Sylv," he said then yawned.

"Let's not get into *that* argument right now." I stared at the water spot in the ceiling; it was shaped like a canoe and I always watched it when sleep eluded me, thinking about the lapping of waves. The previous summer, during a rare, child-free moment, we'd walked together along the Cape Cod seashore. Peering at the lazy arc of the horizon, I'd said, "You can imagine why people *had* to explore it, can't you? It makes me want to hop in a boat and rush out there." Nathan had grimaced, his broad hand between my shoulder blades, and said, "That's funny; it makes me happy to be on shore, enjoying the view."

"Why don't you ever want to 'get into' anything anymore?" he asked now, yawning hugely again. I stared at him, noting his lack of urgency.

"Is it *me* who doesn't want to talk?"

"You like talking to your clients. Maybe I'll call and ask for an appointment."

"Why don't you do that?" I said, meaning it. "You could even take me to lunch. Remember lunch?" My mind flashed on the early days—before babies and home improvement— when Nathan would steal into my studio during lunch breaks, bearing moo shoo chicken and condoms and chocolate, how we'd lower the Venetian blinds, unplug the phone. I couldn't remember the last time we'd done anything in the middle of a workday.

"How 'bout Tuesday? Oh, I can't." He shook his head. "Planning board meeting."

"There's always something." I decided not to mention that Tuesday was my birthday.

"*Jesus,* why do teenage girls have to screech so much?"

"Do you think we should check on them?" I asked.

"Nah," he replied. "Let 'em have their fun."

We didn't talk any more about the swampy territory Hannah's friends might be leading her toward. Nor did we speak of our own sex life—how it had been weeks since we'd even touched this much, my left leg tossed over his right, my long toes reaching for his, pulling them backward. "Monkey toes," he quipped, teasing that if I lost the use of my hands, I could learn to paint with my feet.

"Why don't you do another like that," he asked, pointing to my landscape on the opposite wall—amber farmland, winter trees lifting their skeletal arms to a muted sky.

"Because it's gloomy and tired." I wanted to rip the

painting down, replace it with something brighter, something *not mine.*

"I've always liked that one," he commented as another burst of hilarity erupted downstairs.

"I don't paint anymore. Remember?"

"Come on, Sylv. You're just taking a little break."

"No, Nathan. A 'break' is something you choose. This is different." It irritated me that he laughed off my creative blocks, shrugged over the ache in my hands that had, of late, made painting difficult; it had been over a year since I'd created anything new, aside from the commissioned portraits that paid our grocery bill.

It had also been months since we'd made love, and I wasn't sure why, aside from the daily catastrophe of children and careers and housework, the sheer exhaustion of it, any spare atom of energy siphoned into the construction project. There was his uncharacteristically impetuous fling with the architect, four years before. At the time, I wouldn't have recognized him if he walked up to me in the supermarket—I was that drowning in Emmie's infancy and my own existential despair over how I'd paint again. Nathan had to attend a city planning conference for four days in D.C. while I wrestled with thrush, breast pumps and an eight-year-old who'd reverted to bedwetting—all this heaped injury on the fact of the architect's youth, the nights he didn't call home until the radio dissolved to static. Afterward, he'd come clean quickly, miserably, and I'd work hard to let it go. But there was an ugly block of mornings I'd watched dawn break in, curled into a knot of alarm against Hannah's sleeping back. It wasn't that I lacked empathy. Didn't I know as well as anyone that these things happened? That vows could unravel in a blink? Still, I'd always imagined Nathan and I were somehow exempt from that particular failing, that our blunders would be unique.

In any case, surely we were past it by now. Surely we'd worked it through.

Most nights, Nathan simply passed out on the couch, watching CNN, while I checked e-mail. The lack of intimacy had become routine, commonplace, as hard to disassemble as any rotten habit, and though we lay here touching, equally lonely for one another, I knew we wouldn't make love. After a while, he began to snore—a curse and a comfort. I watched the exposed ridge of his forehead, shrinking cap of auburn hair, hands spread over his rib cage. Quiet hands, calloused, sure as death. Back when we were still intimate, he'd bring me to orgasm almost always, in the lovely old goat paths of our affection. Then there were the nights we couldn't stand the smell of each other, mornings when the dry circle of his goodbye kiss threatened to choke all remaining desire.

I jumped up, moved to the tiny desk in the corner and turned on the computer. It was a compulsion, this checking of e-mail, sometimes with a kind of naive impatience as if I was waiting for something. I remembered how, at one time, I'd believed fiercely in the Second Coming, how I'd pictured it over and over until it seemed real—the spectacular splicing of the heavens, the cataclysmic light seeping forth, illuminating an open-armed Messiah offering total deliverance, or utter destruction, depending on your faith.

Was this what everyone secretly hoped for: the missing piece, unexpected good news, Salvation shooting down like the very hand of God?

Instead, there was the usual slew of spam. There was a note from Hannah's school about fall orientation, and another from my mother, asking if we could *please* plan a visit west.

She would pay our airfare, she wrote. She'd watch the kids so we could have time to ourselves....

And then this one, marked high priority from Tai58: it read, quite simply, *How about this Tuesday? Will be at the Wild Rose at 9, and will look for you, as I do these days. Tai.*

I must have read it seven times, as if searching for hidden meaning in the succinct lines, my ears going numb. I typed: *I'll be 42 on Tuesday. See you there,* then deleted it and wrote: *Where have you been looking? And what are you hoping to find?* This I deleted even faster, amazed at my own impudence. What the hell was I thinking? I tried: *Thanks, Tai, but there's no room for wild roses in my life.* No—even that was playing with fire. I knew it. I sat there for a while, listening to Nathan's deepening snores, the muffled teenage laughter below. The warm, soft closeness of the room was stifling. Thunder grumbled in the distance, like someone clearing his throat before the verdict. I turned off the computer, popped a sleeping pill and lay down next to my husband.

But the following Tuesday morning, my birthday, dawned unremarkable, hot and gray, the domestic rush and clutter punctuated by a small cluster of white daisies next to my coffee mug, and Nathan's barely legible note, "Are we doing anything tonight?" Emmie refused to eat her cereal (it was soggy from the humidity) and poured it into the hibiscus instead; then she proceeded to have diarrhea all over her new dress. Hannah couldn't find her leotard beneath the piles of clothes and magazines in her room, so she ran around the house muttering obscenities like a woman with Tourette's syndrome. The thermometer outside our kitchen window crept past eighty-five. *Fire weather,* my mother used to call this kind of heat. Though, in Massachusetts, you could practically wring the moisture from the air. Here, the heat signaled a different kind of trouble.

The sky pressed over our heads, heavy with the threat of thunder.

Emmie went limp as I was hoisting her into her car seat, making Hannah laugh at my badly suppressed rage, and I managed to spill my coffee at the first stop sign. My orange tank top was already spotted with sweat.

By the time I got the girls to dance camp and day care, thirty-four minutes late, I was biting back tears, feeling like I'd botched everything. The judgment came down like the summary of a bad TV movie: *forty-two-year-old blocked artist struggling to make a living, tenuously married to city planner also wrestling to make a living, explodes at children over socks and house-plants (which are dying anyway), perpetually late and haunted by the past. Is she on a difficult path, or just lost?*

But I was not lost. I was driving on the back road to my studio at 9:09 on a humid Tuesday, the morning of my forty-second birthday, and suddenly I knew where I was going. I took a left on Crocker, a right on Pine, turned down an alleyway, then pulled into the parking lot of The Wild Rose Café. As I checked my lipstick in the rearview mirror, the sky finally opened, spilling enormous drops of water across my windshield—they smacked the glass and shattered.

I had no umbrella, so I just ducked and headed for the door.

For a few months, I would tell this story to myself and to my friend Theresa: *I was driving to my studio,* I'd say, *and the next thing I knew, I was in the parking lot of The Wild Rose.* For a few weeks, I'd play the scene in my mind, like a movie I could rewind whenever I chose. There I was dashing across the parking lot in the rain, sandaled feet splashing in mud puddles, swinging through the café's glass door…. Over and over I'd wonder, at which moment might I have been able to turn back? Was it this moment, as I watched him in the corner, pretending to read the paper? Half a minute went by before he saw me, so I was able to notice other things—the white linen shirt and ragged jeans, expensive leather hiking boots clumped with bits of mud, newspaper vibrating in his fingers. He looked like someone from another life. His foot beat a rhythm on the bleached pine floor and I was still free to walk out, make another choice, until he glanced up. His smile was slow in coming; then it completed his face. Next to him, on the glass table, was a red rose, freshly clipped from someone's garden.

It was the rose that made me want to bolt back across the wet parking lot and descend into the warm safety of my minivan, surrounded by used sippy cups and forgotten socks, empty juice boxes and overdue library books. The impulse shot through me like an electric bolt. Then slowly, calmly, I made my way to his table.

"I knew you'd come." He grinned.

I squelched the urge to tell him how nearly I *hadn't* come, how even now I wasn't sure I'd stay. "How could you have known?" I asked, wiping the rain from my arms with a paper napkin. "I didn't even know."

He didn't answer, just shrugged and poured green tea from a small blue teapot into two mugs, handed me one. "It's jasmine," he said. "Try it."

I stared at the rose on the table, brought the mug to my lips, all the while picturing Nathan's white daisies on the kitchen counter that morning—had I put them in water? Had I even unwrapped them? I held the warm, sweet liquid against my tongue and closed my eyes.

"Nice, isn't it?" His eyes were gaudy behind those glasses, rimmed in extravagant lashes, an edge of bright amber around each pupil. "Doesn't wig you out the way coffee does." Again, I found myself intrigued and repelled by his New York accent, the confident hands on the table, the roguish smile.

"Did our encounter in Ashfield put you off coffee forever?" I asked.

"No, I love coffee, but just on weekends. I love everything I shouldn't have—coffee, cigarettes, wine, you name it. Just have to do it all in moderation or I'm wrecked."

I smiled tightly, resisting the urge to speak my thoughts: *And married women? You do them in moderation, too?*

"What happened in Ashfield changed me in other ways," he said, his fingers diving through his dark curls.

"Oh?" My throat constricted around my words. "How so?"

"Well, I never used to come *here* so much."

"And now you do?"

"Only on Tuesdays." He shrugged helplessly, pushing the glasses up his nose. I realized with a start what he was confessing; that he'd sat at this table, every Tuesday since we'd run into each other over three weeks ago, waiting for me to come in. I set my teacup on the table, hugged my bare arms. The café's air was too conditioned and I longed to be out in the cleansing August rain. Tai refilled my cup, and we glanced around the room, as if searching for the nearest exit.

He cleared his throat, asked about the summer art camps, whether or not I had a space for his son in the fall workshop.

"I know he's a pain in the ass, but I think he's got something, you know? Just needs some guidance."

"He wasn't any problem for me," I said. "Maybe a bit stubborn."

"Won't take anyone's advice. Mine least of all."

"Well, that goes with the territory, doesn't it? Isn't he about seventeen?"

"All of that. And going on forty, some days."

"And five on other days, right? Same with my daughter."

"The whole *letting go* thing stumps me." His hand shot roughly through his hair again. "How much, how soon, how to do it without totally detaching, right? Just to protect yourself from heartbreak." He laughed joylessly. "You'd think a Buddhist would be great at letting go."

"Eli doesn't strike me as a kid who's ready to be let go of."

"He likes you, Sylvia. There's hardly anyone he likes now, over twenty. Not even his mom." He pulled his lower lip into his mouth, let it out slowly. There was no getting around his rough beauty. I assured him Eli could come to my workshop, promised I'd save a space.

"But you could have registered him online," I teased, throwing him off. He laughed, splashing tea down his white shirt.

"I'm always spilling stuff around you," he said as I handed over my napkin. "Next time, I'll dress all in black, like a Goth."

"*Next* time?" I asked.

He cocked an unruly brow.

We were awkward then, chatting about the weather, the war—which seemed to be growing nastier rather than winding down.

"So much slaughter," I said.

"I know, I know. Enough suffering to drown in."

We stared at each other, shaking our heads, our attraction already tired and sweet.

"It's a crazy planet," I noted, at the same moment he was saying, "What a world." Then both laughed as if we were outside all of it, momentarily, looking in.

"Not that anyone has time to notice." He crossed one leg over the other. "It's rush rush, isn't it? Everyone juggling."

"Well, it's hard to find any balance, especially with kids."

"Right. But you have to. Because one day, I turn around and, *holy shit*—my son's almost grown, my parents are gone. I'm telling you. Gone. It all happened so fast, while I was, I don't know, sending faxes or something."

"But how?" I asked, as if really expecting him to have an answer. "Time will always win."

He uncrossed his legs, looked at me as if trying to memorize my features. I felt his eyes navigate my cheekbones, slide down the bridge of my nose to the uncomfortable mole beside my mouth. His hand moved to his own mouth, fingertips brushing his lips.

"Take off your watch, Sylvia."

"Sorry?"

"I dare you. You've been glancing at it every thirty seconds since you sat down."

"Have I really?" I looked away. There were too many people in the café. A student from one of my workshops smiled up from his notebook. A woman from the PTO bustled out carrying a tray of coffees, and my neighbor's daughter worked the register. All of them, ticking staunchly through the requirements of a day—as real and solid as cows.

As I unlatched my watch, slipped it into my black leather bag, I felt conspicuous. Had I done something wrong? Had

I betrayed Nathan already, just by playing hooky, pulling into the parking lot when I knew better, following an impulse because it had been a shitty morning and it was my birthday, after all?

Tai got up to refill our teapot and I thought about this birthday. Everything felt more treacherous and brittle, as if my joints were turning to slate. The night before, I'd noticed the faint but undeniable geography of lines around my eyes, gray hairs starting to spring from my part like electric wires—stiff, untamable, even more unruly than the usual auburn coils. *So this is how it begins,* I'd thought, *the slow unraveling.* I was feeling my body's inexorable descent, the slight thickening of upper arms, the now-prominent veins on the backs of my hands, just like my mother's.

I felt a stab of remorse. It had been weeks since I'd spoken to her, offering my usual list of excuses about why we couldn't come west—work, money, the renovation, how the girls had their summer camps and recitals. They were all good reasons, and she'd heard them all before. We hadn't been west since before Emmie was born.

Tai had sat back down and was talking about his work— he was a landscape designer who wrote books on indigenous gardening—and how he'd starting giving himself Tuesdays off, because he realized that work had taken over his life. He spoke in hyperbole; things were *amazing* or *wretched, taking over his life* or *totally omitted,* and I watched the thick bow of his mouth, wanting to untie it.

"I'm talking too much." He drew his left hand over his brow. "Sorry. I do that when—"

"It's my birthday today," I interrupted. "And I keep thinking *that's* why I'm here, because I needed to do something special, for once. Something different."

"Well." He leaned back in his chair, crossed his arms. "Where do you want to go?"

"To *go*?"

"Clearly we have to go someplace, on a day like this." He cocked his head toward the window. The clouds had, in fact, parted. Strands of mottled sunlight illuminated the steam now rising from wet pavement.

"Oh, I couldn't. I have so much work, and—"

"You said it yourself. You need to do something different." He shrugged and tipped his chair back as if he could take or leave this outing, but his eyes glowed like they would burn holes through the glasses. "You've already taken off the watch."

We were silent for a solid minute, regarding each other. I remembered twenty years ago, stopping at the Grand Canyon at dusk on my way across country: how I'd inched out onto a thin, triangular precipice that jutted irresistibly over the chasm, my legs dangling into blackness, toes tingling with ca-tastrophe.

"Listen." I leaned forward. "I'm just wondering, you know, what this is about."

"About?" His chair scraped back down as he planted his elbow on the table, cupping his bearded chin in one hand.

"I mean, clearly this meeting wasn't about Eli, or my artwork, and, well, I just want to know if I'm supposed to be feeling guilty or something, because—" I was breathless and tongue-tied, my words bumping into each other like logs in a jam while Tai just stared, those bright eyes unnerving. "Well, because I've got enough guilt in my life," I concluded, cheeks blazing.

He nodded, drew in a long breath, then reached out and placed his warm brown hand over my freezing pale one.

"Look, Sylvia, I don't want you to feel guilt. It's a useless emotion."

"Oh?" I laughed. "Some would argue that it has a purpose."

"Hmm. Good for upholding traditional institutions, I guess." He smiled.

"Yes, just think where we'd be without it."

"Everyone would be like me—divorced, no scruples."

"I wasn't suggesting—"

"I just find you sort of insanely lovely. If you haven't figured it out." He dropped his eyes to the tabletop, though his hand remained. My breath caught in my chest, stammered there like a cupped moth. "What is it, thirty-eight? Thirty-nine?"

"Forty-two," I said, face scorching again.

"Okay, then. Happy forty-second. We don't have to go anywhere after this teapot is empty."

"Good. That's good." Air rushed back into my lungs, a pulse in the back of my hand where the skin pressed lightly against his. I thought of Emmie's paper butterfly mobile, translucent wings beating toward the night.

"So. I want to know what you've been painting." He withdrew his touch.

"How about a hike, then?" My words seemed to vibrate in the café's frozen air.

For months I'd replay the scene: sliding onto the passenger's seat of a vintage maroon Saab, checking my reflection in the mirror as we backed out of the parking lot, sped away from the town where everyone knew my face. I'd picture us, tiny and ridiculous, climbing into the heart of the Berkshires on recognizable roads that suddenly seemed foreign, and maybe that's what I was after—a sense of life suspended, action without decision, the illusion that I could look down on myself calmly, as if watching a character in a play.

Only, I didn't feel calm. As we drove higher into the hill-towns, as Tai talked in his deep city voice about his child-hood and asked after mine, my heart vibrated in my throat. The light was impossibly bright through the sunroof, the sky painfully blue. Every bump on the road thrilled and terrified. It was the same feeling I used to get at sixteen, doubting the existence of God; the same feeling at twenty, trying a new drug or man. It was how I'd lived for a time—courting danger, putting myself in harm's way because I *could*. I did it, back then, to let myself know that I belonged to no one, that my mother could no longer control me, my father would never again lay his hand on me. Not even Jesus could claim me anymore.

At twenty-something, I also wanted to quell the mind-warping ache of having lost them—father, mother, sister, God. I wanted answers, and stupidly, thought they would come on the edge of a knife: on the back of some man's mo-torcycle, helmetless and wind-lashed, veering up Pacific Coast Highway in the dead of night; inhaling a line of white powder off someone's smudged bathroom mirror at a party; walking, walking into all the bleak, trashy neighborhoods of the city— East Hollywood, La Brea, Wilshire, Echo Park—just to quell the restlessness that required constant movement, above all, required me to apply to far-off art programs, then get in my car and drive through the hot eye of the country and beyond. *Never be still,* the ache said. *Never stop moving. What you seek may be around the next corner.* Around one of those corners, blessedly, stood Nathan, steady as stone, and he caught and held me in his gentle hands as one catches a bird, stills its frantic beating. For fifteen years he'd held me in his loose carpenter's fingers, fluttering on the edge of the continent, three thousand miles from where I started. I couldn't imagine where I would go from here.

We pulled into a muddy parking lot off a dirt road somewhere west of Plainfield. There was one other car—an old Honda with a dented rear bumper and Rhode Island plates. Tai got out and lit a cigarette before the trailhead map, then offered me one. I shook my head. I'd quit my pack-a-day habit years ago, after many crushing attempts, and wasn't about to start again now. He didn't offer to escort me over the enormous puddle we seemed to have parked in. I just waded through it, hitching my skirt above my knees.

"There's a pretty easy trail here," he said. "Runs along the river for a few miles. It shouldn't be too muddy, although—" Here he stared at my mucky feet in black leather sandals. "I guess it doesn't matter so much anymore."

"I know, I know. These shoes are ridiculous, aren't they?"

"Impractical girl," he scolded, stomping out his cigarette after three drags. "That's probably what your doctor father says—an impractical artist, right? A dreamer."

"My father said lots of things about me before he died. But not that, I don't think." I felt deeply uneasy about the work I was leaving undone, the distance we'd traveled, the sun inching its way to the core of the sky. I started chewing a hangnail.

"Sorry," said Tai, bending over to tighten his bootlace. "I didn't realize."

"Maybe we should go back," I offered.

"We most definitely should," he conceded and laughed, straightening up. "But it's your birthday, and you wanted a hike, right? Besides, there's an incredible view." He took me by the elbow, pressed me into the dark open mouth of the trail. "And you still have to tell me why you have so much guilt in your life."

"Isn't it obvious?" I followed him over a fallen log, onto a path strewn with decomposing kindling and last year's leaves. He leaned down to grab some of the thicker branches, tossing them into the dense woods on either side. I glimpsed the ample outline of shoulders through his white linen shirt. My leather sandals sunk into the rain-soaked earth, making a sucking sound each time I stepped after him, the warm mud oozing between my toes. Each time he heard it, he chuckled. Once, when my foot sank inches into the muck, he had to turn and tug me out, his hand lingering on my forearm before he resumed his resolute pace.

We walked the narrow trail in silence, listening to the river rushing through a small canyon below, the distant cawing of crows and sputtering of grackles, the summer breeze in the treetops, rustling of squirrels and other animals we couldn't see. It had transformed into a gorgeous, rain-washed Tuesday and I could almost convince myself that this was ordinary, that I was just enjoying my birthday with a friend, with no other reason for my racing pulse than exertion. Gradually, the trail widened and we began talking. Tai talked about his business creating wild gardens from indigenous plants and grasses. He pointed out and named some lesser known flowers and shrubs—Bloodroot, Jimson Weed, Trillium, Wild Calla—and told me how he'd had to relearn many of them since moving back east from California.

I talked about my work teaching art to teens, and admitted that I hadn't painted any landscapes for over a year, though I wasn't sure why.

"I just haven't felt much desire," I told him. "Or maybe

I've run out of pictures. Every time I start something, I come up blank."

"Does your husband support it—your art?"

It was the first time either of us had mentioned Nathan. I stubbed my toe hard on a tree root. "Shit," I whispered, hopping in place.

"You okay?"

"Fine. I'm fine." The truth was, I was struggling to keep up.

"You didn't answer my question," he called back.

"Well, it's not like he's offered me a cushy life where all I have to worry about is making paintings."

"That's not what I meant, Sylvia. I'm wondering if he *loves* your work."

"Does anyone love what competes with their needs?" I snapped, shocked at my own defensiveness. I was about to go into my tirade about how things change when there are two children and two jobs and never enough time or freedom or money—how nobody gets their needs met—when Tai halted in front of me so suddenly, I walked smack into him and had to grab his bicep to keep from falling over.

"Shh—hold still." He reached to steady me, placing his left palm against my hip. His back radiated warmth beneath the thin shirt, muscles tense, alert. "There's a great horned owl. You see it?" he whispered. "Right in the top of that yellow birch." I couldn't see anything; the sun's light perforating the leaves momentarily blinded me. I caught traces of sage (his aftershave?), the yeasty odor of sweat and cigarettes. I took a step back. Then, the sharp rustling of leaves overhead, the flashing of two enormous amber wings, and the bird was gone.

"How did you know it was there?" I murmured. Tai

turned and placed both hands on the bones of my shoulders, as if to unmake me. I could count the silver threads in his beard, the crow's feet radiating from each green-gold eye. My heart throbbed beneath my cotton tank.

"I spend a lot of time hiking," he finally said, the jasmine from our tea still on his breath. His glasses started to fog. "And sometimes hunting. But not so much anymore."

Then he let go of me so suddenly, I shivered.

"There's an amazing spot ahead," he called as we started to climb up a steep incline, and I followed again, light-headed.

"I should get home," I blurted. "I don't even know what time it is."

"That was the idea." Turning back grinning, a maple leaf stuck in his hair, he looked like a middle-aged Puck.

At the top of the incline, the woods thinned to a rocky outcropping overlooking a meadow, through which a narrow path meandered toward a small farm bordered by a low rock wall, a white-steepled church clutched in a stand of pines. A perfectly oval, emerald-green lake shimmered from the edge of the view, its banks dotted by the creamy backs of sheep.

"It used to be an old reservoir, but it's not used for drinking water anymore."

"It's so serene."

"Hard to remember the screwed-up world from here," he said.

"Yeah. My daughter would love it—she's always looking for the perfect, pristine New England scene. Funny, for a girl who likes punk and indie-rock, huh?"

"Maybe you could paint it for her," he said quietly. "Maybe this is the view that'll get you going again, Sylvia."

The wind tugged at the ends of my hair, and I closed my

eyes, surprised by the sudden urge to cry. I hadn't realized how hungry I was—for seeing? For kindness? I wondered if I would ever again inhabit that intuitive, rigorous place where art was made. Was it true that Nathan was unsupportive of my work? And did such wondering explain why I was tromping through the Berkshire woods on a weekday, behind a near stranger who smelled like sage? What the hell was I playing at? I felt myself pulled backward into an old, peculiar dream—my body shrinking and expanding at the same time so that I could no longer tell what size I was.

I was startled by Tai's hand in the small of my back.

"Let's get you home," he said.

"Do you come up here a lot?" I asked as we started down the trail.

He turned and smirked at me before replying, "Oh, yeah, I bring all my married girlfriends to this spot." There was an edge to his voice I hadn't yet heard, and my back stiffened. Had I irked him? Was this supposed to be funny? I also didn't know how much time had passed since the café, and was again anxious about the hour, picking up the girls. It occurred to me—not for the first time today—that I'd have to make something up about where I'd been, how I'd spent the morning of my birthday. Or maybe I didn't have to lie; it wasn't as if anything had *really* happened. Relief rushed in as I realized I could still get the girls by three, run to the grocery store, set the table for our dinner with perfect equanimity—

"I don't know why I'm acting like a prick." Tai had stopped in front of me again and was reaching out, his face too near. "It's just…you throw me off balance." He took hold of my upper arms, as if to steady himself.

"Is that right?" And then he was pulling me in and—*Jesus*—kissing my collarbones. Half a dozen impulses shot through: I wanted to shriek, kick him in the shins, dissolve into his smell. Instead, I held my breath, watching myself fall right through my life, floorboards splintering. I don't know how long before his lips found my mouth, his tongue unraveling me, the unfamiliar beard scratching my cheeks, solid hip bones pressed to mine. His tongue was warm, not cool like Nathan's, and tasted of smoke, black tea, Granny Smith apples. Suddenly I was fourteen and hungry, devouring the salty tang of my first boyfriend's lips before the waiting school bus. I grew dizzy, my heart thumping so absurdly it might have beat its way through my breast had his hand not suddenly been cupped there. His thigh wedged between my legs, I sensed the inevitable, terrifying tension at his groin. Finally pulling back, we both breathed hard, touching each other's faces, laughing like idiot children who have found themselves in an amusing amount of trouble.

Then I started to shake, so violently I could barely stand.

"Shh—it's okay." He pressed my hand like a leaf between his, guiding me down the trail.

I was trembling like an addict as I stumbled after him, my thoughts feral and haphazard—predestination, species extinction. The last plagues—how many were there again? What were they called? I was spinning through climate change, brush fires, my father's car on fire, how my mother and I stole off with her lover on an August morning like this one...how the sun turns to blood before it's too late. My brain had come unhinged. It was five, maybe ten minutes before I realized I was apologizing. "I'm sorry," I was whispering. "I'm sorry."

"It's okay," Tai said again. "It's okay, Sylvia." And then he just kept saying it like a mantra, as if, through repetition, it would become true.

★ ★ ★

Riding down the highway, my face tilted toward the open window, I closed my eyes against the day. Wind tangled deep in my hair, my hand nesting in the open hand of a stranger, I understood that this was *it,* the sum total of our mini-relationship—a mishap that we would avoid repeating, and never, ever speak of. We'd see each other and smile ruefully. We'd talk of our children. But there was that thumb caressing my palm, just so, the heat in my solar plexus, the cool breeze against my throat.

Slipping finally into the minivan, I wondered at this life—accountable to no one until the three o'clock pickup, when I'd wander back like a sleepwalker and stare at my children, as if for the first time in weeks. There was that same funny mole on Hannah's left check, new breasts beneath her thin nylon tee. There was Emmie's unruly cowlick, plump elbows and sweet apricot smell. There, the buckling driveway, the annoying hydrangea that needs transplanting and all Nathan's enormous old shoes heaped by the back door. The answering machine flashed like an emergency, the bills piled on the table. All of it, still waiting. I turned on PBS for the girls, climbed upstairs to my bedroom, suddenly exhausted.

An hour later, or maybe two, Nathan slammed the back door, loaded down with birthday cake and takeout, and woke me in the midst of dreaming. I sat bolt upright on the edge of the bed, disoriented in the afternoon light and soaked with sweat, my heart galloping wildly into the past, or away from it; I couldn't have said which if my life depended on it.

1974

AS A PRESCHOOLER, I BELIEVED THAT MY GRANDPARENTS'
house was Eden, the original home of Adam and Eve,
because my cousin Nick told me so. We'd been in Poppy's
orchard at the time, and Nick had plucked a pomegranate to
illustrate, peeling back its leathery red skin with the blade of
his pocketknife. "See," he said, handing me the strange, be-
jeweled fruit. "This is the very same pomegranate tree that
got Eve kicked out of Paradise—try some." And when I hesitated, he added, "It's okay. The damage has already been
done." I popped one of the tiny crimson seeds into my
mouth, feeling its sour snap against my teeth.

Nick was four years older, and I believed everything he said.
Besides, why shouldn't it be true? What better place to begin
the work of creation than here, in the lap of these shining
gold hills, surrounded by ancient scrub oaks and wild California poppies?

We called my grandparents' twelve hilly acres "Orchard
Hill," as if it were an old plantation. Though my mother had

moved from Lafayette at nineteen, when she married Dad, she referred to Orchard Hill as *home*. She said the word as one might utter a prayer, or the name of a deceased loved one, and I understood. Gram and Poppy's sprawling California ranch was home to me, too, though my family had never actually lived there. We'd lived in Riverside and East L.A., Chicago and Oak Park, Tustin and Long Beach and finally, Santa Ana, as we followed the arc of my father's brilliant career. But every summer there was Orchard Hill—Poppy perennially hosing down his Mexican tile patio and recalling the war. Gram refilling her hummingbird feeders under the thick eaves of the veranda, or quoting from the New Testament while pies rose in the oven. Each year, Ali and I wandered up the dirt hill and climbed our favorite redwoods to spy on distant neighbors. Each year, we lay by Uncle Peter's pool with our cousin Sheila, or blazed the fire roads on the back of Nick's dirt bike. It was as if Orchard Hill was safe from the transience and bustle of ordinary time.

Their place was so safe, so private, my mother had decided to keep some of her own precious things there—her old mink stole, her wedding gown and a flock of prom dresses from high school. Every summer, she'd try them on for me, slipping the dresses from padded satin hangers, unfolding the minks from faded tissue paper. Even though the dresses were left over from the fifties, starchy as wrapping paper, they took my breath away. My mother had made them by hand, from expensive pastel taffetas, raw silks and tulles, with neat little bodices and extravagant skirts. Looking at them, I could easily imagine her at fifteen, when she first met Dad at their Seventh-day Adventist boarding school in Stockton.

She was a sophomore and he a senior when they met in the lobby of the girls' dormitory, where he was sitting on the chintz love seat waiting for his fiancée—a buxom almond farmer's daughter named Vivian who always kept him waiting while she exhaustively applied makeup and fussed with her platinum hair. Sometimes Viv would send down her little sister or a girlfriend to occupy her date while she preened. On this particular Friday, she sent Elaine, who roomed across the hall, because she was the only girl available. According to my mother, Viv grabbed her by the wrist as she was going out to vespers, saying, "Don Sandon is down there—can you be a doll and go chitchat with him for ten minutes?" So great was Vivian's confidence, she never imagined that her lateness, on this day, would cost her a fiancé. Elaine, coming down the stairs in her peach taffeta, felt suddenly shy before the somber boy with the glacier-blue eyes. Everyone knew about Don Sandon, about his red-winged temper, his Nebraska farming roots, his father who took off when Don was just nine. Everyone knew he was senior class president, head of the debate team and could handle a shotgun. Everyone knew about his plans to be a surgeon.

Short and slight as he was, people stayed out of my father's way. Elaine, feeling incapable of polite banter, simply sat at the piano near him and played a flawless and tender rendition of Debussy's "Clair de Lune." When she was done, he asked her to play it again, and then again. As she finished the third performance, her auburn hair had ruffled from its chignon and her cheeks were vivid. According to my father, when Viv came down a moment later, he couldn't look her in the eye. By the end of the week, he'd called off the engagement.

I liked hearing about how my mother had to extricate herself from Ronald Forsyth—the other boy who'd been hot on her heels—and how the boys had fought over her.

How beefy Ronald had fractured my father's arm, though not before getting his front teeth knocked out. I loved hearing about the first time Mom brought Dad home one Easter Sunday to meet her parents: he drove her through the Lafayette hills in a borrowed Ford with smoke snaking out the back, his bandaged left arm braced in the window, accidentally backing over my grandfather's prizewinning azaleas while trying to park. It took months before Poppy would speak his name, instead calling him *hey you,* or *pip-squeak.*

Poppy, tanned and oxlike in his Bermuda shorts, had inspected his bruised plants, sniffing the foul exhaust, while my father—six inches shorter and skinny as a barn cat—muttered and kicked the ground before this big man who was everything Dad aspired to be: a self-made surgeon with farming roots who had beat poverty; a man's man who could grow a garden, lay an oak floor and track down a buck. Picturing Dad on the day of the squashed azaleas always filled me with secret pleasure, knowing he'd once been just as terrified of someone as I was of him.

I could imagine, too, how Mom must have felt, at fifteen, falling for a boy of whom her beloved father disapproved. I could feel the fast tightening in the back of her throat, the first taste of rebellion mixed with real terror. This was the father who whipped the backs of her knees with a dog leash, the war hero who taught her how to shoot a .22 and skin a rabbit, the man who had nearly disowned his own son—my uncle Peter—for smoking cigarettes in the school palm trees. The blood must have roared in my mother's ears the day she announced that she was going to marry Don Sandon, with or without my grandfather's consent, consent which Poppy denied after giving Dad a physical exam. "His testes are too small for siring children," Poppy had announced. "No daughter of mine is going to marry a man with undersized balls!" Incensed, she went ahead with her wedding plans.

In fact, until the summer of '74, Mom's one obvious trespass. She'd paid for it dearly—for the first few years of their marriage, Poppy had refused them any help, despite their poverty and my Gram's attempts to intercede.

Things had improved some between them over the years, in part because Poppy knew he was my father's idol. That Friday in late June, they sat in my grandfather's den watching the Watergate coverage with Uncle Peter and organizing their fishing gear for an angling trip. Poppy and Dad would leave in the morning, spend a few nights in the Sierras and be back for the annual July Fourth celebration.

It was the same every year. The men and boys watched TV while the women and girls collected in the kitchen, talking and pitting peaches, pounding dough, shelling peas. I was always amazed by how nimbly my mother slid into this role. Before our suitcases were even unpacked, she'd be dicing onions for the veggie meatloaf. Now she was well into the rhubarb pie, gossiping with Aunt Janie about girlfriends from church school and nodding at Gram's disapproval of the new preacher's wife, who wore too much makeup and who Lolly Schaef had spotted at the mall one Sabbath afternoon.

"Well, what was *Lolly* doing at the mall on Sabbath?" gasped Janie. Mom clicked her tongue in agreement, as if going shopping on Sabbath was among the worst indiscretions she could imagine, as if she wasn't concealing an arsenal of letters in the top of her daughter's closet.

In previous years, I'd tire of this feminine bustle and banter and would sneak in to join the men. Usually, I'd end up in my grandfather's lap, perched on the shiny brown skin of his knees, breathing in his smell of oak leaves, leather and beeswax. Despite Poppy's gruffness, I felt a familiar ease with him that I'd never felt with my father. It made me proud to have such a difficult grandfather who nevertheless treated me kindly. Still, the things men watched on TV bored me, and soon I'd be wandering back into the kitchen like a migratory bird. Back and forth, back and forth, each time unsure of my place, or which alliance I wished to be included in.

This year, for the first time, I felt I had no choice: the womanly repartee suddenly seemed like a code I needed to crack. I was staring at the energy in Mom's hands as she shaped the crust, her eyes darting to the clock as she placed the pie in the oven. Now there were piles of fresh beans to trim, and the men's lemonade glasses needed refilling, but my mother simply unfastened her apron, rinsed her hands. Still glancing at the clock over the stove, she said, "I guess I'll just run to the store now to get a few things."

"What on earth could you need to get, Elaine?" Gram asked, staring over the tops of her spectacles. "We have enough food here for God's army."

"You're getting low on butter," Mom explained, gathering her purse from the table. "And I forgot face cream—I can't get through the weekend without face cream."

"But it's almost Sabbath." Gram tilted her head toward the glass door, through which the hills blazed in afternoon sunlight. I'd heard stories about the early days of their marriage, when Gram wouldn't even flip a light switch or draw a bath after Friday sundown. "Besides, I have plenty of cream," she added. "Don't go wasting money and gasoline on stuff you don't need."

"It's okay, Mom," Elaine said breathlessly. "I've got a special brand I like. I'll take Poppy's convertible. You girls going for a dip in the pool before dinner?"

Ali and I shot each other a glance; of course we wanted to swim with our cousins, but there was something about the way our mother stood, bouncing on the balls of her feet, one hand jingling the car keys. There was something about the tremor in her voice, the eyes jumping to the clock. Even if we hadn't known that Mom never used any cream on her face but Mary Kay (which wasn't sold in stores) we still would have understood that something was up.

"We'll come with you," I blurted, grabbing Ali's arm before she had time to protest.

Mom hesitated a second too long. "Well, you certainly don't *have* to come. There's no need. I'm sure it would be more fun to go see Sheila."

"We want to ride in the convertible, don't we, Ali?" I chirped.

"Yeah, sure," said Ali. Janie had paused over her pile of beans, knife poised.

"Oh, all right," conceded Mom, stealing another look at the clock. Somehow I knew that she wasn't counting out the minutes until sundown. "Let's go, then."

My cheeks buzzed as we slid onto the polished seats of my grandfather's convertible. The warm June wind whipped hair into my eyes and Mom steered us past all the familiar landmarks that suddenly seemed alien—the row of shaggy eucalyptus trees at the bottom of the hill, the white colonial where the senator lived. We passed the Snyders' peach orchard, where Mom had gotten stuck in the mud as a girl, the elementary school and the new BART station, finally arriving at the tiny market where we'd gone, year after year, to collect things for Gram's kitchen. Mom pulled into the lot and fussed with her hair, checked her lipstick. Ali heaved herself out of the car. We both understood our mother needed looking after these days, and it wouldn't do to have her driving all over the East Bay in a Mustang convertible alone.

While Alison flipped through the teen magazines, I followed Mom through the narrow aisles. She filled her basket with random items: some day-old dinner rolls, a bouquet of daisies, a pair of nylons. Then she loitered in the deli section, eyeing prepared salads.

"Mom, Gram has enough food for, like, twenty people." I came up behind her, making her startle. Her hair was drawn from her face, clipped on one side with a slim barrette, and her eyes glittered with extra plum shadow. She batted them dangerously.

"It's almost Sabbath, Mom." Ali appeared from behind the bread rack. "Gram and Poppy will have a *cow*."

"I know, I know." She walked heavily toward the front of the store. Ali sucked in her cheeks. I wondered if she knew what I knew, or suspected—that Mr. Robert most likely lived or worked nearby, since he sent his mail from Orinda. I wondered if he'd been sending Ali letters, as well. I wanted to believe I'd been singled out as his special ally; at the same time, I was ashamed by the thought. So I just followed my sister to the cash register, where she plunked down her *Tiger Beat* magazine with my mother's odd purchases.

"You forgot the butter," Ali said, folding her arms.

"Oh—so I did!" Mom giggled. "Would one of you be a doll and fetch it?"

"I'll get it," I said, not bothering to mention the face cream. For some reason, I couldn't bear her knowing that we were just here to spy on her. It seemed a bit unfair. After all, she was at the end of her errand, getting out her checkbook, fishing in her purse for a pen, and nothing odd had happened. Why hadn't we just gone to Nick and Sheila's?

I continued to chide myself as I carried the bag outside. The sun was red now, slipping toward the bay, and we stood staring at its bright beauty long enough to be momentarily blinded, unable to see the face behind the voice that was calling our names.

"What a coincidence to see you three ladies!" Mr. Robert's voice boomed across the parking lot. "Why, you should have told me that you were planning a trip to my part of the world." His face came into view—the dimples deeper than ever in the fading light. He came right up and hugged me, patting me on the back. "How's my little twerp?" Before I could respond, he was kissing Mom's check. When he got to Alison, she stepped back.

"Who said it was *your* part of the world?"

"*Alison,*" my mother chided. "We were just running an errand for Gram. What brings you to Lafayette?" Ali rolled her eyes. I, too, wished they'd dispense with the pretense about this being an amazing coincidence. How stupid did they think we *were?* Still, I felt an unexpected pleasure at seeing him—the impish smile, the way he called me *his* twerp, the way my mother's eyes ignited, as if she'd been only half-alive five minutes before.

"I live right over those hills, you see," said Mr. Robert, pointing, "and there isn't one decent market, unless you count the five and dime, which is useful for things like, oh, little lace doilies, or twenty-year-old cans of evaporated milk."

"Oh, Robert," my mother said, laughing too loud.

"Mom, we're gonna be late for dinner," scolded Ali.

"Well, we *do* have to get back, but it's wonderful to—"

"Now hold on, just hold on—I think I've got something

in my car for you girls." He turned and jogged, long legs practically *boinging,* back across the parking lot to a silver Mercedes, rummaging in the backseat. Then he returned carrying a rumpled brown bag. He reached inside, extracted a book, worn on the edges, entitled *How to Draw Horses.* "I hear you're quite good at sketching." He winked at me. My sister scowled.

For her, he had a brand-new eight-track of *The White Album,* and for my mother, a perfectly ripe avocado—her favorite food— "To prove that we do have good ones in *my* part of the world." We all thanked him, even my sister, who suddenly seemed awed and speechless; he'd given her the only Beatles album she didn't own. Then he opened all our doors.

"Why don't we meet again, while you all are in town?" he suggested, as if we'd just finished having tea. He moved to my mother's side of the car and handed her a small piece of paper. She shoved it in her handbag before waving goodbye.

By the time we drove back up Gram and Poppy's driveway, the sky was turning indigo and the fog was rolling in from the bay; it rested on the distant hilltops like a sluggish snake. None of us had spoken since we left the market. Maybe it was just too hard to talk in a convertible. But my mind had been busily unraveling the implications of what had happened. Clearly, my mother had planned this meeting with Mr. Robert, but why? Why take such a risk here, at Gram and Poppy's, of all places, when we were supposed to be sitting around the dinner table saying Sabbath prayers? Hadn't she said she wanted to have a "nice, normal family vacation"?

We entered the house chilled and disheveled from the wind, and made our way to the dining room, where dinner

was in progress. Poppy and Uncle Peter were in the midst of
another argument. We heard their raised voices before we saw
Poppy's blanched knuckles gripping his knife and fork, Uncle
Peter's flaccid cheeks, the familiar vein throbbing above his
left eye.

"I'm not saying he's *innocent,*" Uncle Peter yelled. "I'm just
saying it's the status quo, Dad. The Democrats are just as—"

"If we're as bad as the bloody Democrats, we sacrificed
our young men for nothing!"

Only Dad looked up as we came in. Nick rolled his eyes.
Sheila wasn't at the table.

"What took you so long?" Dad whispered, but Mom
didn't answer; she just folded into the chair beside him,
smoothed her napkin over her lap.

"Open your eyes, Dad!" Uncle Peter started in. "Do you
really think this is the first—"

"My eyes are opened, young man," Poppy bellowed, banging his silverware on the linen tablecloth, bits of veggie meatloaf flying from his fork. "*My* eyes saw soldiers in the Pacific
blown to bits for this country, bowels hanging from their
bellies, their goddamn heads shot off."

"Good heavens, Avery," Gram ventured bravely. "Do we
have to—"

"Keep your mouth shut, Mama. You don't know the first
thing about it."

"That's no way to talk to her," Aunt Janie tried in a minuscule voice, but we knew that Poppy would go on—there
was no integrity in the world and folks no longer feared
God—until the sorrow shone in his hazel eyes and he could
no longer talk. I chewed my potatoes silently, secretly happy
for this blessed argument that had diverted everyone's attention from our tardy entrance; only my father seemed to have

taken it in, his eyes drilling into the side of Mom's head. I wondered how long she could keep from looking at him.

Finally, Poppy fell silent and there was no sound but the scrape of flatware on china, the men's bovine chewing and smacking. After a while, he pushed back his chair and walked bearlike across the great room toward his bedroom, shoulders falling. I wished I could run to him, throw my arms around his neck and make him smile, as I used to.

It didn't take Ali and me long to figure out that things were different this year. It wasn't just that fireworks had been banned due to fire danger, or that our father and Poppy would be away fishing for the majority of our visit. We soon discovered that our cousin Sheila, who'd doted on us during past visits, was completely occupied by her new boyfriend, Phil, a sophomore at Stanford, where Sheila was heading in the fall.

Each afternoon while the men were gone, while Gram was napping, Sheila was off with her boyfriend and Nick worked on his dirt bike, Mom, Ali and I took a walk. We walked to the end of Happy Valley Road where the pavement curled around an embankment then dropped us onto a network of fire roads connecting Lafayette with Orinda.

We walked on the dirt roads in the dry heat until we saw Mr. Robert emerging through the dust like a mirage. Each day he came bearing odd gifts—two thin metal flashlights for Ali and me, a book of old cowboy poems, a bouquet of California poppies, a Perry Como eight-track for Mom. We'd greet him, then stand in the middle of nowhere, the fields around us buzzing in the midday heat, and exchange pleasantries as if we were in someone's drawing room. He'd ask us about our family members as if he knew them: he wanted to know what Poppy was growing in his orchard, whether we were sick of veggie burgers (which Gram fed us every single day for lunch) and how would we like to get hold of some illegal fireworks? As he talked, he rubbed a fleshy hand over Mom's sunburned forearm, or fanned his fingers across the curve of her back. Ali was mostly silent during these visits, arms crossed, eyes hidden behind sunglasses, flip-flop–clad feet kicking the dust, though she did perk up when Mr. Robert mentioned his teenage son, Randy.

After a while, Mr. Robert would begin walking us back. The first day, he walked us to where the asphalt took up. The next, he came up Happy Valley Road. The third day, he walked us all the way to the mouth of Gram and Poppy's driveway, my mother's hand swinging high in his. For a moment, I wondered if he was planning to escort us right up Orchard Hill, and my insides knotted. How would we explain him to Gram? But he stopped abruptly at the bottom of the hill, as if he'd smacked into an invisible wall. Then he blew us all kisses before turning and jogging back into the dust.

When we got back to the house that afternoon, I found Nick in Poppy's garage, as usual, stretched out on the cool concrete, working on his dirt bike. I sat down on an orange crate to watch.

"Gotten hold of any illegal fireworks?" I asked.

"No, why? You got a connection or something?" He lay on his side, choosing lovingly from a metal box of tools.

"Maybe."

"That'd be cool, baby face."

I smiled at his bare brown strip of belly, the sandy blond hair falling over one eye. Ever since I'd been old enough to say his name, I'd adored Nick. I loved his grease-blackened fingernails and naughty smile, loved playing war with him in the forbidden bomb shelter. Most of all, I loved riding on Nick's dirt bike. Speeding up the fire roads—my cheek pressed to my cousin's back, head full of hot rumble and exhaust, the dry grasses ruffling by like water—was the closest I'd yet come to any of my dreams.

The summer I turned seven, Gram had broken it to me that girls didn't own dirt bikes, that it wasn't a proper pastime for *young ladies.* I wasn't too distressed by this news because, that summer, I secretly believed I was turning into a boy. It had started in the car, during our trip back from Chicago; staring at my bare, sunburned feet, I'd noticed golden hairs sprouting on the knuckles of my big toes. I took this as a sign—proof that Jesus was answering my prayer and making me a boy like Nick. Soon I'd have freckled boy cheeks, dirty boy toenails, a shock of blond boy hair falling over one eye. Then I'd be able to come and go as I pleased, riding a horse or a dirt bike along the miles of fire roads surrounding my grandparents' house, without anyone telling me to come in, wash up, set the table for dinner. I imagined the transformation would happen slowly, perhaps over months; this way it would be less of a shock for my mother. My father, on the other hand, would be pleased as punch. We all knew that his daughters were sore disappointments. Especially me, since after me there were no more chances. During the last month of my mother's pregnancy, she suffered a uterine prolapse that required a C-section and hysterectomy. When my metamorphosis was complete, my father would throw his arm around my sinewy boy shoulders, ruffle my sandy boy hair and peer into my face like I mattered.

"Can you hand me that wrench in the corner, baby face?"

Nick said, bringing me back. He rarely spoke during these sessions, but seemed to make room for me. There was a mute appreciation between us as he worked, as I handed him the right tool, or brought him a fresh Dr. Pepper from the fridge. It was like being in church—Nick's greasy, lovely church full of squeaky song, tin angels, gasoline that could go up in a breath if you struck a match just so. The air was thick with reverence.

Two days earlier, I'd been at another kind of church with Mom, Gram and Alison. We'd fanned our faces with the yellow bulletins in the stifling sanctuary, hearing about the New Earth that God would prepare for the righteous, once the old, sinful one had been burned to stubble and ash—scorched by wrathful fire for a thousand years. I wondered how God could have gotten angry enough to destroy every single thing He'd made—even the California hills that shimmered gold across the valley.

I asked my mother and grandmother about this on the way home from church that morning. I asked them if God would destroy even the dearest things—the scrub oaks, wild poppies and the does that leaped my grandfather's gates at dusk.

"Yep. Everything that burns," Gram confirmed.

"But why?" I wondered. "Why is God so angry?"

"He's had to put up with a lot of sinful baloney over the ages, hon," Gram said. "He's had to see just about every rotten thing men have done since the beginning of time. I guess that's enough to make anybody pretty darn mad." She said it as if *she* was the mad one, grasping the steering wheel with her knotty hands.

"What about women?" Ali drawled, staring out the side window. "Haven't they sinned, as well? Haven't *they* lied and cheated?" I glimpsed my mother's stony profile.

"Why, sure," Gram said as we began the steep ascent up the driveway. "Women do their share of sinning. But it's the men as are always starting the wars, isn't it? It's them that can't seem to help slaughtering each other." We pulled into the carport, made our way to the kitchen, past Nick working in the garage.

"How come the men never do any housework?" I asked as the four of us busied ourselves with preparations for the midday meal. "And how come they get to go fishing and play while *we* go to Sabbath School?"

"Ha! I don't believe Poppy's been in church since your mom and daddy were married," said Gram, handing Ali the green linen place mats. "He believes he's got a personal arrangement worked out with God. Isn't that typical of a man?"

"Not all men are the same," said Mom, pouring milk into short glasses. "Some are less obnoxious than others."

"Yes, well, obnoxious or not, it's our job to stand by them," declared Gram. "Little Janie doesn't stand by Peter, and if you ask me, that's why their marriage is faltering."

"What do you mean, *faltering?*" asked Ali.

"I'll be surprised if they make it a year," announced Gram. "You mark my words." She placed her hands on my mother's shoulders, peering up into her face. "Poppy won't take it well, if there's a *divorce.* He won't take kindly to it."

My mother tried to move away, but Gram's birdlike hold on her shoulders seemed to tighten. "I can see what's going on, Elaine," she said, over-enunciating. "It's about young women not taking their God-given roles to heart. You hear me?"

"Please, Mom." Elaine squirmed her off. "The onions are burning."

★ ★ ★

July third came and went and still Dad and Poppy hadn't come back. I overheard Mom talking on the phone the morning of the Fourth as Gram and I shucked corn on the front patio.

"Yes, well, I know it's important to get a good catch, but—I know, Don. I know how he is, but you were due back yesterday."

Pause.

"No, we're fine. Just be home for the fireworks or—" She frowned. "Oh, right. I keep forgetting. Well, be back for dinner, then. It's not like we've had a *family* vacation anyway. Not that we ever do."

Pause.

"Well, I'm *here,* aren't I? I'm still here."

An hour or two later, while Gram was napping, my mother retrieved me from the hammock where I was working in my new sketchbook.

"Come on with me, angel," she said. "I'll need your help."

"Where's Ali?"

"She's over at Sheila's. Apparently, the boyfriend has gone to see family today."

We walked down the hill, same as always, only this time we didn't even have to venture onto the road before we saw him. He stood just beyond the gate, wearing denim shorts and a red-and-white striped polo shirt. He had two cardboard boxes beside him, sealed with duct tape, the words *danger* and *flammable* written in red letters across their sides.

"I can't stay," he said. "But I wanted you girls to have some fun."

"Oh, Robert. Where did you get them?"

"Insubordinate teenagers are sometimes useful." He smiled.

"What about the law?" I asked. "What if we get caught?"

"Laws, my little twerp, are for people who lack common sense." He winked, but I continued to gawk, waiting for a better explanation. "If we all just took responsibility for our own actions, we wouldn't need politicians telling us what to do. Isn't that right, Elaine?"

"Ah, I see. Are you taking responsibility for *your* actions?" she asked him. "Is that what you're doing today?"

"That's why I need to get back, isn't it?"

I wasn't sure what they were talking about, but knew better than to ask. I examined the boxes, trying to get a glimpse of the contraband.

"Well, get going, then," Mom finally said, bending over to hoist one of the boxes. "We wouldn't want to keep them waiting." She motioned for me to get the other box, then turned her back on him, trudging up the hill. "Come on, Sylvie," she said. "There's work to do."

"What will we say?" I picked up the second box and followed. "About the fireworks?"

"Just say we got them from a neighbor," she suggested. "Say there was some guy peddling them on Happy Valley Road. After all, it's not *that* far from the truth."

When they arrived at dusk, ice chests bursting with trout, neither my father nor Poppy protested the illicit fireworks as I thought they would. They were sunbaked and smiling, full of bluster about their fishing success. I watched my father lean down to kiss Mom on the cheek as she set card tables on the patio. She paused, then handed him the rest of the silverware and smacked him solidly on the bottom. Uncle Peter took his turn cranking ice cream while Poppy fired up the grill and a few minutes later, Aunt Janie and Sheila arrived wearing white eyelet sundresses, carrying platters of fruit. My father even offered to get out the croquet set.

It was, for those few hours before sunset, just like the old days—Ali and Sheila giggling on the plastic glider while Nick and I set up fireworks on the huge front lawn. Poppy played a few tunes on his harmonica, and Uncle Peter sang badly after too many glasses of wine. Nick offered to let me light some fireworks, and I followed his instructions to the tee, even pulling off, on my last attempt, a stunning sideways roll in the grass that landed me next to my father's knee.

"Come 'ere, sweet pea," he said, using the name he usually reserved for Ali. "Come sit with your old man and pretend you're still my baby."

It was strange and good to lean against his ribs, feeling the brittle thump of his heart, hearing his familiar nasal laugh echo inside him.

As I relaxed more into our comfortable slump, Uncle Peter asked Nick where we'd gotten the fireworks. My heart skidded, and before Mom or I could speak, Nick was explaining that we'd got them from an old friend of Auntie Elaine's.

"Some guy she used to know lives around here, I guess," he said. "Least, that's what Sylvie said." My father's torso went rigid behind me.

"Really, now?" slurred Uncle Peter. "An old boyfriend of yours, Elaine?"

"Oh, sure," Mom answered, examining her toenail polish. "Like I've got time for cavorting around with old boyfriends." She laughed, then got up stiffly and made her way toward the kitchen. My father pushed me off his lap, set his ice cream on the lawn and stood stretching for a minute before going in after her. My insides went soupy, like the ice cream sloshing in his bowl. Ali dropped her face into her hands as

I crossed my legs, trying to enjoy the rest of the fireworks, but this proved impossible, as Nick was getting reckless—lighting three or four fireworks at a time, coming dangerously close to catching himself on fire.

"All right, now, son. Take it easy—party's over," Poppy snapped as thin shards of my parents' argument pierced the screens.

"What's all the damn fuss?" said Poppy as, one by one, Janie and Sheila and Peter stood to leave, brushing off grass clippings. "What the hell is wrong with everyone?"

I glared at Nick, hating him for ruining everything.

But it was my fault, clearly, for forgetting the onerous obligations of secret-keeper. I knew this as Ali and I lay in our twin beds that night, listening to our parents' heated voices ricocheting down the hall… *Don't tell me about respect… If you think I'm going to sit by while you make an ass… What do you care when you weren't even here all week…?*

"It's gonna get *way* worse before it gets better," Ali said through her yawns.

"I hope they don't wake Gram and Poppy," I commented.

"Not all the way down in their room—there must be eight locked doors between us."

"If they wake up, it'll be bad."

"'*Leave my house,*'" Ali imitated Poppy's commanding bark. "'*Don't come back 'til you learn how to behave like happily married people.*'" We giggled, but I felt hollow and chilled.

"If I hadn't opened my stupid mouth," I whispered, "maybe they'd have kept being nice."

"If Mom hadn't been such a *slut,* we wouldn't have to keep our mouths shut."

"They're just friends," I insisted into the blackness. "Mom and Mr. Robert are—"

"Yeah, they've been *friends* for, like, fifteen years," my sister said to the wall. "So how come we're never supposed to talk about it? How come Mom makes us keep all her secrets?" She yawned widely now, pressed her pillow over her head.

"'Cause it will upset Dad. You know how he is, Ali. He won't let her do anything."

"Go to sleep, Sylvie," she mumbled from beneath the pillow. "I'm tired."

I turned on my back, staring at the heavy beams, the whale-shaped patch of light coming from the hall, while Ali's breathing deepened. How could she sleep?

Whatever our mother might be guilty of, I knew I'd failed her, and would have to make it up somehow. I knew this deep in my abdomen as my parents' argument reached a crescendo, their voices now clear and startling as the view from Orchard Hill.

"I don't know why you even came along, honestly."

"Who insisted on a family vacation? Who was it said—"

"You don't know the meaning of *family.* You never have! To you, it means going off on your own little adventures."

"Well, I'll be damned if I'm staying now."

"Be damned, then! You can't go in the middle of the night like some—" I heard the sickening sound of a slap—then silence. My own cheek tingled.

After a moment I heard my mother's voice, quieter now. "Oh, this is rich, Don. Just lovely. How are we supposed to get to the airport without—"

"I don't give a shit, Elaine. Have your boyfriend take you."

"Fine. Just great. Here, why don't I help you."

They were quiet for a good fifteen minutes, after which I

heard the front door creak open and click shut, then our rental car starting in the carport, coasting down the hill, and Mom's soft sobbing. I wanted to go to her, press my nose into her hair, apologize for my part in all this, but I felt paralyzed by dread or guilt, anger or exhaustion; I couldn't have said which.

After a while, I fell asleep and dreamed that a man was digging up Poppy's orchard, carving tiny graves into which he placed small objects—were they animals or babies, or something else? I wanted to see, but was afraid to come closer. When I awoke, the house was dark and quiet. My grandparents' guest room looked the same as always in the predawn light: Gram's Oriental writing desk crammed with photos, the Russian nesting dolls staring from the corner. There, the same Ellen G. White books and red leather King James, the same green brocade chair. If I hadn't known better, I'd have thought nothing had changed. The closet door was open and my mother's old party dresses winked from the shadows.

2004

AFTER MONTHS, PERHAPS YEARS, OF ELUDING MY
mother, I suddenly needed to talk with her, craved the familiar
lilt of her voice. The first time, I called her on a Thursday,
on the way to pick up the girls the week after my walk in the
woods with Tai. Though I hadn't spoken to him since, I'd
thought of him almost hourly, picturing the tendons that
flexed in his forearm when he hoisted me out of the mud,
the coarse heat of his beard in the hollows of my throat. I'd
been hearing his grainy voice in the cave of my ear, saying,
Does he love your work? Does he see what I *see?* I'd peer into my
husband's face—the chiseled English nose, guarded almond
eyes and tapered lips—and see the other man's features: the
gold moons that glowed around each dark pupil, the voluptuous mouth, and a smile so unreserved, in moments, it
seemed insane. I'd been trying to decide, should I call? Should
I e-mail? Or should I try to wipe my brain free of him, take
it as a near miss and thank the gods that nothing more had
happened between us?

"So, you're still alive," my mother said when I called. "I was ready to give up on you." I apologized for my long silence. In a weary, injured tone that was all too familiar, she told me my grandmother was sick again.

"Is it different than before?" I asked, feeling the customary fist of guilt above my navel. "Is she worse, or is this a relapse?"

"More of the same, I guess—intestinal stuff, some bleeding, can't eat solids. It's bad enough that we're moving back to the Bay Area, to be near them."

"Oh, no." My mother had moved so often over the past twenty years, I'd lost count. They'd gone from California to Arizona to New Mexico and back, building custom homes in one gated community after another, like wealthy fugitives. Each time the new house was the *right* one, until it wasn't. We all have ways to outrun our demons. In this latest house, they'd lasted longer than usual, and I'd been hoping they might put down roots. Now this. "I'm sorry, Mom."

"There's really no need to be alarmed yet. Gram could go on like this for years. But the trips back and forth from Phoenix are killing me." I asked if she needed my help, wincing at the possibility. She told me no, that Alison was visiting, helping her locate an apartment.

"How does Ali have time to do that?" I pictured my tiny, ambitious sister—Santa Barbara's Assistant D.A. and mother of two burgeoning, adopted sons. Head of the PTO, chair of the church youth committee. "Isn't she like the busiest woman in the northern hemisphere?"

"Look who's talking. I don't even know how your girls are!"

I apologized a third time, then brought her up-to-date on the girls, Hannah's dance concerts, Emmie's belated potty training, the house renovation…. The school year was fast approaching and soon, I told her, I'd be swamped with work.

"I was starting to think that you'd all packed up and moved to Canada or something," Elaine said, voice still glacial. "Flown the coop. Became ex-patriots."

"It's not like that hasn't crossed my mind, with this awful war," I confessed. "But I might rather go to Wales." I had imagined it often—Holyhead, Colwyn Bay, towns I'd never even seen. My friend Jules was Welsh and said there were places along the coast where you could walk for miles without seeing anyone. It would be important to see no one, and to stay on the very brink of land, the sea clamoring for miles beside me. "Anyway," I told my mother, "if I did go away, I wouldn't take Nathan and the kids."

"Ah. It's that way, is it?" In the traffic circle at the dance camp now, I spotted Hannah talking to a friend by the side entrance, lean and elegant in her leotard and cropped pants.

"Sylvie?" Mom's voice had softened. "What's going on that you want to run off to Wales?"

"Nothing. It's just… I wondered, you know, if you and Dad ever tried to work things out. If you thought about seeing a family therapist, or anything like that."

"We didn't have family therapists back then." She'd resumed her icy, abbreviated tone, and I knew I wouldn't get far in this line of questioning; still, something made me persist.

"It was the mid-'70s, Mom. Everyone was seeing therapists."

"Not in our circles. We prayed together. We tried seeing our pastor, but I don't remember all that much—"

"Just tell me, was it more about what went wrong with you and Dad, or more about your feelings for Robert?"

For a moment I thought she'd hung up on me. Then she near whispered, "I suppose I was in love." She heaved one of her signature weighty sighs. I considered telling her that the dream was back—a strange man falling from sickening heights, his body battered and breaking on rocks as I watched—but now Hannah had climbed into the van and she *had* to get to CVS for hair ties and double-A batteries. I told my mother I'd call back soon.

"Why this sudden interest in things that happened thirty years ago?"

"I know, it's ancient history. Best not to upset the ruins," I tried for humor; she didn't laugh and we said our stiff goodbyes. But driving to the park that afternoon, I remembered that they had tried, albeit feebly, before the end. I recalled those last few months, the trips to Tijuana, the night swimming, the botched vacation at Orchard Hill. The memories stacked up like black suitcases shoved in a closet: all you had to do was crack the door and they all spilled out. While I pushed Emmie in the swing, I remembered the strained family dinners where my father drank too much and stormed off to his study, the sunset rides in his Corvette where he drove too fast, too close to embankments. I chased off a shudder.

The park was empty and cold that day. A few dirty clouds scudded across the horizon.

Hannah came toward me, her chartreuse skateboard tucked under one arm.

"Let's go home, Mom. I'm starving and I need Daddy to fix my skateboard wheels. They're, like, all funky again."

"Good idea." I snatched up Emmie and headed toward the car, trying to prohibit the images that seeped around the rim of every thought now—his imprudent smile, warm hand cupping my heartbeat, desire rising and striking, sudden as a snake. I handed Emmie a juice box, buckled her firmly into the car seat and squared my shoulders. "I'll make something special for dinner," I resolved to my daughters. "Maybe Daddy will be home by five, for once."

But Nathan wasn't home by five, or five-thirty. At six o'clock, the girls and I sat down to turkey burgers and sweet potato fries without him. At six-twenty he called, breathless, with another perfectly solid excuse: he'd had to run to Home Depot after work because the plumber was coming to hook up the downstairs bath at the site, and we still hadn't gotten fixtures.

"I can't have the plumber there with no toilet, can I?" he barked and I barked back.

"Nathan—Laura Forbes is sitting for a portrait at the studio in like forty minutes!"

The line was silent, then, "Shit, Sylvie."

"Don't you ever write things down? Do you realize how important—this job could bring in several thousand dollars!"

"I forgot, okay? I wrote it down but I forgot anyway. Sorry. I can be there in an hour."

"Right, but that's twenty minutes too late!" My blood was roaring behind my eyeballs, heart swelling with justified rage. In some awful way, it felt good. "Why do you *always* forget? Why is my work never on your radar screen?" It shook me, the force of my need to rage at him. I couldn't remember the last time we'd had a really good fight, and wished I were the kind of woman who smashed things. I could imagine taking down the crystal water goblets his mother had given us, winging them one by one onto the tile floor, though it was too dramatic, of course—far more than the situation called for.

"Just hear me out—" Nathan started, but Emmie chose the moment to drench her T-shirt with apple juice and start wailing, just as Hannah sprang from the table and blasted the stereo.

"Can you please just cut me some slack here?" Nathan said at the same time I was yelling, "I've got a circus on my hands!" Then silence again, as Kurt Cobain screeched in the background. I moved to turn off the music, saw the neighbor twins pounding on the front door, asking Hannah to come to TJ's for soft serve. Now Emmie's complaints were escalating over something unrelated to the spill, something to do with Hannah hiding her pink pony.

"Han, get in here and do your dishes!" I called, feeling the headache take root above my ears, as always, the insidious tendrils inching along my forehead. "And where's the freaking pony?" I remembered how Tai had smoothed the hair from my temples on Route 9, how that one simple gesture—his hand, my hair, wind grating over the exposed skin of my forehead—had interrupted the tension, altered the landscape irrevocably.

"I haven't even showered, bean," I explained to Nathan, using the old nickname not so much for effect as to see how it felt. "And Laura Forbes is supposed to be there with her daughters in—thirty-three minutes now. How long will this errand really take?"

"You know, Sylv," he shot back, unmoved by my feeble tenderness, "you're always on my back about finishing the goddamn house, and when am I supposed to do it? In my sleep?"

"So now the house is all *my* idea? I think I'd rather have a partner again," I said, cringing at the bite in my words.

"Listen, hon; I had two hearings today, the King Street sex

shop scandal is blowing up in people's faces. I work forty-five hours, you know. I don't run my own show."

"What the hell's that supposed to imply?"

"Just—nothing. I just wonder if you know what a luxury it is to be in charge of your own schedule."

"I work hard, too, Nathan." I felt my voice weakening, resolve buckling under the weight of new guilt.

"Why is Laura Forbes so important all of a sudden?" I swore I caught a note of suspicion in his question, but before I could defend myself, our connection crackled and faded. I could hear him saying, "Tell her it's something to do with the kids—make something up if you have to. Lord knows you're becoming…" Then the line went dead, and later, I hadn't the heart to ask him what he thought I was becoming.

School started. Hannah bounded into eighth grade like a Labrador diving into water—she'd been born a teenager, I always told Nathan. Emmie barely got potty trained in time to commence preschool. Nathan finally finished the downstairs bathroom in the new house and it seemed that life's ordinary disorder would resume, without further incursions. Then, during the second week of September, I received an e-mail that made my breath stall.

Am trying hard to regret kissing you in that stand of birches.
Winter is too long here and is coming too soon. I hear my father's sermons in my head and some of them are true, but I still can't regret that day with you. —T

I sat there for a long moment, staring into space, my vision blurring. I inflated myself with breath, deleted the message.

Then I retrieved it from the Deleted box in a panic, like an addict pulling cigarettes from the trash. I wrote back.

How do you get late-blooming roses to thrive? They are so lovely but mine are all leaves and thorns this year, refusing to flower. Thought you might have the answer...
—S

I called my mother again that afternoon, en route to the studio for my first teen watercolor fall workshop. "Did it feel like you had a choice, Mom?" I blurted at the intersection of Binney and Pine, when she answered the phone in a breathless tone. "Or did it feel like, somehow, you were driven by outside forces?" I downshifted and gunned it through the stop sign, narrowly missing a highschooler in a Honda.

"What on earth are you talking about, Alison?"

"It's Sylvie!"

"Oh, Sylvie—twice in one month?"

"I just want to know if you felt you had a choice."

"A choice about *what?*"

"When you got involved with Robert." As I pulled into the parking lot, I realized my arms were vibrating, my feet buzzing, as if I'd just stepped down from a rickety carnival ride. I rifled through the back for brushes, coffee cans, rolls of bright paper.

"Sylvia Lee," Mom said after a pause. "What's going on with your marriage?" Her tone was businesslike now, demanding.

"It's not that. It's just..." I stood in the parking lot, breathed in the afternoon sunlight angling over factory build-

ings, the Mill River murmuring solidly nearby. "I think I
need to sort out what happened back then."

"Oh. I don't know if I'm up for that conversation right
now."

"You never are." I closed my eyes, tried a different
approach. "How are you, anyway? How's Gram?"

"Pretty much the same, I guess. Your sister found us a cute
place in Walnut Creek, so we're moving at the end of
October."

"Wow. Good. *Is* that good?" I gathered up my supplies,
attempted to walk into the building balancing everything,
phone tucked under my chin. I'd forgotten my keys somewhere. The coffee can of brushes slipped from my elbow grip,
clattered to the asphalt, so I straddled the rest, trying to reach
the brushes, but now everything was falling.

"It's fine, honey. It's what we need to do for now. Sometimes, you just have to do what's needed, regardless of how
you might be feeling. Does that make sense?"

"Yes, but—"

"And one *always* has a choice," she said. "Or just about
always."

"Yes, but—" I let it all topple to the pavement, heaved a
sigh.

"I'm going to have to call you back, Sylvie. Some people
are here to look at the house."

One always has a choice; it echoed in my head like a hymn
as I stood before my first group of teen artists that day, explaining about blending and background and white space and
light. I repeated my mother's words to myself when Tai's son,
Eli, sauntered in, wearing big shorts and a black New York
T-shirt, trying so hard to look cool, my chest prickled. I

chanted her advice as I leaned over Eli's painting, noticing the familiar field of walnut curls, the candy-green eyes rimmed in ebony, the delicate left hand trembling as he held brush to paper. There was something off about him: he couldn't make a straight line. His horizon was all skewed and the brush too wet—he tossed it across the studio, where it clattered into Izzy Fletcher's chair leg.

"Eli, Eli." I placed my hand on the smooth skin of his wrist. "You have to ease up, man."

"This medium is bullshit," he said, gritting his teeth. "I can tell it's not my thing."

"It's really hard," I said, handing back the brush, peeling a new sheet of paper. "You have to just let it be a throwaway from the start, understand? Take the pressure off. Decide you're going to recycle this fucker before you even begin, okay?"

He looked up then, smiled his broken, cynical smile—not at all like his father's. "I like it when you use profanity, Ms. Sandon. It inspires me."

"Yeah? Well, maybe I'll swear some more if you finish the assignment, okay? Just hang in there." But he didn't hang in; twenty minutes into class, he got up and left, tossing his crumpled papers in the wastebasket.

I forced myself not to follow, tried instead to focus on the other students—there were seven left, and they all needed my help. "Watercolor is deceptively difficult," I kept saying. "You have to let go of your expectations." I paced the studio, my feet smarting in decades-old cowboy boots. I had a sudden, bizarre impulse to rush home and scour my closet. I pictured fifteen years' worth of shoes and jackets and tights heaved onto the center of the unmade bed.

"So just let's get a wash today, guys. Just get this first step done." I circulated among my remaining students, trying to stay focused, but my eyes kept darting to the doorway, wondering if he'd come back, wishing I could help.

Sometimes you just have to do what's needed, regardless of what you're feeling, I mused as they filed out the door an hour later. I couldn't believe my mother had given me advice that resonated, but there it was. I called home to check on the girls.

"Can you grab a pizza or something?" Nathan's voice splintered with exhaustion. "I can't deal with dinner prep tonight." We'd been clipped and guarded with each other since the argument, each keeping track of our own contributions, each watching the clock. It always came down to time, and who was doing more, or working harder, or getting a sliver of need met once in an age. When did life get so *flat*? How did people remain alive to one another?

The pizza would be twenty minutes, so I decided to do some work of my own: inhaling, I sat down at my easel, took out a clean sheet and began. But the colors were all wrong today, the grays too muddy, the bristles stiff in the joints. The tendons in my hands ached like an old injury, and I had the wrong kind of mind—I knew it. The kind of mind where nothing was enough. Unscrewing a tube of cerulean blue, I flashed on the early days: Sundays, Nathan and I used to walk the dirt road behind our house and climb the railroad bridge by the fairgrounds, where we'd watch the parachutes come down. We'd sit side by side, listening for the high drone of the airplane, poised for that perfect moment of silence as the engine was cut, our eyes scanning the atmosphere. It was a contest: who'd be first to glimpse the small, bright specks—three, four, five of them piercing the cloud cover, falling weightless as paper clips toward the earth's magnetic swell? He always grabbed my knee when he spotted them and I'd stop breathing; I could practically feel the wind pulling their cheek muscles taut. Then, the *whoosh, whoosh,* as one after another parachute opened, tugging the divers temporarily heavenward, buoying them in the clear July sunshine so that for a moment, it must have felt as though they would never descend.

Sighing, I dabbed at my watery mistakes with a sponge, wiped off my palette knife, tried again to get the shade right.

And then suddenly he was beside me, his breath alighting on the ridge of my ear like a soft, treacherous moth.

"Roses aren't native to New England," he whispered, "they're transplants, like us."

Even without looking, even after all these weeks, I'd have recognized that particular dark flavor of sage and garden dirt and smoke. "Don't stop working," he said, reaching to tug a stray curl from my eyes, tucking it behind one ear. "I want to watch you for a while."

I can barely remember what we talked about that evening, leaning on our elbows at the worktable, fingertips brushing across the metal expanse, my heart resounding in my ears. I think we spoke of gardening—my late-blooming roses and acidic soil, how to add peat and work in compost. I'm sure we talked about Eli, how he'd stormed out, how he'd been storming out of classrooms and kitchens and therapists' offices since his parents' divorce. Tai spoke of his ex-wife, who suffered from agoraphobia, how it started with bridges and Chinese restaurants. I thought of Nathan, who had done nothing, not really, to deserve my disloyalty, whose most egregious crime was that of working too hard, too long, for our mutual dreams and in the grind of it, somehow losing the original joy.

I don't remember the exact words we spoke in those forty-five minutes before I picked up the black-olive pizza, went home to my family; just that his lips fanned out inside the oval of his beard, broad and lonely, and it reminded me of the Northern California coast for some reason—a kind of beauty shot through with loss. His eyes were clear and creased, as if they'd taken in the world and found it dire, and funny. A scar hovered beneath his left eyebrow. I ran my index finger over that pale ridge and saw him shiver as something passed through him. I wanted to place my finger, just so, on the very thing that moved me—was it the sensual mouth? The strange, ocher-rimmed pupils? That crazy smile with its shadow of ruin?

I can't recall what we said as we parted, after our second devastating embrace, but something had shifted. He didn't kiss me in the darkened studio, or later, in the empty parking lot, and I wondered why, and wished for it all the more.

One always has a choice, my mother had said, and I believed her. Why, then, did it feel like a passage had opened and I'd not walked, but fallen through?

1974

THERESA CHAPMAN'S HOUSE WAS NESTLED IN A CLUMP
of eucalyptus on three acres at the top of La Loma Way, about
a ten-minute walk from our house. So many pale pink oleanders grew in front that I missed the house the first time I
came, and might have walked on by if I hadn't heard the
barking. Theresa's mother was a potter who also took care of
her war-damaged son and bred border collies. There were
other animals, too; a palomino mare grazed in a triangular
pasture, unfazed by the dog racket, and up the hill, three
pygmy goats stood like statues on a mound of stone. In the
months to come, this place would become my sanctuary.

I thought Theresa the luckiest girl in Orange County. Dad
had never allowed us to have pets, aside from one diabetic
hamster and a tank of lethargic goldfish. Mom said it was
because of the dogs: when Don was just a boy in Nebraska,
his own father, in a fit of drunken rage, had taken all the
family dogs behind the barn and shot them in the head, one
by one. Apparently Dad was unable to speak for six months

following this incident. Even after he regained his voice, he never forgave his father.

I was standing at Theresa's front door, trying to decide whether to knock or ring the bell, when a small, muscular woman came around the side carrying a bucket. Her hair was gathered in a loose ponytail, and she wore rubber boots and Bermuda shorts beneath a soiled purple tee. She held up a gloved hand, motioning for me to come around back. I knew from the amber eyes and freckled skin that she was Theresa's mom.

"Theresa said it was okay if I came." I followed her across a patio cluttered with clay pots.

"She's up in the barn." She pointed toward a brick path, swiping at a smudge along her cheekbone. She was pretty, in an unkempt sort of way. My own mother wouldn't have been caught dead in such a getup.

Since my father had gone away, she'd taken some modeling jobs for a few local boutiques, and her wardrobe had expanded to include metallic gold tube tops, hip-hugger shorts and a scary assortment of wigs. Two Sundays ago, I'd discovered a redhead flipping the avocado omelets, and just this morning she'd been wearing white gaucho pants and a green paisley halter, her bobbed-and-dyed hair a brunette bubble floating above her shoulders, which were freckled brown from the yard work she'd taken over since he left. She glowed, like a woman newly aware of her own appeal. I had stood in the hallway, watching her through the same wooden slats through which I'd spied my father ransacking her desk a month earlier.

"I don't know, Sammy. It sounded like a hotel lobby. He might've just been having a drink, though." And then, "I've no idea when he's coming back—maybe never." She laughed grimly, twirling the phone cord around and around her wrist, as if it were a tourniquet. Up until that moment, I'd almost believed the story she'd been telling everyone: Dad had left Orchard Hill early because he had an emergency "work situation" and now he was attending a medical convention and visiting his cousins in Vegas. She'd been so convincing.

Why would she lie to me, of all people? I wondered as I reached the Chapmans' horse barn, peered inside the half-open door. Hadn't I earned the right to her confidences?

I found Theresa cleaning one of the two stalls, hair pulled back the same as her mother's, jeans splattered with manure. The other stall housed a well-groomed bay gelding. I opened my palm to receive his soft, whiskery muzzle.

"I didn't know you had horses," I said, my voice thick with jealous awe.

"That's Georgie. He only likes a few people, so I guess you must be groovy. The one outside is Magdalena."

"What are you doing?" I asked.

"Shoveling shit—wanna help?" She tossed me a shovel and we worked in silence, flinging horse manure into a wheelbarrow. I loved the sharp smell of the soiled shavings, the small bulge of Theresa's biceps as she lifted and flung horse apples. She flung one at me; it landed with a muffled thud on my thigh.

"What are you staring at?" She laughed.

"Nothing." I flung one back.

"You were." She tossed a shovelful in my direction. "You were looking at my fat butt."

"Your butt's not *fat*." I lunged toward her, shoving a handful of hay down her shirt.

"Compared to your snake ass." She pushed me into the shavings.

When her dad came into the barn a few minutes later, Theresa and I were covered in pine shavings. He stood in the doorway, hands on hips. He was a contractor, and had the ropey body and leathery face of his trade. His brown hair was silver-tipped and a smile threatened to break through the stern gaze.

"You must be Sylvie." He shook his head at our dishevelment. "You girls get cleaned up, Terri—we're taking your mom's stuff to the craft fair. I need help loading the truck."

"But, Dad—Sylvie just got here!"

"Don't make me ask again, you hear? Sylvie can come back." He turned and left the barn, but not before winking at me; for some reason, my throat tightened with emotion.

"Can you come later?" Theresa stood and brushed the shavings from her legs. "My dad's always making me do stupid chores."

"At least he's *around*," I said. A fat white cat waddled into the stall, slunk around my legs and I reached to scratch her head. "Jeez, how many pets do you have?"

"That's Persia—she's about to pop." Theresa sucked on a strand of copper hair. "You want a kitten?"

"Yeah! But my dad won't let me." I scooped up the pregnant cat, felt her sweet vibrations against my neck. "He's like that."

"But if he never comes back, you can do whatever you want, right?"

A few days later, on the morning of my twelfth birthday, my father called to sing to me. I heard someone paging Dr. Remming behind a clanking noise, and I realized he must be at the hospital. I wanted to ask where he'd been staying, when was he coming home, but was stunned into silence by his nasal baritone, wavering over the notes of the birthday song. I hadn't heard him sing unaccompanied since two summers before, during a road trip to the Sierras, when he'd uncharacteristically burst into song: "If ever I would leave you, how could it be in springtime...."

Even more surprising, my father had tried to teach me to fly-fish on that trip. He'd taken up the sport during the previous spring and spent obsessive hours practicing in our swimming pool, tugging at his big rubber waders, casting his fly into the Jacuzzi. Alison and I sometimes hid in the living room to spy on these elaborate practice sessions—we'd peer through the corner windows, waiting for him to catch his fly on a bush so that we could throw ourselves to the floor in convulsive laughter. I suppose we wanted revenge for all the times he'd asked us to sit in the belly of some boat in the near dark, damp and yawning. Dad wanted us to be tiny sportswomen so desperately, he'd drag us out of our sleeping bags before dawn on every camping trip, parade us down the dock, telling us that whoever caught the most fish would get a dollar, or a candy bar, or a ride on his shoulders.

I always wanted to ride on my father's shoulders, careening into tree limbs and bumping my head on ceilings as he lurched around pretending to be Bigfoot. But even for that rare pleasure, I couldn't pretend to like fishing.

By the time I stood watching him fly-fish on the banks of the Feather River, he'd gotten quite good, his arm moving fluidly as a dancer's, feet planted on the slippery rocks. "If you wanna be *really* expert," he informed me, "you have to get into a kind of rhythm with it." I yawned. I was supposed to be memorizing his technique and guarding his orange fly box. I felt honored by this charge—he had asked *me* to join him, for once—but also burdened, and restless. I couldn't help wondering what Mom, Gram and Ali were buying at the outlet stores in Grass Valley.

"Pay attention now, sporto," my father called from the center of the river. I nodded and squared my shoulders, noticing his use of the old nickname. "You're not going to learn a damn thing if you just stand there yawning."

"I'm watching," I blurted, and we locked eyes for a tight minute before he went back to his sport. I frowned at his supple form, wanting to run away. Instead, I picked up a handful of pebbles and started tossing them into the river a few feet from where he stood. One, then another, *plunk, plunk*. My father, mistaking the *plunks* for the splashes of jumping trout, suddenly became excited and aimed his fly toward the spot where I'd thrown my stray rocks. "You see that, sporto?" he yelled. "Did you see that sucker jump?" Delighted, I continued to plop sly stones in the river, maneuvering my hip-booted father farther downstream, like a neat remote-control boat. "Now we're onto 'em, kiddo!"

We spent over an hour like that—me tossing stones into the river, him following eagerly after, chasing our imaginary splashing trout, until finally, exhausted and fishless, he looked up in time to see me lob a big, square rock over his head. I remember his face, foolish and blank as the recognition settled in, and the creeping shame in my own stomach. It was then, I think, that the rivalry between us sprouted flowers and thorns.

We walked back to the cabin in silence, him marching a good ten feet ahead. I still carried his orange fly box, but as we walked up the cabin's steps he turned to pry it from my hands. I held on, refusing to turn it over—as much as I'd hated my fishing lessons, as thoroughly as I'd ruined our day together, I couldn't give up my charge like this, with such obvious defeat. I held on churlishly.

"Damn it, Sylvie," he growled, grabbing my wrist. "What are you playing at?"

"I want to hold it," I said through gritted teeth.

"The goddamn game's up," he snapped. Then he loosed my wrist and backhanded me hard across the face; my feet left the steps and I found myself sprawled on the ground. The box had come unhinged and my father's flies were scattered in the mud and sticking to my clothes. I plucked one off my T-shirt and looked up, but he had already turned away, slamming the door.

I stood, swallowing blood and the need to cry. Then I began collecting the flies, replacing them in their minute compartments, the browns with the browns, the yellows with the yellows, the tiniest ones hooked into squares of Styrofoam, as if everything depended upon this meticulous arrangement. Each fly was beautiful in its symmetry and palette, and I could imagine how they'd sprung to life in his hands. Each had so clearly required his attention, forethought, maybe even love. Each had turned out just as he'd planned. I admired and hated them.

So I didn't know what to say when Dad came back a week before school started, driving a brand-new car. His white Lincoln was gone, and in its place was a bright red T-top Corvette. He came home on a sweltering Sunday morning and took Alison for a ride around the neighborhood. I felt the blood drain from my temples as they sped down the street, Ali's hair rippling like a banner. I had to sit on the lawn with my face between my knees.

"Well, Sylvie." Mom plopped onto the grass beside me. "I wonder how long he'll be around."

"Is he staying?" I tried to sound as cool and detached as the grass poking into my thighs.

"He might be, I'm not sure yet." She pulled her knees to her chest, started peeling the polish from her big toe. "I guess it all depends." *On what?* I wanted to ask. *On whether we say the right thing about his new car? On whether we stop getting letters from Mr. Robert?* "Do *you* want him to stay, angel?" she asked without looking at me.

"I dunno," I said. Although he'd left before—for a weekend or a week—this time it had seemed easier for the three of us to spill into the sharp hole he'd made. We sat on the kitchen counters rather than at the dinner table, eating potato salad and Jell-O from round Tupperware containers, banging our bare heels against the pine cabinets. We spoke to each other in double Dutch and pig Latin, created fruity concoctions in the copper blender, made over each other, teasing each other's hair into frenzied shapes. Mom hauled Ali and me to all her Mary Kay parties, where we worked as models. While the women oohed and aahed over our youthful complexions, our mother worked the room, doubling her sales. When we returned home from these expeditions, she'd curl on the living room floor for hours.

I figured things must be pretty bad when she started appearing at my bedside. I'd wake from a bad dream to see her silhouette sketched into the moonlight. "Just wanted to make sure you were okay." Her breath was sharp and light, like kumquats. "Wanna come sleep in my room, angel?" I'd nod, grabbing my pillow, and trail after her down the long hallway. I slept in a tight line on my father's side of the bed those nights, pressing my face into his powdery scent.

One morning, Mr. Robert showed up with a potted bougainvillea, a white bag of croissants and an enormous orange. He set his gifts on the entryway table, ruffled my hair. "Hey, twerp—next time I see you, we'll ride horses on the beach. How does that sound?" But before I could answer, he seized my mother's shoulders and whispered, "It's done, Lainie. I've served her the papers." Then he kissed her long and hard. Her eyes fluttered and her neck went slack, like a sunflower stalk whose magnificent head had become too heavy to support. I didn't know what Mr. Robert's message meant, but it seemed to unearth her. After he left, she called in sick to her modeling agency and spent the day thumbing through old photo albums.

Mom's friend Sammy started appearing in the afternoons, bearing bottles of pickled okra and red cherry peppers. On smoggy summer evenings, the two women would lay by the pool in bikinis, nibbling Sammy's offerings, their middle-aged bellies luminous and soft against the warm cement. Mom would dip her long hands in the water, splash her face with a resigned laugh, forgetting to censor her talk in front of my sister and me.

From what I could gather during these conversations, men were pretty much the same wherever you went—rude, unfathomable, more transient than petunias—and though it was best to stay away from them, they seemed the only subject worthy of conversation. A few days before Dad's return, Mom said something to Sammy about Mr. Robert being "more human than most of them," and Ali countered with, "What's the point, Mom, if they're all so grodie?"

"Yeah," I echoed, "besides, you have *us*." My mother looked at Alison, then me, void and flustered, as if we had suggested that purple elephants grew on our plum trees—as if we'd handed her something useless and fantastic.

"Well," she finally said, "it's like having a car. I mean, just because cars are dirty and difficult and expensive to maintain, you wouldn't want to be without one, would you?" I nodded, wondering what kind of a car Dad would be in her metaphor. A black limo? A Ford pickup like Theresa's dad drove? A silver Mercedes like Mr. Robert's?

So as Dad and Alison pulled back into the driveway in the red Corvette, as he showed off the eight-track player and the shiny engine, I decided that my father had chosen the perfect vehicle to represent him. This car was mean, quiet and fantastically fast, he explained, and if we played too near it, the alarm might go off. It was an impractical car, Mom protested, made of fiberglass—much more fragile than it looked—and might shatter into splinters if you crashed it. My father assured us he had no intention of crashing.

After we'd fiddled with every button on the dash, our parents led Alison and me into the family room and sat us around the oak game table. My mother sat beside me and Dad stood behind Ali, rubbing his hands as if to warm them. Then Mom asked, in the voice of a ten-year-old, what we thought of their marriage.

Ali laughed—it sounded like a bark. Then we all fell silent while Dad cleared his throat as if trying to dislodge something. Finally he said, "Your mom and I have been talking about whether I should stay. And, well. We don't know."

"What do you mean?" wailed Ali, her cheeks still pink from her ride in the Corvette.

"You see," Mom said too cheerfully, "what we mean is—how would you girls feel if we got a *divorce?*" We were quiet again, digesting this word that each of us had thought, but no one had uttered aloud. Dad clicked his tongue. Alison put her face in her hands and started to sob. I felt as if the top of my scalp was going to fly off like a Frisbee.

"I'll hate you both forever," I blurted. My parents looked as stunned as I was, and Mom whispered, "Why, Sylvie!" I wasn't sure why I'd said it; after all, it *had* been nicer, in some ways, with him gone. I couldn't have explained—not for years to come—my urgent sense of apprehension. So I told myself it was because divorce was a sin—I'd heard Pastor Wilkins say so in one of his sermons. And besides, the kids at school with divorced parents weren't doing so hot.

"So," Dad said, "is that how you feel, too, Ali?"

"It's not fair," she answered between sobs. "Why can't we just be like *normal* families?"

"Oh, Ali, sweetie." Mom grabbed Alison's wrist and Ali yanked it away. "Oh, honey, please." Her eyes brimmed, and I felt sick, knowing that if Mom started to cry, I would, too, and that would leave only Dad, and we were always doing that to him—leaving him out.

"Why can't you just live separate for a while, and write love letters back and forth?" I suggested. After all, this seemed to have worked for Mr. Robert. "Maybe that would straighten things out." Elaine bit her lip, then started to laugh. I noticed how big her teeth were, square and perfect, like horse teeth. We always teased her about the size of her mouth, but those teeth were the most beautiful part of her face. Now she was laughing painfully, clutching her ribs. Soon we all were laughing, as if I'd said something hysterical. The laughter was metallic, like a bundle of silver wires being pulled too tight, like something was going to give.

"Well." Mom sighed, blotting her eyes with her ring

fingers. "Okay, then. Here's what we're going to do. We're going to work this out, God willing. We're going to hang in there."

"Really?" Ali looked up, dubious. Dad hoisted his left eyebrow.

"There's no reason why we can't, is there, Don? Other couples have done it with worse odds." She sounded vague, as if reciting something she'd once read in a magazine, in a dentist's office. *Does this mean no more Mr. Robert?* I wanted to ask.

"Right. Of course we can, if that's what we want." Dad gazed at her pointedly. "People just have to want things bad enough. We're a family, after all. A *family*." He nodded, his hands claiming Alison's shoulders. Then, as if unsure what else to do, he dropped his chin, shut his eyes and murmured, "Let's pray."

We all followed suit, though I fluttered my eyelids open enough to see him reaching for Mom's hand, her thin fingers curling around his crooked pinky as he mumbled, "Lord in heaven, bless this family with Your grace and help us to do Your will, in the name of the Father and the Son and the Holy Spirit, Amen." I felt like I was in a TV movie, an After-School Special.

"So it's settled then?" Dad cracked his knuckles. "I'll just bring in my things?"

He hesitated, wincing. Mom smiled feebly. I tried to remember if I'd ever seen him kiss her mouth the way Mr. Robert had. Would we still go horseback riding on the beach? Dad headed for the garage and Ali bounded after, eager, it seemed, to reinstall him. My mother and I stayed put. I took her hand, which felt brittle and freezing. "The heat must be getting to me, angel," she muttered. "It's unbearable. Let's go make some iced tea, shall we?" Then she got up and walked down the hallway toward her bedroom.

That night, Mom made overcooked lasagna and we ate around the dining room table like normal people, napkins smoothed over our laps. We talked about school schedules, my mother's modeling (which Dad suggested she give up, now that he was back), Dad's new partner. Ali seemed her old, buoyant, pre-teenage self, filling up the silences, chatting about ninth-grade teachers, her plans to try out for the cheerleading team in September.

"Over my dead body," muttered Mom.

"What's so bad about it?" Dad opened a bottle of red wine, offered her a glass.

"Yeah, Mom. All my friends are trying out, and besides, it's good exercise."

"You *know* I don't drink wine, Don. That hasn't changed in the past three weeks."

Then, silence.

"Theresa's cat is having kittens in a few days." I realized that now—while we were trying out happy domesticity—was as good a time as any to ask. "She said we could have one if—"

"I won't have you cavorting around in one of those getups, Ali. Hanging out with Leslie Brown every Saturday night."

"She's a pretty cat," I insisted. "Half-Persian, I think. You'd like her, Ali."

"You can't shelter them from the world forever, Elaine," muttered my father, helping himself to more lasagna.

"Leslie's a totally sweet guy," said Ali. "You just don't like that he's black. And anyway, it's not a *getup*—it's a skirt and halter top!"

"I'd take care of the kitten myself," I tried. "I'd even change the litter box and—"

"In any case, Ali, those football games are all on Sabbath, so it's out of the question."

"Oh, I get it. It's okay for you to wear halter tops, but not me?"

"Why can't we just have *one* little pet like everyone else?" I practically screamed. They all stared at me and I winced, anticipating a slap. Instead, my father was watching me with interest, one eyebrow raised, so I continued. "It's just— Theresa has like sixteen animals. It's just one kitten I'm talking about. It might cheer people up around here."

"We'll see," Dad agreed, refilling his glass. Then he winked, ever so slightly, and for the first time in many months, I felt the stirrings of hope.

After dinner, he suggested we all take a ride in his new car.

"There's not enough room for all four of us," Mom protested, referring to the so-called backseat, which was big enough to fit a large duffle bag, maybe, or a dog.

"The girls can squeeze in back," my father insisted, slurring his *r*'s. "Don't you think I'd buy a car with room for my babies? Don't you think I might consider that, Elaine?"

"I'm not suggesting you didn't, honey," she said, clearing the last of the dishes. "I just doubt it was your primary concern."

"What the hell's that s'posed to insinuate?"

"Besides," she trilled, piling things in the sink, "you've had too much to drink."

He was silent, swilling the wine in his glass. I could see his jaw muscles flexing, his tongue probing the back molars. I, too, was worried he'd had too much, but even more worried that he'd storm out again, drive off to wherever it was he disappeared to when he got mad. So I said, "Come on, Mom, I haven't been for a ride yet. Ali got to go already—"

"Yeah, and I wanna go again," my sister chimed.

"You won't regret it, ladies." Dad tossed the keys high in the air, caught them in one fist. I was surprised and encouraged that he could manage this, and my mother must have been, too, for she agreed, wiping her hands on the dishrag and following us out the door.

The warm breeze rifled the eucalyptus branches as we drove up La Loma to La Sierra to Skyline Drive, where Stacy Frey—Theresa's other best friend—lived. Stacy's dad didn't have a red Corvette, though; she and all her big, blond brothers could never fit in the back of a sports car, I mused as we made a sudden sharp left, veering into the blackened foothills.

I grabbed my father's headrest. Ali and I barely had enough room to sit sideways on the bench seat, our knees colliding in the center. I was spooked and thrilled by the engine's deep roaring, the night wind ripping through the T-top and ravaging our hair, tires squealing around each bend as we rose higher and higher—high enough to see the lights of Orange County shuddering below. The air was sharp with the memory of brush fires. My father swerved to avoid a huge tumbleweed lurching down the road, and Mom just leaned her head back, clenching her eyes the way she did on roller coasters, giving in to the ride. I wanted to give in, too, but I couldn't. It was like the moment at the carnival when you look around and understand how makeshift it all is; how ramshackle the machinery you've been trusting your life to.

As we rose round another bend, I wondered: Was my

father exciting or just scary? I remembered the drives to Tijuana, when he insisted on stopping in the middle of the desert to shoot at coyotes, the night swims where he switched off all the lights without warning, turning the pool inky black, the camping trips where he got us so worked up with Bigfoot stories, we couldn't fall asleep. I remembered all the Christmas nights when, after the presents were opened and the decorations removed, my father would chop the Christmas tree into brittle thirds. Then he'd shove them crackling into the fireplace, humming carols, nearly burning our house down while Ali and I screamed, as we were screaming now, blazing up Saddleback Mountain in my father's amazing toy—flying through darkness.

2004

THOUGH I AVOID SEEING HIM IN PERSON, THE E-MAILS come every night now. I read them late at the corner desk, after Nathan has given up on the ten o'clock news, slumped sideways on the futon couch. After I check the girls and recheck them, I pour myself a glass of red wine, settle into my mother's green antique chair—the one Nathan calls my *boudoir chair*—and turn on the computer, hands throbbing, fingers trembling like a junkie's.

He writes strange things, tells me a hundred ways to let my garden grow wild, writes the scientific names of plants because I want to know: *Rhus aromatica*—fragrant sumac; *Viburnum cassinoides*—Northern wild raisin. He writes about a high meadow we've both visited, separately, on the northern California coast near Goat Rock, where the cows follow you to the lip of the sea, their brown eyes like the eyes of spirits. He writes about the first time he saw me, at my art opening two years ago—how he knew then our paths would collide.

I dissect his syntax, lean into my restlessness, surprised that it feels like grief.

Saving the e-mails in a file marked "household liabilities," I bury it deep within two other folders, shoved in an inconspicuous corner of my hard drive. Sleep comes late and badly. My dreams are thick with hard, broken bits of the past, like pieces of beach glass turned smooth by time and tossed back out again, onto the raw shores of consciousness.

"You're telling yourself it's okay because you haven't consummated it," says Theresa sagely on the phone one afternoon. I've confessed to my old friend because it's impossible to keep anything from her for long.

"It's not like adultery in the biblical sense," I try, cradling the remote with my shoulder while I tend to my neglected garden, fingers raking around the bases of overgrown basil plants. There's an unmistakable chill in the air, this last week of September.

"So, what is it?" Theresa's voice is both kind and mocking. "An escape from intimacy with Nathan? A stage for your childhood demons?" In the background, I hear the insistent snorting of Bella, the Morgan mare she uses in her therapeutic work with clients. "Some sort of deferred revolt against the Adventist church? Oh, no, wait—you did that already."

"Don't psychoanalyze me, Terri. You're my best friend."

"What are friends for, Sy?"

"Look, it's not really the same as—"

"As what? As what your mom did?"

I sit back on my heels in the mud, my hands too filthy to grip the phone. "You don't understand," I say, tossing weeds into a pile. The last of the summer squash is barely visible through tangled masses of mint. My mother was right about mint—you can't allow it free rein or it will devour everything else in the garden.

"What, I don't understand because I'm not married? Because I haven't got any kids?"

"Oh, Terri, shut the hell up. That's not what I meant." How can I even begin to explain it to her—this undeniable feeling of undertow, the deep distance from which I'm watching myself, as if there's no real danger of drowning?

"Look, I've got a client in fifteen minutes. Anyway, it seems like this conversation deserves a face-to-face."

"Sure, but I haven't got time to drive to Vermont," I explain. "I haven't even cleaned my house since Hannah's birthday party."

"Nathan has his problems, but he's got a pure heart."

"Meaning I don't?" I wipe my hands on my shorts, wishing my closest friend wasn't a shrink. I remember a therapist I saw briefly in my twenties, who loved to use gardening as a metaphor for self-improvement. You "work the soil" and lay the foundation for growth. You "compost" the lessons of the past; cultivate patience, accepting the perennial grace of seasons. You sow the seeds, tend the new growth and *blah blah blah. But it's more complicated,* I always wanted to protest. There are boulders and tree roots, storm fronts and longing, someone's decomposing old work boot. There are the things you forgot to harvest, weeks of torrential memory, the three-hundred-year-old bricks of a shed foundation. Some days, you're too damn tired to weed. Sometimes, you let nature have its way.

"It's just—it's the thing you *swore* you'd never do, Sy—the same thing as your mom," Theresa concludes. We are both quiet a moment, during which I can picture her securing the

bulky saddle, waiting for Bella to exhale before she cinches
the girth.

"No." I stab my trowel into the soil. "It's not the same,
because I'm not involving my *children,* am I?"

"But they will be involved, eventually, if it's taking up this
much space."

"This much *space?*"

"It's taking up the same amount of psychic space as if you
were screwing him," she says tiredly. "And sooner or later, you
will be."

"I have to go," I snap. "I have to get cleaned up."

"Sylvie. I don't mean to piss you off. I just—"

"I have to pick up the girls and go shopping for dinner,"
I state as if to remind her that I am still performing my duties,
still a conscientious mother and wife with responsibilities to
fill.

All through dinner and homework, bedtime stories and
algebra problems, my desire sits breathing beside me, impa-
tient and warm as a living man. All through teeth brushing
and dinner dishes, laundry sorting and good-night kisses, I
am as frantic in my skin as a dog on a humid night—I can't
stand myself. I can't help it.

He writes about his German shepherd, Yuki, and her obsession with the hawk that lives in the white pine out his
kitchen window. He tells me about his Rabbi father, his
mother going crazy in a second-floor walkup in Queens,
dreaming of Indonesia. He worries about Eli. He writes
about a baseball field where he fractured his cheekbone, his
guilt over locking his brother in the broom closet when he
was nine. He begs my stories, and I give him fragments. I tell
him about the brush fires I used to walk toward, a tornado I

watched careen by our apartment in Chicago when I was four. I was raised on apocalypse, I tell him. He writes back, quoting Neruda: "Let us build an expendable day / without winding the hours…That day of all days that came bearing oranges…" His messages are, by turns, corny and mundane, insightful and self-pitying, clinical, horribly sexy. My nights hinge on them.

There are other e-mails, too, of course, all the usual junk—marketers and creditors, NEA newsletters, client inquiries. My mother writes that she is packed, again, ready to move to their new apartment. My grandmother is doing poorly, she says. I might want to plan a visit. There's the occasional stray e-mail from Hannah's friends, too, which I forward to her in-box, though one night I open one from her friend Ava, which reads: *"Joel Stimpek is going to the party at Leyla's on Sunday. It's a no-brainer, Han. He thinks you're hot! Don't be such a ballet geek!"* I close the message immediately, save it as Unread. It occurs to me that Hannah could do the same with my messages, but I dismiss this thought—teenagers aren't that interested in their parents' lives and Hannah is no exception. These days, she barely seems to notice Nathan's and my existence.

Today, the first Sunday in October, Rosalyn Benton, our Ashfield neighbor, has let her goats stray onto our property again. There are five of them this time. When we arrive at the site, they're tearing off strips of Tyvek paper and pooping on the newly rebuilt front porch. For some reason, I imagine them in Beatrix Potter outfits—little blue knickers and stiff corduroy jackets—and start to laugh.

"Can you drive over and get Rosalyn?" Nathan says irritably. "Tell her to come get her animals under control. And grab a couple coffees while you're out, would you?" But I don't want to go to Roz Benton's. I'm afraid of this neighbor, with her translucent turquoise eyes and cracked yellow fingernails. She always reminds me of a mermaid, hauled against her will from the sea. She's a retired social worker, or so the locals say, who supposedly never recovered from the loss of her son to Vietnam. Now she makes her living on goat cheese, yarn sweaters and psychic readings, a genuine leftover from the sixties. There are many like her in these hill towns, too many to account for the alarm I feel at the thought of driving to her cottage.

"We'll just walk the goats back home," I offer. "The girls and I will take them."

"Uh-huh. And how, exactly, are you going to manage it?" Nathan stands in the gravel driveway, long fingers fanned over hips. I find myself thinking about the first time we met: I was twenty-six, broke and strung out in a rented dump with four other women, including Theresa, who had lured me to Northampton in an attempt to rescue me. That house was listing like a sinking ship, with starlings' nests in the porch eaves and so much old paint caked on the sills and trim, it took us a week to pry the windows open. Nathan, a late-blooming undergrad and sometimes carpenter, came to repair a fence for our psychotic greyhound, Byrneman (after David Byrne), who'd bitten the mailman twice and the slumlord once. But Byrneman merely rolled over for Nathan, exposing his soft, freckled belly. "You can't ignore a man who has a way with animals," said Theresa, who was forever trying to fix me up with someone nice for a change. "You have to give him a chance if *that* dog approves."

Watching him glower at Rosalyn's goats, I wonder what happened to the gentle idealist who drove me to the hardware store that first day, instructing me on drill bits and the death of affordable housing, then offering to mend our porch roof for free. Afterward, he sat beneath it sipping Irish whiskey out of a Yankees mug, tickling Byrneman's belly, speaking about his passion for Adirondack furniture and his father's heart attack with a tender naïveté that made me look twice, despite the narrow eyes, a certain softness around his jaw.

"How are you going to manage it, Sylv?" he repeats. "Have you got goatherding talents I've yet to discover?"

"It's only a ten-minute walk to Roz's place. We've got carrots in the ice chest. We can *lure* them home. The girls can help, right, Han?" I yank my daughter's iPod earplugs from her head. "You'll help me take the goats home, won't you, sweetie?" I over-enunciate.

"Yeah, sure. Whatever."

"I can help, Mommy," pipes Emmie, hugging the neck of the littlest goat. "I know how."

"Oh, do you?" Nathan's expression finally cracks. "We've got a whole family of closet goatherders?" He laughs. "What about coffees?"

"Why don't you run to the market yourself?" I shrink from his gaze. "Take the car." The truth is, I'm shunning the Ashfield Market, where Tai likes to have his Sunday coffee and paper—avoiding the inevitable moment when we run into him again, and I have to navigate my unruly feelings in front of my children, or God forbid, my husband.

As it turns out, Rosalyn's goats are equally unmanageable. Twenty minutes into our expedition, we aren't much closer to the property line than when we started. Hannah attempts, with carrots and as much patience as she can muster, to entice the animals through the leaf-strewn woods, while Emmie and

I act as sheepdogs, herding them this way and that, trying to stop them from stumbling into the river.

"They're not very bright, are they?" notes Hannah, flinging another handful of carrots onto the soft ground.

"Or maybe they just don't like carrots." I clap my hands behind the tiniest one, who keeps threatening to bolt. Emmie seems to think the whole thing a terrific game; she's barking like a border collie, laughing and darting through leaf debris, pretending to nip at their heels.

"I think she's found her calling," Hannah says drily.

"Well, I'm glad she's enjoying herself. We might be out here all day at this rate." Through a stand of pines, a few minutes later, I can finally see one of Rosalyn's outbuildings at the edge of her meadow.

"Just a little farther," I pant. "I think they're starting to get the hang of it."

And it does seem that the goats are beginning to cooperate: we get them to wander in a straight trajectory for a while, somehow enticing them onto the arched wooden bridge spanning the stream that serves as a property line.

Then, everything happens in an instant. Emmie runs onto the bridge, too close behind the animals, causing a wave of panic among them. She sprawls on the boards just as the mother goat lashes out with a sharp hoof that catches Emmie hard in the forehead. She howls, startling the kid, who scrambles off the edge of the bridge and falls a good four feet into the water. I call for Hannah, who is already wading into the river to rescue the goat. Then I turn to inspect the gash on Emmie's head, which is bleeding copiously into her left eye.

"Good God," I gasp as the adult goats scatter over the bridge and across Rosalyn's meadow. Hannah emerges from the water, soaked to her hip bones, clutching the kid to her chest. I can't hear what she's saying over Emmie's wails.

"Just put him down," I suggest, searching my pockets for a tissue—anything to mop up the blood. "He'll follow the others."

"There's something wrong with its hind leg," Hannah yells. "I don't think he can—" She catches sight of Emmie's wound. "Holy shit," she breathes, eyes round as fifty-cent pieces.

I squint up toward Rosalyn's cottage, weighing my options, then unwrap my sweatshirt from my waist and use it to clean Emmie's gash. She quiets momentarily. Blood soaks through the white cotton, turning it neon red, and at the sight of this she begins crying in earnest again, while I beat down a stiff wave of panic. Trying to recall what I know about head injuries, I remember a time when my sister ran through a sliding glass door at Gram and Poppy's and the blood pooled shockingly, though it turned out she only needed two stitches. Ali was out cold that day. At least Emmie is conscious and screaming mightily. Her Hello Kitty T-shirt will never come clean. With the help of Hannah's pocketknife, I rip one arm from my sweatshirt and tie it around her head as a kind of tourniquet. "Can you carry that little guy up the hill?" I ask Hannah, heaving Emmie onto one hip. "Rosalyn Benton may be weird, but I bet she'll have first-aid supplies."

The first time I met Rosalyn, she as good as cursed us. She'd walked over to introduce herself a week or two into the renovation, just after we'd discovered the complete lack of insulation in the kitchen. Nathan and I were slumped on the decaying porch steps, debating whether to tear apart the Sheetrock or blow in insulation, when Rosalyn emerged from the woods, her gray hair shining in the 5:00 p.m. light. It was early September, and she held a bouquet of Queen Anne's lace and a pound of goat cheese, as if there was any place to store such things at a construction site. Still, I was touched by her hospitality, until she opened her mouth.

"The family that lived here before didn't fare so well," she said in her even therapist's tones, her watery eyes unblinking.

"I'm starting to get that," said Nathan wryly.

"The poor man lost his way, couldn't keep up with the place. You may have heard…."

"We heard that there were money problems," I offered. "We heard his poor wife and child died in a car accident and—"

"That's what some people say." We were all silent, regarding each other warily.

"Well, I guess you think something different," suggested Nathan after a pause.

"John Kauffman shouldn't have stayed on here after his wife was gone," Rosalyn said, glancing around at the stripped siding, the overflowing Dumpster, the crumbling porch steps. She shook her head sadly. "I hope it goes better for you people, but they say houses have their own auras."

"Yes, this one has the *aura* of about seventy thousand bucks in renovations." Nathan chuckled joylessly.

"I hope it goes better for you people," Roz repeated. "Let me know if you want me to do some energy cleansing." And then she walked away, leaving her offerings on the railing.

"I think she just cursed us or something," I said after she'd disappeared down the road.

"Please, Sylvie. You're starting to sound like the old-timers in town."

"What did she mean by 'energy cleansing'?"

"I don't think I want to know," he said, dropping his head in his hands.

Now Rosalyn stands before me in her tiny, dark kitchen, inspecting Emmie's wound, while Hannah pats the russet head of the injured goat Roz has stashed in a laundry basket. I glance at the odd assortment of clutter: herbs and chili peppers hanging from the low rafters; jars filled with beans, legumes and dried mushrooms, unidentifiable mossy bits, shells. The windowsills are lined with pieces of driftwood, painted wooden animals and ceramic goddesses. Though as crowded as any room I've been in, it seems clean. I'm starting to feel less panicked when Roz announces, "I'll just make a healing poultice, then. To stem the bleeding."

"I'm afraid she might need a couple stitches," I whisper over Emmie's whimpering head. Roz stares up, those wide eyes startlingly beautiful in her withered face.

"Aloe leaves can be quite useful for—"

"We just need a good-sized bandage, if you've got one. And maybe some ice."

"Of course. But it might be wise to brew some calendula and nettle—"

"And then a quick ride back to our place, if it's not too much trouble." I try to communicate gracious disinterest with my whole person.

"Uh, Mom, I'm, like, totally soaked here." Hannah indicates her river-sodden jeans.

"Ah—it's always the little ones who suffer when we go wandering." Roz nods gravely, rummaging in a cabinet under the sink.

"Excuse me?"

"Think of my Daniel…" She wafts back to the table, unwraps two brown bandages and secures them to Emmie's forehead. Then she freezes, scrutinizing my daughter's face. "Why, she looks just like Lucy."

"Lucy?"

"Yes—" she says, her hand starting to tremor, like one of those bobble-headed dogs on a dashboard. "The children are the ones who pay," she concludes.

"Look, we were just trying to get your goats back to you, Roz," I say. "I didn't mean—"

"Of course. Of course you were. And I'm sorry for the trouble my darlings caused you. They've never been able to keep away from John Kauffman's old place." She pats Emmie's thigh. "Looks like I can't, either." Plucking the kid from the laundry basket, she tucks him under one arm and leads us out the side door, to an ancient VW bus. I climb in, hoisting my trembling four-year-old onto my lap, struggling to keep the ice pack—wrapped in Rosalyn's now-bloody gauze scarf—pressed against her wound. Hannah ambles in behind us, tailed by three of the goats; at the sight of this, Emmie stops whimpering and lets out a delighted squeal—a good sign.

"It's all right," chirps Roz. "The sweet dears like a ride to town now and then." As she backs out the long driveway, Hannah falls forward and the goats scramble onto the vinyl seat beside her. She crosses her arms, scrunching hard against the window.

"More exciting than hanging out at the mall, though, isn't it?" I tease. She rolls her eyes as we bump down the dirt road.

"I'm filthy and freezing."

"Just hold on, Han. There's a change of clothes in the car."

But when we pull into our driveway, there's no sign of Nathan, or the minivan.

"Brilliant," drawls Hannah, who is being nibbled by one of the goats.

"I want Daddy to fix my boo-boo," Emmie whimpers.

"He's probably just gone for coffee." I place a hand on Hannah's damp leg.

"Yeah, but you never can tell with Daddy, can you?"

I check Emmie's saturated bandages, knowing Hannah is right. Nathan's the only person we know capable of turning a ten-minute errand into a major detour. I know his lateness isn't a personal affront, but something more complicated and benign—a kind of childish idealism about time mixed with his inability to gauge the big picture, and spiked, most likely, with a dash of passive aggression.

"My head hurts, Mama," Emmie says again, swamping me with fresh panic.

"Okay. Listen, Roz, would you mind taking us to the market? Nathan might be there with the car." But Rosalyn is absently stroking the kid in her lap, staring at our unfinished house.

"We ought to do some energy work around that foundation," she lilts.

"Right, but—can you take us to the center of town?" My voice is now sharp with irritation.

"Anything for the little ones." She pulls onto the paved road. Hannah makes a face.

"You still think it's brilliant there's no cell phone service up here, Mom?"

"Don't worry. We'll find him," I say. But as Roz idles in front of the market, I can't spot our car anywhere on the street or in the parking lot. Still, I decide we should get out; there's at least a working phone here, and I sense that Roz, now muttering something about Mercury being in retrograde, will not be of further assistance. As I'm thanking her for the ride, she blurts, "There's Tai Rosen's car. Surely he can help you."

"You know Tai?" My stomach churns into a pretzel.

"Oh, sure. Helped me with my garden some time ago. Sort of famous around here."

"Is that right?"

"One of the only people around who understands about labyrinths. Are you friends?"

I pause, perhaps long enough for her to detect something in my features, for her eyebrows float to her hairline, those aqua eyes glinting—no longer dreamy.

"We've got to go." I offer my hand, which she turns, holding firmly in her own. "Thanks again for your help," I try, but she's busy examining my palm.

"Would you look at that," she mutters. "Cleanly divided."

"Sorry?" I withdraw my hand from her cool, sinewy fingers.

"Your life line is divided in two. What do you make of it?"

"I don't know, Rosalyn." Antsy to get away from her, I lift my injured girl from the bus. "I don't know what to make of anything, just now."

The Ashfield Market is empty, except for Eveline, two young women in black at the back table and Tai, of course, reading his paper at the counter. My insides lurch to make room for this new piece of chaos, and I shift Emmie higher on my hip bone. He glances up as we enter, his surprise turning to consternation when he sees the look on my face, my bloodstained toddler and sopping teenager. My already rushing heart gallops so violently, it threatens to knock me clean over. "We're looking for my husband," I say in what I fear is the voice of a nine-year-old. "Emmie's hurt—we need— Did you see Nathan come in?"

"Sylvia." Just that one word—quiet and insistent as a

prayer—and my breath finds purchase in my lungs again. "I don't even know what your husband looks like."

"You after Nathan? He came in looking for fasteners." Eveline appears behind Tai. "I sent him to Williamsburg, to the hardware store. We haven't got— Lord Almighty, what happened to the child?" At this, Emmie begins crying again and Hannah mutters an obscenity.

"I think she needs a couple stitches. I don't have my wallet, or, anything."

"You'll come with me," Tai insists. And then, more softly, "I can take you."

I stare into his face, studying the features that have become too familiar, though they aren't—I rarely see this abundant mouth, the vivid eyes, except in my thoughts, reading his e-mails, sipping my guilty wine. His torso suddenly seems too long, as if some whimsical, sadistic god has heaved him heavenward by the armpits. Growing nauseous, I wonder if I've somehow orchestrated this whole event, sacrificing my youngest just to feel the simple heat of this hand resting on my forearm.

"Take us to the hospital," I whisper. "If it's not too much trouble."

For the second time in two months, I am speeding in the maroon Saab, listening to Tai's reassurances, only this time they're directed at Emmie, falling asleep between Hannah and me in the back, her wounded head on my lap. Theresa's warning echoes in my mind: *your kids will be involved eventually, if it's taking up this much space....* Why is it that when your life's falling apart, everyone becomes a bloody seer?

"Weird, how this guy seems to be around when Emmie

gets hurt," Hannah whispers, and I look away, frightened of her uncanny ability to read me.

"It's lucky we ran into him," I say, but find myself wondering if he is, in some karmic way, responsible for these mishaps.

"Don't you think we should call Daddy?" Hannah asks. "Shouldn't we at least leave a message?"

"You do it, honey. You've been waiting all day to use your cell." The thought of calling Nathan at this precise moment catches my voice, pinning it mouselike somewhere behind my breastbone. "Tell him we couldn't find him anywhere—tell him we waited at the site and Emmie needed help, and we ran into—"

"I'll just tell him what happened," she shoots back. "I'm not gonna *lie*."

"Of course." I clear my throat. "I wasn't asking you to."

Tai drops us off at the emergency room door and I thank him perfunctorily, expecting not to see him again for days or weeks, swallowing the dry ache in my throat. So a few minutes later, as we're behind the front window admitting Emmie, I'm surprised to spot him in the waiting room, rolling back and forth on the soles of his cowboy boots, hands shoved in his back pockets. Hannah spies him, as well.

"Why is that dude still here, Mom?" she whispers as I'm filling out the paperwork with one hand, gripping the sleeping Emmie with the other. "Are you guys friends or something?"

"Yes, well—sort of," I answer. "Han, can I give you Emmie to hold? You need to keep this ice pack pressed to her forehead." She nods and I situate Emmie on her lap, hoping this will provide sufficient distraction to shut her up.

"How do you know him?" she insists.

"His son Eli was in my printmaking workshop," I say, relieved to have something tangible to offer. "Remember Eli Rosen, Isabel's friend?"

"Yeah, he's kind of a loser, isn't he?"

"*Hannah,* that's cruel." I sign the last sheet of paper, hand it to the admitting nurse, who secures a wristband around Emmie's inert arm. "And no, he's not—"

"Isn't it kind of weird for some random dad of some random student to be hanging around like that, waiting for us?"

"He's just concerned," I explain. "And he's not 'some random dad.'"

"Right this way, please." The nurse leads us into a narrow white room. I lay Emmie on the bed and peel off the bandage to inspect her gash. Though it's no longer bleeding much, it grins up threateningly, flowering purple along the edges.

"I'm still dampish," Hannah complains as I cover Emmie with the thin hospital blanket. "No one thinks about the girl who's slowly freezing to death. So long as there's no blood."

"My poor baby. You want me to get you a hospital johnny?" I tease, gratified that we're moving on to other topics. And then...

"So, how come this Tai dude isn't just a random dad?" I'm amazed by her tenacity, and I start to wonder if she suspects something, but how could she? What could she possibly know? Still, I decide to give her a meatier explanation.

"He's someone we know from Ashfield, Han. A landscape designer—okay? Lots of people know him up there. He might be helping us with the landscaping on our new place," I add, regretting the lie at once.

"He is?"

"Well, maybe, yes, probably. I just said so, didn't I?"

I'm rescued by the E.R. doctor, who enters the room with a bit of a flourish, asking for details. He inspects Emmie's wound and proclaims that she'll need half a dozen stitches. "We might even be able to accomplish it while she's napping." He winks. "You must watch her for signs of concussion, although I don't think it's likely, from what you've said…."

Hannah becomes so engrossed in watching the procedure, she forgets about the inquisition. I've never felt so relieved to see a doctor.

Half an hour later, though, as we're leaving the E.R., Emmie's forehead stitched up with bright blue thread, we run smack into Nathan and Tai, chatting affably in the waiting room. The air squeezes from my lungs as I hoist Emmie up my torso. Hannah sprints to embrace Nathan, as if she's missed him for days. Tai peeks around Nathan's shoulder, cocking an ungainly brow. I try to breathe the way I've been taught in yoga classes—slow, deep breaths, all the way to my navel, one, then another—as if this can save me.

"You're done already?" Nathan pries himself from Hannah. "I was just coming back."

"And I was just about to go," says Tai.

"He was a fast sewer," I say. "Must have taken home ec instead of shop." Maybe my lame attempt at humor will relieve the crushing tension in my ribs. It is strange and horrible to see them standing here side by side. At six-two, lanky as a basketball player, Nathan towers five or six inches over Tai, whose more muscular arms are crossed over his chest. Nathan peers at the patient, who beams.

"See my stitches, Daddy? Aren't they pretty?"

"They're certainly *blue*." He laughs. "No more goatherding for you, little girl."

"Doctor says I'm brave," she announces, while Hannah clings to Nathan's sleeve.

"Did you get my cell phone message, Dad? Did it come through?"

"Not right away. Got what I could from Roz—you know how she is—and then Eveline told me you'd been abducted by this character," he gestures at Tai, who grins impishly.

"I gather you two have met?" I ask, my ears starting to buzz.

"The City Hall renovation—three years back, wasn't it? Tai GC'd the landscaping." Nathan shrugs, apparently nonplussed.

"I didn't realize—" Tai starts.

"I'm brave, Daddy," repeats Emmie, trying to recapture her moment of glory.

"Of course you are, baby—"

"Mom says Tai's doing the landscaping on our new house," Hannah interrupts, and now both men are staring at me— the dark almond eyes beside the pale green, the auburn eyebrows and the black all rising together. I open my mouth to explain, but my voice has fled the scene, deserting me. Instead, there's a lump in my throat the size of a ripe plum.

"Yeah, we did discuss it in the market one day," Tai offers after two beats, delivering me with grace from this unwieldy pause. "It was my idea. You see, I created some of those original gardens, back when it belonged to John Kauffman."

Now it's my turn to raise an eyebrow.

"Is that so?" asks Nathan. "Well, now. Isn't that something? Although I have to say, I'm not sure we can afford you, Tai."

"Ah—well, you know." He glances at me, unsmiling. "You might be surprised."

★ ★ ★

Emmie falls asleep again on the way home. Hannah's plugged into her electronics, and Nathan is brooding. He apologizes for not being there when we needed him most. He suggests having Tai to the property, getting an estimate on the work. Squirming, I question the practicality of hiring a landscaper. "We may as well find out what it would cost us," he insists. Then we stumble into an archaic silence. I think again about the day we met—the day Nathan sat on my porch and told the story of his father's heart attack. He'd been home from college for the summer, helping his parents, and was in the midst of staining the back deck when he heard his dad's strangled call from the shower. For weeks after I heard the story, I'd pull out this image, turning it like a stone: Nathan, his coveralls spotted with deck stain, clutching his dying father in the shower, slipping on tiles. For weeks I'd picture him there—a compelling mix of strength and humanity, heroism and helplessness as he wrestled his dad's spent body to the bathroom rug, struggled to press life back into him. Here, I'd thought, was a man with a clear outline, a knowable size and density. Here was a man you could count on.

I remember how precisely I fit in his armpit, the first time he slung his clean, heavy limb across my shoulders. I thought I could live forever in that shallow cave, listening to the granite thud of his heart. For months I fell asleep without sleeping pills or wine, just that constant clear pulse against my kidneys.

Now I sleep on the opposite side of our king-sized bed, buttressed by pillows, front and back—a habit I picked up during my pregnancies and refused to shed—Nathan, a body-width away, warm as the endangered earth. Night after night, I curl into my solitude, reaching for some black-dream depth—unquenchable, gorgeous, immense.

★ ★ ★

As the four of us are pulling into the driveway late that afternoon, hauling our things back into the little rented house, I decide the duplicity must stop. *I* have to stop it. Only one walk in the woods, one kiss and at least a dozen e-mails, and already I'm in over my head, struggling for light and clarity, dazzled by the complications, the implications, past and future. As I stew a pot of my mother's red bean chili, I'm remembering how her affair snowballed, gathering heft and momentum, involving first one and then another—children, parents, spouses and ex-spouses, ending in fire and funerals. I hook up Emmie with a coloring book, nuzzle the top of her head, set the table for dinner, shoring up my will. As I kiss Nathan's prickly cheek—he's heading back up to the site for the evening, to finish the work left undone—I'm inwardly composing the e-mail I will send, carefully selecting the words that will discontinue this madness. Theresa will be pleased with my clearheadedness, my newfound resolve.

A resolve that's slipping as I settle into the boudoir chair at 9:45 p.m. The kids have been asleep for an hour, and Nathan is not home, still not back. I've been pacing the house in the chill night, staring out the blackened windows, struggling against the weighty pull of seduction.

Finally I turn on the computer, sip my wine and am undone by the new message in my in-box.

S: Night comes fast this time of year, rising like a blade. Today, watching the faces of your lovely daughters, your husband, I willed myself to let it go. Then sat with that for a while…. All afternoon, walking in the fall woods with the dog, chest aching, mind naked as a stone.

There is no holding on to beauty, is there? But on my

walk, a pileated woodpecker rapped and called and rapped again against an oak, wanting into that sacred darkness—the very heart of the tree, where history lives.

I can't deny this longing any more than I can willingly lose a fist, an eye.

There is just no way to rise gracefully into the next day.

Meanwhile, squirrels keep vigil outside my walls, scratching and gathering, fueled by hunger—they know winter's coming, though they don't understand from where. Sometimes, I'm stunned by the sorrows of this world, Sylvia, but then I think of you, your real skin beside me, heat rising into what only we can create, if we choose. There is just this one intersection in all of time—blue and deep as earth, wild as ocean.

Don't we want that? Isn't it ours?

1974

I STARTED SNEAKING INTO MY FATHER'S STUDY THAT
fall. The worst things had not yet happened, but I felt a heavy
sense of foreboding, and it seemed to bear my father's name.
Every day after school, I'd creak open his oak door and stare
at the wall of bookcases where Dad's fishing and shooting
trophies shimmered. The room felt dark despite sunlight
spilling over the walnut desk, the deep red rug, the cupped
leather chair where I tossed myself each day, like a baseball
caught in a fat mitt. I'd sit there, blank as a sinking stone,
staring at the strange, primitive trappings of my father's world:
the worn bindings of medical books, the sex books in the top
left-hand corner (too high to reach), the sad eyes and musty
forehead of an antelope he'd shot, the long shiny nose of his
rifle.

He was planning a hunting trip to Montana, and the
packages had arrived all through September, carrying sleek
L.L.Bean boots and flannel vests, hunting knives and shotgun
shells, camouflage pants. On late summer evenings, I often

stared at him as he polished his new guns during *60 Minutes,* and I burned with a sullen protectiveness toward the pheasant or deer that my father was hoping to kill.

A murderer—that's what he was, I decided a few days before he left for Montana. I was sitting in my usual corner of the study, staring at the hunting gear and suitcases on the floor when it struck me and I stood up, filled with a thrilling new resolve. I went to his desk, took a pad of his prescription paper from the top drawer and wrote that word—*murderer*—on each of the creamy white squares with a red pen. I liked how the word looked as I wrote it again and again on those blank pages with his name printed at the top. I liked the righteous shrug of the *r*'s, the round, upside-down smile of the *m*.

I was thinking about finally climbing up to have a look at those sex books, the day I wrote the murderer notes and placed them carefully in all the folds and creases of my father's suitcase and hunting jacket. I tucked one underneath his briefs and another inside his black leather shaving kit. Then I moved his office chair against the bookshelf, so that I could reach *The Joy of Sex,* which I slipped under my shirt to take to Theresa's.

After all, my mother refused to answer any of my questions that fall. She wouldn't tell me how boys got erections or what a diaphragm was. She wouldn't explain about *Roe v. Wade,* or what Helen Reddy meant when she sang "'Cause I've heard it all before, and I've been down there on the floor. No one's ever gonna keep me down again…." She wouldn't tell me whether we were going to see Mr. Robert again, either, or what it meant that he'd *served* someone papers. (I kept picturing him in a waiter's uniform, the mysterious papers hidden beneath a serving dish.) She wouldn't explain about *orgasms,* or why she got that look on her face when I asked. So when I pressed myself against the Jacuzzi jets one August afternoon, when my body dissolved into itself, my toes curling up in the heat while the stars fell from their holdings, I thought maybe I was ill, or had damaged an organ. The southern California sky was overcast for once, the air heavy with coastal fog, the house eerily quiet. I sank farther into the warm water, checked my pulse, then decided to have another go.

Theresa and I tried to answer our own questions. We lay on her white eyelet bedspread in the blank warmth of after school, *The Joy of Sex* spread open between us. We stripped down and compared bodies in her full-length mirror: Theresa's looked like a woman's, with kiwi-sized breasts and wisps of coppery hair in all the right places. Her torso curved in just below her rib cage, then swelled gently below her navel, while mine was all angles, my breasts nothing but little kumquats. I felt like an alien, an in-between thing. At my age, Ali had already had her period for a year.

"You're shaped like a boy," Theresa appraised and I shot back, "Just because *I* don't have a huge ass!" Then we mauled each other with pillows until we were giddy and flushed.

"I'm going to die when my dad gets home from Montana," I told her a few days after I'd planted the murderer notes.

"He won't kill you." She stretched across her bed, brushing the wall with her fingertips. "At the very most, he'll ground you and I can sneak through your window."

"We don't get grounded in my house." I imagined him opening his suitcase in the hotel suite, finding the notes, his features curdling with our old disappointment.

"Well, if he kills you, can I have your skateboard and your Elton John records?"

"Sure," I said, "why not?" And we spent the rest of the afternoon making out a will. Theresa wrote and I dictated who should get my belongings when I was gone—the album collection, the Tolkien hardbacks, the skateboard…. Afterward, she appeared almost gleeful about the things she was going to inherit, and agreed to let me ride her horse. I trudged behind her up the path to the stables, wondering if people who are dead feel homesick for what they've left, or if they simply go to sleep while waiting for Jesus. I wondered if I would make it to heaven, or if all the evil things I'd done—the murderer notes, the Jacuzzi jets, the shoe-box letters—would keep me out.

Touching the flanks of Theresa's warm gelding, Georgie, was like touching the sun. It was better than prayer or my mother's lemony cheek at night. Theresa made a stepladder with her fingers, so I could hoist myself onto Georgie's back and ride the ring, nowhere to go but in circles. But riding was soaring. I wanted to fly wild as a deer through some hushed forest. To be kissed by someone like Leslie Brown, my sister's new crush—to caress the thick veins on his black forearms. I wanted to make out with John Riley from school, to make my father hit me because I had it coming. I could make him do things he'd regret, could plan the violence. I wanted to know that it was *mine,* coming to me, as deliberate as the dadada-*da* of the horse's hoofs against hard, unyielding dirt.

Two days after my father left for Montana, my mother came to my room at dawn, tugged back the curtains and announced we were taking a trip of our own. She stood before the window, allowing the yellowish light to frame her—a full-length halo. She held an armload of my underwear, washed and folded, and began stashing it in my dresser, ignoring for once that my clothes were rumpled and inside out, shoved in all the wrong places. Her cream-colored button-down shirt was cinched in a quick half knot above her jeans.

"Where?" I rubbed my eyeballs and sat up. "Where are we going?" She perched on the corner of my bed, patted my leg briskly through the blankets.

"Have you been warm enough in here, angel? It's been awfully chilly."

"I'm *fine.*" I brushed the hair from my face. "What trip? What about school?"

She spoke quickly now, as though she might run out of nerve to say all this: we were driving up the coast, to a bed-and-breakfast where they had little individual cabins, some horseback riding on the beach, maybe even Hearst Castle—had I heard of Hearst Castle? She smiled weakly, a plea in her gray eyes.

"What about school?" I asked again. "What about CJ?"

"You can miss a day or two, honey. I'll take care of it. We'll get the neighbor boys to feed the cat." She picked at a loose thread on my quilt. "Mr. Robert is taking us," she said, staring at me now with a steady, pointed gaze.

"Really? Does Dad know?"

"Of course not." Her eyes grazed the walls of my room, like a sparrow in an attic. "He'll be gone for over a week," she explained. "Hunting." I knew by the way she took my hand—firmly, with a conspiratorial squeeze at the end—that we were not to tell Dad about this, ever. I longed to confess about the murderer notes, but it seemed unwise, as if any more wickedness would tip the precise balance of this moment, send us reeling into some swampy place.

"So," she said, standing and brushing lint from her thigh. "Get dressed in something comfortable, okay? I'm going to talk to your sister."

"Okay." I lay in bed for a minute after she left, wondering what my father would do if he ever found out. Would he leave again?

Since he'd been back, he seemed to crave only quiet. He wanted silence in the living room and in the rose garden, silence at the dinner table and in the car. More and more, I found myself pressing against the still edges of his anger. I couldn't help myself. It was like stepping around a coiled snake in the road, wanting to poke it with a stick, make it move.

I had even brought home one of Theresa's new white kittens, which I named Calamity Jane, before he'd granted permission. He said nothing, but the first time CJ sharpened her claws on the sofa arm, he sent her sprawling in one pitiless stroke. I flew to where she crouched, collected her in my arms and glowered at him. He glared right back, daring me to contradict, doubling my pulse. There was an undeniable allure to this antagonism, a kind of charged intimacy I shared with no one else. Still, I knew I shouldn't push it too far. Picking up CJ, I retreated to my room, but that night, I continued speaking double Dutch at the dinner table, after he'd twice asked me to knock it off.

"Hibey Ibalibi—Dibon't yibou thibink thibat thibis ibis iba nibut hibouse?"

"Pipe down and eat your dinner!" He grabbed my forearm, which would bloom lavishly purple next day. I winced, suddenly recalling the story of his own father, shooting the dogs—where had Dad been? What had the violence sounded like?

"Please, Don—that's enough." Mom's voice seemed to come from across the neighborhood, though she was sitting right next to me. "Please don't, sweetheart."

"I'm not your sweetheart, last I checked." Dad released my arm with a final yank. "And I know what's enough." He looked at all his women, one by one, focusing on my face last. I tried to swallow the shame scorching my chest. Then he left, trailing profanities, taking his wineglass with him. I knew he was right to go. I was bratty and uncivilized. I had too much hair.

"You don't have to *curse* about it," Mom called, but it was too late. After his office door slammed, she dropped her face into her hands. But looking up a minute later, her expression was neutral, and she began eating again. "Finish your dinner, girls." She sighed. "Just ignore him. It's going to be all right."

But it wasn't all right. His hands were treacherous and surprising, like bats bursting from evening caves. And I was the noise in the darkness, the intrusive shaft of moonlight that called them. His hands would startle from their places next to his plate to crash into my cheeks, grab my chin, yank the napkin from my hands. And on those evenings when he was tipsy and playful, firing up the Jacuzzi, lighting the fire pit, singing along with Andy Williams—even then his hands were erratic, grabbing me around the waist, snapping my training bra, tickling my armpits, his laughter hot and nasal in my neck.

When he was distant and preoccupied, I craved his touch, missed his critical stare. I'd try getting close while he worked in the garden, watching as he snapped dead roses from the bush. In his rare good moods, he'd tell me about his work—a patient who had recovered well, a new nurse at the office—and I pictured how steady his hands must be during surgeries, those fitful fingers contained and precise in their white latex wrappers. I could imagine my father's hands graceful enough to cut into someone's sick heart and heal it, stitching a life back together.

Filled with a sad hunger that nothing would quell, I began to pray before bed each night. I didn't pray the way I'd been taught in church, knees and head bent, hands clasped as I whispered *Now I lay me down to sleep, I pray the Lord my soul to keep….* Instead, I sat on the edge of my bed and repeated words, phrases, in a kind of greedy, rocking chant. I kept my eyes open, staring at the bright Jesus hologram I'd won in Sabbath School for my recital of the Ten Commandments— the picture distorted as I turned it, so that Jesus seemed to wink at me.

On the way to Big Sur, Mom laughed so hard she peed her pants. Every time we passed a falling-down shack or roadside outhouse, Mr. Robert would slow the car and say, "We're here!" He was an amateur ventriloquist and could throw his voice into any corner of the car. He became Richard Nixon, Archie Bunker and Felix the Cat. And he sang. As we drove through L.A., he invented a song about the headless orphan boys who worked in the top of the Arco Plaza. Even Alison, who sat hunched against the window, was starting to giggle by the time we reached San Simeon.

As we were waiting in line at Hearst Castle, my sister sidled up to me, looping her arm through mine. "What do you think?"

"I like him okay." I was staring at a huge bronze-colored map of the San Simeon Mountains, wondering how it would be to ride horseback over all that land. "He's nice to her."

"I guess. Dad can be nice, too."

"Sure, sometimes." We were trying to settle into some

harmless phrases. I sensed that she didn't want to tell me her real feelings, but we needed to be friends for the weekend— good friends. Ali sighed, running her fingers through my curls in an odd fit of tenderness. I leaned into her solid torso.

All through the tour, Mom smiled at us across small distances. It seemed half a dozen tourists always separated us from her and Mr. Robert. She winked and nodded, as if we were old friends she'd spotted on the other side of a room, at a party.

We rode horses on a perfect beach at sunset, then ate dinner in a seaside pizzeria that was practically empty and smelled of burnt crust. Bouncing on the red vinyl seats, Ali and I begged Mom to let us play the hulking jukebox in the corner. Mr. Robert gave us quarters, and Alison jumped up to punch in songs by Buddy Holly, the Beach Boys, Elvis. I wondered what had come over her—she hated Elvis. But when "Hound Dog" came on, Mr. Robert pulled my sister to the middle of the restaurant, where they did a giggly jig between tables. Mom smiled, playing with her newly bleached bangs.

"You look like Julie Christie with your hair that color," I said.

"Oh— Good heavens, Sylvie," she exclaimed and then laughed, patting my hand. "Don't shred the napkins, okay?" A minute later she stared at me and asked, "Do you like him?" She sounded expectant as a schoolgirl, and in that instant I knew what she was planning, if only she could marshal her courage, if only she could plant us firmly on her side. My vision started to blur and I placed my open palms on the tabletop, to steady myself.

"Yeah. He's funny." A slower song clicked on and Ali

crashed into the booth, forcing me to scoot over. Mr. Robert bowed before Mom, offering his hand for the next dance. She followed him to the makeshift dance floor, where they swayed and laughed, clattering into chairs; then, in one silky gesture, Mom placed each of her shoeless feet on top of his black shoes, laced her fingers around the back of his neck. She tucked her head into his shoulder, her body sagging as if she'd just released a hundred-pound burden.

Ali jabbed me with her elbow, but I couldn't stop watching—her arms resting on his shoulders, his hands on her buttocks, her back swaying as if she had started to soften and privately dissolve and wouldn't stop until they were far from here, on the road north, in some hotel where they would look at each other and laugh because it had been so easy, so simple to leave us behind. She stretched up and kissed his neck. Then turned suddenly, as if she'd remembered leaving her pocketbook somewhere; she looked over to where Ali and I sat drinking our sodas. Stiffening, she slid her hands to his shoulders and smiled—a toothy, uncomfortable smile, accompanied by a fluttering wave.

I waved back. Ali whispered, "Quit staring like an idiot." She ordered a chocolate milk shake from the waitress who was stacking our empty plates. After the waitress left, I told Ali she was a pig, that she'd been stuffing her fat face all night.

"Go to hell, brat," she said.

"Why don't you just shut up?" My rage shot toward her, like boiling water from a kettle—as if she was the one responsible for this tumult in my belly.

For two days, the four of us slept in a cabin by the sea. I liked the scent of the place—the damp salty wood, the furniture that smelled like metal and cheese. But I felt a little sick,

OUTSIDE THE ORDINARY WORLD 163

watching my mother and Mr. Robert kiss each other's lips before migrating to separate cots on the sunporch. I stayed awake for hours, staring at the knots in the ceiling, wondering how it would be if this was our life—this odd absence of violence, this sweet pit of loss like an echo behind my heart.

We took the scenic route home, but I didn't want to sightsee anymore. I got out the sketch pad and pencil set I'd bought in the Big Sur gift shop. While Mr. Robert sang, while Mom exclaimed—how voluptuous the coastline! How treacherous this highway we'd taken!—I just stared into my book, drawing small rounded hoofs, the soft curve of my mother's neck. I drew horses' ears, Mr. Robert's ears sprouting stiff silver hairs, Alison's knees and horses' knees.

"Why, we have a budding artist on our hands," Mr. Robert chimed and I winced, wondering what he meant by "budding." It bothered me. A few weeks earlier, when Mom handed me the stiff ivory training bra in its wrapper, she'd referred to my breast lumps as "cute little buds." Could she have told him? Mortified, I finally asked her in a gas station bathroom, as she crouched above the filthy toilet. "Did you say something to Mr. Robert about my bra? Is that why he said I was budding?"

She laughed, throwing back her head. "Oh, Sylvie, you slay me! You're so silly. Come here." She stood up, zipped her pants and, still laughing, reached for my hand. I pulled away.

"Leave me alone," I said.

"What's the matter, honey, aren't you enjoying the scenery?" Mom kept asking as we drove down the coast. "Can't you try to be a *little* bit nice?"

"She's just being a baby," Ali said.

"It's puberty, Elaine," explained Mr. Robert with a laugh. "She'll outgrow it in about six years."

"Leave me alone, okay?" I whispered. "Just leave me alone." It became a joke then. Every time Mom or Ali asked a question, Mr. Robert would reply, "Just leave me alone." He even made a song about it as we drove south on the Santa Ana Freeway: "Oh, leave me alone / you big buffalo bone / I'm so tired of the nonsense you sing. / Just don't say a word / you discouraging turd / 'cause I think you're a big ding-a-ling!" Everyone laughed, and even I had to grin as I drew another horse's head, the nostrils gaping like eye sockets in a skull. As we neared home, I drew faster, filling up the entire notebook, deciding I would will it to Theresa, along with the skateboard and the records.

I came home from school the following Thursday and his smell was back in the hallways. I walked through each room, saying, "Dad?" my heart quivering. Still, the only signs of his return were a new Ping-Pong table in the family room and his suitcases, tossed on the floor of his study. I peeked in at all the familiar things—the trophies and guns, the sex books in the upper corner. I wondered if he'd missed the one I'd taken, and whether I should borrow another. I was starting to move his chair to take down *Everything You Always Wanted to Know About Sex,* when his hand gripped my shoulder. I jumped and gasped.

"Moving my furniture for me? Or were you going to leave some more love notes?" His eyes were painfully blue in his tanned face, his chapped lips twisted in a wry smile. Everything about him seemed shockingly real.

"Dad—I just. How was your trip?"

"It was great, actually. Fantastic. Why, does that disappoint you?" His clasp on my shoulder tightened. Then he steered me toward the door, pushed me roughly through. "Now, don't let me catch you messing around in here again." That was all. I stood in the hallway, relieved and oddly disappointed.

"Fine," I muttered to his closed door.

The next day, a Friday, Ali and I came home from school to find packages on the kitchen table. "Go on and open them," said Mom, who was preparing for Sabbath dinner. "Robert sent you something special." My present was a set of shiny paperbacks—one on every horse breed known to man. For Ali, he'd sent a brand-new eight-track of *Elvis: His Greatest Hits.*

"Shows you how much *he* knows," said Ali. "I don't even like this music." She thrust the present at Mom, leaving the wrapper on the floor, and stalked down the hall. Mom looked stunned, but I wasn't the least bit surprised. Alison had recently begun a full-fledged rebellion against our mother that included cheerleading practice (because Dad said it was okay), Saturday night dance parties and Leslie Brown escorting her several times a week from the school bus to our driveway, where the two of them would loiter extravagantly, kissing and touching each other's hair. None of us knew that she was just warming up. Our mother's threats and objections seemed sadly ineffectual, especially in light of her own guilt.

The alliances had been drawn, and my mother and sister were no longer on the same side.

"Well, I hope you like *your* gift, honey," my mother said in a small voice. CJ looped around my leg and I picked her up, held her tight against the pain in my diaphragm.

"Yeah, I like it. Did he send you something, too?"

She indicated a small opal hanging from a gold chain around her neck.

"Wow. Are you really going to wear it?"

"I'm wearing it, aren't I?"

★ ★ ★

She was still wearing it at Sabbath dinner that night, fingering the oval stone as my father described his hunting trip, the pheasants he'd shot, the wildlife he'd seen. He and Ali were eating the pheasant heartily, while Mom and I picked at our lentil loaf. No one said anything about what the three of us had done while he was gone. I kept my mouth shut, afraid of saying something that would give us away.

After a while, he took a sip of his wine, leaned back in his chair and said, "So, sporto—how 'bout that Ping-Pong match? You think you're ready to take on the old man yet?"

Earlier, I'd watched, entranced, as he and Ali played. Stunned by the simple camaraderie that floated between them as lightly as the white ball, I studied how my sister smoothed over Dad's blunders, or held her tongue when he did something sneaky. She didn't even seem to care about winning. I couldn't quite fathom this, and when he finally turned to offer me the next game, I'd refused. "Not now," I sulked. "Maybe later."

Now he was studying me with quiet displeasure. "Here I brought home a new toy and you haven't even tried it—some thanks I get. You afraid the old man will beat you?" His voice was private and mocking. He drummed his fingers on the table four times before I put my fork down, glared at him and said, "Okay, then. Let's go."

Though I hadn't played much before, I found myself hitting the ball in a kind of determined trance. Each time the ball soared over my head or dropped soft and treacherous close to the net, I strained to reach it, my hands precise and self-willed, my feet quicker than my brain.

"Hey, you're not bad," he said, slamming the ball across the net. "Hey, you're pretty damn tough," he added as we began yet another round.

After an hour or so, he stopped refilling his glass and fell silent. Then there was only the slap and clatter of our match, punctuated by Mom's remote attempts to get me away from him and to bed. We swayed together for what seemed like an age, bobbing and thrashing like palms in a Santa Ana. He was a better player, but I could return anything he dished out. *I'm good at this,* my body screamed as I watched him grow frustrated and darkly amazed.

Mom and Alison eventually gave up and went to bed, and still we danced along the table's edges. He wanted to beat me. I could feel it in the rhythm of his playing, his laughless eyes. My only advantage was that I wanted it more, wanted it so much, it was the only thing in the universe. The world had swallowed itself and shrunk to the size of a tiny white sphere that connected me to him in this delirious contest which, finally, I won. I set my paddle on the table, trying not to gloat, and went to my room.

As I was about to pray that night, he tapped on my door, peeked inside. "Can I come in?"

"Sure," I said, though my body tightened with surprise. I placed my Jesus hologram on the night table, quickly tossing a book of rhymes over it. My father strolled around my room, hands in pockets, like a tourist in a mildly interesting museum. Then he poked his head into my half-open closet and my heart seized. From where I sat, I could see the pine box of letters on the top shelf, next to my mother's illicit shoe box. Was he going to reach for it? Is that what he'd come for? I wondered if I would faint.

But he turned instead and sat stiffly on the edge of my bed, reached over and took one of my hands. He held it up so that our palms met face-to-face, one bigger, one small pressing up.

"Look at that," he said, shaking his head. "We have the same hands."

"We do?" I allowed myself to breathe again.

"Yep, see, same curved fingers, same bony joints, same crooked pinky."

I stared at our hands, meeting in the air and stuck there like friends.

After a minute, he placed my hand back in my lap and touched my shoulder. "You could be a surgeon with those hands," he said. "And especially with your determination. I had no idea... I think maybe we have a lot in common, Sylvia." He shook his head, as if seeing something for the first time that had been right in front of him all along.

I nodded, staring into the jigsaw puzzle of his expression, the deep blue of an iris, the crisscross of lines beneath his eyes. I didn't think I wanted to be a surgeon, but I said thanks anyway, because he had never sat on my bed like this, never looked at me and said I was good. My thigh muscles were clenched beneath my nightgown and I was trying to smile, wanting to love him, wanting so much.

After he left, I promised Jesus that I would behave from now on—no more secrets or sex books, no more Jacuzzi jets or lies. For a few months—until Darian Woods came to town—I would actually keep this promise.

Finally I slid under the covers and clicked off the lamp, wishing my father had stayed, wishing he would come back and say one more thing. I stared at my bedroom door, the sweet crack of light above it.

2 0 0 4

DRIVING TO TAI'S HOUSE THIS FIRST TIME, MY CAR
pulled up Route 9 as if by some colossal magnet, I'm wondering if I've passed the point of no return. Or maybe there's
not a single moment but many—many points on this prodigal
path, beyond which the decision to step off gets progressively
harder. I could still make it back in time to help Nathan wash
the dinner dishes and quiz Hannah on her algebra. I could
say my plans with my friend Jules were canceled, could undo
the lie. I might stop the car now, or a moment from now,
might pull into the Hess station or the mini-mart, the Look
Restaurant, the lumberyard. That road to the left leads back
home. I could take it.

Take it, I tell myself, even saying the words aloud into the
car's quiet interior. My voice startles me—it sounds so thin,
naked as a bone, but I don't obey. Maybe it was too late the
day I walked into The Wild Rose, the day of his mouth on
mine in the birches by the river.

Somehow, impossibly, I keep driving, looking for the exit to Route 112. I even have a page of directions to his house and soon I'll have to look down at it, squinting into darkness. I can no longer pretend that I just *happened* to run into him, my life a series of chance encounters—accidental or fated— somehow involving no choice. The dwindling embers of this sunset remind me of California, the clouds so streaked with crimson and gold.

Pulling to the side of the road, I'm overcome with something like homesickness. I rest my forehead on the cold plastic steering wheel, waiting, breathing, while the engine clicks. Is this the magnetism of self-discovery or self-destruction—both of which have always had equal pull in my life; I've never been able to keep them straight, never been able to tell where one lets off and the other begins. "This desire demands everything," Tai wrote in an e-mail this morning, in a seeming fit of desperation. So why are we following it?

At the Ashfield property, a couple weeks ago, I followed him through my overrun gardens while he talked of moisture, soil composition and disruptive species—lily of the valley was invasive, and someone had planted too much phlox. The dogwoods needed attention, and did I know we had a natural wetland area, north of the barn? I wrote notes on a clipboard, feigning professionalism. We were pretending we could work together this way, without incident. Nathan was up the hill, obsessing miserably over his trim, radio blaring.

We had argued again that morning—one of the last warm Sundays in October. He'd taken the girls kayaking on the lake and had forgotten to apply sunblock to Emmie's china doll skin. Now she was bright and puffy as a seared tomato. I had swallowed my rebuke—he'd *taken* them, after all—but I'd been silently fuming. So when I came out of the house an hour later, speckled with plaster, to find him prying off the newly installed cedar clapboards, I lost it.

"Oh, my God, please tell me you're not doing this! Dan just sided this last weekend!"

"I know, but it's all out of level," he sputtered, continuing his work with the crowbar.

"It's *fine,* Nathan. It looked—just fine. That stuff costs a fortune!" Emmie and Hannah were squabbling over the ladder ball set in the driveway. I pretended to ignore them. "How much out of level could it possibly *be?*"

"The water table's a good quarter inch out of whack." He heaved another twenty-dollar board onto the pile. "It's screwing up the corner board alignment. Dan's a good worker, but his details—" Here Emmie erupted in wails of indignation, and Hannah stormed off toward the house, kicking the game apart on her way; one of the plastic ladder ball tubes smacked me in the shin.

"This family sucks," Han said, slamming the back door. I shut my eyes, forced some deep breaths. These are the moments when you picture yourself turning away, slipping behind the wheel and just driving into silence.

"Nathan, we were supposed to move on to roof trim today, right? The siding was fine."

"Believe me, Sylv, I'd like nothing better than to move on."

"*Really?* Because it seems like—"

"Give me some space here, would you?" he snapped.

"All I ever give you is space," I began, just as Tai's car pulled into the mouth of our driveway, inching down the long drive, kicking up a horrible ruckus in my chest.

"Can you deal with him?" Nathan sighed. "Landscaping *was* your idea."

★ ★ ★

It all felt surreal and slightly sickening. I tried not to walk too closely beside him, tried not to notice the soft, ripe fit of his jeans, the well-built wrists protruding from rolled-up shirtsleeves. Tried not to feel the way his presence set me to a new frequency as we traversed the outskirts of my property, talking.

"This kind of border just begs to be broken up." He indicated the boundary of the old garden, where someone had planted a swath of daylilies. "The lilies want to be integrated, not used as a wall...." I took down more notes, thinking I could listen all day to that voice. He nudged his glasses up and grinned at me. "The plaster in the hair is a nice touch."

"Oh—yeah. Lovely, isn't it? I'm a total mess today."

"It's perfect, actually. A woman who can hang her own Sheetrock," he teased, causing my cheeks to ignite. We walked silently as my face smoldered.

"Rosalyn Benton said you know all about labyrinths," I offered as we tromped through the blackberries, boots smacking in sludge.

"She did, did she?" He chuckled. "Good old Roz."

"She said you're sort of famous around here."

"Is that so?" He ripped at some sumac, smiling inscrutably. "Well, it doesn't take much to get famous around *here,*" he said. "Building a stone labyrinth on your property qualifies you—good enough for the locals." He scratched a few notes on my clipboard, standing so close I could smell his morning coffee and toast, the sweet tang of sweat and shampoo. "You've an amazing piece of land, Sylvia. You'll never run out of landscapes here."

I asked what he knew of the previous owners. "I know what most locals around here know. Jennie and John

Kauffman were a pretty miserable couple. She was paranoid, depressive—kind of like my ex, only much worse—and one day she and her five-year-old daughter ended up in their car, at the bottom of the lake."

"Jesus! That's awful. Did she do it on purpose?"

"No one knows. There was an investigation. They decided it was an accident. She'd had too much Valium and driven off the road. This was back in the late eighties."

"Did you know her?" The wind blew a clump of curls into my eyes and Tai reached to brush it away, then caught himself, stroked his own beard instead.

"No. I met Kauffman when he was still deep in mourning, though. He stayed on for a decade. Letting the place go. It wasn't pretty." As we trudged up the hill, I shivered at the thought of Jennie Kauffman plunging down the embankment, the terror in the little girl's eyes as the car filled with lake water. Tai turned suddenly, swept up a fistful of clay and held it before me; for a brief, fascinating moment, I thought he might smear it across my face. "Sooner or later, darling, everything returns," he stated then spread the earth over his own ropy forearm.

Then he beamed his madman smile, and I knew I'd end up at his house, somehow.

June bugs smash their weighty bodies against his windows as I walk in. Or no. Those can't be June bugs, because it's early November, and winter's breath is already on the air, stinging the skin of my cheeks. It's just the rain, grown suddenly boisterous in this instant as I walk through the door into warmth and his smell.

"Come on in," he says, too politely, I think. He's trying to tell me something with the tilt of his head, one eyebrow raised high as a flag in warning. "I tried to call you," he whispers.

"Let me take your coat." He peels off my leather jacket with the stiff formality of a cocktail party host. And then I see Eli, sitting on a white couch in the open living room, bordered by blind windows. "Eli—look who's here," Tai says, more in his normal voice, the voice I've come to crave like a drug—a voice like warm tar, asphalt after rain. Eli stands. He's surprised to see me, and rightly so—almost seven o'clock on a Thursday night, and I don't exactly live around the corner—it's taken over an hour to find my way to this cottage in the Plainfield woods. He comes across the wide room and I rack my brain for what to say, why I'm here, while Tai deserts us to take something from the oven. I catch the fresh, yeasty odor of bread.

"Eli. It's wonderful to see you." I gather up my poise, smoothing the tremors from my voice as if I'm twelve again, at one of my mother's makeup parties, entertaining the doctors' wives. I glimpse my own reflection in the liquid glass—maroon lipstick, black V-neck sweater and jeans, hair swept up. The room isn't large but gives the illusion of space, with rough-hewn furniture and exposed beams. A fire jumps on the grate. There are books and Japanese prints against the walls, a hunting rifle slung over the hearth. Eli shoves his hands in his pockets, rocking on his soles the way Tai sometimes does. Tom Waits's off-key blues keens from the stereo. I wonder how fast I can bolt back through the door, dive into my van and void this mistake.

"Sylvia wanted to talk to you about your artwork," Tai calls from the kitchen.

"Uh, sorry I haven't been to class," Eli mutters, and I realize with shame and relief how close I was to throwing myself into his father's arms a minute ago. "I've just been, like, kind of hanging by a thread at school." He's playing the naughty boy, staring at his feet, twisted with guilt of his own. I'm the teacher, here or anywhere. He doesn't suspect anything, I don't think. Not yet. Tai comes out wearing green oven mitts, setting a loaf on the pine table, next to a bowl of olives. Then he opens the French doors and whistles.

I try to play along. "Eli. It's just—you've got a gift, and I hate to see you throw it away," I say. He nods. Yuki, Tai's white German shepherd, bounds toward me. I put out my hand for her to sniff, stifling the urge to call her by name. Surely Eli would find *that* dubious.

Tai leads me across the room, seats me on the low couch facing a pine coffee table adorned with a vase full of some orange flower I can't name. Eli sprawls on floor pillows near the fire. I sit on the edge of my seat, stiff-backed, trying to exude teacher-ness with every fiber.

Tai hands me a glass of red wine as Yuki settles in beside Eli, lets out a halfhearted growl and drops her head on her paws.

"So, you really think I've got something?" Eli says after an impossible silence and I realize that he has bought it—this story about his art teacher driving up a mountain through a November rain to talk to him about his endangered potential. He is seventeen, after all, turbulent and self-absorbed. It wouldn't occur to him that I've come here for any reason other than this. I center myself again, trying to breathe.

"Of course—you're very talented," I tell him. "And not just that; you've got a special *vision,* Eli, a really unique way of seeing the world." I steal another sip of wine, glance at Tai, who is sitting at the pine table now, head resting in his hand, eyes shut.

Eli has sat up and is attentive, ready for more information about himself. I sense that he needs this talking to—he's hungry for some crumb of direction or encouragement.

"Look over here," I say, standing and pointing to the wall beside the hearth, where Eli's framed print hangs—one he finished in my workshop last spring. "Look how you created a sense of tension with the diagonals in the buildings," I tell him. "And these windows invite the viewer in, almost making us feel like voyeurs...." I'm drawing on all my old MFA bullshit, and yet, I also know I'm speaking truth. He is gifted.

"But it takes way more than talent to make great art," I conclude. "It takes really hard work, Eli. It takes incredible persistence and dedication. And you have to be willing to make mistakes, make a mess of it. Throw away ten, fifteen pieces for each one you keep, you know? 'Everyone has the right to make an ass of himself,' as Maude says to Harold."

"Huh? You lost me there."

Tai lets out a laugh from his spot at the table. I'd almost forgotten he was there.

"Never mind," I say. "The important thing is that you should study, and work hard, because without that, talent is about as useful as a turkey sandwich."

"Wow. You've got some funky metaphors." Eli stands and stretches luxuriously, checks his watch. He's heard enough, I gather. I find myself noticing how he's got his father's compact muscularity and fine bones. "You're losing me a little, Ms. Sandon," he says, "but I totally appreciate this advice. It's, like, kind of amazing that you came up here."

"Well, you know. You're worth it," I try, burning with shame.

"Well, maybe I won't enlist after all," he smirks, looking

at his watch again. I shoot Tai a look. He nods and shrugs. "I wish I could, you know, hang out and shoot the shit with you guys some more, but Zac's coming by—"

"You heading out?" Tai asks.

"Yeah, we're gonna hear his brother's band at Pearl Street."

"Right. And then?" Someone honks from the driveway and Eli walks to the front door, grabs his jacket off a hook.

"I'll probably crash at Mom's, if that's okay."

"It's her night, after all," Tai says. "Glad you came by." He hands his son some money, thumps his shoulder. "I'll just chat with Sylvia a minute. You be careful."

Eli starts out the door, then turns around, smiles his crooked smile.

"See you in class, Ms. Sandon," he says, and then, "You be careful, too, Dad." Then he's gone, and there's nothing left to divert my attention from where I am, why I've come.

As Tai shuts the door behind Eli, leans one knotted forearm against it, I start to tremble again. I'm all jammed up with some thick emotion I can't name or release. Tai sighs deeply. "Well," he declares, shaking his head. "That was just— incredible." He comes toward me, the jade eyes glinting, the rogue-boy smile electric. "Really something."

"Is he seriously thinking of enlisting?" I collapse onto the sofa. He clicks off the stereo, and I take a hefty gulp of wine, clutch my elbows to contain the tremors overtaking me in waves.

"Not after hearing so eloquently about his artistic merits and the value of perseverance!" He settles on the sofa near me, plucks an olive from the bowl, shaking his head. Though we aren't touching, I can feel his warmth through my jeans. "You were pretty convincing."

"Well, it was all true. I mean, I may have exaggerated a

little." Tai hands me an olive, and I shake my head no. "Do you think he believed me?"

"Yes! Though I'm not sure he believes *that's* why you're here. He's not a stupid kid." He rifles his fingers through his hair, as if trying to dislodge some irksome thought. "He thinks I'm a scoundrel," he says tiredly, stealing the wineglass from my hand, putting it to his own lovely lips. "But I bet you'll see him back in class." Setting down the glass, he places a hand on my leg, still shaking his head. "Christ—you're shivering."

"I can't be here," I say. "Eli suspects—"

"He'll keep his suspicions to himself." He faces me on the couch, traces the outline of my elbow. "He's a private guy."

"But it's not fair to him!" A bubble of panic expands in my throat. It's as if I've woken from a dream to find myself in the wrong house, wrong life. "It's a—a burden he shouldn't have to carry." Saying it, I can feel the exact weight and texture of that burden, its particular size and density—a painful, familiar cyst. I stand up to leave.

"I don't think he'll take it on that way." Gripping my hand, he pulls me firmly back onto the sofa. The tremors have conquered my body now—a full throttle 7.2 earthquake.

"Tai, I don't know what the hell I'm doing here. I can't stay."

"Of course you can't *stay*." He begins massaging my right hand, eyes deep and steady as rivers. "You've got your kids to get back to. But you can finish your wine, right? Besides, it's pouring. And I can't send you off shaking like an epileptic. It's not safe."

At this I laugh a little.

"Here, let me do this properly," he says, positioning himself on the coffee table's edge facing me, scooting in close. "Is this the hand that aches?"

"Sometimes. Mostly when I paint."

After a few silent minutes, he moves to my left hand. The pressure and warmth of his fingers on my palm, my wrist, the muscles of my forearm begin to calm me; the shaking subsides. Suddenly I'm aching for a cigarette, though I haven't smoked once in fourteen years.

"Do you have any of those Camels you sometimes smoke?"

"They're in the fridge," he mutters, his fingers rolling over the tendons in my hand. "I've had my two for the day, but you're welcome to them." He's intent on his work now, head down, hands efficient and surprisingly skilled. Staring at them, I feel a single strong beat of desire.

"How can you be so damned disciplined?"

He looks up, surprised. Then he laughs, takes his glasses off and sets them on the table. "If I were so *disciplined,* would I really be seducing my son's married art teacher?" He exhales, pressing his fingers into his eyes, shakes his head. "Tell me, Sylvia—should I send you home?"

I nod. For an instant, I allow myself to go there—that dim, ever-shrinking room in my consciousness where I *don't* choose this, where I get up as I should and leave my hunger behind, sealing the door shut. Then I look at Tai and pat the sofa cushion beside me, my blush rising like fever. He hesitates. A shadow casts over his features; there's regret, a shade of fear, some raw susceptibility I haven't yet seen. A moment later he's beside me, his hand buried in my hair, and there's nothing left but to kiss him the way I've wanted to, all these months since that sultry August Tuesday. Now, like then, I'm overcome by the simple heat rising from his core, the earthy, familiar scent. I've heard about the power of smell resonating in some meaty, illiterate room of the brain; how scent can startle memory from its hiding. A kumquat, or a lone sprig of eucalyptus still has the power to evoke whole years of my childhood, and I believe I married Nathan, in part, because he smells like my grandfather.

Tai's scent—like apples and black tea, soil and smoke—now invokes something else: an old, inarticulate longing, so necessary and sharp there's no refuting it this time, and for a while I'm spinning in it, without memory or the words to shape it. I can't kiss him deep enough, can't unwrap him fast enough. We're sliding off the couch cushions, bumping into coffee table legs, tangled in our clothes, laughing and then—deadly serious.

I'm shivering again. He asks if I'm cold. I tell him I don't know—I don't know hot from cold, dark from light, wrong from right. I don't know what I'm doing, I tell him. I don't even know if I'm really here. "Well, let's find out," he says. "Let's find out if you're here." He picks me up, carries me through the French doors to the open deck, holding me against his bare torso and jeans in the pelting November rain—freezing rain, or maybe sleet—tiny glasslike shards sear my shoulders and thighs. I scream into the darkness, shocked by how right that feels. I wouldn't be surprised to look down and see my skin bruised by cold, bloodied by rain. I'm sure I must deserve this. I curl into myself while he throws his head back, laughing. "You're here!" He brings me back in when I'm numb, sets me on the rug too close to the fire, feeding it more wood until I'm stinging with heat.

Then he's unraveling me in the silence, with hands and eyes and tongue, his face strange in the firelight, primitive almost, without the glasses. I'm entering some bright, burning country—leafless, wild. Tracking my fingertips over his olive skin, I'm struck by the potency and fragility of blood and breath and bone—these intricate, insubstantial casings that separate us, keep us alive.

For a moment, two moments, three, we're part of the same organism: some outrageous sea creature washed up and tangled on the shore, terrifying, beautiful, beyond hope.

The tears come later, my back pressed to his unfamiliar chest, his heart beating my spine. Outside, leaf shadows twist and fall like embers. He's whispering something into my hair and I'm listening but not, noting instead the inner geography—landmasses have altered. The planets have come unmoored, just like in the Last Days. They will surely fall.

Or maybe nothing has changed.

Yuki lets out a long, forlorn whine. Then she lumbers across the room and butts her head into my side, hard, making me laugh.

"Are you here yet?" Tai asks, wiping my cheeks.

"I don't know." I don't say what I'm thinking: that my secret will weigh heavy in my bones, isolating me from the people in my life. The loneliness is at once bleak and weirdly consoling. I press my lips to his salty palm, as if to find some thin sustenance there.

"I'll have that cigarette now," I say.

I return home after midnight. Stepping over the threshold is like crossing the continental divide. Hannah's schoolbooks and magazines litter the sofa. Emmie's dolls are strewn—headless and disrobed—across the living room rug. The TV's blue light pulses from the den and I know without looking that Nathan has fallen asleep putting Emmie to bed, that he lies there still, one long leg dangling off the pink quilt. I start to gather the toys from the floor, but my head is reeling and I have to sit in a dining room chair, rest my cheek on the sweet oak of the table.

When I look up a few minutes later, Hannah is standing on the stairs, ghostly in her white nightie. "Where have you been?"

"Oh, hi, sweetheart. I went out with my friend Jules. Remember? She's in the studio across from Mommy's." I can't believe I just called myself *Mommy* to my teenager.

"You're late," she scolds, the same intense fretting in her brow as when she was five and eight and ten. I resist the urge to run over and embrace her. I know I must reek of cigarettes.

"I know I'm late, honey." I rest my head in my hand. "We watched an old movie, then got carried away talking." The lies stick in my throat like old bread. Somehow, I never imagined this scene, never envisioned that I would be justifying myself to my daughter, while Nathan snores upstairs, oblivious.

"Nana Elaine called twice," she says after a long pause. "She wants you to call her back—it's important."

"Okay. I'll call her in the morn—"

"I think you should call *now*, Mom. She sounded weird." Then she turns and floats back up the stairs so gracefully, I can almost convince myself she's a dream.

I sigh. I'm dizzy, spent and raw with guilt—the last thing I want to do right now is talk to my mother. Still, a sharp sliver of worry causes me to pick up the phone, dial the new number. Her voice sounds strained, asking me why I'm up so late, and I repeat the story I told Hannah. I hear her uneven breathing over the phone, and wonder: at what point did she realize it was too late to return? Did she feel herself step over some invisible boundary? Look around at the topography, the weather, as if taking stock of her new country? I'm summoning my nerve to ask her when she interrupts my thoughts.

"I'm buying you all tickets to come west for the holidays."

"Okay, but—"

"Gram's dying," she states. "I think this might be her last Christmas."

1975

A NEW GIRL ARRIVED AT OUR SCHOOL THAT WINTER.
Short black hair and wide animal eyes, she was pretty the way
some boys are pretty. Dry and dirty around the edges, Darian
Woods had falling down socks, flower print dresses and black
fingernails always in her mouth. The other kids teased her
because her clothes were old and wrong, but I found ways to
watch Darian while she picked at a cuticle or stared into space.

One day at recess, I gave her my 3 Musketeers bar while
no one was looking. She stared up with surprise in those
round black eyes.

"You sure?" she asked. I nodded, noticing for the first time
that her cheeks were covered with a spray of fine freckles, as
if someone, long ago, had misted her with mud and the
specks had been fading little by little. Soon they'd be gone. I
wanted to get over to her house before that happened, I
decided, as she took the candy bar and walked away, heavy
in her boyish hips. "Come over and play sometime," I called
after her.

"She's creepy," Theresa observed as we waited for the school bus and watched Darian walk toward her house. I stared at my best friend, my secret searing my throat. "She lives under the Garden Grove Freeway," Theresa continued, handing me a stick of gum. "I hear she lives in a shack. Sometimes she doesn't wear underwear."

She giggled in a throaty, confidential way, and I almost confessed my obsession with Darian. But my mother pulled into the parking lot just then, driving a pink Mary Kay Cadillac.

"Isn't that your *mom?*" Theresa jabbed me hard with her elbow.

"Ow—I think so." I peered into the car's rosy windows. It *looked* like my mother, except the hair was wrong, so I simply gawked until the horn honked twice—my signal to get in.

"Well?" Mom asked as I slid onto the pink leather seat. "What do you think?" Her shoulder-length locks had been shorn and now curled around her ears, making her head look smaller. I felt like I was in one of my nightmares, slowly comprehending that the woman I'd been mistaking for my mother was a stranger.

"You cut your hair." I tossed my book bag onto the floor. "It looks, um, nice."

"That's all you can say? Here I show up in a brand-new Cadillac—which I earned with my own hard work—and all you can talk about is the haircut?"

"Yeah, well, it looks different."

"I know, angel," she said after a pause, pulling onto La Loma Street. "It's awful. I look like Helen Reddy or some awful thing."

"No, it's pretty. More Florence Henderson than Helen Reddy."

"Well, hair grows back." She sighed at the stop sign, waiting for two women pushing strollers across the street, staring at our pink car. After they'd passed, one giggled behind her hand. "Hair is one of the few things in this life we can afford to screw up," Mom said.

"Why are you picking me up, anyway? How come I'm not taking the bus?"

"You *could* act happy about it," she scolded. Then she explained that she had choir practice at the church. She'd gotten the solo soprano part in the Easter cantata again, and she didn't want me home alone all afternoon. Ali was busy with cheerleading practice, and who knew when Dad was coming home. "He comes home when it suits him," she said.

"What will you do with the Jaguar?"

"I've been working very hard to get this car. Not that anyone's noticed," she complained as we pulled onto Riverside Freeway. "So, I suppose I can sell the Jag if I want to, right?"

"I guess." I shrugged. "But, I thought Dad didn't want you doing Mary Kay?"

"I suppose it's okay for him to come home in whatever crazy, souped-up race car he wants, right? But *I* have to ask permission?"

She did have a point. Still, my neck went hot thinking about what my father would say when he found out. Lately, he'd been at her to give up her "hobbies," as he called the part-time modeling and Mary Kay. His idea was for her to start a medical transcription business. The market was good, he said, and he could supply her with a steady stream of clients. But Mom had other ideas. She rarely contradicted him directly, but later, in the kitchen, or in the car on the way to the market, she would confess to Alison and me that she hated medical transcribing, that she'd just gotten the certificate as a way to put *him* through school. "I gave up all my dreams for him," she told us again and again, and I always nodded in sympathy, though Ali would roll her eyes and mutter, "*What* dreams?"

The sun was dropping when my mother and I pulled into the driveway next to her green Jaguar XJS with a For Sale sign propped in the back window. Dad's Corvette crouched in the garage. As we made our way past it, I couldn't help feeling comforted—it was so red, so outrageous. Almost as ridiculous as the pink Cadillac. How could he object?

"So you think you're selling the Jag?" were his first words as we walked into the kitchen. He stood at the wet bar, and didn't look up as he poured himself a drink.

"Well, that's a nice way to congratulate me." She took items from the Sav-On bag—cans of beans, a bottle of Windex—banging each on the counter with a thud. I slid onto a high kitchen stool, feeling queasy.

Dad claimed the stool next to me, gripping his sweating glass. "It's great you won the regional sales—thing. But we're *not* keeping that car."

"Look, honey." She spread her hands on the counter. "The Jag's got over sixty thousand miles." She inhaled, then reminded him, in a reedy voice, about the transmission problems, the sticky thing with the back window, how expensive it was each time they took it in. "So I don't see why you're so upset," she concluded sweetly, turning her back.

Just then Ali banged through the back door in her emerald-colored cheerleading outfit, golden hair cockeyed, cheeks as rosy as Mom's new car. I suspected Leslie Brown was not far off.

"What's that hideous thing in the driveway?" she asked as she tossed her backpack on the kitchen chair. "And what did you do to your hair, Mom?"

Mom shut the cabinets with a loud crack. "I'm telling you, I get no respect."

"Ali's right," Dad said. "If you're sick of the Jag, I'll get you something else—a little Audi sedan or something. But *that* car is an embarrassment."

"Oh, really?" She spun around, eyes glittering. "And I suppose your two-seater macho penile race car isn't embarrassing? I suppose that doesn't cause the neighbors to snicker?" Ali froze in front of the open fridge. Neither of us had ever heard her talk to him this way.

"And what's to laugh about, exactly?" Dad's left hand kneaded his thigh. I could tell he was deciding whether or not to take her on. At the same time, he seemed strangely diminished, wilted like old lettuce. I could see the scars from his recent hair transplant, neat rows of painful pink dots gleaming along his forehead.

"Nothing to laugh about, honestly." Mom's voice was reaching a crescendo. "Just that everyone in the county now knows about Don Sandon's midlife crisis."

He raised his hand along his face in an odd, protective movement. I'd seen him do this before, usually in the midst of arguments with Poppy. He explained once that his own father used to wallop him daily and this was just a leftover reflex, like shutting your eyes in a bright light. But I'd never seen him do it with Mom. Ali shut the refrigerator, gaping.

"And what about your little midlife crisis, *Lainie?*" Dad moved to the bar and stacked new ice in his glass. My heart thudded. He never called her "Lainie." It was Mr. Robert's name for her and apparently we all knew it. "What do the neighbors have to say about that?"

My mother laced her arms over her belly, as if trying hard to hold herself together there in the center of her kitchen, trying to keep all her separate parts from flying into space. Something about her gesture, the frailty and hopelessness of it, made my throat sting. "Just pour yourself some more gin, Don," she whispered.

"I will," he growled. "I'll have as much damn gin as I want." With that, he filled his glass and retreated to the family room, clicked on the evening news.

I watched him settle onto the orange couch, though he was anything but settled. The air around him vibrated, and I knew he hadn't given up. I decided to steal out of the kitchen before she could enlist my help, before she and Ali could launch another argument, before the pink Caddy resurfaced, before Dad could pour his third drink. I'd sneak down the hall to my room, as I always did these days, squeeze through my window and escape up the street to Theresa's.

If I were lucky, Theresa would let me ride Georgie and feed the collies. Maybe Theresa's mom, Rose, would invite me for dinner, and when I called home, my mom wouldn't be too angry to say yes. If it was a regular Tuesday at the Chapmans', Rose would make do-it-yourself tacos with guacamole, Theresa's dad would push us on the rope swing, and her brother Davey would play Neil Young songs on the harmonica. We'd laugh so hard, Theresa would squirt milk out her nose. Then we'd lie on her bed painting each other's toenails, reading Tolkien, forgetting our homework until the last possible second before my mother came to collect me. Some days, I loved Theresa more than myself—so much, it was like a thorn piercing the soft hollows of my throat. Some days, it was impossible being friends with someone so blessed.

The house was quiet and cool a few days later when Darian came over. I took her to my room first, to show off my Elton John posters, my model horses, my impressive collection of books. She didn't seem moved by any of these things; she just shrugged and slumped on the edge of my bed, removing her shoes and socks. Her toenails were filthy and jagged.

"I can't stand shoes, can you?"

"Not really." I stood before her blankly. Then I bent down to take off my own shoes, tossing them on the pile in my closet. With Theresa, it was so easy, so simple to fall into our schoolgirl gossip and confession, but this girl was different, sitting there with her legs tucked under her worn dress, her brave, expectant eyes. Talking didn't seem like an option. "Do you want to play horses?" I asked. "Or listen to some music?"

"Nah. Don't you have a pool?"

"Yeah, but it's February."

"I don't swim anyway," she said. "But we could look at it." I nodded and she bounded into the hallway. I followed her to the entryway, where she opened the sliding glass doors, sauntered into the backyard as if she knew this place by heart. As she walked toward the pool, then around it twice, I continued to follow, watching the back of her black hair, her dirty round calves. Finally she plopped on the low brick wall bordering my father's rose garden.

"This is cool." She grinned, swinging her legs back and forth, staring into the blue water.

I felt a slow, peaceful curiosity with Darian that I hadn't felt around anyone—not even Theresa. My new friend didn't seem to care that she was unkempt or unpopular, and while

I was with her, I didn't care, either. Time slowed and spread out around her and we didn't talk much. So I started inviting her over often and she always came. Unlike Theresa, Darian never had better things to do—horses to groom or dogs to feed. She wandered the periphery of our well-tended lawn barefoot and sighing.

During her third or fourth visit, Darian commanded me into the bushes with her. "Let's play a game," she said.

"What game?"

"Let's play Fuck Island."

"What's that?" I giggled, my face growing warm.

"I'll show you." She motioned me onto the ground. I did as I was told. Twigs and rocks bore into my back as Darian huddled over me, whispering, "Fuck Island is where you die unless you fuck someone every four hours. You have to keep doing it, to live. Wanna be the girl?"

"I don't care." My heart hammered and a leaf fell into my face.

"Good," she said. "We'll take turns. You be the girl first—where do you like it?"

"What do you mean?" I stared up, terrified and excited. Standing above me, surrounded by leafy branches, Darian looked as strong as any boy. She smiled—her upper lip stuck to her teeth. She had a pear-shaped mole on her cheek. Suddenly she dropped to her knees, slipped her hand into the waist of my jeans and shoved her fingers between my legs. I gasped. She touched me through my underwear, moving her finger up and down.

"Do you like it here? Or here? Tell me."

"Uh—there," I whispered, easing my legs open, guiding her finger to the right spot.

"Pretend my finger is a dick—a boy's dick and we're fucking now. Get it?"

"Yeah." I closed my eyes, my body going limp and prickly as Darian moved her hand back and forth, up and down, a little too hard.

"We have to do this every four hours, or we'll die."

"If you say so," I whispered.

But we did it much more often than that. In fact, it was nearly all we did on those high February afternoons. We did it in the empty hours before my mother returned from choir practice. We did it under the bushes or behind my father's gardening shed. Twice we did it in the orange grove at the end of Darian's street, cushioned by soft, dry dirt, citrus in our hair.

I felt that she was taking me apart and putting me back together again, each time, with her bare hands, teaching me a strange new ritual with which to greet the growing darkness at my center.

I arrived home from school one March afternoon to find my grandmother at the kitchen sink, loading the dishwasher.

"Gram—what are you doing here?" I tossed my things on the kitchen table, glanced around for my mother.

"Don't clutter that table, honey. I just cleaned it." She peered over her glasses. "I'm just tying up a few loose ends around here."

I experienced, again, the unsettling sensation of dreaming. Gram and Poppy hadn't been to southern California for years. In fact, as far as I knew, they hadn't really left Orchard Hill—aside from going to the market or the post office—since 1970. I rubbed my eyes, willing myself to awaken. Then Gram's arms were around me, her real, warm bosom pressing my neck, her familiar smell of old linen flooding my senses.

"Is Poppy here?"

"Oh, heavens, no. Poppy wouldn't get on a *plane*—not for all the avocadoes in Mexico." She pulled away, resumed her work. "Your mom's in her room, getting ready for choir."

Walking down the long hallway to the master bedroom, I could tell by the sound of Mom's voice that she was talking to Sammy. I crouched on the blue shag carpeting to listen.

"I just picked her up at John Wayne Airport a little over an hour ago."

Calamity Jane slithered from Mom's closet and purred against me.

"No, I had no idea," she continued. "She said he called on Monday. Wouldn't tell me what he said, just that we needed her *help!*"

There was a long pause. I held my breath while CJ stalked away, tail twitching.

"I'm telling you, he brought her here to keep an eye on me or—*Sylvie!*" Mom had appeared around the corner, wearing nothing but her pink lace panties and bra, clutching the powder-blue phone.

"What?" I made my face blank.

"As if I need more spies in my house! I've gotta go, Sammy." She hung up the phone, then reappeared, hands on her hips. "What are you doing slinking around?"

"I'm not *slinking*. I just came from school. Is Gram really spying on you?"

Her gray eyes narrowed, as if she believed I'd become part of the conspiracy against her, then she turned and began dressing. "She's here to keep an eye on you girls. So I can go to choir practice without worrying what you're up to," she concluded, slipping on a pair of black gaucho pants and a chartreuse sweater—the same one she'd worn in San Luis Obispo a few months ago with Mr. Robert. I wondered if she knew, somehow, about my afternoons with Darian. But how could she? She fastened the opal pendant around a neck that seemed gazelle-like without its usual adornment of hair.

"You're not supposed to wear jewelry to church," I scolded.

"Gram's here to help out for a few days, so please behave," she said, walking past me down the hall. When she got to the bedroom door, she stopped and looked back, contrite, and held her arms out. I flew into her embrace.

"I'm scared, Mom," I said, surprising us both.

"Next time I'll take you with me, angel." She traced her dry fingers along my cheek before turning away.

Once Alison had gotten over the shock of finding Gram in our kitchen, we spent a rare afternoon cooking together. The three of us constructed an elaborate enchilada casserole, created a fruit-nut salad and baked oatmeal cookies from scratch. We worked painstakingly for hours, as if preparing a complicated elixir that could cure our family's ills. As we cooked, Gram talked, telling all the familiar stories about her childhood in Walnut Creek and her marriage to Poppy: how she rode horseback to school each day, how Poppy came courting when he was a medical student and she just a teenager, how they had to sell blood at the local hospital to earn enough money for their wedding bands....

"There was no honeymoon, of course," she announced, fingering her ring. "But no matter. Your grandpa was handsome as a movie star. I thought I was the luckiest girl in L.A.—right up until he needed to take a bath."

"What do you mean? What happened?" Ali perched on

the counter, bare feet dangling. This was a story we hadn't heard before.

"Well, Avery wanted to take a bath on our wedding night, and the tub was dirty." She placed the casserole into the oven, then eased herself into a kitchen chair. "So he asked me to go on and clean it."

"On your *wedding* night?" Ali asked, at the same time I was saying, "What did you do?"

"I thought he was joking at first." Gram shook her head, eyes watery, staring into a room of the past that neither my sister nor I could enter, but I could imagine it—the unadorned walls and curtainless windows of Poppy's student apartment, his finely muscled torso gleaming above a white cotton towel as he braced one arm in the door frame. I could imagine the square yellow bathroom tiles, the dirty tub looming behind him, my petite grandmother perched on the edge of the quilt in her rosebud nightgown. I could even see Poppy's tapered lips mouthing the next, horrible words that Gram now related, "Get in there and clean the damn tub, Blanche."

"Jeez—did you do it, Gram?" I asked again, sitting down in the chair beside her.

"Of course I did." Gram's tone was suddenly businesslike. "I cleaned that tub like I meant to scrub the tiles right out of the grout. I had married him, after all, for better or worse." She removed her spectacles and polished them on the hem of her blouse. "And he did turn out to be a pretty good husband, all things considered."

"My dad would never make Mom do that," Ali said.

"Yeah, but he does other things," I said.

"Even so, my dears, it's a woman's sacred duty to—"

As if on cue, our father rustled through the back door,

jingling his keys. He slapped a pile of mail on the counter, then stopped short when he saw us.

"What are you three doing sitting in the dark?" He flipped on the light switch and I squeezed my eyes against the glare. "Where's Elaine?"

"She's practicing in the choir, Donald." Gram stood and removed her apron. "At the church—where you might be more often, if I may say." My father blinked like a stunned animal, then cleared his throat and asked when dinner would be on. "Elaine will be home near seven," Gram answered. "We'll eat then."

He pinched his nostrils and disappeared into his office, snapping the door shut. My belly tightened with rage at his rudeness. He couldn't even greet Gram properly, though he was the one who'd summoned her! I blamed him, in that instant, for every mean, self-centered thing the men in our family had done. I wanted to run to his office door and kick it down, demanding he come out, explain himself. Instead, I stalked into the laundry room, retrieved my yellow skateboard and made my way outside, slamming the door behind me.

The asphalt smelled hot and metallic after a brief rain. I glided toward Theresa's house, but stopped at the top of the street, staring up the row of oleanders that led to the Chapmans' driveway. Somehow, I couldn't bear the thought of Rose whistling while she fed the goats, the sweet smudges of paint along her cheekbones, happy yapping of dogs. I turned instead, made my way back down La Loma in the dusky light to the corner of Mesa Verde—a long, dark street that sloped toward the freeway, then dipped into an orange grove on the other side. I picked up my skateboard and walked past houses that grew progressively shabbier until I came to the green stucco with barred windows. It seemed to huddle in its weedy yard.

"Come on, then—don't just stand there," Darian's mother said when she opened the door. With her wispy dark hair and bleached, freckled skin, she was pretty in a haggard sort of way. She wore a flowered housedress, her gray apron covered with bright red splotches—for a second I thought these might be blood, until I smelled the garlic and parsley and wine. "Dar's in her room," she said, waving her stained wooden spoon in the general direction of the backyard. I followed through the living room and into the kitchen (which was the size of our guest bathroom), stood near the cracked counter while Darian's mother returned to her cooking, one hand braced on her back. She stirred sauce in a dented silver pot, taking sips from a wineglass and talking to herself.

"Long past time. Isn't that just the way." She seemed to have forgotten I was there. A fat yellow dog snored next to the refrigerator and the windows were streaked brown. Finally I worked up my nerve and cleared my throat. She startled and swung round, flinging bits of red sauce across the counter.

"Holy mother of Christ, girl—have you been standing here this whole time? I told you, Dar's in her *room*. Down the hall and left. It's the only one there," she said.

I found Darian lying on a throw rug in the middle of her bedroom floor. She was staring at the ceiling, her eyes tiny slits, lips moving. She didn't stir when I came in and sat on the corner of her twin bed; just continued mouthing her silent sentences, hands clasped over her rib cage. Was she praying, perhaps, or memorizing something? There were a few books on the night table, and a King James on the bed, but no toys to speak of, except a collection of plastic statues lined up on the windowsill, a floppy stuffed dog splayed across her pillow. The room smelled like graham crackers.

Finally she opened her eyes and gazed at me. Her black hair was fanned in a perfect dark half circle above her round skull. "'Bout time you came over," she said.

"What are you doing?" I asked. "Were you sleeping?"

"No. I don't sleep on the *floor*. I was saying my Hail Marys."

"What are those?"

"Don't you have to say Hail Marys?" She sat up, crossing her legs, and stared, slack mouthed. I shrugged and shook my head. "How do you get pardoned for your sins?"

"I don't know. I pray sometimes, if that's what you mean. I go to church and all that."

"But what does the priest tell you to do after confession?"

"Oh, we don't have that," I corrected, beginning to understand. "We're not Catholic."

"So, how do you get absolved?" she asked, picking at a loose thread on the hem of her dress. "How do you get pardoned?"

"Well, we ask for forgiveness and then try to do a lot of good deeds, I guess, to make up for the bad ones." I crossed my arms, glanced around the tiny room.

"But who tells you how many good things you have to do for each bad thing? How do you know when you've made it up?" She seemed genuinely concerned for my soul, and I realized that this was the most she'd ever spoken to me at one time.

"I don't really know." I was getting antsy with this conversation, my obvious lack of answers. I wanted to play Fuck Island, or go home. "I guess when you've done enough good deeds, you're supposed to feel less guilty or something. You're supposed to have faith."

"And what about prayers for protection?" she asked, rubbing the pale skin of her legs. "Aren't you worried something will happen?"

"You mean, like the end of the world? Like Jesus coming or something?" She seemed terrified of something—something she had to hold her whole self rigidly against. I reached awkwardly to touch her knee, but she jerked away.

"Darian? Are you mad? Do you want to do something else? Play Fuck Island or something?"

At this she looked up, grim and ghostly—the tough, sexy tomboy spooked clean away. "Wanna know where I learned that game?" she asked. The yellow dog waddled in, jumped on the bed and started licking my knees, and I let him, though it gave me the creeps. I wondered if it was true what Theresa and the other girls said about Darian—that she had already been with boys in that way. I started to get edgy thinking of it, but then she stood, hugging herself. "I don't want to play that anymore," she said, looking down at me with something like hatred, but this was duller, flatter than any hatred I'd seen.

"Fine. We don't have to. It wasn't *my* idea anyway, remember?" I knew then that I would not play with Darian again, and was surprised by the release flowing through my arms and legs, making me sad and dizzy. Still I waited. I wanted her to say the game had been *her* idea; that I'd only gone along with it. I wanted her to free me from the heaviness of this room, this dark sweet conspiracy. But she just stared with those saucer eyes, then snorted, patting the dog's head. After a while, she moved to the window and began showing me all the plastic saints on her sill. They were all women, all with a special, saintly task. She held them so gingerly. I nodded, pretending to learn their names, and by the time she was done her mother was yelling at her to come eat and the darkness was spreading like scandal.

It was fully nighttime when I got home, but the pink Cadillac was not in our driveway. I set my skateboard down, made my way into the house.

"Hey, weirdly." Alison was doing homework at the kitchen table. "You're in trouble."

"What for?"

"You're kidding, right?" She looked up from her book, sucking on a strand of hair. "It's eight-fifteen, Sylvie. You kind of missed dinner. Dad went to look for you at the Chapmans'."

"Oh, shit." My stomach dropped. "Where's—"

"Mom's not home yet. Said she was stopping at Sav-On, like we *believe* that."

"What about—"

"Gram's gone to bed and Dad's going to *kill* you, so if I were you, I'd, like, apologize or something."

"Tell him I went to bed." I grabbed the Cap'n Crunch box and made a beeline for my room, but my father intercepted me in the hallway. Stepping out of the bathroom, he seemed perfectly collected, except for the red-rimmed eyes, worry lines like fissures between the dark brows, his clamped fists.

"Where the hell have you been?" I caught the sickly reek of alcohol, and my heart started banging like a loose shutter in a windstorm. When was it that he'd started drinking so much?

"Sorry. I was out riding my skateboard. I didn't realize—"

"Just like your mom, huh, sporto?"

"*What?*" The pressure in my chest switched from fear to fury.

"You aiming to be exactly like her?" Another question I couldn't answer. It seemed I was turning out just like her whether I aimed for it or not. I hugged my cereal box.

"I'm going to bed."

"Oh, no, you're not." His voice was soft, venomous. Maybe he really *had* mistaken me for Mom. "You're gonna go eat a decent dinner. Your grandma worked all afternoon."

"I *know,* Dad. I was working, too, for your information," I began. "I'm the one who—" But his hands were loaded springs, crashing across my face, grabbing my shirt and hurtling me into the linen-closet doors, which snapped shut so loudly, I thought they'd broken.

As always, the violence was quick as a car wreck; before I knew what had happened, I was sprawled on the tiles and sunk in shame, my pants soggy and something warm leaking from my nose. The cereal was scattered down the hall and into the entryway like so much confetti, across which my father was walking, smashing cereal into the grout with his loafers.

Gram stayed with us for almost three weeks that winter— long enough to reorganize the linen closet, bake a month's supply of lasagna, recite most of the New Testament aloud and lecture Mom several times on *a wife's duty.* Though I liked having her, I wasn't sure she was having the effect Dad had hoped for. After all, we were still sneaking coffee breaks whenever Mr. Robert was in town. Still getting letters filled with promises—my carved pine box was bursting. I'd even started writing him back, figuring it was time to take things into my own hands. "I'd like a place with pretty green pastures and no fighting and a few horses," I wrote. "How about you?"

All the same, my Gram did have influence. A few days after

she returned to Lafayette, I came home from Theresa's to find Mom sticking mailing labels onto brochures at her desk, which Gram had reorganized. Next to her sat a fat Rolodex containing dozens of doctors' names and addresses. I flipped through it. She swatted at my hand.

"You're messing up my order, honey."

"Does this mean you're doing the transcription business after all?" I asked.

"That's what it means." She didn't look up from her work.

I slumped at the kitchen table. "So, you're not going to be home in the afternoons?"

"You're old enough to look out for yourself a bit, Sylvie."

"Where's the pink Cadillac?" I asked.

"I gave it back to the company."

"What?"

"It was never really mine, honey. I *earned* the right to drive it, that's all." She continued peeling labels off a long sheet, securing them to the pale blue brochures that read "ELS Transcribers—Fast, Reliable, Accurate: we work behind the scenes to make you look good."

"It was never really mine," she said again, as if speaking to herself.

Staring at the back of her neat corduroy jacket, I couldn't have begun to explain the fury and betrayal I felt. I wasn't sure what any of this—the car, the job—had to do with me. I hadn't even liked the Cadillac. "Are you going to do everything Dad says from now on?" Mom turned around, stared at me over the tops of her new magenta reading glasses.

"Look, angel, the pink Caddy was a cop magnet. I got my *only* two speeding tickets in that thing. And this business will help me save up some money. Dad is right sometimes, okay?"

"What do you need to save up money for?"

"Oh, I don't know. Maybe we'll take a special trip this summer, to horse country or something." She turned away, resuming her project.

"We *who?*" I demanded. "*We* like the people who live here? Or do you mean *we* like Mr. Robert and us?" She was silent. "Mom?" I had no idea which answer I was hoping for, but it didn't matter, because she wouldn't give me either.

On the night of the Easter cantata, I went to the church early with my mother to help the choir set up. My father and Ali were arriving later. I couldn't remember the last time Dad had been to church with us. Perhaps this was his way of trying to show support for one of Mom's "hobbies." Or maybe he was rewarding her for getting rid of the car, starting the business, doing what he said. Maybe he thought these things meant she was still his.

The choir members—plump elderly women and balding men—all knew me by now. All of them dowdy in their burgundy choir robes except for my mother, glamorous in her Florence Henderson do. I helped them all find their robes and black satin shawls, helped them set up shallow bleachers at the front of the sanctuary. Some of them called me "Elaine's little clone." They teased me about how my mom should be a star with that voice, and maybe I would be a great artist one day, too. I thought they were joking, having a little good-intentioned fun at my expense, until later, when I watched her transform into Claudia.

She delivered her lines in a voice powerful and ethereal, arms spread, eyes rolling back and closing as her clear soprano rose to such heights, I thought the stained glass might shatter, or maybe my heart. It occurred to me then that my mother really could have *been* someone. As Pilate's wife, on bended knee before the choir, she begged for the life of Jesus, pleaded for fairness, pardon, absolution, real tears dotting her choir robe.

For some reason, I found myself thinking of Darian and her saints. Since that day in her room, I'd been careful never to look at her, and she hadn't said a word to me, just stared at me once—a long, vacant waiting that I felt on the side of my face all through social studies. The next week, she was gone. According to gossip, her mother was an alcoholic and she'd been taken to an aunt in Eugene, or maybe a foster home. Nobody knew for sure.

The day before Easter, I'd ridden my skateboard down her street, stopped in front of her house. The lawn was weedier than ever, and one of the windows boarded up. Tucking my skateboard under my arm, I crept around the house, through a tangle of faded oleanders, to Darian's bedroom window. Peering in, I thought I saw her for an instant and jerked back, then realized it was just my own face reflected in the milky glass. I looked closer. The saints were still there, lined up and dusty on the sill. They looked ominous and hopeful, their faces pointing to the world outside. I wondered if she'd abandoned them on purpose, or if she just didn't have time to gather them together. I wished I could get inside somehow, and take them for myself.

2004

I FIND MYSELF WANDERING INTO THE UNITARIAN Meeting House, the morning after my night with Tai. Between an optometrist appointment and a meeting with my accountant, I push through the plain oak doors, surprised they aren't locked against me. Nathan and I have come here on a dozen occasions, testing it out, but each time I've felt somehow discouraged by the narrow podium, the bleached ceiling beams like the ribs of some great whale carcass. Today I sit in the empty sanctuary for fifteen minutes, hoping for clarity maybe, or virtue, or at least a respite from my sledge-hammer of guilt, but all I feel is a familiar old silence.

Several days later, I try the First Churches on Main Street and the next day, St. John's on the corner of Chestnut. Here, the air is heavy with incense and flowers adorn the altar. Stained-glass windows along the walls depict every hour of Jesus's days leading to the crucifixion: Gethsemane, Judas's betrayal, the last-ditch redemption of the thief on the cross. I am still intimate with these scenes. Maybe, then, life is a series of reenactments—chasing down new frames for the stories that stalk us. I choose a seat in back, near the confessionals, remembering Darian and her saints. I've always envied the Catholics their rituals, but what would I even say, if I were allowed to whisper it to a priest—that I've made an art of my restlessness? Become my mother at last, despite the years and miles between us? And what of the other secrets, deeper even than Tai, that hover like smoke on the outskirts of memory?

After a few minutes I get up to leave. What I'm seeking won't be found in a church. I need to move through eddying leaves, glimpse new snow on the Holyoke Range, hear the thirsty call of migrating geese. I need a landscape big enough for this longing, air sharp enough to cool my inescapably primal thoughts—hot curl of laughter, bright well of an iris, his hands tracing my jaw, mapping my hip bones, unhinging me. His e-mails are all wild metaphors that stalk my dreams, catching me at the center.

"What are we doing?" I ask him, staring at the ceiling. "What is this about?"

"I don't know yet," he whispers, trolling his fingers through my insubordinate curls. "It's about mining for God, isn't it? Living near the bone."

"Can God be found in deception?" I ask. Weeks into this, I'm wondering if we're even wading in the same river: two thirsty vagrants, both seeking some strong, bittersweet tonic.

"God is anywhere you find yourself opening, right? Bowled over by life."

"Are you talking rebirth? Second chances?" I gaze around his room at bookcases filled with titles on Buddhism, masonry, mythology. Poetry by Neruda, Ginsberg, Mary Oliver. Facing the huge corner windows, his drafting table is blanketed with sketches and file folders—drafts of the land-scaping book he's writing. I want to memorize each thing, as if these details could answer something. At the same time, I wish I could delete him entirely.

"Maybe rebirth, but not escape." He straddles me beneath the off-white quilt. "This can't be about escape."

"Why?" I laugh. "What do you have against escapists?"

"Nothing, really." The splashes of gold in his green eyes look like tiny brush fires. "I come from a long line of escapists—workaholic Rabbi father, depressive mother."

"Me, too. Except for the Rabbi part."

He plops down on the bed beside me. "My little brother died of heroin. My family was so good at escaping—well, they're not here anymore."

"Tell me about that." I stroke the lone, misguided curl that creeps down his neck, surprised at how hungry I am for his losses.

"Mmm, it's a long story—suffice to say that I try to stay present." Flashing a knavish smile, he falls back on the pillows. Then, suddenly somber. "This isn't about running from your life, is it?" I look away from his dark beauty, stare out the bedroom windows; November branches scratch at a sky as hard as slate. Beyond the hemlocks, I see vestiges of his wild garden, the Zendo he built from cedar, his stone labyrinth, which is supposedly what I came for today, why I drove up this mountain in the middle of another Tuesday, abandoning work.

"We didn't even make it to the garden," I note. "We lost our way, like last week."

"I know. But I don't feel lost." He bites the fleshy part of my hand, then stretches like a cat. I stare at the curved mistake of his spine, hard error of a bicep, inky mishaps of his brows.

"Maybe we're looking for salvation," I say. On the opposite wall hangs my painting, of the view from Orchard Hill—scrub oaks in the fog, amber hills and that scraggly old water tower. I remember painting it, five or six years back, standing on Gram and Poppy's lawn while Hannah played nearby. Maybe someday I'll understand this need to study a picture of my childhood from the refuge of someone else's room. But right now I can't quite believe I'm looking at that view from here, like this.

"Not Salvation with a capital *S*," Tai comments now. "I can't offer that." Sitting on the edge of the futon, he peels me from the comforter. "But maybe with a small *s*." With a calloused finger, he sketches the outline of one breast, the ghostly lattice of stretch marks left from nursing. "Come outside with me," he offers. "I'll show you how to walk the labyrinth." But I'm reluctant to move. I feel heavy and drowned as a drunk, my insides still warm with him.

"Do all Jewish men have such lovely smooth chests?" I ask, as if it's the most natural thing, touching a stranger this way, killing off the life I've made with a flick of the wrist.

"Ah—an adulteress *and* a racist." I can see he's teasing by the curl of his mouth, but that doesn't stop the burn of rage in my belly. I sit up, swing my feet onto the cool wood floor.

"I need to go."

"Sylvia. I'm sorry." His hand on my back is still unfamiliar, precise fingers kneading my shoulders. "I was just playing—you know that, right?"

"I have to leave anyway," I snap. Emmie will be finishing rest time by now, Hannah going off to drama or history? I can't remember which it is on Tuesdays and this suddenly seems pathetic, inexcusable. I miss them fiercely, as if I've journeyed to the very edge of the earth and stood on its craggy precipice, peering into the depths. It's impossible that

I've just been away a few hours, in the middle of a school day, unmissed. And what of Nathan? Does he sense, in the quietest part of his bones, how far I've traveled? *I belong to no one now.* I wonder if this is the very same loneliness that once caused my mother to enlist me as her confidant.

"You've grown sullen," says Tai, withdrawing his touch.

"*Adulteresses* tend to be. The guilty are always morose, right?" I stand, slipping on underwear and bra, aware of his appreciative gaze, how stirring it is to be seen. However moody, guilty, afraid, I'm also not done here.

"*I'm* not morose," he points out. I turn to stare at him propped on an elbow, the sheet falling over his hips, skin especially olive against the ivory quilt. Everything here speaks of ease—pale walls and rice paper shades, canvas chair and sleeping dog, expanse of cool linen, his smile.

"That's because you're a Buddhist," I sulk. "I haven't quite mastered your art of quiet surrender yet. Besides, *you're* not betraying anyone."

"Right, but a Jewish Buddhist is always guilty." He reaches for me. "Don't go off angry."

"I'm leaving," I repeat, though the thought of it exhausts me.

"Here, let me teach you the art of quiet surrender," he teases, pulling me easily back down, pinning me to the bed.

"I don't know what we're doing, Tai," I protest as he unfastens my bra.

"Maybe it is about second chances," he whispers, tracing the swell of one hip. "Or, how about second comings?" He smiles, sliding his hand between my thighs.

By the time we emerge, the sun is slipping down the arc of the sky and I still haven't seen the thing I came for—the backyard design, the labyrinth. "It's like us," Tai says as we drift to his door, Yuki trotting circles around us. "A bit past noon, edging toward evening. It's my worst time of day. I can't believe you're leaving me to it."

He walks me to the driveway, leans me hard against the cold van. I've grown used to the scratch of his beard, the taste of his tongue, how thirsty I am. Like whiskey, his kisses don't quench; they just deepen the craving.

"Here—" he whispers, extracting himself from my arms. "I want you to have this." He digs something from his pocket, pushes it into my palm—a rough bluish stone shaped like an uneven heart, the size of a silver dollar. "It's an agate. I found it while walking the beach north of Big Sur, when I lived there. Keep it." He curls my fingers snug around it.

I slide it into the front pocket of my jeans, where it will live for a while. Then I will myself into the car, recalling something Theresa once read me when we were both graduate students—how everything is memory and genetics: how we speak and dress, the ways we falter, those we're drawn to—was it Freud? I remember asking her, *What chance do I have?*

Skidding down the mountain, following a sharp arrow of geese, I'm confronted by the things I've left undone: brochures I abandoned at the printer, clients I've failed to call back. I'm running out of supplies at the studio, have yet to pay this month's bills. I forgot the girls' appointment for flu vaccines, and Theresa has left three messages on my voice mail—in the last one, she just sighed, "Sylvie, oh, Sylvie." My hands throb against the steering wheel and the road before me undulates. I pull onto the shoulder for a moment, hazard lights flashing, allowing the traffic to shudder by until I can gather my wits for the agony of reentry.

But I'm still dazed as I walk through Cloverdale preschool. I feel uncivilized among all the young mothers with their neat ponytails and ski jackets, their tote bags and wholesome smiles. Jillian Alstrom's mom asks if we can please arrange a playdate after Jilli's Music Together class, and I just nod dumbly, my bedroom hair flopping into my eyes. I am soiled and feral, unfit to be the mother of this child with the strawberry ringlets who clings to me. I wouldn't be surprised to look down and find that my jeans were unzipped, my boots missing.

"Can we go get ice cream, Mama?" Emmie asks as I hoist her into the car seat.

"Ice cream in November?"

"I want chocolate with chocolate sauce and chocolate sprinkles and a chocolate cherry." She giggles, amused by her own excess.

"Okay, honey." I laugh. "We just have to pick up your sister first."

But when we get to Hannah's school, she's not there. I'm ten minutes late, so I decide she's probably gone inside. My love stupor is falling from me like a damp towel as Emmie and I clip through the tiled hallways, searching. When we walk into Hannah's homeroom, the teacher, Ms. Weiss, is already turning over chairs, setting them on desktops. I tell her we're looking for Hannah and she frowns and cocks her head.

"She went home with Ava Selinger. They took the bus to Ava's house, remember?"

"Uh, no, I *don't* remember. I didn't—"

"She brought a note. It's right over here." She grabs a tiny slip of notebook paper off her desk and hands it to me. On it, in a fairly good imitation of my terrible turkey scrawl, is a note granting permission, signature and all. My stomach clenches. This is so unlike Hannah, I can't quite believe it, and I tell Ms. Weiss so. "I don't think she's ever done anything like this before," I mutter, chewing my thumbnail.

"Yes, well, there've been quite a few uncharacteristic behaviors lately." She glances at Emmie, unsure what the little sister should hear. "I've been waiting on a reply to my e-mail."

"You sent me an e-mail?" I'm remembering all the unopened messages in my in-box—the newsletters and grant deadlines, the pithy Christian forwards my mother sends…. Reading these messages *not* from him is always an unpleasant jolt, like coming out of a warm bath into the drafty fall bite of our house. I let them pile up, save them as Unread. Still, wouldn't I have read anything from one of the girls' teachers?

"Oh, dear. Well, that's the trouble with the new technology, eh?" Ms. Weiss smoothes her bobbed gray hair behind her ears. "E-mails are always so—"

"What's going on with Hannah? Is something up?" The pain in my wrists is firing up again. My eyelids feel singed.

"We really ought to meet. I don't have time for a conference this moment."

"Can you just give me the general *idea?*" I clutch the edge of a table while Emmie totters off to attack the chalkboard and colored chalks.

"Just small, worrisome things. Nothing too egregious, but quite uncharacteristic—"

"*Like?*" I struggle to stay poised, but it's difficult. I'm as jagged as a bread knife.

"Well, like a lot of missing homework assignments, which is unusual for Hannah, and a disruptive verbal fight with another girl—Isabel Fletcher, to be precise, though not a lot came of it—and the stolen calculator, and the math test."

What fight? What calculator? "This is the first time I'm hearing about this stuff." I crumple onto the edge of a chair she hasn't upturned yet.

"Well, it *was* all in the e-mail. The cheating was strangest, but look, Ms. Sandon, we need to set up an appointment." She continues her work of upending the chairs. "I just can't take the time right now."

"How about tomorrow?" I'm getting out my appointment book, my pen is poised, but Ms. Weiss can't offer me a conference until next week, the Wednesday before Thanksgiving. I take it—women like me can't be too choosy, after all.

Driving to Easthampton to pick up my teenager from the Selingers' house, I recall the night Mom and I drove to Orange to collect Ali from a club where she wasn't supposed to be. Elaine still had the Mary Kay Cadillac, and I hid in the back, teetering between elation and mortification as she pulled up in front of The Blue Wave, catching my sister smoking a joint on the curb, Leslie Brown's big black hand foraging under her tube top. My mother's outrage was absolute as she dragged poor Ali into the pink car, announcing that Leslie and every other randy young boy were prohibited for the remainder of high school.

I can't quite muster up my mother's brand of self-righteous wrath as I walk into Ava Selinger's basement at 4:00 p.m., though I should be furious. Ava's parents aren't home and the girls are playing pool with two high school boys. Hannah takes one look at my face and grabs her backpack, comes to the car without a fight. It's just not her nature to be seditious;

I'm thankful for this, and try to go easy on her during the drive home.

"Did you think I wouldn't *notice?*" I ask after a sticky silence. "Did you think I'd just shrug and go on home when you didn't show? Or—or what?"

"No, Mom. I just—I don't know, okay? I don't *know* why I did it." She's sitting alone in the rear seat of the van, staring out the window, ignoring her little sister, who keeps turning around, begging Hannah to put Barbie's dress on for her.

"Well, could you come up with a couple ideas?" I ask. "Because I really don't know what to tell your dad about all this." Some fear or uncertainty keeps me from mentioning my conversation with her teacher. I decide to wait until I have more information.

"Ava wanted me to see her new pool table. And then her neighbors showed up. That's it—end of story."

"Okay. And since when does that need to involve forgery and—and going AWOL?"

"I can't do this," Emmie whines, thrusting the blue Barbie gown at Hannah.

"You weren't around, okay?" Hannah snaps. "I tried to call you, like, *fifteen* times. Did you even check your messages?"

I swallow, squeezing my eyes shut. Of course, I haven't checked my messages once today—not at the studio, not at home. My cell phone's been on, but there's no service in Plainfield. *What if there was an emergency?* Impatience with myself shoots out toward my daughter instead. "That's no excuse," I tell her. "It doesn't give you license to lie."

"Why does *Dad* have to get involved in this, anyway?"

"Because," I say, turning behind the high school, veering into our street. "Because, Hannah, he's your father and I just don't feel comfortable—"

"Keeping secrets?" she inserts.

I stare at her in the rearview mirror—the almond eyes and thick auburn brows exactly like Nathan's. Then she glances away, just as Emmie bursts into frustrated sobs, hurling the blue gown *and* the nude Barbie over the front seat and into my lap.

Thanksgiving is an everlasting affair and I'm smiling stiffly through it, trapped in the aperture of my mind. As always, we gather at Nathan's sister's house in Amherst—the same lovely cape where Nathan grew up, went to school and dropped out, ran away from home, came back. The same house where he first got drunk and laid, and then finally, where he and I got married, fifteen years ago under the catalpa trees. I love Nathan's family—his earnest, school administrator sister and brilliant professor brother-in-law, his two hard-drinking twenty-something nephews and his dotty, intellectual mother. I even love Richard, Nathan's antagonistic older brother who always tries to stir up an argument. But today, I might as well be in south Texas for how connected I feel.

I'm smiling through it, trying to engage in conversations about politics, about the casualties in Iraq which the media never covers, McCarthian threats to our freedom of speech—all of us comfortably on one side in this liberal northeast college town, all of us assured of our rectitude, except me. I'm sitting on the black leather recliner in the corner, spinning outside the circle of light, a space traveler between worlds. Still tasting the smoky tang of my lover's kisses, still feeling his imprint between my thighs, I wear my guilt like a veil—it obscures my vision of this family, muffles my hearing. Somewhere, in some other universe, I can discern Emmie's happy shrieks as her big-boy cousins toss her on the frozen lawn.

"I want to give you the name of my acupuncturist," says Nathan's sister, Shelly, leaning in close as she hands me a small square of yellow paper. "She's really terrific, Sylvie, and Nathan told me you've been having some somatic symptoms."

"*Somatic* symptoms?" I stare at her over the rim of my wineglass.

"The tendonitis—I hope you don't mind. I noticed you rubbing your hands earlier."

"Oh, right. Thank you." I take the paper, slipping it into my back pocket.

"It can help with marital issues, too, if you know what I mean," she says, winking. "Dan and I once went the better part of two years." She peers down at me, real concern in her round chestnut eyes. I smile and nod, mortified that Nathan's been telling Shelly about our sex life, or lack thereof, when he won't even broach it with me.

Hannah comes across the room like an emissary, hand held out, and asks if she can have a glass of wine—her first? I give her my half-drunk glass of Pinot Noir, still adrift in an ether of unspeakable thoughts. My in-laws turn and stare. Nathan looks at me like I've gone round the bend, and I realize Hannah has asked *me,* not him, because she knew I'd say yes. I remember my half-hour conference with her teacher the previous day, cataloging the symptoms of some new trouble—is it just adolescent rebellion? The long overdue assertion of her independence, or something more disturbing? I haven't told Nathan anything yet.

Why haven't I told him? I wonder, as my sister-in-law pours me more wine, calls us for dinner. Are Hannah's transgressions somehow webbed into my own? Do I fear that one confidence, pulled up into the yellowish light of our bedroom, will unearth them all?

Now we're all seated around the long table in my favorite sunroom. Always before now, this house has felt safe and full of heart. On the day of our wedding, surrounded by new family on the sheltered lawn, I beamed with the fortune of an adopted stray—never again to roam. Under the catalpa trees, I spoke homemade vows about finding my lost center, surrendering to the beauty of mortality while Nathan wept, grasping my hands so tightly, my fingers went numb.

"So what've you been doing for *fun,* Sylvie?" Richard asks in his affected drawl. He passes me the beets as I recite the litany of my days—the art classes and studio hours, Hannah's performances, my ailing grandmother, the upcoming trip west…. He nods, then whispers into my ear, "How come you look so damn *radiant?*"

I feel the flush spreading like an infection over my throat and forehead, and quickly turn my attention to Emmie, clambering onto the chair next to me, demanding Jell-O. I ask Shelly to please send it down and busy myself loading up Emmie's plate. Hannah is at the end of the table, enjoying the ribbing of Caleb and Andrew, her two beefy cousins. The rest of them are discussing Ron Laughton, a professor friend of Nathan and Dan's from high school who is leaving his wife for a twenty-five-year-old grad student. I'm so nauseated, I doubt I can eat a bite.

"You have to wonder how many months *that* relationship will last," mutters Dan.

"You're right, Dan," concurs Clara. "Relationships begun in secrecy don't fare well."

"What'll poor Ron do when his midlife crisis winds down

and he's stuck with a twenty-five-year-old across the table?" says Shelly.

"What's so awful about twenty-five-year-olds?" Andrew pipes in.

"My mother's still married to the man she had an affair with," I find myself saying. Now they're all staring down the long table, waiting for more. "I mean, I don't know how blissful they are, but it lasted." Nathan clears his throat, too loudly, I think. Perhaps I've embarrassed him by stating the truth, bringing up my impossible family.

"Yes, but with a *student*," Clara continues. "It's different."

"It's the children I worry about," says Shelly.

"But how can you blame Ron?" asks Richard. "Nobody wants to live in a cage. Now, if you open the cage door, tell the prisoner they can come and go at will, they might decide to stay."

"Come on, Rich. Let's not go there today," suggests Nathan.

"Traditional marriage is too small a container—Ronnie's just a case in point."

"Just because a loving relationship feels like a cage to *you*, Rich," snaps Shelly.

"What's Uncle Richard talking about, Mommy?" Emmie tugs on my sleeve. Everybody laughs. Then the table grows quiet.

"Well, he's talking about how we can't always make others happy," I venture, "even those we love." She blinks, so I try again. "Sometimes, people just need different things."

"Like, when Hannah won't play Polly Pocket?" She frowns at the memory of this betrayal, fresh from the morning.

"Yes, sort of," I concede after a pause. Hannah guffaws.

"Honestly, though, Sylvie," Richard persists. "Don't you

think your folks' marriage would have improved if your mother could've had her lover on the side?" I feel the heat singeing my cheeks again, hands hurting. I drop my fork, staring into my mashed potatoes.

"That's enough, Rich," says Clara. "There are children present."

"No, it's an interesting question," I manage to respond, looking up. "I don't think my parents' marriage was mature enough to weather an open arrangement. I don't know many that are." I don't say that maybe the secrecy was part of the appeal for Elaine—the idea of having something no one else could access. Somehow, I'm realizing this for the first time.

"Your face is the same color as the cranberry sauce, Mom," Hannah says cruelly.

"Is it?"

"Yeah, you ought to do something about that blushing, Sylvie," teases Richard. "People will start thinking you're guilty of something."

Everyone chuckles. Just as I'm about to melt into the dhurrie rug, darling Emmie knocks her strawberry milk across the turkey platter, necessitating an abrupt transition as the women stand in unison. By the time we sit back down, the conversation has thankfully shifted to home improvement. Nathan and Dan are commiserating over how long it takes to install exterior trim, especially on these old, irregular houses where nothing's level, nothing's plumb.

It's getting dark and suddenly I'm worn out by all this socializing. I'm craving the dark woods around his cottage, the sweet, earthy aroma of his bed quilt, snow softly battering the windows. The restlessness begins at the root of my spine. I'm wondering if I can slip out for a smoke right now, maybe even call him. Will he be with Eli? Having dinner with the ex-wife? Home alone?

I'm startled by Nathan's lanky hand pressing my shoulder.
He's standing behind me, clearing his throat to get everyone's
attention. Then he proclaims that next year, *we* will host
Thanksgiving, at our Ashfield house overlooking Apple
Valley. "I know it's been years, and nobody here believes I
can finish anything I start."

Richard snickers.

"We love you anyway, Nate," croons Shelly, collecting the
dishes.

"Yes, but it *is* about time, honey," chimes their mother. I
reach back to squeeze Nathan's forearm, hating myself for
somehow joining the conspiracy to undermine him. Hating
him for refusing to get angry. This is how these dinners go:
Rich holds forth and Nathan is lovingly derided until I come
to his defense.

"Anyway, I'm sure you think we'll be in Tyvek forever,"
Nathan says. "Including my wife." He squeezes my collar-
bone. "But next fall, we'll be done."

"Or, at least moved in." I amend, hoping to keep his
promise within the realm of possibility. "And you guys can
come up there for a change and leave the dirty dishes." At
this, Nathan leans over to kiss my cheek, Hannah watching
intently from across the table.

"You look sexy," he whispers. "How about messing around
with me later on?"

But once we're home and the girls finally asleep, I decide
it's time to talk about Hannah's offenses, and he explodes,
short-circuiting the remote possibility of romance.

"Why the hell hasn't this come up? How long have you
known she was in trouble?"

"I only found out about it last week, Nathan. And I don't

know that she's *really* in trouble. It could just be normal eighth-grade stuff. Didn't you ever get into mischief at that age?" I continue rearranging the refrigerator, making room for all the leftovers Shelly has plied us with.

"Hannah's not the kind of kid to *steal* a teacher's calculator so she can cheat on a math test!" he proclaims, banging a Tupperware container full of stuffing on the counter. "It'd be one thing if it was just grades, or boy trouble, but this just feels *wrong*. For her anyway." He retrieves the cognac from the cupboard above the fridge, pours himself a glass, then offers me one. I decline. I feel uneasy enough without the blur of more alcohol.

"It doesn't seem *that* outrageous, does it? I mean, think about what some of her friends are up to! Ursa Abbott was suspended for selling drugs, for Chrissake. And that Loughman girl—what's her name?—who dropped out of school last year to have her illegitimate kid down in Florida?" I'm trying to sound unruffled by our daughter's petty crimes, but deep down, I know he's right. Hannah's one of those kids who earns As despite her learning issues, leads community service projects and performs in the *Nutcracker*. I'm one of the moms other parents avoid at PTO meetings, because they don't want to hear how great my kid's doing. Sure, she's had her problems: she talks too much on the phone, can't sit still for five minutes, has a tendency to pick up "strays." Her room looks like the tragic conclusion of a hurricane. And I'm not sure we'll ever recover from her colicky infancy.

"Remember how she used to cry for five, six hours at a time?" Nathan asks, smiling thinly as if following my thoughts. "Remember what complete basket cases we were?"

I nod, recalling those early, brittle months, our nerves splintered, how we stumbled into the middle of every night in shifts, bouncing our bawling infant, how Nathan drove her for hours through the winding hills. How for eight heart-breaking days we attempted sleep training, gripping each other in bed, weeping together while our tiny daughter shrieked into the dawn.

"She's always been high-strung," I tell him. "She's just wired that way."

"So, Sylvie," he scowls. "Are we supposed to feel smug because other people's kids are in worse shape?"

"That's not what I was—"

"We're supposed to be reassured because she hasn't had her first abortion yet, or what?" He slumps onto a stool at the counter, drops his head into his hands. I can almost see the disenchantments of his forty-five years—our house, his job, the intricate knots of family, the endless toil tugging his tendons, failure's shadow stalking him. I resist my habitual impulse to squeeze his shoulder, run my fingers over his spiky hair. I can't bear to touch him just now, with the memory of another man so freshly inscribed in my skin cells. And not for the first time, I'm seized by a sickening urge to confess—*why not just have out with everything?* Instead, I shove my hands in my pockets and discover Tai's heart-shaped agate nestled against my groin. The edginess that's gripped me of late takes hold again. I need a cigarette, a solitary walk in the dark.

"Let's just see how things pan out," I whisper, clutching my elbows. "In three weeks we'll go to California for Christmas. Maybe seeing her grandma and cousins will snap her out of it. We can plan some special time with her, without Emmie."

He's silent now, looking at me sideways.

"Nathan? Don't you think that's a reasonable plan?"

"Yeah. Only, I'm not coming west with you." He drains his glass, sets it on the counter.

"What?"

"Not this time—there's just too much work to do on the house."

"I see. And it doesn't matter to you that my grandmother's dying? That you may not—"

"No offense, Sylvie, but your gram has been 'dying' for the past ten years."

"I think this is different." My rage is bubbling to the surface now, laced with ten years' worth of quarrels in this kitchen, the slow erosion of hope.

"We haven't seen my family for four years. We haven't even—"

"I know. Look, I can come Christmas day if you want. But it seems nuts to spend six days, when there's so much to do at the site." He isn't saying anything about how far we've been sliding, how distant he feels, but I see it in his closed-door expression, the tilt of his jaw, arms clenched protectively over his heart. Maybe he senses my betrayal, the way a dog smells fear.

"Okay," I finally say. "I'm not going to force you to come." The truth is, part of me is relieved. Part of me needs the extra bubble of space his absence will provide—space in the bed beside me, space for my mind to wander and spin, space for missing Tai.

Now he's cataloging all the tasks he wants to accomplish over the holidays, all the things needing his attention more than the girls and I: milling up the trim, laying the mudroom tiles…. The list goes on, unrealistic as ever, and my restiveness builds to a painful pitch. I lace up my boots, rummage in the cubbies for mittens.

"You going somewhere?" Nathan pauses in his diatribe.

"Just for a walk."

"Another walk, huh? I think I'll catch a few scores then."

"You do that. Have a nice sleep on the sofa."

"Oh, Sylvie. Cut me some slack, for Chrissake."

But before we can get into it, I'm busting out the door, rushing into the night. November air slaps my cheeks as I squint at distant constellations, fumbling to light one of the cigarettes Tai has left with me. Then I inhale deeply, as if taking my first real breath after a long dive underwater. I move fast in the darkness, wishing I had a dog to justify all this walking to the neighbors who pass me in their cars, or peer out their windows. The moon casts an ephemeral light on the Fullers' barn, the abandoned paper mill, the Lutheran church spire, the distant black line of the Berkshires just beyond town.

In Tai's bed next week, I'll feel myself begin to sink beneath the questions and conversations, beneath guilt and silence, flesh and floorboards, beneath years of erasure and disenchantment, beneath the wild frozen earth to a time before everything came apart.

1975

ONE SUNDAY MORNING IN APRIL, MY FATHER WOKE US all early and said he had a surprise—just the thing our family needed—and we had to get out of bed and get moving. He looked a little crazed. He clearly hadn't slept much, seemed wired on coffee and was cultivating a beard that now covered his face in random, silvery-black patches.

The three of us dressed as quickly as we could and squeezed into the Corvette, my mother sending Ali and me worried glances. The last time Dad had done something like this, three years back, it turned out he'd bought a dairy farm in Modesto that went bankrupt within months. Lately, he'd been talking about wanting to buy his own winery.

"I hope this isn't one of your crazy investment schemes," Mom said as we veered onto Newport Freeway. He just kept driving west, weaving in and out of the fast lane.

We parked at a private marina in Newport Beach, unfolded ourselves from the Corvette. Mom squeezed my fingers as we followed Dad and Ali across the parking lot and down a series of shifting wooden docks bobbing with yachts of every size. My sister was practically skipping with excitement by the time Dad halted before a gleaming, forty-foot sailboat. As we stood gawking on the dock, he explained that he'd been learning to sail on Saturdays, investigating currents and navigation so that the four of us could sail to Catalina Island on weekends, or maybe down the coast to Ensenada. He was even thinking of entering some amateur races.

"Cool." Alison climbed aboard without hesitation, running her hand over the bright blue sail covers as if surveying her rightful inheritance. "This is so *totally* awesome."

"I thought you might like it." He handed us all sun visors and matching red Windbreakers with the boat's name embroidered across the back in block letters. We were supposed to suit up now, I gathered, become a team.

"But, Don, I haven't the faintest idea how to sail." Mom's face was pale with shock.

"You can learn," he said, hoisting her onto the starboard deck. "I'll teach all of you."

He'd named the boat *Allegiance.*

But it turned out that my mother couldn't learn, despite several weekends' worth of trying. She had severe seasickness that no amount of Dramamine could cure. After two hours of motoring around in the fog, that first day, Mom miserably puking into a bucket, we gave up and headed in. My father stood at the helm, scowling beneath the brim of his red *Allegiance* hat, as if personally affronted. I could read what he was thinking in the weave of his brow, the muscled knot of his jaw: we'd never even made it to the open sea. We'd never even hoisted the goddamn mainsail. Somehow, she'd managed to overturn another dream.

Still, he had no intention of giving up his nautical aspirations—not after all he'd invested. He joined the Newport Yacht Club, hired a small crew of local sailors and continued to spend his Saturdays at sea, while Mom, Alison and I went to Sabbath school and church. Occasionally, we lunched out with Mr. Robert. In June, Dad announced his ambition to enter the Ensenada Challenge at the end of the summer. He and his crew would be gone for the better part of three weeks. This was just the opportunity my mother had been waiting for.

We left in the cool dawn, huddled like refugees in our blankets. As Mom pushed us into the back of the big silver Mercedes, I asked, "What about my stuff?"

"Your things are in the trunk," she said, tucking the blanket tighter around me, fastening my seat belt. "Ali, give one of those pillows to your sister."

"Why are we up so early?" Ali asked, shoving a pillow into my face. "What time is it?"

"It's five-fifteen in the morning—practically time for breakfast." Mr. Robert slid into the driver's seat, smiling— a jolly captor. He smelled of aftershave, nylon and cold morning air. He squeezed Mom's hand once before starting the car, backing out of the driveway. I nestled farther into my cocoon of blankets.

My father had left the previous morning. He'd been in a rare cheerful mood as he packed his duffle bags and sailing gear in the Corvette, slammed the trunk. He'd even kissed us all twice, promising presents and asking Ali and me to take good care of our mother. "You hold down the fort now, my sweet peas," he'd said, ruffling our hair before he drove away. I'd felt a sharp stab of guilt, knowing that we wouldn't need to take care of Mom, since Mr. Robert would soon be assuming that job.

We were on our way to Wallowa, in Oregon's far northeastern corner, where Mr. Robert owned a cabin. By the time we crossed the state line, leaving California's parched landscapes for Oregon's wild green ones, my father was already navigating the open seas with his mates.

The Wallowa Valley looked like Eden compared to Orange County's looping freeway overpasses and smog-choked skies. Extravagant fields opened before us, dotted with wildflowers and giant rolls of hay. Big-bellied horses flanked homey farmhouses and brooks tumbled from the snowcapped mountains growing on the horizon. Mr. Robert narrated the sights and my mother wrapped her fingers around his wrist, while Ali continued reading her book.

I just stared, picturing myself on one of these farms, tending the horses, exploring the countryside like a young Annie Oakley. Our secret trips with Mr. Robert always had this effect, luring me into the bright, seductive rooms of fancied lives. If we lived in one of these clean Oregon farmhouses, I could have Theresa up for a weekend that would leave her weak-kneed. I'd had Theresa over a handful of times in the past year, but she never stayed long. After all, what was a pool compared with her menagerie of animals and her groovy, permissive parents? Only once I'd asked her to dinner and it was a terrible mistake: my mother served warmed-over pizza, Ali came in late complaining of a headache, my father didn't show and Mom sat silent through the whole meal, forehead in her hand. As I was walking Theresa back home that night, she draped her arm over my shoulders. "Sy, you can come to my house anytime you want," she offered, and a lump of gratitude and shame worked its way into my chest.

But if we lived up here, we'd eat dinner around a table overflowing with farm-fresh produce. Mom would play piano while Mr. Robert sang his ridiculous songs, and Theresa would laugh so hard, she'd pee in her pants. Then we'd ride the horses across open farmland until she exclaimed, "I can't believe I spent years riding around a stupid ring!"

From then on, Mr. Robert didn't have to work so hard at wooing me. I didn't even mind that his cabin was small and unkempt. "I'm afraid it's a bit rustic," he apologized as we hauled our bags through the narrow kitchen. "And no one's really cleaned since—well, since last time I was here." He shook out a cobwebby gingham curtain.

"It smells funny." Ali made a sour face.

"*Alison,*" Mom scolded. "I'm sure it will spruce up just fine with a little cleaning."

"It's the river you smell," Mr. Robert said. "The moisture works its way into things." He led us to the great room, which housed an enormous stone fireplace. Pictures lined the hearth. There were several of Mom—at the beach, in a hotel lobby, standing in a meadow somewhere—and I wondered when they'd been taken. In some she looked quite young. The other photos were all of Mr. Robert's children. It seemed there were two boys and a girl, about my age. "That's Randy and Lou, and this one's Lisa." Mr. Robert pointed to each one. "They're all teenagers now. Lou just turned twenty, in fact." I knew Mr. Robert had children, but I'd never considered them as actual people, with birthdays and pimples, feelings and graduation gowns, and now here they were, staring from their frames as if demanding an explanation. They made me uncomfortable, so I turned my back on them to investigate the shelves full of board games, a few old Zane

Grey hardbacks. I ran my fingers over the broken spines while Ali examined the two hard couches.

"Where are we supposed to sleep?" she asked.

"Well, there's the double bed, which is passable," offered Mr. Robert. "And I thought you girls could put your sleeping bags on these couches." He seemed suddenly ashamed, an unpracticed host moving to pull back the curtains and crank open the windows. Instantly, the cabin was full of soft light, the sound of rushing water.

"It'll be sort of like camping, girls," Mom piped in. "Only with a few more comforts." She needn't have assured me. I'd already discovered the cedar deck outside, overhanging a frothy mountain river.

"That's the Wallowa River," Mr. Robert called. "It's got one heck of a current, and it'll freeze your batoozies off, but I try to cross it each year. Just beyond those trees are the stables."

"*Horse* stables?"

"That's right, little twerp. You can go riding every day if it suits you." I resisted the urge to grab Mr. Robert's slack, embarrassed cheeks and kiss him.

"It'll feel just like home in no time," Mom said, joining me on the deck.

"Yeah, if you happen to live in a bear pit," muttered Ali.

My sister continued to sulk as we drove to town for groceries and cleaning supplies. She and Mom had been at war for months now, waging daily skirmishes over Ali's clothes and makeup, friends and pastimes. And, of course, Leslie Brown.

"So, Mom," Ali said slyly as we pulled up to the western storefront of the Joseph Market. "I can't quite figure out the math on this problem."

"What's that, honey?" Mom's tone was decidedly cautious beneath its sugary coating.

"Well, there are three beds in that cabin, and there are four of us—how does that work?"

"For your information, Miss Smarty Pants, there are *four* beds." Mom's nostrils flared as she faced Ali in the back. "There's a cot out on the sunporch for Robert, and maybe you'd have noticed, if you hadn't been so busy complaining."

"Good." My sister struggled to keep her expression placid. "We wouldn't want you getting in trouble."

"You just watch your own backside, young lady." Mom was breathing hard, trying to pull the emergency brake on Mr. Robert's car. "And let's try to have a good time while we're here, okay? Let's just try to be happy."

"Well, she can't control *that,* can she?" Ali grumbled after Mom disappeared behind the milky shop windows. "She can't force us to be happy here."

For my own part, I soon decided that I would stay in Wallowa forever. Each morning in that cabin, I woke to the river's gentle rushing and the smell of Mr. Robert's cooking. I'd hear my sister's even breathing across the room and Mom's quiet laughter spilling from the kitchen. A strange sense of peace nested in my ribs then, like a gray bird in the rafters. I didn't want to move much for fear that it would take flight in the country air and never return. So I just lay snug in my sleeping bag, looking at the chinks of brilliant light dotting the cabin's sides. Finally, I'd get up and wander in to Mom and Mr. Robert, giggling near the stove, feeding each other samples from stacks of golden pancakes or cartons of fresh berries.

Mr. Robert loved to make breakfast. Ali and I stared at each other over the plastic tablecloth, amazed and skeptical at the spread—fried grits and tomatoes, eggs Benedict, blueberry nut waffles. We'd never eaten such breakfasts. And we'd never seen our mother quite this jovial. She wouldn't even let us do dishes, but whisked them happily away, insisting we go out and enjoy the good weather. "It won't last forever," she said.

After only a few days in Wallowa, Ali and I discovered the main drag, where boys in their cars, or their father's cars, went cruising. We walked that street on the way to the lake and back each day, and sometimes several times between. When Mom needed dish soap from the market, when Mr. Robert wanted the paper, when anyone craved a soda or an apple, Ali and I volunteered to go. Mom eyed us as Ali lay on the bed to zip herself into her shorts, as I bobby pinned my hair, trying in vain to make it straight. While Ali lined her lips, I tore off T-shirts and cutoffs, trying to find the article of clothing that would accentuate my tiny breasts. "All that just for a loaf of *bread?*" Mom asked from the doorway, arching a critical brow. But she didn't interfere with our flurry of vanity. After all, she was in no position to preach propriety, and Ali and I made the most of our mother's guilt as we waltzed out the door.

Finally on the main drag, we heard Led Zeppelin blaring from the smoky recesses of pickups and custom vans. Sometimes the boys would honk and yell, making my stomach seize. But it was always Alison they wanted. "Hey, you, in the tight shorts," they yelled. "Hey, foxy blondie—you want a ride in my boat? A drag on my roach? A spin on my wheels?" Freckled boys with burnt cheeks and wicked smiles; dark-skinned boys with arms draped across open windows; boys on dirt bikes, their tattoos and dust screaming out something I couldn't fathom. They made my toes ache, my head spin.

I watched Ali sauntering down the road on her tanned legs, riding fully on her fifteen-year-old hips; I was grateful and furious that they didn't call for me.

"I bet you girls didn't know that Indians lived here once, did you?" Mr. Robert offered over pasta at the lodge. "Old Chief Joseph lived in this valley with his tribe, until the land was taken by the government. There are statues of him all over this town."

"Wow," drawled Ali. "How fascinating."

"Old Chief Joseph—he was a stubborn man. Didn't want to leave this place. Haven't you heard of the Chief Joseph Dance, Alison?"

"What's that supposed to be?"

"All the kids up here do it. It's a rage with those boys who follow you down the road." He pushed his chair back and stood, then did a silly, jerking dance around the table, head bobbing, hands glued to his sides, chanting a mock-Indian rhythm—half Chief Joseph, half Steve Martin, with a dash of John Travolta. Mom and I were doubled over by the time he took his seat. Even Ali cracked a smile, holding her napkin over her face.

"Oh, Bob," Mom gasped, wiping her eyes. "The things you'll do for a laugh. Thank goodness there's no one else in this restaurant!"

"Poor old Chief Joseph," Mr. Robert said, sipping his wine as if nothing odd had happened. "Loved this valley like his own flesh and blood. But how can you blame him?"

"*I* don't blame him," I commented, glancing at the dark lake through the lodge's windows. "I would want to stay here, too."

"I wouldn't." Ali twirled a strand of spaghetti around her fork. "It's way too dead."

"Well, now, that's debatable. Isn't it, twerp?" He looked at me and I stared into my plate, ashamed to be counted on. "Now, the kids up here who live on horse ranches have plenty to do," he went on. "Just think, Alison dear, if you had crops to water and horses to tend."

"Sounds like some nerdy idea of fun that went out of style a hundred years ago."

"Maybe you couldn't hang around the mall every weekend, but you'd have cleaner fun—more family-oriented fun." Mom said *family-oriented* as if it were a strange, foreign dish that she was trying out before she ordered it. "I think families stay closer, living in the country."

"Right, Mom." Ali looked as if she were going to spit. "The only problem is, we're not a family, are we?" She tossed her napkin in her plate, stormed off to the bathroom. *Just like Dad,* I thought. The three of us stared down at our half-eaten food.

"Well, I suppose she has something there." Mr. Robert smiled sadly. "I suppose she does have something there, doesn't she, sweetheart?" He pried Mom's hand from its clutch on the table and pressed it to his lips, then he winked at me. In that instant, my affection for him took root, blossoming in my belly.

And it continued to blossom during the next week as Mr. Robert took me for early morning horseback rides, on trails that wound around alpine lakes and into pine groves. We talked on those rides, about his childhood in Walla Walla, his regrets about parenting. "I messed up with my own kids, don't you know, twerp? But I sure would like another chance."

We talked about Chief Joseph, too—a fierce warrior who didn't want to fight. "'I will fight no more, forever,' that's what he said, Sylvie. One of the greatest warriors in history." Mr. Robert repeated the famous words, swaying atop his gelding. "But sometimes you have to fight for what you love, don't you? Sometimes you just have to fight like hell, regardless of the consequences, or even whether it's right."

Later, Mom and I were sitting on the deck steps, tossing peanuts to the ground squirrels when she turned to me, placed her hand on my knee.

"So, Sylvie, I need your advice."

"Okay." I puffed myself to my full stature, smoothed the worry from my face. "What?"

"You're growing up, Sylvie," she went on. "And you must have opinions on things."

"On most things, I guess."

"Well then, do you think we should keep trying to work things out with Dad? Or should we live with Mr. Robert? What do you think?"

Then she stared at me hard. I could hear my own heart swishing in my ears, my mother's heavy, expectant breathing. My cheeks blazed.

"I don't know." The words came out like a cough—dry and crumbly.

"No, of course you don't, angel." She rubbed my knee. "Of course not. But you must feel *some* way about it? You're nearly thirteen—a teenager!" She said this as if it were a foregone conclusion that at thirteen I should be able to manage my destiny, all our destinies.

I couldn't look at her, so I stared at the tumbling river, the pines creaking in the breeze, the horse stables winking between them. I caught the faint, earthy traces of someone's campfire.

"I think we'd be happy with Mr. Robert," I finally whispered, looking her in the eyes, which softened with some thick emotion—was it sorrow? Relief? Hope? Then she nodded and took my hand, lacing our fingers together and gripping so hard, I could no longer tell where her hand let off and mine began.

"So how 'bout a swim, ladies?" Mr. Robert had appeared on the deck behind us, wearing navy swim shorts, his eyes glittering with mischief. "You ready to cross that river?"

The next morning I had a stomachache and could barely bend my arm, which Mr. Robert had bandaged too tightly after I'd whacked it on a rock, attempting to cross the river. It turned out the Wallowa's current and depth was greater than we'd bargained for. Though we'd tried for an hour, none of us had been able to make the crossing.

Today was foggy, and Alison and I gave up our ritual teenage parade to the lake. I wanted to forgo adventures for a while, to sit in a warm corner with a book. It was a new feeling, this quiet waiting, this deep desire for solitude, and I fed it all morning, sitting in a rocker on the porch.

Around midday, I went to the bathroom and discovered a reddish-brown stain on my underpants. I stared at it, mortified and relieved. Could it be? Was it really? I inserted a finger, just to make sure, drew it out coated with blood. Then sat stunned and elated for a few minutes. Ali was having her period, too, so I helped myself to one of her pads, deciding that I would keep this to myself, for the time being. I didn't want my mother and Mr. Robert to have it.

Later, I was sitting at the kitchen table, making my way

through Mr. Robert's stack of horse books, when he came rushing into the cabin, slapping a sheath of white papers against his thigh. "Come on, everybody; I've got something to show you!"

"Well, show us, then," Mom said. For hours, she'd been removing green plastic dishes from the cupboards, stacking them on the counter, sweeping the shelf paper with a damp sponge. "What is it?"

"Can't show you here," he announced. "You'll just have to come with me if you want the surprise." He stood behind Mom, trickled his stubby fingers down her spine and landed on her right buttock, which he squeezed. My own stomach squeezed in turn.

"Alison's not here," I said.

"Well, then." Spinning around, he arched his eyebrows. "Why don't you just go and find her?" The edge of impatience in his voice made my heart stumble.

"But I don't even know where she is. I haven't seen her since breakfast."

"It could take Sylvie all day to find her, Robert!"

"She must be at one of your old hangouts, right? She must be out there somewhere." He opened the door, indicating, with a mock-chivalrous bow, that I should exit.

"Okay, okay," I said as I trudged into the foggy day. "This surprise better be good."

"Believe me, it will be."

I walked down Main Street, irritated and exiled, kicking rocks in the mist. There were a few cars cruising the street, despite the bad weather, but none slowed or honked. I tried to walk like Ali, leaning into my hips, swinging my shoulders, head high and flirty, but I just felt gawky and exposed.

Then a voice behind me was crooning, saying, "Hey, baby. Hey, cute thing—what happened to your arm?" I looked back long enough to see the cream-colored Jeep, the blond head and rusty-colored forearm out the side window, the white glint of a smile. I whipped back around, excited and full in my new body.

The Jeep sped up and passed. A second later I heard Ali's rough laughter behind the old hamburger stand. I steered myself toward it, hearing other voices now, boys' voices, jagged as metal slicing through my sister's giggle. They sat in a circle on old crates in a clearing a few yards away. Three boys and Alison. What was she doing? And then I smelled the familiar musky burn, saw the joint they were passing, my sister's bare shoulders, her cardigan in a heap at her feet. I stood there until Ali spotted me. "Hey, weirdly. What's up?"

"Mr. Robert has a surprise. You're supposed to come home. Like, soon." My voice sounded so thin and young I wanted to cut it out of me. The boys' eyes all scanning me for trouble or possibility. They looked older than Ali, arms tense with new muscle, faces shadowed with stubble. One of them, a lanky black-haired boy, had his hand on Alison's thigh and was running his fingers down her leg, around her kneecap and back up.

"They want me *home*, huh?" Ali's voice was mocking and lazy.

"Is she cool?" the blond stocky one wanted to know.

"She's a cutie," the black-haired one added. "Maybe she wants to play with us, huh? You wanna party, little sister?"

"She's too young," Alison snapped as if she were angry, or jealous. I felt a brand-new thrill race through me. "She doesn't smoke, but she won't tell, either. Will you, Sylvie?"

"What do you think I am, some kind of nerd?" I cocked my hand on my hip. The boys snorted and guffawed. "Come on, Ali." I was starting to feel weak-kneed. "Just come on home, please?"

"Go on yourself, Sylvie," Ali demanded, but her voice cracked. "Say I'll be back for dinner, okay? Tell them I met some girlfriends at the lake."

I turned and hurried back up the street, holding my bandaged elbow, stumbling hard into the divide that had opened before me. I didn't want to follow Alison into the place she was heading, but I no longer knew what to turn to.

A horse was the answer to everything, I decided as we walked around the one-thousand-acre ranch, peering into outbuildings and watching the palomino foals nod over the fence. *A horse is the answer,* I thought, walking between Mom and Mr. Robert in the hazy light. I wasn't sure what it was the answer to, but I could imagine myself riding hard over that land, the animal moving beneath me, my love for it making me strong. A horse would make me real, I thought, while Barbara, the real estate agent, bubbled over about the condition of the barns, the freshwater well, the historic farm-house, which she was saving for last.

"Just wait 'til you see the house," she kept saying to Mom, winking as if at some joke only for women. "I want you to get the full impact of this place from the outside in."

"Well, I think I'm getting it," Mom chirped, dodging a pile of manure. "I'm just about ready to see the house, actually. I'm ruining my shoes."

"Oh, goodness, why didn't you say so?" Barbara stared down at Mom's white leather sandals. "Didn't your husband warn you we'd be walking around the property?"

My mother looked void, and I winced, dreading the next sentence: *Oh, no, this isn't really my husband. My husband is on a sailing trip....* I desperately wanted the real estate agent to believe in us as a family, so I held my breath, waiting for the words that would expose us as liars and frauds. But Mom just cleared her throat and hooked her arm through Mr. Robert's.

"No, he didn't warn me about any of this," she said as we climbed onto the porch. "It was a surprise."

"How romantic! I wish my husband was more that way." Barbara led us into the spacious farmhouse kitchen.

"I like to keep her on her toes." Mr. Robert grinned and I felt glad, just then, that Alison hadn't joined us; she surely would have given us away with some sarcastic, well-timed comment.

Ali would just have to get used to all this, I thought as the three of us drove back to the cabin. She'd come around, once she saw the farmhouse, the big corner bedroom upstairs that would be hers, the four-poster beds and the game room in the cellar complete with pool tables and air hockey. She would just have to love it, I told myself, as my mother and Mr. Robert talked quietly in the front seat about oil heat and well water.

"But you haven't told me what you really think, Elaine."

"It's amazing. Obviously, it's gorgeous, Robert, but a bit premature, don't you think?"

"Imagine, though, darling. All I'm asking you to do right now is to imagine how it could be. What we *could* have. That's all. I didn't mean anything else by it."

"Do the horses come with it?" I asked, leaning over the seat.

"The horses, the furniture, the cattle, even the kitchen

utensils. The owners are moving to their penthouse in Seattle, giving up the country life for good, I gather."

"That's stupid of them. I'd never leave if I lived on that ranch," I vowed.

"Well, we can't even afford *that* ranch, so just get it out of your head," Mom said.

"Of course we can afford it, Lainie. We can afford anything we want."

"We're not a *we* yet, Robert. And no, we can't afford to talk this way."

He was quiet, staring at the road ahead, though he did reach over and place his big hand on the nape of her neck, as if to massage the doubt right out of her. I sat back in my corner, feeling a longing so sharp and confused, it was as if an insatiable, toothy mouth had birthed itself inside. Or maybe it was just cramps.

"Can we go out to eat tonight?" I whined.

"We'll see, angel. We'll see."

But we didn't go out that night—our last one in Wallowa—because the concierge from the lodge came to the cabin with an urgent message: Sammy had called. There was no phone at the cabin and she'd been trying to reach us for seven hours, apparently, to tell Mom that Dad had capsized *Allegiance* off the coast and was in a San Diego hospital, being treated for hypothermia. We needed to come home.

A week after my father's accident, we gathered around the piano to sing Sabbath hymns. I was shaken by his transformation: he'd dropped fifteen pounds and seemed as pale and transparent as a sheet of typing paper beneath his sailor's tan. His beard was full, speckled with silver, and he clutched Mom's shoulder as if still finding his legs. He shut his eyes as he sang—"Shall We Gather at the River?," "Standing on the Promises," "Revive Us Again"—his tremulous tenor wavering beneath her clear melodies. He'd always been self-conscious about his difficulty carrying a tune, so Ali joined in the harmonies and their voices created a unified front.

I tried parroting my mother's part but my own voice broke with emotion. It was too much—everything, too much. Finally overcome, I crawled under the Steinway and lay on my back, looking up at the inner workings of the instrument, watching my mother's long pale toes hover over the pedals. I couldn't recall when we'd last done this—all four of us singing, all of us gathered for a unifying purpose.

My mind kept returning to Wallowa, to Mr. Robert's jokes and promises, Mom's hand swinging in his, her face tilted toward the sun while her husband strove to prove himself on the open seas, failed to read all the signs of a fast-approaching storm. I pictured Dad bobbing in the Pacific, almost meeting his end while his crew struggled to cut the rigging and release the mainsail, then begin the agonizing search for their lost captain. In the hospital last week, Dad's face had gone slack and ghostly as he told the story: how the rain made it impossible to float on his back; how he felt each part of his body go leaden and numb; how he panicked, even prayed. "I thought, you know—that was it," he'd said, squeezing my mother's fingers. "And even though I was scared shitless, it seemed as good a way to go as any, out in the water, doing what I loved. But then I thought of you girls, and everything I'd miss—" Here Alison burst into sobs beside me. My own sorrow was jammed in a thick, complicated knot behind my breastbone.

Listening to him sing "How Great Thou Art," my mind

began whirring with questions I didn't dare ask: Why hadn't he been wearing his lifeline during the storm? Why hadn't he lowered the sails? Why had he been so reckless? Did he know where his family had gone—that we hadn't *really* been visiting Sammy's parents in Grass Valley?

Now they'd stopped singing and Dad had requested "Clair de Lune"—his favorite, the song that first brought them together. She still played it as if her very heart was beating in the piano's great heart, all her lost love and longing surging through her fingers into the instrument, shattering the air. Tears gathered in my ears, muffling the music, so I didn't hear when my father finally left the room.

The next day, Mom and I were driving back from her new office, the traffic piling up around us like dishes in a sink. It was a typical late summer day—we couldn't see the San Gabriel Mountains, but we knew they still shimmered, breathtaking and muscular behind the veil of smog. We couldn't see the Pacific either, half a mile to the west, but we knew it turned, bright as a marble, just behind the cinder-block walls and freeways.

Mom pulled to the side of the road, to let the engine cool. Resting her head on the wheel, she sighed long and deep— was it despair that moved her? Exhaustion? Resolve? Then she raised her head. "What in the world should we do, Sylvie? What should we do?"

"Do about what, Mom?"

"About this mess we're in." She stared at me in the passenger's seat, eyes brimming. "Dad says he's been changed by the accident. He says he wants to try again."

"Oh—wow. What did you say?"

"I said I'd have to think about it. Sylvie, he says he doesn't even care about Robert anymore, that he's willing to let the whole thing go, and I want to believe him, but—"

"Do you want to make it work?" I asked.

"Of course. Sometimes I want it more than anything. But we've tried so many times. Our *whole life* has been about trying, and trying again." She wiped her eyes with the back of her hand, uncharacteristically smearing her makeup.

I sighed and stared out the window, at the cars creeping like slick roaches, the new housing developments going in along the highway. Suddenly I hated it all so much—this dreary tract-housing world we lived in. I thought of Mr. Robert's pancake breakfasts, the hikes through fragrant pine groves, horseback rides to alpine lakes, the one-thousand-acre ranch. I pictured Dad in the hospital—blue and bloated, eyes panicky above the plastic oxygen mask. I remembered his ring scraping my cheekbone, the cereal box flying from my hands.

It was an easy decision, really. It took less than a minute for me to look my mother in the eye and say, with all the forced assurance I could muster, "I think we'd be happier with Mr. Robert, Mom. We'd be a whole lot better off on a ranch with Mr. Robert—you'll be sorry if you blow this chance." I didn't say anything about horses, nor did I say aloud that she should divorce my father, demolish our family, but those were the words that came next. I felt them hanging in the air between us. The weight of those words pulled us together, our heads nearly touching in the still warmth of the car. I wouldn't even have been surprised if she'd asked me to switch places with her and drive, so she could have a little rest. Instead, she just nodded, a sad smile wavering on her lips, and started the engine, pulled back into the snarl of traffic. I knew what she was feeling: she was sad at the knowledge of what she'd have to do. She was terrified, elated and grateful, too. She was thankful and sorry that I'd taken part of her burden. I knew all these things about her in an instant, though I couldn't have said what I felt, just then.

2004

FLYING OVER THE GREAT LAKES, MY DAUGHTERS SETTLED beside me, the portable DVD players that Nana Elaine sent open on their laps, I'm thinking again about migration—the geese that slice through our November mornings, the monarch butterflies Emmie's preschool is studying. The improbability of traversing such distances on such seemingly fragile wings.

How does it start? Are they gripped by a sudden restlessness, an inexplicable ache born in the breast and shimmering outward, like a rumor, until the whole flock, clan, colony is alive with pain—the only cure for which is flight? Do they fear the oncoming threat of winter? Do they long for their destination, or is it pure movement they're after?

Do they dread the miles they have to cover?

This morning, as Nathan was driving us to Bradley Airport, I was stricken with dread about this trip.

"I think I've lost my homing device," I told him, and he misunderstood.

"Is that what all these late-night walks are about?" he asked, shooting me a worried look. "Are you trying to get lost—to see if you can find your way back?" Funny, I thought, how for him "home" means our tiny slanting duplex on Eastwood Drive; for me, it's somehow always meant California—the place I ran from.

I didn't answer. Didn't have the heart, so early in the morning, to slice through our layers of dissonance and explain it to him. I couldn't even explain it to myself. Was I fearful of the flight itself—hurtling through the atmosphere inside seventy thousand pounds of man-made steel and burning oil? Was I panicked by the thought of leaving him, or Tai, or the minuscule corner of the continent that has become my all-consuming universe?

Now the captain announces that we're over Lincoln, and Hannah jabs me hard in the ribs.

"Ow, Han."

"Isn't that where your dad was from? Grandpa Don?"

She's never called him this before and at the words *Grandpa Don,* a thorn of pain pierces me. It's as if she's handed me a brand-new bundle of loss, with its own specific texture.

"Yes, Han." I finally find my voice. "He was born there."

"It looks so—*flat.* Did you ever go there, to visit?" I stare at her fine, angular cheeks, the heavily lidded eyes, amazed that this line of questioning would be sufficiently engaging to distract her from *Harry Potter and the Chamber of Secrets.*

"No, I never went," I tell her. "My dad moved with his parents out to San Francisco when he was just a boy, and his father sort of disappeared a few years later."

"What d'you mean, *disappeared?*" She pulls off her headphones, presses Pause.

"He went off to law school in Arizona or something—at

least that's what he told them—and never came back. There was probably another woman."

"That's so harsh. What did they do, after he left?"

"My grandmother, Virginia Jean, worked in a barbershop for a while before she fell ill. She had diabetes and a broken heart, I imagine. They struggled big-time. I think that's why my parents married right out of high school—he didn't have any other family left."

"He had a tragic life," she announces in the dignified voice of the adult she so nearly is.

"I suppose." I shut my eyes for a second, stunned that my daughter doesn't already have this information, that she's never heard the story. But, of course, who would have told her besides me? My own mother seldom speaks of him, and she wouldn't have heard it from Alison, who we rarely see. For my own part, I've assiduously avoided passing down my broken family history—at least anything that smacks of the betrayals and losses that I fled. But I suddenly feel I've deprived my children of something enormous. I turn to give Hannah more of the details, but she's already gone back to Harry Potter. On the other side of me, Emmie is singing aloud to Dora the Explorer, oblivious to the stares and chuckles of fellow passengers. I try to lose myself in the airline's glossy catalog, full of unbelievable contraptions like self-watering houseplants and musical pet-potties. Then we hit a patch of turbulence. Seized by a fresh wave of nerves, I drop the magazine. No one else seems the slightest bit anxious.

Have I acquired a phobia in the years since I've been on a plane? Maybe I'm scared to see my family, after all this time, worried they'll detect my secret life. Afraid of their judgment, estrangement or indifference. Or perhaps dreading how inevitably they'll have changed—my own mortality mirrored back in their lined and falling faces, their diminishing beauty.

But when we arrive in Oakland, I see that Alison's face has not fallen one millimeter in the past half decade; her beauty is anything but diminished, though she has a sort of stretched, surprised look—clearly one of the perks of marrying a plastic surgeon. She struts across the terminal like an ambassador in her cropped chartreuse jacket, black pants and spike heels, her bleached blond hair twisted in a sleek knot at the back of her head, lanky adolescent boys galumphing behind her. She stares straight at me for twenty seconds before the recognition creeps across her face. I wonder how much *I've* changed since the last time she saw me, four years ago when she came to visit following Emmie's birth.

"You're so thin." She looks me over as if unsure I'm the right passenger off this flight.

"Well, haven't just squeezed out a baby this time, have I?" I reach to embrace my nephews, Donny and Ben, ages fifteen and eleven, who hug back half-heartedly—do they even remember me? Donny's grown at least a foot—he's black-haired and lanky as a yearling colt, his hands huge at the ends of scrawny forearms. Ben is stocky and fair, a sarcastic twist to his chapped smile, cheeks glazed with pale freckles.

"And where are your girls? You didn't leave them home with Nathan, did you?"

"They're just over there, looking for the bags. For some reason they find this whole air travel thing entertaining," I say.

"Jeez—I can't imagine," Ali concedes, and without warning, she grabs and hugs me tightly—the same old vise grip around my neck that I've always had trouble managing.

Even in her most affectionate moments, Alison is an abrasive woman, but I suppose that comes from serving as Assistant D.A. for ten years, and being married to Kurt even longer.

Now Hannah's calling from the moving belt—she's toppling with my enormous bag. Ben and Donny sprint off to help and Emmie's wandered away again. *Where is she?* I'm clutched by momentary panic, but when I turn around again, my sister is holding her on one hip. Ali's eyes are moist and her voice buckles. "So this is the gorgeous little niece you've been keeping from us. How could you, Sylvie? How *could* you?"

So begins the six-day parade of guilt. Dragging our baggage to the sidewalk, I learn that it's been hell here, absolute *hell,* that Gram's hanging by a thread—that Poppy's in one of his deep, Biblical funks and Mom's had to upend her entire life because Uncle Peter is useless, *useless.*

"And Sylvie's gone and run off to the east coast," I add, trying to smile.

"Yeah, well—" She arches her perfectly waxed brows. "Thank God Robert didn't mind moving back here. He's been a saint, actually. He's out playing golf with Kurt right now. They barely have room for us in the apartment but I wanted to let you and the girls stay at Orchard Hill. I've been here so much. I'm doing half my job through faxes and e-mail!" All this as we're standing curbside in the breathtaking California day—this fragrant golden air unlike anywhere else I've been—waiting for Mom to collect us in her aqua Suburban.

I sit up front with my mother. Ali has insisted on sitting beside Emmie so she can "get acquainted." As I fasten my seat belt, Elaine appraises me over her dark glasses, then squeezes my hand. "It's high time you came," she scolds. At sixty-seven, she's still elegant, though a bit more careworn than the last time I saw her. She pulls away from the curb just as the police officer is coming to move us along.

"You look tired, angel," she notes, veering onto the freeway. I laugh.

"I guess I'm the only woman in my family who ages. Must be something about the east coast winters."

"You won't say that when you see poor Gram." She bites her lip.

"So I hear. Sorry it's been so hard, Mom."

"Well—it's just life." She sighs. And then, "That's quite a getup your eldest has on," she delivers with a wry smile, as if Hannah's ripped jeans and cropped *Wicked* T-shirt don't bother her in the least.

"It's just a T-shirt and jeans." I brace myself.

"Yes, but why all the rips and safety pins? Did she do that herself or did you buy the pants that way?"

"Ah. The jeans come that way, believe it or not. Nathan and I have decided to choose our battles."

"I'm surprised Nathan's not here," she says a few minutes later, as we shoot through the Caldecott Tunnel. I glance behind at Alison, who is good-naturedly reading Emmie's pony book for the third time. Hannah and the boys are swapping iPods in the back.

"He might come Christmas eve," I answer, knowing he probably won't.

"So then, everything's *good* with you and your husband?" Mom whispers as we enter Happy Valley Road. She's tap-tapping her nails on the steering wheel, obviously onto something. It's so *like* her to launch right into this, to start probing and criticizing in the first five minutes of my first visit in five years. *She still has no boundaries with me.*

"Things are as good as can be expected, Mom," I snap. Does she really think I'm going to launch into a treatise on my marital issues right here, with my children in the back and my sister now leaning over the seat, ears poised?

As we start the ascent up Orchard Hill, Mom says quietly, "That's fine, Sylvie—you can keep your secrets."

Who was it who taught me about keeping secrets? I'm thinking a few hours later, standing in the narrow kitchen with its familiar cracked yellow tile, its custard cups full of buttons and peanuts, aspirins and safety pins. Nothing here has changed, including my mother, who trained me in duplicity early and well, making me what I am today—a woman who can walk this line, inhabit parallel worlds, carry a lifetime's worth of guilt without flinching, hold a secret as exquisitely as if it were one of these Wedgwood teacups Gram still insists on using, though one seems to shatter every couple years. This one has tiny roses painted on the sides, reminding me of Tai—of that first rose he offered, of his weakness for these extravagant transplants.

Only a dozen hours into my trip, I'm missing him more than I want to, shocked by how insistently my mind wanders back—to the thick, resonant voice in the cave of my ear, his thumb stroking the fleshy part of my palm, the disquieting shards of light in his eyes. As I face my family's accusations—that I've abandoned my heritage, failed to stay in touch, become a liberal Easterner—I'm continually warding off these illicit thoughts, or drawing them close like the threads of a protective cocoon. I keep reaching into my pocket, fingers curling tight around the rough blue agate.

The last time I saw him, he'd appeared during the annual Open Studios that our building hosts before Christmas. I'd decided at the last minute to participate, opening my doors and displaying a dozen of my landscapes, along with a sampling of student art. Eli's work was represented, of course—I'd hung two of his best watercolors on the center wall—and part of me was anticipating father and son, watching the crowds, feeling a tiny explosion of disappointment each time someone *else* walked through the door. Still, I was somehow unprepared for the moment when he finally entered in his chocolate-colored tweed blazer and worn jeans, Eli close behind.

I was talking with the director of development and a board member from Smith College—a conversation that should have mattered to me. They were asking if I'd ever considered teaching in an academic setting. One was saying she'd like to send two artistic nieces my way, the other asking how much for that piece with the harbor? I should have given them every molecule of my attention and salesmanship, but all I could do was steal glances over their shoulders, wondering when I'd get away. He was sipping wine in the corner, laughing with my petite friend Jules, who owned the studio across the hall. Was he *actually* flirting? So convinced of his appeal? Was there a shade of cruelty I'd never noticed before in that sensuous smile? I was blazing with jealousy, regretting the moment when the world became divided into Tai and Everyone Else. When was it that he hijacked my wits?

The Smith women introduced me to the art museum curator, who had the audacity to take my time talking about Lesser Known Impressionists. I thought I would die of agitation and longing as the curator droned on about Berthe Morisot and Mary Cassatt—a topic I normally would've found interesting, had my lover not been walking toward me, jump-starting my heart.

And then he was taking my elbow, mercifully, saying, "Would you excuse me, ladies?" Flashing a radiant smile. "I just need to speak with Ms. Sandon about one piece before I go." I was muttering my apologies, dissolving into the solid warmth of his shoulder as we traversed the perimeter of the studio.

"I can't stay," he whispered. "I'm taking Eli to the movies tonight, but I wanted to see you, before you go west."

"You smell yummy," I said.

"Do you think people would suspect anything if I bought *all* your paintings?" he asked. "Well, except that one with the boats."

"Oh? Why don't you like that one?" I pulled away, feigning offense.

"Too cheerful," he remarked. "It feels like a facade— doesn't have the intensity of your other ones somehow."

"Well, I'm not *only* gloomy, you know." We had stopped before the paintings and were standing a few feet apart, pretending to talk shop. He'd trimmed his beard closer and was wearing the sagey aftershave that I loved. My head seemed to float several feet over my body, though I hadn't had any wine. I handed him a business card, just to be cute. He looked at it, pulled out a pen, and scribbled a few lines on the back, then slipped it into the pocket of my black silk jacket just as Eli sauntered up.

"Your paintings look great, you know," I told him. "They're the centerpiece."

"You won't believe this, but that woman in the furry hat just asked if they were for *sale*." He was flushed, running his fingers through his hair in a Tai-like gesture of mock humility.

"See what I'm telling you, Eli? Aren't you glad you came back to class?" I pressed.

"Yeah, but what do I say? Are they for sale? And how much? I've never even flipping thought about what I'd charge."

"Start at five hundred," Tai instructed, and when Eli raised an eyebrow he shrugged and said, "You can always come down."

After Eli left, Tai took my hand as if to shake it and pressed it between his own—the exact gesture he'd used to calm me in the Plainfield woods, after our first kiss. I suddenly felt I was made of glass—brittle, transparent—all my need and treachery apparent to anyone who might look.

"If I don't see you before you go," he said, "just try being with the family you've got." He released my hand.

"Are you speaking Buddhist again?" My heart was dropping like a pebble through a bog. I felt him preparing to go, taking all my energy with him.

"*My* family's gone, Sylvie. Parents, grandparents, brother… Except I do have one great aunt in Florida. And a cousin in Brooklyn. The point is—just enjoy them while you can, *if* you can. I'll be here when you get back." He pulled himself away, collected his son and left without another glance, only minutes before Nathan and the girls came bustling in, tardy and tousled, bearing white carnations and a cheese platter. Nathan looked haggard and Emmie's eyes were puffy—she'd clearly just had a meltdown over something. I hugged them all, feeling wretched and faithless as a tomcat.

Strangely, it feels wrong to be at Orchard Hill without Nathan, unsettling to be three thousand miles from his grounding presence, the comforting weight of our shared history. Painful to picture him at the construction site alone, tromping back and forth through the Ashfield snow, the distant sound of carolers reaching him through the pines.

The water has boiled. I fill the rosebud teacup with Postum and warm milk, the way Gram likes it, then bring it to her on the living room sofa. In the five years since I've seen her, she's shrunk to the size of a nine-year-old child, her veins knotted beneath tissue-paper skin, eyes sunken and cloudy. She's a woman teetering on the brink between worlds, unsure, from one second to the next, which way she'll lean.

Now she holds out a crooked hand to me and I take it in my own. Her bones feel as fragile as a bird's wing, and I can sense the nearness of death. My eyes start to fill and I will myself to stay composed. I don't want to alarm her.

I sit down on the corner of the couch, setting her Postum on the table beside her and tossing a crocheted throw blanket over her lap. She smiles grimly.

"Your daughters are spirited, Sylvie," she croaks. "Just like you, and your mom."

I laugh nervously, pushing away my inclination to hear an accusation in her words. "Yeah, they have minds of their own," I say. Gram looks at me and nods—I can see in her milky irises that she's chasing some thread of memory.

"Don't talk to that runaway girl, Mama," grumbles Poppy as he shuffles past the room, apparently done with his nap. At ninety, he's still striking, albeit diminished, his shoulders now bowed under the weight of years and Gram's illness. "That girl's a deserter," he calls back, winking once before he disappears into the kitchen.

"I hope this, this—*independent spirit* doesn't complicate your daughters' lives too much," Gram says now. "I hope it serves them."

"Times are different, Gram," I note. "Women *have* to have

spirit to survive." But she doesn't seem to have heard; her eyelids are lowering. Mom is setting out Christmas decorations in the den. She hasn't stopped working since I got here. Just as I'm preparing to leave Gram to her nap, her eyes fly open and she says, "How's that house you and Nathaniel were redoing?"

"Nathan," I correct. "We're still working on it; a bit of an albatross, actually."

"Oh, my." Her tiny face crumples. "Hasn't that been going on for an age?"

"Nearly a decade," I admit. "There was more work than we thought, and Nathan doesn't like to hire it out. That's where he is now." I resist the urge to add, *That's where he always is.*

"It's important to have a *home,* Sylvia," Gram rasps after a pause—it's costing her vital energy to talk to me. "I don't know what I'd have done all these years without Orchard Hill…. If I'd have stayed married, even without it. Our home reminded us—" she trails off. I feel I should let her alone now, let her sleep, but I want the conclusion of this thought.

"Reminded you of what, Gram?" I place my hand on the powdery, soft skin of her forearm. "What did Orchard Hill remind you of?"

"Oh." She smiles sadly, her head quivering. "Just—there were things we both wanted. Good things. Things worth working for."

I don't know what to say to this. My mind flashes to the first time Nathan and I saw the property in Ashfield, the first time we sat together on the crumbling front steps of our house, sharing a bottle of Chianti, savoring the view. Hannah was wrapped in fleece, asleep on the picnic blanket under the apple tree, so we spoke quietly of our dreams: how we'd renovate the outbuildings into a studio for me and a shop for him; how we'd grow blueberries and tap the sugar maples for syrup, fill the old coop with chickens and the pond with koi. We'd even have horses and teach Hannah to ride on trails that wound through the Berkshires. I remember how the afternoon light slanted across the planes of his face; how I felt like the luckiest woman alive.

"Here, Gram—you've forgotten your Postum." I pick up the cup to hand to her. Just then Emmie crashes into me, spilling the brown liquid all over my silk jacket, down my jeans to the antique Oriental rug. Gram smiles, and it's this more than anything—this uncharacteristic disregard for her precious things—that makes me understand she is letting go.

Two days later, we're standing in the circular driveway—Ali, Kurt, my cousin Nick and I—debating how much freedom to grant our children. Nick's seventeen-year-old daughter, Ursa, wants to take Hannah, Ben and Donny to the mall. Emmie's napping, and the teenagers are eager to sneak off before she wakes and demands to be included.

"Why not play tennis or golf?" insists Kurt. "Do something *wholesome,* for crying out loud." He picks lint off his Ralph Lauren cardigan.

"Yes, why slum it with the *mall rats?*" asks Alison. I stare at my sister in her burgundy cashmere, wondering if she's forgotten her own "mall rat" days.

"How much trouble can they get into in a few hours?" I wonder aloud.

"Let the kids have some fun, for God's sake," bellows Poppy from the lawn chair by the garage, where he's been observing, legs sprawled before him, straw hat propped over his eyes.

Just as I'm fishing in my pocket for cash, laying down some ground rules, Mom emerges from the guest room, looking shaken, and takes me by the arm. "I want to talk to you, Sylvie." She leads me across the driveway. "Let's go for a little walk."

We start down the hill in the fog, Mom's arm linked too firmly to mine, her face stony, though when she finally speaks her voice is melodious, betraying nothing. "The kids are off shopping?"

"Yeah. I hope they can stay out of trouble for a few hours."

"More than we can say for you, huh, angel?"

I'm silent, trying to keep pace with her down this treacherous hill. She suspects something, of course—that much has been clear since our ride from the airport—and I've decided not to offer her a thing, to float cool and impermeable outside her radar. Still, I'm not prepared for what comes next.

"Do you love this man, Sylvia?"

"What man?" I halt at the entrance to the orchard, next to the pomegranate tree. Pulling my arm from hers, I cast her a steady gaze, trying to ignore the adrenaline swamping my veins.

"The man that wrote you this." She hands me one of my own crumpled business cards. I stare down at the familiar logo until she turns it, so that the handwriting on the back is legible.

After these crowds are gone, I want to kiss your beautiful pussy on that table in the corner where I first saw you, and forfeited my heart.

My first, unbelievable response is regret that I haven't read this before—that I might have missed an opportunity to be with him one last time before I left. Relief that he still wanted me despite his seeming detachment that night. Then I look into my mother's remote gray eyes, the elevated chin, arms crossed over her flat belly. She is still lovely in her plum turtleneck and ivory cords, still righteously self-assured, after all we've been through. My face starts to smolder with anger and shame. It's as if not one minute has passed since the day she caught me masturbating in the bath when I was twelve. As if the world hasn't turned inside out since then.

I turn from her, start walking farther down the hill.

"I didn't mean to snoop," she calls after me. "I was just trying to clean your jacket."

"Well, I wish you wouldn't." I march toward the iron gates. "I wish you would stop trying to take care of people! I'm perfectly capable of cleaning my own jackets and managing my own affairs."

"Sylvie, wait! Where are you going?" She's behind me, trying to keep up in her slick-soled loafers.

"I don't know. I need to walk," I practically shout. Then I twist my ankle and stumble, losing my clog. My mother catches my arm.

"I'm not here to chastise or preach," she pants. "Though I do think a relationship with the Lord might be crucial during such—"

"I'm forty-two years old, Mother," I interrupt, struggling to get my shoe back on.

"I know you're old enough to make your own choices, honey—obviously, since you've chosen not to even be a part of this family for nearly a decade!"

"That's not true, exactly—"

"I just want to give you a little advice." Her eyes soften and fill. "If you'll take it."

For a while we just stand there, facing each other outside the spiked gates. I remember the day—almost thirty years ago—we stood in this exact spot, accepting contraband fireworks from Mr. Robert, how she snipped at him for being with his family that day, how she told me to lie.

"How can you advise me about infidelity or marital responsibility, or whatever it is you're going to say?" I cross my arms against the damp, heavy air.

"Because I've been there," she snaps. "I know how intoxicating it is to have a man's desire and secret devotion—to be adored, seduced, *seen*—married life pales in comparison!" She's trembling, whether from the cold or from emotion, I can't say. Somehow this gratifies me. "But it's a dangerous game, Sylvia. It will tear you apart," she concludes.

She's right about that. I want to ask if she ever felt she was falling through her life, pulled down through dream and memory by a force larger than gravity. I want to know if she felt the splintering pain of it—a terrible, fruitful pain like birth, a pain you can't stop because you have to know what's on the other side.

"Maybe my situation is different." After I say it, I realize with a start that this is just what I've been telling myself, how I've been justifying my actions—my story is different than hers. I sigh, putting my hands over my face. She touches my arm, pulls me back.

"Do you *love* this man? Is he worth risking everything for?"

"No—I don't know," I blurt, my hands flying out insanely, grabbing at the ends of my hair. The weight of despair squeezes my chest, as if I'm being shoved into a corner, pinned by something massive and invisible. "Yes," I whisper.

"I love him, okay? And I love Nathan, too, Mom. I love Nathan, too." The tears spring out of their own accord, despite how hard I'm holding them.

"Well." She grips my upper arms. "Then saving your marriage will be the hardest choice you ever make, Sylvia. And the most important."

"How can you say that?" We're both shivering now, like saplings vibrating in an earth tremor. "How do you know, Mom? You didn't save your marriage. *We* didn't save it! We threw Dad over for someone else, because—because I told you to. Because we wanted to be happy, right? And now he's dead and there's no way we'll ever know, is there? There's no one who can tell us how that story would have gone!"

"Is that what you think?" Her face is chalky; she looks as if I've slapped her. "You really believe that you, at age twelve, were somehow responsible for my choices?" One thin hand floats over her mouth, the other still grasping my arm.

"Well—I did tell you to." I wipe my face with my sleeve, pull in a tattered breath. The rain starts, softly at first; I can see it beading on her carefully sprayed hair. I start pulling away again. "I need to walk, I need to walk for a long time."

"You can't go off now. Emmie will be up soon. She doesn't want Alison or me. She barely *knows* us. She'll want her mommy." I pause and sigh, turning back. She's right again. My daughter will wake grumpy as she always does. She'll be inconsolable if I'm gone.

She places her hand on my cheek. "The reasons for our family coming apart were far more complicated than that, sweetheart. Sometime, when we have more time—"

There are so many things I could ask her, standing on the border of Gram and Poppy's property. But the rain is starting to soak through our clothes and Emmie will wake any minute. I know I'm running out of time for this conversation.

My mother offers me her arm and we start up the long hill together.

1975

THE SUNDAY BEFORE LABOR DAY, MOM DELIVERED HER final answer, while Ali and Theresa and I splashed in the pool during a rare, perfect summer afternoon. At the time, we knew nothing about the fateful conversation occurring on the other side of the house, but later my mother would tell me.

He was in the garage, doing some typical Sunday task amid the ten-speeds and dust, the flashlights with burnt-out batteries, hammers hanging down like question marks against the white plaster. Perhaps he was waxing the infamous red car the day she told him—something that made him shudder with satisfaction. He was waiting for her answer, sure she'd want to give their marriage one more chance. At least, I want to picture him that way, assured and hopeful, his manhood settling and shifting in his joints, but feeling okay, really, until she came in.

I imagine her wearing a pair of white and green palazzo pants, a slim white halter, shoulders freckled and warm from the sun. Maybe he was thinking, "How thin she looks!" or

"She's still beautiful!" Or perhaps he was wondering how he looked to her. He was still handsome, wasn't he? At the very least, he was rich and getting richer—chief cardiovascular surgeon at the hospital now, head of his practice. He could give her almost anything she wanted.

I can feel the tingling in his toes and fingers as he dropped the chamois cloth, felt the words a moment before she spoke them.

"I don't love you anymore, Don. I want a divorce." Did she say that? Did the grim lines around her mouth soften into sorrow? "I'm tired of the struggle." I can picture my mother there so clearly, every mole on her shoulders, the slight sag of the forearms, regret hardening to resolve in those wide gray eyes.

She said he cried then. Did his head drop slowly into his hands until she pried his fingers away? Or did he wait, holding tight to his grief and shame the way a child holds a bruised shin, fingers laced over the hurt? I can imagine him holding on, watching her leave, opening the door to his car and getting in. I can picture him sealing himself in with his sorrow while my mother went back to her housework, while we girls screeched in the yard, practicing cartwheels off the diving board, as if it were an ordinary Sunday afternoon.

Sammy came for dinner that night. I wonder now if my mother invited her out of fear. Dad had undercooked the leg of lamb, but we all ate it bloody and pink—even Mom and me, the vegetarians of the family—afraid to say anything that might push him over the edge of his loaded restraint. At the time, I couldn't imagine what had caused this shift. Just that morning he'd been practically jovial as he clipped the roses, filled my shirt with fresh tomatoes off the vine. Now his jaw muscles were as tight as guitar strings as he sawed into his meat, filling his glass again and again, splashing dots of red wine across the ivory linen tablecloth, which Mom didn't even try to salvage.

"Are you girls looking forward to your new school this week?" Sammy tried, unaware of the nerve she'd be hitting, unprepared for the geyser of complaint this would unleash.

"No, we're not looking forward to Seventh-day Adventist school," Ali started. "We're not looking forward to leaving all our friends and riding the stinking bus for an hour every day to some ugly old school that doesn't even have a cafeteria."

"*Alison*—that's enough! It will be a welcome change," Mom countered. "I'm hoping there will be fewer distractions, and that the girls can concentrate on important things for once. A change of scenery is sometimes good for the soul, right, Sylvie?"

"I guess," I said, stuffing a glistening sliver of meat into my mouth. I didn't really want to go to the Christian school either, but I decided to keep quiet.

"It's an asinine move," my father said after an awkward pause, opening a fresh bottle of wine. "The public schools in this neighborhood are exceptional, Sammy. This Palmwood is a step down. Not that anyone wants my opinion."

"I want my children to learn something besides how to sneak out to dance clubs on Saturday nights," Mom clipped, looking at Sammy.

"*Your* children?" Dad growled.

"When was the last time you went to a teacher conference?" Mom said, returning his stare. "When was the last time you drove around looking for your kid at midnight, or had to drag her out of a nightclub?"

"Jeez, Mom, you make me sound like a fucking criminal," said Ali.

Mom raised her hand in the air, then caught herself, brought it back down to her lap, trembling.

"Go to your room, Alison." Her voice clenched. "Stay there until your mouth is clean."

"Fine!" My sister threw her napkin on the table and stormed down the hall, slamming her bedroom door. After a pause, Mom apologized to Sammy and we ate the rest of the meal in silence, as we so often did. Calamity Jane sulked in from the kitchen and twined herself around my legs. I fed her pieces of the bloody lamb when no one was looking.

Immediately after dinner, Sammy got up to leave, making excuses about an early shift in the morning. Mom followed her outside, where they talked for a few minutes on the front lawn before she came back in and disappeared down the long hall toward her room.

Then only Dad and I were left at the dirty table as the sky turned tangerine and magenta. I sat with him in the quiet dusk, though every cell of me was screaming to go. "I guess everybody's leaving tonight," he said after a silence. "You going, too?"

"No," I said. "I'm not leaving." I finished my ice cream, taking careful bites in the shadows while my father poured himself a final glass of wine, draining his second bottle.

"Well, I wouldn't blame you." His voice was wrecked and rusty—a piece of old farm equipment dragged across the Nebraska prairie. "I know I haven't been the best dad in the world. These last couple years haven't been easy."

I stared at him in the near dark, utterly at a loss.

"My own dad was a terrible father—even worse than me. D'you know that?"

"No. I mean yes. I mean—you're not such a bad dad." My throat felt as if I'd swallowed a fistful of dirt. "We all make mistakes." It was all I could come up with. For years I'd revisit this comment with shame and longing. If only I could have said something else: that I'd only ever wanted his love. That I was sorry for my part in everything. That I forgave him, even for the things he hadn't yet done. We live forever with the words we don't say.

"That's for damn sure," Dad said, tripping on his consonants. "But let's try not to regret the past, shall we? Life's hard enough, Sylvia, without regrets. You just have to do what you can, and hope for some pardon along the way—okay?"

"Okay," I said, thinking this was the saddest and truest thing he'd said to me.

After a while he emptied his glass, cracked his knuckles and slurred, "Well, sporto, guess we're left with kitchen duty, eh? Best clean up this mess."

"Yep." I quickly started clearing the table while my father emptied the dishwasher. His movements grew more manic and careless as he worked. Then he dropped a crystal wineglass, and it shattered against the tile.

I gasped.

"Goddamn it," he said, and then we both turned to see CJ hunched on the counter, licking the juice from the leftover meat. Dad leaped across the room.

"Don't—" I started, but he was already shoving my cat under one clenched arm, where she hissed and squirmed. I followed him, pulse thudding in my throat as he marched to the screen door, slid it open and tossed CJ onto the patio. She crouched there, dazed.

"Jeez, Dad, she was just hungry," I snapped, opening the door, scooping my stunned pet off the ground and bringing her in. "You don't have to be such a jerk!"

My father pounced at once, pulling CJ from my arms by the scruff. She tore at my skin, clawing the air as he hurled her onto the patio again—this time with such force I thought he'd broken her—then slammed the door, wrenching it off its track. When I reached for it, he yanked my arm, eyes bulging, insane. He looked like a man with nothing left to lose.

My own anger boiled in my throat now, shook me to the core. I wanted to foam like a rabid dog at him, curse and claw and tear him up for every cowardly thing he'd ever done. My fury expanded me, made me bigger than him, my heart steely and stupid. I stepped around him, pried open the screen door with freezing fingers.

"Don't you defy me again," he whispered, and I paused, considering this, my crazy heart pounding beneath my breasts. After a moment, I lifted CJ off the pavement where she still hovered, terrified. I carried her through the door, held her close to my body in front of my dad, as if to show him what it was to hold a thing, to care for and love a thing. For an instant, it seemed we'd reached some silent under-standing—I thought I saw a blue flash of recognition in his eyes. Then he was on me, the cat flying, his fists grabbing my hair, wrenching my neck backward, unearthing me. I crumpled to the tiles and he dragged me to the family room like a dog, arms flailing, orange carpet rising fast to meet my face. Just when I thought it was over, the point of his shoe caught my back, my ribs and arms, his feet kicking and kicking until my limbs curled up, mouth full of snot and carpet and a scream that never got out.

Then he was gone. I heard him grab his keys off the counter, rattle the shutters on the back door. The clock ticked hollowly on the mantel, and my breath came back in a sickening rush. I smelled something rancid and realized with a shock that I had shit in my underwear. After a minute, I rolled onto my back, felt my face, my neck and arms. There was no blood, though my body throbbed in places. No broken skin, no proof of this moment except my hot soiled underwear, which proved nothing but my dirtiness. I lay there for a while, hearing the faint, tinny sound of Mom's voice at the far end of our house. Her talk fluttered on for a while and then there was a stark, awful quiet. I got up and went to the bathroom, to clean myself.

Later, I lay on their bed in my nightshirt, listening to her yell at him over the phone. Alison sat scrunched in an armchair in the corner, looking green. I had told them everything, even allowed Mom to lift my nightshirt and see the bruises, already spreading and turning purplish. I'd told the story in a clipped, matter-of-fact voice, like a reporter, and a few minutes after my stilted confession, Dad called with his own.

"You made her *defecate* in her underwear," Mom kept saying. "You made her *defecate,* do you realize?" Each time she said that word, I got smaller and sank farther into the bedspread until I was no more than a speck of lint floating in the air between them, so small that I couldn't utter a word when she finally put the phone to my ear. "He wants to say sorry," she told me, but all I heard were my father's thick, horrible sobs. Then the line went dead.

That night, I started having the dream—a man I couldn't recognize fell from an impossibly high cliff, his body tumbling like a rag doll, battered and breaking against rocks while I stood by, watching. I had a vague feeling I'd pushed him, or at least given a little nudge. A Santa Ana wind was brewing when I woke panicked and hot, and I couldn't get back to sleep through the racket. I lay on my bedroom floor, running my fingers over the marks he'd left on my arms and back— a map of fire. I was listening for his return, but there was only the dry, frantic clapping of palm fronds, people's trash barrels knocking down the street. Sometime after midnight, the streetlights sparked out and my night-light went black. I heard sirens, and in the darkness my body seemed to swell as though it would fill the house. The weight of my dread pressed down like water—vast, immovable.

After a while I got up, stood on tiptoe to reach the pine box and the Kinney's shoe box in the upper corner of my closet and brought them, bulging with contraband, into the night. It was nearly impossible to light the fire pit in that swirling Santa Ana, but I kept at it, lighting match after long wooden match, holding each letter firm until it caught, curled and blackened into flame, until the boxes were finally empty. Bits of ash danced and dispersed across our patio.

Then I climbed the fence, joined with the wind. I walked up La Loma to Crestwood to Skyline Drive, wind thrashing my hair, dirt pelting my eyes. Tumbleweeds the size of televisions cartwheeled across the road and I felt I might walk forever, over those mountains, across whole states and through other lives, until the land ran out. I walked until an orange dawn bled over the San Gabriel Mountains, until I could no longer feel my toes, when my mother finally drove up beside me, her face ashen, and told me to get in.

Somehow, I knew. Maybe her waxy cheeks and swollen eyes confirmed my knowing, or the fact that she didn't yell at me, not really, for walking through the foothills all night alone. Perhaps she sensed that my life was already on fire without the fuel of her wrath. As we coasted down our street, I glimpsed the moon—a tender sliver of light upturned over Highway 5, beyond the Pacific. It looked so irreproachable, that moon, so ridiculously pure and remote. I stared at it as I took in my mother's broken, mechanical words, anguish and horror pumping through me like a drug. Still stared at it as we sat in the driveway, Alison rushing out like a wild thing to bury her face in my lap.

"It's Daddy, it's Daddy, it's our daddy," she wailed, pressing her grief in my open hands, though neither of us had ever called him this in his life.

Shortly after 2:00 a.m., he'd crashed his beautiful Corvette on Newport Freeway, hitting the center divider at ninety-five miles an hour. The shattered car had flipped and spun like a toy across the highway, then exploded into flames. There was no way he could have been saved, according to three witnesses, who all described how suddenly the car ignited in that wind, how fiercely it burned—so intensely, catastrophically bright, it hurt their eyes.

That was the image I held on to, after all the others were gone.

2004

THE STORM HAS SETTLED IN FOR THE DURATION. RAIN taps relentlessly against the skylights as we set the table in Gram and Poppy's dining room, and I'm suddenly reminded how the rain came after he died—in torrents, in buckets. How the moisture slid right down the parched, wind-battered foothills, flooding the gutters of our neighborhood, washing away lawn clippings, Ping-Pong balls, grocery receipts. Ali and I watched from the corner windows, dazed and speechless in the orange family room chairs, missing our first days of school. I remember wanting to run into the deluge and lie in the backyard. Maybe then the rain would take me, too.

It's dusk now—gray light falls over Gram's deep walnut table, the ancient linen curtains, the Mexican tile floors layered with Oriental rugs. Poppy's grandfather clock ticks from the corner of the living room as Alison and Mom and I bring in platters—sautéed green beans and lasagna, garden salad, lentil loaf and cheesy bread. It's the food of my childhood, and I could almost convince myself that I'm a girl

again, except that my hands ache like a catastrophe, and the words my mother spoke out in the drizzle echo in my head—
Do you love this man? Is he worth risking everything?

Since our conversation, an undeniable weight has settled in my mind and chest, and I can hardly bring myself to make the requisite kitchen small talk, can barely meet my mother's meaningful sidelong glances. When I look at her, my eyelids sting. Though we've spent an hour preparing this meal, I have no appetite for food. My dread is compounded by the growing darkness, and the fact that our teenagers are not home from the mall yet. Hannah called nearly an hour ago to say that they were on their way. They should be back by now.

"Do you want me to call Han again?" I ask Ali as we place the remaining dishes on the table, call the men in to supper. "I left a message ten minutes ago."

"I know—I just tried Donny's phone and he didn't pick up." Ali flops down in a chair, looking spent. A few fat golden strands have slipped from her chignon and her bruisy dark circles are visible beneath fastidious layers of concealer. The faint network of lines around her eyes are in the same pattern as mine, the same as our father's—I could almost find him by tracing a finger over my sister's skin.

"I'm starting to wonder if we should call the police," she says.

"The *police?* Come on, Ali," I half whisper. "They're just being teenagers, testing out their limits. They'll be back soon—I'm sure of it." She nods, but I feel less confident than I sound. I don't want Ali to know how little I can predict what Hannah might do these days.

Gram calls for water from the living room sofa, unable to walk the six yards to the dinner table, unable to eat solid food.

Poppy goes to her, fills her cup. Earlier, I watched, entranced, as he fed her a bowl of applesauce—spoon by tiny silver spoon, her shrunken mouth opening and closing like a baby bird's as he whispered endearments. "There you go, little mama. That's my girl." Then he wiped her mouth with a soft cloth, rearranged the pillows behind her head. These small, nurturing gestures seemed so natural for him, so effortless, that I begin to wonder if this tenderness toward her has been there all along, masked by the habitual dismissals and gruff demands. Perhaps there are worlds between every couple that none on the outside can detect, I muse as everyone comes to the table—Mom and Robert, Alison and Kurt, Uncle Peter with his new "lady friend." As I seat Emmie beside me, trying to pry the chess pieces out of her fingers, I'm wondering about the marriages in this family. Sheila and Nick are both on their second. Since his divorce from Janie, Peter bounces from one relationship to another. Mom and Robert have reached an amenable but rather proscribed middle ground. Alison and Kurt seem jointly addicted to their acquisitions and status.

As for me—I've been obsessing over the text message I received an hour ago.

Been trying not 2 do this but things bleak here…Eli's enlisting. Miss you, world flat w/out you….

It's taking every fiber of my will not to rush out into the rain to call him.

As my grandfather offers his familiar inaudible prayer, I stare around the table at my family. Despite the rigors of Adventism, the sanctity of marriage and the influence of Poppy and Gram's nearly seventy-year union, none of us are doing so great in the relationship department. There is no map here showing me the way.

Sonia, Uncle Peter's new Russian girlfriend, asks how I like living back east. "Peter tells me you're the *Bohemian* of the family."

"Bunch of damn communists in that part of the world," mutters Poppy, helping himself to salad.

"Not exactly communists, Avery. Just bleeding-heart intellectuals," explains Robert, winking at me. I smile, grateful for his support, despite the irony.

"She has a successful studio," Mom asserts. "She's a talented painter."

"This is yucky, Mama." Emmie smashes two fingers into her lasagna. I don't have the energy to argue with her tonight. I'm watching Mom mouth something across the table to Robert, who nods at her. If thirty years of marriage has done nothing else for them, it's enabled him to read her lips, the precise tilt of her head, the imperceptible hand gesture. Nathan and I have yet to master this subtle form of communication.

In the middle of dinner, a car hums up the driveway, blessedly and finally. Ali jumps and rushes from the room, intent on meeting the kids head-on. I stay at the table, trying to get Emmie, who's climbed onto my lap, to open her mouth for a green bean. I'm in no hurry to confront Hannah at this moment or to join in my sister's righteous tirade.

A few minutes later, as the men are arguing over Tiger Woods' dominion in the golf world, Ali calls my name sharply. I plop Emmie in Mom's lap and make my way to the spare room, where Hannah and Ben are slumped side by side on one of the twin beds, their heads lowered before my sister, whose face is livid and blotchy.

"You wanted to know how much trouble they could get into in a couple of hours," she snaps. "Well—now you know!" She yanks Ben's chin upward so I can see the tiny silver stud on the left side of his freckled nose. Hannah has a similar adornment. "They pierced their noses, of all things—without permission and without any thought to the consequences of their actions," my sister announces in her best Assistant D.A. voice. "And Ursa and Donny, who know better, did nothing to stop them!" I glance at the older children: Donny leaning against the wall, scratching his head in forced nonchalance. Ursa cowers in an armchair.

"You've proven yourselves pretty incapable of handling the kind of responsibility we trusted you with." Hands braced on hips, feet spread wide on the tile floor, my sister cuts a formidable figure, despite her small stature. I find myself sympathizing with her boys, and with all Santa Barbara criminals. "And you have to take those—*things*—out of your noses, however it's done. Right, Sylvie?"

Hannah looks at me, arms crossed, eyes beseeching. "You never said I couldn't, Mom," she says softly. Alison barklaughs at this.

"We never said you couldn't, like, hijack people's cars, either. But some things shouldn't have to be spelled out!"

"Let me see it." I inspect the tiny azure stone, embedded in the tender ravine along the side of Hannah's nostril. "Well, actually, Ali, nose studs have never made it to our *forbidden* list. I mean it's not really the same as stealing cars—"

"Don't tell me you're going to let her keep it!"

"Can I keep mine, too?" Ben pleads.

"Absolutely not! It's fine and well for you, Sylvie." My sister spins round to face me, gold eyes blazing, hair fallen from its clip. "But *my* family still belongs to the Church."

"Right, of course, Ali." My pulse quickens. "I can see how that complicates things. Much simpler being heathens like us. Come eat dinner, Han." I turn to leave the room, jaw clenching.

"Oh, that's just great." Alison's voice has shed its professional veneer. "Just leave the mess to me. Just—just run away, little sister—you're so good at that!"

I swing back to face her, heart thumping in fury. "I'm sure you'll figure out a way to micromanage things back under your control," I snap. "That's what *you've* gotten so good at."

I'm breathing with difficulty as I make my way back toward the dining room, where Emmie is now calling me. My desire to sneak out for a smoke and an illicit phone call is waylaid by the sound of another car in the driveway; most likely Nick, come to find Ursa. I decide to meet him first and explain things—to cushion him from my sister's rage—so I open the massive front door and step out onto the rain-slick patio.

But a second later, it's not my cousin who emerges from the new car in the carport. It's Nathan, grinning broadly as I gape at him. He comes toward me through the mist, like a figure in a dream, clutching his navy duffle bag. His left wrist is encased in a white plaster cast.

"What are you— What *happened?*" I ask, stunned.

"I couldn't really work anymore," he says. "So I decided to join you."

Later that night, Nathan tells the story again before the fire, while Hannah, Emmie and Ben decorate the Christmas tree Kurt has set up. Ali offered to drive Robert—still recovering from a bout of bronchitis—back to the apartment, taking Donny and leaving me with a chilly hug good-night.

Knowing my sister, it will be weeks before the old affection seeps back into our rapport, though she ought to be appeased. Hannah, in an uncharacteristic fit of selflessness, offered to take her nose ring out, too, and now she and Ben both sport inflamed-looking little holes. Every so often, one of their hands floats up to investigate the injury.

"So anyway," continues Nathan. "This storm was a bi—a doozy," he corrects, remembering not to curse in front of my family. "Ice and rain and sleet—in New England we call that lovely combo a 'wintry mix,' like it's a cocktail or something."

Only Kurt laughs at this joke. My dislike for him lessens a notch.

"Anyway, I'm working on the stairs, replacing some treads when I notice water dripping down the hallway wall—some sort of leak, right?" He gestures with his uninjured hand.

"Don't tell me you went up there to fix it?" my mother calls from the dining room, where she's polishing silver. She's been remote since Nathan arrived, floating on the periphery of every conversation. I wonder (not without a hefty dose of irony) if she's uncomfortable holding my secret, afraid she might inadvertently give me away. "Don't tell me you climbed on the roof in that weather, Nathan Jones?"

"Well, I did, Elaine. I had to do *something*—I mean, the water was dripping onto the brand-new treads."

"Sounds like you oughta just put that house back on the auction block," remarks Poppy from the couch. He's sitting by Gram, whose chin is slumped on her chest.

"Aren't there people you can *hire* for this sort of work?" asks Kurt, a look of extreme distaste on his pale features.

Nathan laughs grimly from his seat on the stone hearth, long legs stretched before him. Despite his fall, his face glows from the limelight, the warmth of the room, the days spent working outside. Sitting on a hard blue chair facing him, my cell phone still burning a hole in my pocket, I find myself thinking what an attractive man he is; but it's a detached appreciation, as if I'm taking in the beauty of a stranger.

"I knew there were a couple of shingles that needed replacing up there," he continues, "so I took up my pry bar and some flashing to make a temporary patch. Well, it isn't long before my pants are soaked through and they trip me up as I'm coming down the ladder, and—" Here he holds up the cracked wrist. Emmie trots in from the guest room with a fistful of markers, ready to embellish the cast.

"Daddy, Daddy," she's chanting as she settles on the floor near him.

"Jeez, Dad," says Hannah, hanging a glass angel on the tree, "you're lucky you didn't get seriously messed up!"

"I know. And here's the really strange part. Apparently, I hit my head on a rock when I came down and was knocked out. Just lying there like a rag doll in the flower bed. In the middle of an ice storm. You can imagine." He winces. "I don't know how long I would have stayed there either—it could've been bad. But our crazy old neighbor Roz Benton comes by in her VW bus and sees me. Calls an ambulance."

"Roz just *happened* to be coming by at that moment, in the middle of a storm?" I narrow my eyes at him as the chill spread over my shoulders, down the length of my spine.

"That's like totally psychic or something," says Hannah.

"She's been weirder than usual." Nathan shakes his head, peering up at me. "She comes by at all hours, sometimes on foot, sometimes in her bus. Says she's looking for Lucy—must be the name of one of her goats."

"Lucy?" I remember the day we stood in her kitchen after the goat accident—how Roz remarked that Emmie looked like someone named Lucy. "I think Lucy's a person—someone she used to know."

"Is this neighbor dangerous?" asks my mother.

"No, nothing like that." Nathan chuckles, holding out his cast for Emmie to draw on. "I've heard people say she's got early signs of Alzheimer's. But I'm sure glad she was wandering around that night. I'll tell you one thing—the whole incident made me rethink my priorities." He stares at me, then down at the purple ballerina Emmie has drawn on his cast.

We're all quiet until Gram wakes and begins coughing—a deep, tearing sound that rattles her fragile body over and over. I can almost hear her bones knocking. She's clawing at Poppy's blue sweater as he startles from his seat, grabs a handful of tissues from the coffee table and holds one to Gram's mouth, patting her back. When he removes the tissue, it's splotched with blood. The coughing subsides, but Gram looks purplish. I swallow a lump of sorrow and alarm.

As I wash my face before bed, memories of my father's dying continue to surface—that feral wind followed by a lashing rain, as if the earth itself were raging and then weeping. Theresa sitting on the corner of my pink quilt two days after the accident, saying, "You'll feel better after the service—I did, after my Nana's funeral." She and Rose had filled our kitchen with sunflowers and bags of ripe avocadoes, and now she stroked her fingers along my cheek in a gesture that was strangely maternal. Her own tawny, freckled cheeks glowed in the afternoon light and I didn't tell her about the recurring nightmares, the broken man who dropped through my dreams, the perpetual feeling that I was growing and shrinking at once. I could no longer tell what size I was. When I spoke, my voice was dim, then deafening, and I doubted a service of any kind was going to help.

Besides, my mother had decided against a funeral. She wanted to remember him as he was, she said. She didn't want to dwell on the gruesome parts, didn't want others whispering about the odd and tragic circumstances of his death. And she just wasn't up to having people around. Still, over the next two weeks, an endless stream of visitors wound through our house, needing coffee, bringing soup, murmuring in the courtyard.

I stayed in the kitchen near my mother, at first, wrapping the cakes in cellophane and brewing more coffee, suddenly understanding the need for company after a loss: the necessity of feeding and washing and answering the door kept me from caving in on the images burning at my core. Standing at the kitchen sink, stacking dishes for Mom because she refused to leave her bed one morning, I couldn't stop my mind replaying the scene—his car hitting the center divider at a hopeless speed, flipping across the highway and shattering like a roughly handled plaything. I couldn't help wondering: Was there a flash of sorrow or regret before the end? An instantaneous vain yearning for the living?

"Why didn't you call, after you fell?" I ask Nathan as we lay in our parallel twin beds in Gram and Poppy's guest room. Hannah and Emmie have moved into the den, to accommodate their father. "Why didn't you tell me?" I'm startled and ridiculously hurt by his seeming distance, and the fact that he hasn't once kissed me—not even a peck—since he arrived.

He's silent. By the dim hallway light, I can discern the outline of his square cheekbones, the fine lips and tapered nose. I remember first taking in those features that scorching

July day when he built a fence around my yard—how he reminded me of a cross between John Hurt and Chevy Chase, only sweatier, and more handsome. How he listened to the English Beat on his boom box, hips swaying a little when he thought no one was watching. His attentive kindness was like a balm, soothing the chafe of too much transience, too many wrong men. Now he just looks like himself, or rather, a spent, weathered version of himself.

"I guess I figured you had enough to deal with. Or maybe I felt ridiculous," he adds.

"Ridiculous?"

"I might not be able to work on the house for a while," he states flatly, as if this is the worst news he's ever had to deliver.

"Clearly." I laugh. "Although I suppose, knowing you, you'll find a way to lay tile or something with one hand."

"Actually, I've laid most of the tile already. Did the mudroom floor using remnants from Richie Littleton's job. There are all these gorgeous little hexagons—sort of a mosaic. I think you'll like it."

"I'm sure I will." My old tenderness for him nudges me like a dog. His consistency, his faithfulness to the dream. "What will you do with yourself once the house gets done?" I tease.

"I'll make furniture in the converted barn." He doesn't miss a beat. "While you paint."

"Really?" I'm stunned by the realization that—even after all these years—there are slivers of him I don't recognize, desires I haven't learned by heart.

"Anyway, I won't be able to do much for a few weeks," Nathan repeats. "And we're just about out of money. Our credit's tapped out." He tries to cross his arms behind his head, then winces, remembering the wrist, and turns to me instead. "It's a serious problem," he concludes.

"We've got more than one," I tell him after a pause.

"I know we do." After he says it, I discover that my hands are burning, and the room has started to tilt. "How has it gotten like this, bean?" Nathan says into the gulf between our beds. "When did we stop paying attention?"

I'm loath to utter a single word. Afraid that if I even part my lips, the truth will shoot free like fire, ready to ignite the last threads tying us together, devour everything dear. Instead I probe my memory, trying to locate the exact moment—or series of moments—when our marriage began to stumble: Was it the unrelenting grind of parenthood or the stress of home improvement? Was it my unexpected pregnancy with Emmie or his hurtful indiscretion with the architect? Or does it go back further? Maybe I'm just hardwired for disloyalty.

"There was that woman—" I start, unsure of what I'm after, where I'm going with this.

"Oh, Sylv." He exhales. "I really thought we'd gotten past that. I thought you knew—"

"I just wonder, you know. What was going through your head?"

"It was one night," he says. "I was drunk, exhausted, careless. We were in a terrible place—you know that. You were so far away then, so preoccupied, and I was just— Believe me, I wish I could take it back."

"But what were you *thinking,* that night, Nathan? Why were you willing to take such a risk?" My heart is laboring painfully now; it's difficult to even draw a breath.

He turns to face me. "At the time, I guess it felt like I was losing myself—babies, houses, the job…. Losing you, too, everything we'd loved about each other. You were *so* pissed off all the time."

"Was I? It's all kind of a blur."

"Yeah. It was like, this last chance for lightness, discovery…. Kind of like the moment on the starting block in a swim meet—the second before you plunge into the cold. You need to remember what you're made of, or something. Whether you're still *in* there. I know it sounds completely asinine."

"No," I whisper, lacing my aching fingers over my chest. "Not completely."

"Listen," he says after a long silence. "I know I've been an idiot about the house. Preoccupied, stubborn, maybe a bit obsessive…"

"A bit?"

"Okay, maybe a lot. But somehow, I thought when I saw you out *here*… I had this fantasy—if I walked in your grandparents' front door, you'd melt or something. That the distance would just melt." He chuckles bleakly. "Silly, huh? To think it could be that easy."

"Yeah." I pull the electric blanket to my chin. I feel chilled and waterlogged, swollen with sadness and deceit. "I guess I've been preoccupied, too," I offer. "Worried about Hannah. Worried about Gram."

"Well. Gram's clearly on her last legs. I had no idea." He yawns, seemingly relieved to shift to another topic. "I'm sorry I doubted it, Sylvie. Sorry I made light of it."

As his breathing slows and extends, I'm searching myself for an honest emotion: Am I truly wounded by his earlier indifference? Or is my anger just an excuse to stay separate, and silent? One thing's for certain—I know I won't sleep this night.

★ ★ ★

Two days later, flying over Arizona, I'm thinking about Gram's last words to me. My bags packed and ready in the entryway, I'd knelt down beside the couch and took her brittle hand, stared into her clouded eyes and apologized. "I'm sorry, Gram," I said, struggling for words. "Sorry I didn't come sooner, that I didn't bring the girls out to—" I broke off as she patted my arm. Outside, Ben and Donny were chasing Emmie across the emerald lawn while Han rocked beside Alison on the glider, absorbing the light. My sister and I had restored a tentative equilibrium, reached our usual unspoken agreement *not* to talk about things, just to pretend the quarrel never happened.

"Your place is with your family," Gram said softly.

"I know, Gram. Somehow, it's been really hard to get home these last few years," I sniffed. My mother came up behind me, touched my shoulder.

"You'll miss your plane, if you don't leave now," she said. "Nathan's waiting."

"No, Sylvie." My grandmother gripped my hand, gathering her breath for a final thought. "*This* isn't your home anymore. Make your home where you've chosen to be." Then she pressed my fingers to her lips before closing her eyes again, turning her face away.

But how? I wonder now, staring at the vast expanse of terra cotta desert below us. *How do I do it, Gram? Who will show me the way?*

1975

MY MOTHER AND MR. ROBERT WERE MARRIED AT THE end of the school year, in an Adventist chapel in Monterey, nine months after my father's death. Coming down the aisle on Poppy's big arm, Mom grinned up at Ali and me—so blushing and unsure, she seemed more like a teenage bride than a thirty-eight-year-old recently widowed mother of two.

Throughout the service, the idea of my father rattled around my head like an empty can. While the preacher droned about God's will and second chances, while Mom and Mr. Robert read their vows and kissed primly before the congregation, my father circled my thoughts like a shadowy moth. I heard his nasal laugh echo off the dance floor as Lane Aluminum's CEO toasted Robert, "The best damn salesman to grace our corporation." And when Poppy refused to call Robert by name, referring to him as "Number Two," Dad winked and nodded, like he knew all along we were headed for trouble.

Mom didn't speak of her own misgivings for a while. When she and Mr. Robert returned from their honeymoon, she seemed rested and resigned, if not ecstatic. The thousand-acre Oregon horse ranch had given way months ago, to blueprints for a modest, three-bedroom tract house in the east San Francisco bay, but Mom seemed to take this in stride. "Robert has to work," she'd announced after the New Year, as if it had been evident all along. "He can't just uproot his whole life!"

As the movers hauled her Steinway through the new front doors, unloaded our sagging box springs, dropped our crates on the freshly paved driveway, Mom orchestrated with a bright voice and terse smiles, but I knew better. I saw the way she stood apart from her husband, embracing her own ribs. I noticed how she touched Ali's angry forearm—as if seeking absolution—and fell silent at meals, her face going pallid in the middle of a conversation.

It wasn't just the tidal wave of loss, the shock and sleepless nights—all three of us wandering the house in silent shifts for months after he died, pursued by nightmares. Mr. Robert had changed, too. Gone was the goofy, cowboy-booted captor who'd made us pancakes at Wallowa. That was vacation, of course, and this was real life, his businessman's life that we'd signed on with for good.

In this new life, Mr. Robert left at seven forty-five each morning, wearing his uniform. (It wasn't really a uniform, but that's what Ali and I called his blue-gray suits, white shirts, maroon ties and striped socks.) He returned every evening at five-fifteen, kissed my mother's cheek, patted her ass, poured himself a martini and settled in front of the TV, where he'd nest until dinner. By then, he'd have removed certain parts of the uniform—the jacket and shoes and tie—

and unbuttoned the top two buttons of his shirt, so his gray chest hairs sprouted around the empty buttonholes. He'd sit on the brand-new couch, hitching his pants to reveal shiny, hairless calves. I'd go in to him sometimes and sit beside him—something I'd rarely done with my own father.

"Hey, twerp," he'd always chirp, and then he'd start changing the channels, cradling the remote loosely. He'd jump from sports to weather to news and back again, never staying on anything long enough to get a story from it, and soon I'd get discouraged and leave. Sometimes, I wondered if he'd tricked me—maybe once I was gone he'd congratulate himself, take a deep sip of his drink and settle into one program all the way through.

Ali stayed in her room almost all the time now, organizing. Since Dad's accident, she'd been obsessed with order and had already arranged her new room—books by author, magazines by title, photo albums by date. She'd color-coded her sweaters and the last time I went in, was folding her underwear in shoe boxes to take to boarding school. I wouldn't start school until September, and had no one to talk to. I had even given my skateboard to Theresa, imagining I wouldn't need it in our new neighborhood because I'd have a horse. I had pictured rolling fields dotted with shiny equine backs, but the only horses I saw around here were kept in tiny corrals angled up dry hillsides. From the highway, you could see lots of these triangular pens sandwiched between new Tudors or colonials—houses so shameful and stark along the freeway, they seemed like naked hitchhikers, showing themselves blithely to every passing commuter.

To make matters worse, Theresa called in late June to say that she and her family were moving to Vermont in September. Rose, a native New Englander, had inherited a five-hundred-acre Morgan farm outside Brattleboro, wherever that was. It may as well have been Tunisia. "I hope you'll come out," she said. Then she asked how things were in my new town.

"It's great here," I lied. "There are horses everywhere you look, and no smog!"

The air *was* cleaner in Danville—on that point I had to give Mr. Robert credit. And there were some buzzing golden hills behind our house; if I hopped the fence and picked my way up the artificial creek, between backyard gates and swimming pools, I could slip out of the development altogether.

"My mom wants to know if you're doing any painting," Theresa asked. "She says you have talent." Rose had started giving me art lessons a month after my father's accident. What began as a blessed diversion had blossomed into something like a calling. It turned out I loved the soft smear of paint on my fingertips, the grainy skin of canvas. I loved everything about painting—the greasy pull of the dishrag against my forearm, the tiny but infinite worlds I could create. But I hadn't had the heart to unpack all my supplies, in this new house.

"I walk now instead," I told Theresa. "There are hills forever here."

Leaving all the houses behind, I'd climb through the widest stretch in a saggy barbed-wire fence and emerge in the foothills of the great Mount Diablo. There I could wander for whole bright hours without smelling a car or looking at my stepfather's face. I could make my way through desiccated oak groves, could stretch my skinny legs and shout to the blue-white heavens until dinner without having to confront any evidence of my mother's and my mistake.

But evidence continued to present itself. In this new life,

Mr. Robert had real teenage children who often came to kick at the driveway, nursing bent cigarettes, and an ex-wife who called in the middle of the night. I'd wake in my room, which still smelled of nylon carpet and fresh paint, to the phone ringing in the blackest hours of morning, then Mr. Robert's exasperated words. "Yes, Bee, I know you feel that way. How much have you had to drink, Bee? Where are the children—can you put Lisa on? This is really going to have to stop. You have to pull yourself together, Beatrice. I'm going now. No—there's no need for *that* kind of language." Then my mother's sleepy, plaintive voice, and soon the phone would ring again; Mr. Robert would go through the whole thing again before unplugging the cord from the wall. Sometimes Mom's words became rushed and angry, like sharp little winds cutting through the house, and once I heard her gentle sobbing, accompanied by Mr. Robert's tired, "There, there, Elaine. I know it's all been hard."

I waited for her confession, but it didn't come. She was quieter than usual as she completed the tasks her new home offered. She looked old all of a sudden, the gray half-moons below her eyes every bit as dark as during the weeks after Dad's death, the grooves around her mouth setting. Sometimes I sat with her or read to her while she ironed Mr. Robert's shirts or practiced her golf on the living room carpet, but we couldn't rustle up much conversation. We were going to make the best of it—that's what she seemed to say in her sturdy glances, her mustering sighs.

Finally one Saturday morning, in the car en route to our new church, my mother looked at Alison and me and said, "I'm sorry I wrecked our lives, girls, but we're just going to have to make what happiness we can." That was all. She looked back at the road before her then, dabbed the corners of her eyes with her ring finger. Alison said, "Jeez, Mom. Get a grip," and stared out the window for the rest of the ride. I didn't know what to say, so I just touched Mom's arm, held her hand in my lap all through Sabbath School. And in the middle of the sermon that day, my mother's hand in mine, I decided to give myself to Jesus. What else could I do? He looked so patient and paternal in his stained-glass glory, towering behind the minister, a lamb tucked under his arm. Pastor Trumble was talking about preparing for the Second Coming—that glorious event when Jesus would appear in the sky, carry us off absolved to His Father's house in heaven and I thought, *Yes, this is the answer!* I didn't know how long it would take, all this redemption, but I decided to wait for it.

Then in July, the real trouble began. The heat suddenly bore down like a flat boulder over our heads. It was so hot, the soles of our feet blistered on the patio. They said it was a drought year—no rain since March—and the hills behind our development crackled in the midday sun. My stepfather said it was earthquake weather, and stayed home for a few days, lounging in his underwear and socks, martini in hand.

"It's fire weather," my mother pronounced.

"It's the end of the world," said Gram, who'd started coming to Sabbath School with us each week. "Jesus is coming," she said. "That's the reason for all this heat."

I liked this last explanation the best. I liked the idea of Christ ushered in by the catastrophic heat, his presence breaking the cruel sky, a fury of storm clouds following, raining salt tears over the land.

Instead, Mom's prediction came true; fires cropped up in the hills again. It seemed a perfect way for the world to end, and I pictured us all spinning toward heaven in a wheel of cleansing fire. Two fires, then three, then four fires raged under the tearless sky, circling Mount Diablo's bald crown like a ring of bright hair. Mom and I felt the heat as we stepped onto the driveway, though the fires were still several miles away. If we stood there for a few minutes, bits of ash would float down and stick to our arms. My mother's face was spotted with it.

"Isn't fire one of the last plagues?" I asked hopefully. "Isn't that one of the things in Revelation? One of the big things before planets fall? Before Jesus comes?"

"I don't remember, angel," she said, wiping the soot from her cheeks. "Let's go inside and make something cold to drink."

My walks got more risky. I'd slip out of the house when my mother was busy and climb through the fence, making my way on fire roads toward the source of heat and smoke. It was the same feeling I'd have later, as a student at UCLA, walking through the streets of East Hollywood, La Brea, Echo Park, L.A., legs pumping, mind spinning, winding my way toward danger as if I needed to walk to the very edge of ruin.

Seven houses in the surrounding foothills caught and burned. Five developments, including the one next door, were evacuated. But not ours. So life continued as the fires raged, becoming an ominous but familiar part of the landscape. Mr. Robert watered the deck every morning, doused the driveway. Mom took Ali and me clothes shopping in Walnut Creek and I watched, stunned, as Ali assembled a new persona for boarding school: pumps instead of platforms, cardigans with shoulder pads. She sauntered off to Petites with Mom, leaving me in Juniors, where I tried on earth shoes and macramé belts by myself. I told myself it didn't matter; we'd never seen eye to eye. Afterward, we staggered out of the air-conditioning like travelers returning from a journey; then we remembered, and glanced up to see what new damage the fires had wrought.

Finally they died down, leaving massive black scars on the hillsides, air murkier than the worst L.A. smog. It was in this sooty aftermath that Lisa, Mr. Robert's nineteen-year-old daughter, came to our house, her face smudged with mascara, to tell us that Beatrice had drunk herself to death.

"She's dead, Daddy," she sobbed, while Mr. Robert patted her back, Mom, Ali and I standing helplessly aside. "Mommy killed herself," Lisa sniffed, "And now we have nowhere to go. Me and Randy have nowhere to go."

"Well, of course you do." He looked over her shoulder at my mother. "You'll come stay with us, that's all. We'll just have to get a bigger house, won't we, Elaine? We'll figure it out." Mom said nothing, just hugged her elbows, bracing herself for the penalties of this new life.

It seemed a fitting ceremony for the beginning of our new family: all of us clothed in black, huddled in the scant shade of a Moraga cemetery, breathing the gritty residue of ashes. The service took place at graveside, as Beatrice had requested. Mr. Robert stood to one side of the casket beside Lisa and Lou, greeting a smattering of family and friends. My mother, Ali and I sweltered on the other side, not exactly innocent bystanders, but not insiders, either. This tragedy was not ours. A few people who knew Mom came up to give stiff condolences. The rest of the crowd eyed us with curiosity or suspicion, and Beatrice's younger sister from Portland downright glowered from behind her Chinese paper fan.

Randy, who was Ali's age, stood alone, smoking on the

margins in his black Levis, Calvin Klein T-shirt and sunglasses. He looked dangerous and tragic—a maltreated stray that might turn on you if you tried to pat it. But after a few minutes, Ali took a deep breath and marched over to speak with him. I watched in admiration as she approached him in her black chiffon sundress, flinging her gold hair over a shoulder. He reached to take her outstretched hand. I couldn't hear what they said, but I saw him push his dark glasses to the top of his head, toss his cigarette into the dirt. Apparently, Ali alone knew how to reach this boy. By the end of the service, they were embracing.

But a few weeks later, Alison had deserted us all for boarding school. The rest of us left the bright little tract house in Danville for a hulking split-level in the charred foothills one development over. This second house had six bedrooms and still stank of cigarettes from the previous owners, who'd been so spooked by the fires they fled to Seattle. This new town was called Alamo, and as we moved our things out of the U-Haul, once again lugging boxes through doorways and up stairs, I kept thinking of the famous Texas battle, parched soldiers hiding out in ditches, bodies strewn about.

"Isn't the Alamo where everybody got killed?" I asked Mr. Robert as he helped Lisa carry her bed into a downstairs room. "Isn't that where everybody got slaughtered?"

"Yes, but they held out for a good long time before it was over," he said, dropping the mattress on the floor with a thud. "Where do you want this thing, Lisa?"

Lisa shrugged and pointed to the darkest corner of the room. We would be neighbors now, inhabiting adjacent rooms in the cellar, our exhausted, newlywed parents above us. Lisa and I would share a bathroom, a hall closet and a phone jack, so I watched her closely. Her round, black eyes reminded me of Darian Woods's, and she had the habit of placing her well-manicured fingers over her lips, muffling her voice. Once or twice that day, I caught her staring fiercely at my mother's back. I decided I liked her, though she was odd and acted younger than her nineteen years. Unlike Randy, Lisa seemed to understand that humor was needed; she kept surprising me with well-timed witticisms, spoken from behind her pink hand. She called us the Bradys from Hell and poked fun at the tacky decor while her brother stormed through the hallways, stoned and furious, kicking at boxes. I knew just how he felt, but I wished he wouldn't take it out on the rest of us. When I tried to make friends by carrying a crate of record albums into his room, he accosted me on the steps, grabbing it from my arms.

"Keep your hands off my stuff." I smelled the familiar tang of alcohol and backed away. He was already losing his hair in front. "Got it, *Saliva,* or whatever the hell your name is?"

After that, I stayed out of Randy's way. It wasn't hard to do, since he was usually locked in his room, listening to Aerosmith and Kiss. I wondered how long it would take Mom to figure out that her stepson was smoking pot all day. The sultry odor seeped into the hall no matter how many towels he stuffed under his door. Lisa, on the other hand, was almost never in her room. She sat on the family room sofa from breakfast until bedtime, eating Doritos and Cheez Whiz, watching talk shows and circling employment ads in the newspaper.

A few weeks after our move, it occurred to me that Mom and Mr. Robert were rarely home anymore. He was working longer hours all of a sudden. My mother had joined the ladies' golf league, was singing in the choir and volunteering on three committees at our new church. I knew what she was up to, and often asked if I could accompany her to the ugly brick building in Pleasant Hill. While she practiced choral arrangements or sat through committee meetings, I wandered the playing fields out back, the dilapidated classrooms of Pleasant Hill Adventist Academy, where I'd soon be starting eighth grade.

Eventually I found myself wandering down the middle aisle of the church sanctuary, sitting in an empty front pew and staring up at the massive face of the Savior. He looked benign enough, although there *was* something missing—a certain empathy or pain. This wasn't the bloody, tortured Jesus of the crucifixion, who'd presided at our old church in Tustin. This was the post-resurrection Jesus. He'd been through it all, and had the mellow, self-satisfied look of the immortal. With His gauzy robes and sun-streaked hair, He seemed almost complacent, and I wondered if He could see me from the sanctuary of His Father's kingdom. I wondered if He could hear me when I prayed to Him each night, after Mom had left my room.

She always said she just wanted to tuck me in, but once she'd shut the door and sat on the edge of my bed, she'd start to cry.

"I don't know what to do." She'd squeeze my hand in her thin fingers. "I don't know where to turn." I strained my mind for the perfect advice, trying for an expression that would ease her pain. She talked about her ambivalence toward Mr. Robert's children, her hatred of this new house. She missed Alison and Sammy and, yes, my father. She missed all their old ways. She even missed his anger, God help her. If only they'd found a way to work things out. If only she could have saved him; if he hadn't been so rash. She didn't know this man she'd married, and she thought about leaving, finding a place closer to Gram and Poppy's, just the two of us…. But she always came around, resolving to stick it out, make the best of the life she'd made.

"I couldn't bear the scandal of a divorce, now, on top of everything else," she said one night, and I felt my heart curl up and retreat, like a marsupial seeking darkness and shelter. Then she wiped her nose across the back of her hand and I was startled by a desire to slap her—my fingers vibrated with it. I nodded as she talked, hugging my own arms to avoid doing any more harm, pretending to listen.

That night, I dreamed that Jesus was approaching in the eastern sky and I was on a beach, all tangled up in the damp sand with my sister's old boyfriend, Leslie Brown, his big hand rummaging between my legs. Just as I was about to come, I heard the heavens cracking open and looked up at the tumultuous, bright sky. Jesus's disappointed face shone down from the fist-shaped cloud. Then a tidal wave conveniently towered up—immense and shining—to smother our misconduct. I woke with my heart thudding in the darkness, my nightshirt sticky. Unable to fall back asleep, I wandered the house until dawn, taking in the new smells, the odd shapes, the eerie feeling of other dreams being dreamed so near—stranger's dreams.

"He will come like a thief in the night," Pastor Trumble assured us. "And all but the most devout will be surprised at His coming. Two of you will be sitting side by side, and only one will be taken. The other will be left behind…."

I sat in our second-row pew with Mom, trying not to

notice the mulchy brown stare, long hands and shapely ass of Russell Schmoll, the tenth-grader who played the organ.

"All but the most faithful will beg the rocks to fall upon them, to cover their utter wickedness," droned the pastor. "But the righteous—" Here he opened his arms to include those of us in the front pews. "The righteous will rejoice in the utter certainty of their faith!"

I started to watch and wait. I wrote down everything I ate and fasted on Fridays. After church, Mom and I always drove to Orchard Hill, and while Mom and Gram prepared lunch in the cool kitchen, while Poppy watered his garden, I'd stand on the edge of their wide front lawn, trying to picture Christ's coming. I'd pick a cloud on the horizon—maybe that dark fisted one hovering over Alamo. Yes, that could be it, hanging silent above my own neighborhood. I needed to *see* that cloud, His hands reaching forward, that perfect, paternal smile. But whenever I came close to imagining it, I just felt tiny and afraid. Standing for hours in my disappointment and yearning, I knew I was a sinner of the worst order—a masturbator, a conspirator, a she-devil of a girl. Jesus would pass right by as if I were simply a smudge on the otherwise perfect lawn. I needed to muster up the appropriate exuberance. I needed to *focus*. But I grew weary of the task; my eye was drawn down from the heavens to that ghostly water tower, or the silver-black ribbon of fire road that strung together two knotty oak groves. I started wondering what shades I would mix to conjure the bleached amber hillside, and whether I'd use a brush or palette knife to capture the exact texture of the field.

"What in the world are you doing out there?" Mom called. "Why don't you come eat?" So I went. Once again, I'd been lured from my vigil by the smell of lasagna, the familiar sounds of my grandparents' voices, the beauties of the earth. I was fleshy, after all, unfit for redemption.

School started, and I went to Bible class every morning at Pleasant Hill Adventist Academy, where Mr. Marks talked about the joys of baptism by immersion. I'd seen this a few times—the robed believers springing from the water, cradled in the preacher's arms, conviction sparkling on their cheeks. Walking to the girls' bathroom after class one day, my Bible pressed to my breasts, I knew what I must do. If I couldn't be cleansed by fire, I'd be purified by water. I imagined emerging from the baptismal, absolved and full of confidence—my transgressions washed away like stubborn stains in a detergent commercial.

My mother took me for weekly counseling sessions with Pastor Trumble, who warned me of the dangers of adolescence. "The temptation of the flesh is strong," he said, massaging his knee with his chubby hand. "But you must resist, and study your New Testament, and keep yourself pure in the eyes of God, no matter what your peers are urging you to do. Are they urging you?" he asked a little too eagerly. I told him not to worry, that my sins had little to do with people my own age.

In the car on the way home, I quoted whole passages from memory—The Beatitudes, The Lord's Prayer, The Ten Commandments, The Twenty-third Psalm.

"Randy was arrested for drunk driving last night," Mom told me. "We'll have to pay a stiff fine, and Bob and I now have to drive him everywhere."

"I'm sorry, Mom," I offered, "but we shouldn't judge him. Especially since he just lost his mother. Jesus says in the New Testament that—"

"I know, Sylvie. It's just hard. Bob's talking about sending him to his grandma in Eugene and I feel so guilty, but— if I'd known things were going to turn out this way…" She sighed.

"Everything will work out for the best, if you give it to the Lord," I tried. "'But rather seek ye the kingdom of God; and all these things shall be added unto you.'"

"I suppose that's true. That's from the Psalms or something, isn't it?"

"Luke 12:31," I said, turning my face away.

I believed, during those first few months of the school year, that being baptized would take away my aversion toward my new family. It would erase the stinging rage I felt around my mother, the horror and guilt about my father, the grief that often smothered my senses like a layer of damp wool. Maybe it would even mend this ache between the two halves of my rib cage—some days, it felt like God himself had slid a silver knife into my breast, splitting me in two. Baptism would fix all that, I knew. I imagined that everything would be brighter, after I emerged, cleaner, more whole. I would gasp with wonder and gratitude, like Dorothy emerging from her dingy, beaten house and stepping into the colorful landscape of Oz.

Instead, I came out of the baptismal coughing, having gotten some of the sour, chlorine-rich water up my nose. Pastor Trumble slipped as he brought me to my feet and we stood clutching each other, waist deep in the chill water, tangled in his heavy, slick robes. The first thing I saw when I opened my eyes was not God's face, but Pastor Trumble's matted black nostril hairs and wide red chin as he stammered, "I'm sorry—I'm terribly sorry."

I shivered all through the sermon that day—hair cold and slimy on the back of my neck, infection brewing in my left ear—smiling tightly when Mom whispered how proud she was, how grown-up I seemed, what a beautiful little *lady*. Russell Schmoll winked from behind the organ, so I stared right back. I couldn't look at Pastor Trumble's shiny face, or at the stained-glass Jesus receding behind him.

2004

I STILL HAVEN'T CALLED TAI BY THE TIME WE DRIVE home from Bradley Airport the day after Christmas. Then there's the unpacking and the washing, the bills and recycling, the Christmas tree to disassemble. Nathan does what he can with one arm, but keeps bumping his cast and cursing, so I send him for groceries. Our plants are dying and the driveway hasn't been shoveled. Through it all, I fight off the desire to call, like tamping down a stubborn brush fire at the base of my skull. Emmie requires help with her new train set and Hannah wants a chess partner. The fire creeps over my scalp, seizes my forehead, migrates to the troublesome tendons of my hands.

I wake up sweating in the middle of the first night, and the second, seeing his words—*Eli's enlisting...world flat without you*—flash across the greenish expanse of my mind. I can't go back to sleep and float through the house wraithlike, thoughts spiraling: *I have destroyed all our chances for happiness....* On the third night, I hear my father's distinctive nasal twang calling, "Now you've done it, sporto." I whip around, tune in more closely, but there's only silence. I remember the haunted string of nights following our wedding, how I woke Nathan at one-thirty, two and four-fifteen, my mind a flapping shutter of memory: how my new husband would force himself awake, hold me in the broken dawn and read the poems "Song of Myself" or "Sunday Morning" aloud for hours, until sleep claimed me or the shaking subsided. I want to go to him now, curl into his spoon, claim my sweet marital comfort—but it's no longer mine.

Then the storm rolls in and Emmie's the first to get the fever and sore throat that spreads to the rest of us by Sunday. The last four days of 2004, snow falls in thick white clumps the size of marshmallows—thirteen inches in all—and we're marooned in the king-sized bed, the girls damp and dozing while I dole out Tylenol with crippled fingers.

The fever lifts but we aren't well. We bump around the house exchanging tissues and grumpy condolences, playing in shifts with Emmie, who alone remains energetic and has overtaken the living room—now dubbed Fairy Land—with her train tracks and doll furniture and blocks. She invents a new game about a Wish Fairy, with the power to grant one all-consuming wish to each of us in turn. "My all-consuming wish," Hannah finally moans, tossing herself on the sofa, "is never to play Wish Fairy again!"

When we can no longer abide dramatic play, the four of us settle down to family movies. Hannah has to repeat every movie two or three times, whether she likes it or not, and I'm uncomfortably reminded of myself, during the weeks after my botched baptism: despondency had set in, and I wandered the house in the same pair of powder-blue sweatpants for days, until Mr. Robert brought home a big-screen TV, a

VCR and a stack of old movies. During Christmas break that year, he set everything up in the basement and proceeded to educate his patchwork family about cinema. His favorites were black-and-white films that featured Katharine Hepburn and Spencer Tracy. We teenagers crept from the dank solitude of our bedrooms to watch.

"What is this weird shit?" Ali asked about *The Birds*.

"Don't you have anything more current, Dad?" asked Lisa.

"Is this supposed to be a horror flick?" Randy rasped.

Robert just laughed—a rarity those days—and said, "Grab a seat and shut up, would you? They don't make movies like this anymore." I eyed the new entertainment system suspiciously. I hated everything about that house. I hated how the rooms all seemed miles apart, how you could get lost in the hallways, how my mother avoided coming downstairs for fear of running into her stepchildren. But even she descended during the Cary Grant movies, taking her place beside me on the green basement couch.

I fell in love on that couch, with the Hepburns and Marilyn, with Jimmy Stewart and Grace Kelly, Bogie and Bacall. For glorious hours, I'd lose myself in their dry wit and simple antics, the tight story lines with satisfying endings. For two weeks before life clanked back into place—before Alison returned to boarding school and I spun back into restless despair—I stayed on that couch, transported to a world without compromising scenarios and senseless tragedies. We'd watch together—some of us staying, some wandering off— laughing at the funny parts, sighing in unison. Every now and then, I could almost believe we were a family.

"We can't keep on this way," Tai says when I finally sneak out of the house to call him, in the midst of *The Sound of Music*. "I think we should probably just stop, Sylvia."

I feel the air leave my body, as if I've been slugged hard below the ribs. It's New Year's Day and I'm the one who's been poised to say this, mustering the shreds of my will. Now he's stolen my line, and I feel cheated, chastised, bereft.

"Why?" I hear myself ask in a minuscule voice.

"Listen to what you've been saying." He laughs bitterly. "You sound awful. You've lost fourteen pounds and you're living on Advil. You can't paint. Your marriage is crumbling."

"Jesus Christ," I say, incredulous. "What did you think— that my marriage would be thriving right now? All it needed was a healthy dose of adultery?"

"It's making you miserable," he pronounces.

"So, now you're the guardian of my happiness? Why didn't you think of that *before* you started all this?" I'm shivering, and far enough from home to light my lone cigarette, pulling warm tatters of smoke into my lungs, which contract in protest and gratitude. "Are you blaming me for Eli's wanting to enlist?"

"No," he says. "I'm hoping he'll snap out of it before his eighteenth birthday."

"I feel like you're punishing me."

"Good God, do you think I'm getting some sort of— Do you think this is what I want?"

"What *do* you want?" I round the corner of Lupine and it occurs to me that I'm walking the same escape route I go solo each night, so I veer left, just to be different.

"I think it's what you want that matters right now."

"That's not fair," I snap. I'm walking furiously, hunched against the brittle air. Light snow starts sifting down again like dust. *Will it ever stop?* I can't believe I live in a place where the weather hurts, that I'm smoking with a fever and a sore throat.

Can't believe I'm being dumped by the man I've risked everything for—don't believe it, really. His voice has lost its usual resonance. It's like he's speaking practiced lines through a metal tube.

"Sylvia?" he says after a minute. "Are you still there?"

"Fuck you," I conclude idiotically, dropping my half-smoked cigarette into a storm drain. "Isn't it obvious I don't know what I want?" I swerve onto the dirt road running beside the Fullers' barn, straight into the hard-bitten cornfield. "Anyway, I don't believe you."

"Oh? Why not?"

He's chuckling, the bastard. "Because your diaphragm's not in it," I say. Tears freeze on my cheekbones as I crunch through the corn stubble. "And you wouldn't be laughing if this were really the end."

"Where are you, darling?" It's his normal voice again—the one I loved even before I loved him.

"I'm in the middle of an arctic cornfield. And you're probably sitting by the fire, right?" I close my eyes. I can see him there so clearly in his baggy pants and black sweatshirt, wineglass grazing the voluptuous wave of his mouth. I can see every vein in the warm hands, the thick stubble on his neck below the close-trimmed beard, white crescent scar over his left eye, the almost cruel joy of his smile—easy edges of his front teeth beside the wolfish canines.

If Emmie's Wish Fairy were to appear just now and say, "Go ahead, make your wish—" I'd be hard-pressed to utter a single thing. I want to be burrowed beside him by the fire, his fingers tugging the roots of my hair, the edge of his beard scraping my throat. At the same time, I'm desperate to be back in the life I've chosen. I want our family back to normal and the dream revived. I want to want my husband again. Want us happy and unscathed. In the next breath, I just want to walk alone along some windswept sea for weeks, never speaking. There are so many things I want, and each comes at a price I can't pay.

"I want to be good," I tell Tai, winded. "I'm so bloody tired of feeling guilty."

He's quiet for so long, I wonder if he's hung up on me. Then I hear the breath leave his chest. "All right, Sylvia." He sighs. "Then that's what I want for you, too."

I slump down in the snow, sit right down in the damp middle of the road and put my head against my knees, tiny flakes collecting on the sleeves of my black jacket. It's nearly dark, and my aching hands are finally numb with cold. I've walked too far. Nathan and the girls will be wondering where I've gone. They'll want me to see the end of the movie with them—the part where Maria and the children hide from the police in the Abbey and then they all burst out triumphant over the shining Alps—a happy ending; the kind we all want.

"Please don't tell me what you're about to tell me," Theresa says when I finally call her back in the middle of January. "Just lie to me, Sylvie."

"What kind of lies do you want, my friend?"

"Tell me you quit the crazy e-mail affair, that you didn't sleep with the tree guy—that you came to your senses."

I click off the public radio background drone, slide on my sunglasses against the morning's glare. "Okay." I sigh. "Nathan and I are about to go to Portugal for our second honeymoon. When we get back from our trip, we're moving to our finished house. So, I'm calling to see if I can buy a couple of horses, to put in our renovated barn this spring."

"Shit, Sylvie," she says after a pause. "I hope your lies to Nathan are better than that."

We're both quiet as I drive through Haydenville. It hurts to grip the steering wheel, so I'm driving with my knees.

"And he's not a *tree* guy," I sulk.

"Oh, Sy."

"Anyway, I've resolved that it's over," I tell her, but it comes out sounding like a question, misery welling between my words.

"When have resolutions ever worked for you?"

"Wow. I hope you're a bit more supportive to your therapy clients."

"I'm sorry. I just—I wish you and Nathan could recognize what you have, before it's too late." I hear the clank of dishes and picture her in the kitchen of the old Vermont farmhouse she inherited when Davey died and her parents moved to Florida—the house she hoped to fill with children, if only she'd found the right man. It doesn't seem quite fair, the math on this problem; no wonder she's fed up with me. "Besides, I'm not your therapist, Sy; I'm the friend who dragged you out of Hollywood when you were hell-bent on self-destructing, remember?"

"You're starting to break up," I say, truthfully. "I'm losing you."

"How convenient. Where are you?"

"I'm on my way to Ashfield. I'm visiting our neighbor and meeting the phone guy, okay?"

"Well, call me when you're out of the hills." The line crackles. "I'm not done lecturing you."

I toss the phone into my bag, trying to remember resolutions that stuck, wanting to prove Theresa wrong—if only in my mind. Surely there were times when, full of resolve like clear March sunlight, I kept a promise, did the right thing? I got myself out of L.A., didn't I? Got into a graduate program, married Nathan and got through two pregnancies? Started a business? Clearly there were times when I managed to quit whatever was killing me just then: the cigarettes or the drugs or the man, whoever he was, that was tearing me up or turning away.

Back then, I only loved the ones who couldn't love me, the ones who'd devour you for their lunch break and roll out of bed, car keys jangling. They brought lines of white powder and bottles of Wild Turkey, straggled into my life mean and battle-bloody, their busted childhoods like limbs needing amputation. When they started to get too restless or needy or mean, when I'd had enough of sucking them off or washing their filthy laundry, when I sensed them inching away or getting too close, I'd put an end to it—get in the car, change my number, tell them I had AIDS, say I was married. Then I'd walk around the city, leaning into my losses, peering at people in cafés and bus stops, deciding they were all just as lost as I. Especially the ones who clutched their lovers' peacoats, dangled along on sleeves.

Back then, at least I had the famished comfort of never caring too much. Now it seems there's too much to care about—everything to lose.

Though her bus is parked next to the house, Roz Benton doesn't come to the door. I'm just about to leave the banana bread on the porch when I hear her voice chiming from the back meadow. I follow it around the garden, through the goat-trampled snow to her barn.

"There, there, darlings. Don't go abusing one another—

you're trampling your feed, Dalton. Good Lord, look how pregnant you are, Bitsy, fat little whore. Get off her—"

"Excuse me, Roz." I poke my head into the warm animal stench of the goat house. "Sorry to disturb you—the girls and I made some banana bread." I hold out the foil-wrapped packages. "We heard what you did for Nathan."

She's still patting the pregnant nanny goat, staring, so I continue, "The week before Christmas? When Nathan fell off the ladder?"

"Oh, yes," she says, waving off my words. "Always a struggle over at that place, isn't there?" She pours feed into several pie tins, then comes toward me, beaming weirdly. "Let's make some tea, shall we?"

"Actually, I really can't stay. I've got to—"

"You can tell me all about the man who fell—off the roof, did you say?" As she pushes past me up the hill, I check my impulse to run, to be done with the exchange, free of this barmy old woman. *She's got no one but those damn goats,* I tell myself. *And she* did *save your husband's life.* I sigh and follow her into the kitchen, where she busies herself with a teapot and loose tea, hand-thrown mugs and milk. Finally taking my packages, she peels one loaf from its foil, sets it on a warped pine board and cuts off four thick slices.

"If dear John can't keep up with the repairs, he ought to sell the place," she remarks, setting the bread on the table. My stomach twists. Is she really so far gone? Or was it just a slip?

"You mean *Nathan,*" I correct. Her aqua eyes drift to mine. "Nathan and I own the house now, Roz." I catch myself speaking as if she's hearing impaired.

She turns to retrieve the boiling kettle, forgetting the oven mitt and scorching her hand, which she shakes rapidly in the air.

"Here, I'll get it," I offer. "Why don't you sit—I bet you've been working all morning."

"I'm just fine, my dear." But she sits anyways, sucking the burnt finger. "You're the one who needs to relax."

I laugh as I fill the teapot with steaming water. "That's probably true." I bring our mugs, the pot, the honey and milk to her round table. Steam curls between us.

"Of course it's true—just look at you. Your aura's all muddied."

"I wouldn't be at all surprised." I smile, offering her some bread.

"Well, it is. You're the one with the divided life line—I remember now."

"Yes, Roz—I'm Sylvia." I reach across the table, touch her wrist. I had no idea it was this bad. She takes my sore hand and turns it, just as she did before, staring into my palm. Then she reaches for my left hand and does the same.

"Plenty of passion, but changeable, divided," she mutters. "You do like to complicate things. The heart line's broken— see these three shooting up from it?" She nods, sucking her front teeth. "Two lines of attachment—hmm. The past has more sway than it ought. And you've got this vertical one cutting deeply through your life line. I've not seen one like that before. Did you say you were a Pisces?"

"Leo."

"Well, the two hands are distinctly different, so there's hope." She releases my hand and blows on her tea. "Everything you've been running from is before you."

"What do you mean?" I ask, becoming interested.

Her eyes, unblinking, start to water. "You have work to do."

I sip my tea, shifting in my seat. "You know, my hands

often hurt," I tell her, hoping for some grain of insight, despite my skepticism.

"Mmm. The hands are self-expression, dear. Creativity, efficacy, change…" She moves her own root-like hand through the air as if to shape it.

"So, what do you think it might mean, one's hands aching?" I try again.

"You have work to do," she concludes unsatisfactorily. I sigh, setting down my cup. I want to tell her that I have *literal* work to do—I must clean the studio, balance my books, prepare for winter workshops, which start next week. But I'm afraid my to-do list would read like Arabic to her. As I'm preparing to make a cordial exit, she startles from her seat.

"Where's Lucy?" she asks, beginning to search around the small room.

"You mean one of your goats?"

"No, no, my girl." She's suddenly frantic, peering under the table, behind the ratty couch in the adjoining room, then back to the kitchen, grasping her rough skirt.

"Who are you looking for, Rosalyn?" I stand, unsure if I should offer to help, or call someone. Should I take my leave now, while she's so distracted?

"Lucy—Lucy Kauffman," she snaps, swishing past me and peering into the bathroom, the mudroom, the hall closet. "She was here just a moment ago!"

It hits me, finally, and I understand that she's stalking a child's ghost. Haunted by memory. When she sweeps by me again, I reach for her elbow, try to hold her steady.

"Do you mean John Kauffman's daughter?" I ask. "Is that who you're looking for?"

"Here she was, just a moment ago—you mustn't let them

take her!" My heart contracts with pity as I guide her back to her seat, both of us breathing hard.

"It's okay, Rosalyn. The Kauffmans don't live here anymore." I rub her forearm, trying to hide my own alarm. "Let's finish our tea." She continues to glance around the room with a folded brow, presses her left hand over her face.

"What did you say your name was?" she whispers, receding into the chair cushions.

"Sylvia." I sit beside her, a fast chill rolling along my spine. "Listen, Roz, that was a long, long time ago," I try. "Lucy's safe now, she's—she's safe," I stammer.

After another moment, she stands briskly—all business now—and retrieves something from one of the high shelves near the fridge. "Here, Sylvia," she says, clear as glass, and hands me a small bundle wrapped in brown paper, tied with green string. "I've been meaning to give this to you."

"What is it?" I ask, but I can already smell the familiar strong scent.

"White sage." Then she begins to clear our dishes, though I haven't finished my tea or touched my bread. "It's for energy cleansing. You'll need to burn it around the foundation. You'll certainly need to do that."

"Thank you." I'm at a loss, flabbergasted by the seismic shifts in her demeanor. I bring my cup to the sink, pour out the leftover tea, shaking my head.

"And now, my dear, if you'll excuse me, I should really milk my poor goats."

"Yes, of course." I retrieve my coat from the chair back. "Thanks for the tea, Rosalyn."

As I'm making my way through the snow to my van, she appears in the side doorway, wiping her hands on a lavender dish towel. "Give my love to John," she warbles. I turn, my lips parting to correct her—then I stop myself.

"Did you know him well?" I ask instead. She cocks her head, so I try again, "Do you know the Kauffmans well?"

"Oh, yes." She's shutting her eyes on the morning's white brilliance, nodding. "He was my lover," she says, clutching her tea towel; then she slips back into the kitchen.

My mind is buzzing as I bump down Roz's long driveway, take a left onto Route 112. As the pieces of the puzzle clunk into place, I reach for the phone, wanting to tell Nathan what I've discovered. I can just imagine him shaking his head, chuckling. *So Kauffman was doing Roz Benton—the old devil....* Then I remember I have no cell service up here, and maybe it's for the best. The implications of what I've learned are troubling indeed. Did Jennie Kauffman know that her husband was having an affair? Is *that* why she drove herself and Lucy into the lake? Did Kauffman stay on all those years out of grief or inertia, or because he was in love with Roz and wanted to be near her? I imagine the two of them, slowly going mad in their cocoon of secrecy and remorse, losing track of years while the house and grounds fell to rubble around them. I laugh aloud, though it's not the slightest bit funny.

Approaching the turnoff to Plainfield, I'm overwhelmed by the need to see Tai. With no time to hesitate or reason, I swing sharply, dangerously onto State Highway 116. *Just for a moment,* I tell myself. *Just for one cup of tea and a talk—that's all, Sylvie. That's all you can have.*

But I'm already regretting it as I spot four cars in his driveway. Aside from Tai's Saab and landscaping truck, there's a Ford Ranger and a CR-V. He's talking to two young men in work clothes; they're all staring down at oversized sheets of paper rolled out on the hood of his car—blueprints for something, I'm guessing. I'm about to turn around when he spots me and comes forward, frowning. I crack my window. "Sorry," I say. "I was going to turn around."

"No, no, it's fine," he responds. "These guys are about to leave—I'll just be a few minutes."

"It doesn't seem like a good idea, Tai. I was just being impulsive."

"I like your impulses. Can you give me five minutes?"

I park near the shed, then wander behind the house, not wanting to engage with his workers, not wanting them to consider me or my errand. I pick my way across his stone patio and down the narrow garden paths, recently shoveled. The sun heats my shoulders; the snow is melting into tiny rivulets that run wild through his winter garden, the breeze unseasonably warm. Before me, the Berkshires roll west in a thousand shades of mauve and gray and chocolate.

I stop beside the labyrinth, which he's cleared of snow. It's a huge, circular, mazelike structure, about a foot high, and looks ancient, though of course it's not. Perhaps that's the appeal, I muse—a shape that recalls some piece of our deep, communal past. I imagine how he milled each stone from the earth, contemplated and shaped each before adding it to the pattern—it must have taken months. I'm making my way toward the entrance when I hear him crunching up behind me. Yuki appears and stuffs her cold nose into my ungloved hand, then bounds over the landscape, stopping here and there to poke her tongue into dissolving snow.

"It's so warm today," I say, squinting into the shining east as he comes near. "Must be January thaw—seems to happen every year around now."

"It's global warming, darling, as sure as I have this annoying hard-on," Tai says in his loamy chuckle. "What brings you?" He reaches to push a curl off my face—a routine gesture that suddenly irks me. I bat his hand away, resisting the urge to kiss him. It's been twenty-eight days and my heart is stomping, energy shooting through the soles of my feet, scorching the frozen ground.

"I'm not suggesting climate change is a liberal hoax." I smile. "But *this* is a typical New England January thaw." I can't fathom why I'm talking about the weather. I'd thought I wanted to tell him about Roz and the Kauffmans, but now that I'm here the idea of such gossip seems ludicrous. "There's a storm predicted for tonight," I say brainlessly.

"Did you drive all the way up here to give me the forecast?" He laughs, hands shoved in his pockets, slow rocking on his boot soles. I know his habitual tics and poses, know this body—each vertebrae and pockmark, slight indentation of the breastbone, the dark nipples and well-muscled thighs, the pale appendectomy scar above the sudden sharp swell of his cock. Sometimes, I'm frightened by the sense that I'm breathing beneath his skin instead of my own.

"I was thinking I might walk the labyrinth."

"Oh—good. Well, here it is." He indicates the entrance with a mock-cordial sweep of his hand. "Help yourself." I nod, wondering if we can pull off some sort of friendship, pull ourselves back from the precipice we'd been inching toward.

I hesitate by the first snow-dusted stones.

"Is this like a maze? Are there choices about which way to go?" The naked arms of surrounding oaks weave in a sudden gust, as if warning me away.

"It isn't a maze—there are no wrong turns," he tells me.

"There's just the next step." Yuki trots to his side, panting. As he reaches out instinctively to stroke her, I feel an insane stab of envy. His love for this animal is so unquestioned, so uncluttered.

"But where's the exit?" I ask. "Where will I come out?"

"You come out the same way you go in," he explains. "The entrance and the exit are the same. You follow it all the way in to the center before you come back."

"I see. Is that supposed to be a metaphor for something?"

"Sure, if you like." He grins inscrutably, placing one warm hand in the small of my back, urging me forward. "Some people get into the symbolism," he says, "and others just do it for the experience—sort of a walking meditation." I catch a scrap of his lush, earthy scent. A shaft of sunlight sears through his glasses, illuminating the otherworldly green of an iris.

"No one should have eyes like yours."

"The idea is to walk mindfully," he states as he ignores my comment. "Just stay open and notice each step, each thought, then let it go."

"Okay. Mindfulness." I take a tentative step. But the truth is, I don't want to do this meditative walk, this labyrinth thing. We're fools to pretend like this when all I really want is to take his hand, pull him up the stone path, across his deck, into the cottage glowing with early light.

"Some people say that when you get to the center, you'll find what you need to let go of. But I'm sure you'll get your own meaning." He comes up behind me, gives another little shove, but I don't go. Instead, I turn to face him; there are inches between my mouth and his throat.

"I don't want to do it," I breathe.

He steps back, nudges up his glasses. "Why not?"

"I already know what I need to let go of." I stare at the full rise of his upper lip.

"Okay. Then, why are you here, Sylvia?"

It's a good question. I want to say that it's not right, ending things over the phone, but none of this has ever been right. Maybe I've come to say goodbye; only, that doesn't make sense either, since I'm yearning for the stillness of his white room, that sensation of floating together just outside the ordinary world. I feel anxious to resolve or revisit something. Or is this just an excuse for bad behavior?

"It's more complicated than I thought," I say.

He inhales long and sharp, then blows out slowly, head falling back until he's staring at the sky—in frustration? Surrender? His Adam's apple looks painful against the rough brown skin of his neck, and I find myself thinking how easy it would be, really, to kill a man.

"I don't know what to do with you," he growls, looking me in the eye.

"Yes, you do."

At this he turns and walks to the cottage, Yuki tripping on his heels, and I feel like a dirty, unwelcome child, standing alone in the midst of his frozen garden. I can't believe it's come to this—me, a forty-two-year-old mother, wife and business owner.

"Come have some tea," he calls from the deck before disappearing inside. "Let's talk."

But we don't talk much—at least not right away—it being twenty-eight days and January, with the sun streaming onto his futon, the fireplace crackling with birch bark. We leave our mugs of tea to cool on the table. By the time we get back to them, they'll be ice cold.

Still, it's different this time. He's jagged and greedy in a way I've not experienced him. I feel raw and exposed afterward, sickened by our lack of restraint. Sprawled across his sunlit sheets before noon, I can't see how we'll ever have the strength to end this. And not for the first time, I watch the ugly scenarios unfold: Nathan's heartbreak and grim fury, the girls choosing sides, mediation perhaps, the house sold off and our assets divided, extended family splintering.... I'll need to enlist my mother's help just to afford the narrow, south-facing apartment over some professor's garage where I'll live with my part-time children: Mondays through Wednesdays and every other weekend? Every other Thanksgiving and Christmas? I imagine them huddled in the backseat, driving to and from their dad's place, duffle bags in hand, Emmie clutching Pink Bunny, Hannah's withering glances.

And what of Tai? Will I have him over on free weekends? Will this love or obsession or whatever it is weather the annihilation of my present life?

He's sitting on the edge of the bed now, his dark head in his hands, and I am triply liable for drawing him back in after he'd set his will against me. As if I need more guilt.

"I'm sorry," I say, and he turns and touches my arm.

"Don't be—that's not what I want to hear you say."

"What do you want to hear?"

"Oh, I don't know." He chuckles wretchedly. "That you'll love me forever? That you'll run off with me?" He crawls onto the bed, threads his arm through mine.

I'm desperate to remember when I used to feel this way about Nathan, that first summer when we couldn't get enough of each other. I'd ambush him on the stairs the moment he came home from his ten-day construction gigs in Long Island. More often than not, we never even made it to the bedroom. Sometimes, afterward, we'd sunbathe on the roof outside the landing. He'd read me Walt Whitman and Wallace Stevens, sipping Diet Coke through green plastic straws. We'd commiserate about our fathers' deaths, the trials of being the youngest. I knew without question that I'd marry him. Knew it the first time I laid eyes on him, really— his impossibly lanky legs spread before him on the porch he'd just mended, the steady hands and handsome English features, eyes that took me in with the helpless pleasure of a captive—

"Run off with me, Sylvia," Tai whispers. "I have a friend with land in the Santa Cruz Mountains. He has three cabins he never even uses."

"And what, we'll live off the land? Become ascetics?" I chuckle, but he isn't laughing. I turn to stare at him, propped on an elbow. His eyes are the intense color of antique glass. It takes me a moment to understand that he's serious, another to allow the fantasy—cover of coastal fog rolling through cedars, the overgrown garden engulfing our rough-hewn hippie cabin, two rickety chairs on the porch facing a vast, untenable quiet.

"I—I could never leave my daughters, Tai."

He pauses two beats longer before saying, "Bring them, then."

There is an ancient, familiar pressure in my chest. I close my eyes. "They love their father," I finally blurt. "I couldn't— wouldn't ask them to make that choice." Not a sliver of me doubts this, despite the mayhem in my heart.

"Well." He sighs deeply, falls back onto the pillows. "At least tell me you're tempted. Some little part of you?"

"Of course. But I thought you were against escapism?" I tease.

"Ah. Now you know all my secrets."

"You know mine, too," I say, but we both know it's not true. There are certain things that I've never talked to him about, certain subjects I won't broach.

"Tell me your *darkest* secret." He reaches for my hair.

I laugh. "You are my darkest secret."

"Mmm, I don't think so—if that were true, I'd know."

"What's yours?" I ask. "You go first."

"Ha—I should have known you'd try to bargain with me."

"Why should I go first? You started it."

"Fair enough. Okay, then." But he's quiet beside me, staring at the ceiling beams, black lashes unblinking as if peering into some crumbling room of his past. A shiver of pain twists his forehead; he takes my hand, rubbing it between his own like an amulet.

"You okay?" I ask.

"I watched my little brother die," he says without looking at me. "More or less, anyway. I didn't realize it was happening at the time—I thought he was just nodding off. We were hanging out with friends, New Year's Eve 1981. Listening to old Dylan albums, drinking whiskey, shooting up. For me it was just a recreational thing, but for Matt—" He shudders. "I didn't realize how serious it was, how far he'd gone." A tear streaks past the crow's feet, across the veined skin of his temple. I reach to whisk it away before it slips into his ear. "You know some of this already."

My throat constricts with sorrow, his losses pulling hard at my own. "My God—it must have been terrible."

"Well, it's the things you don't know at the time that kill you later, right? The things you think you *should* have known. I was his big brother. Should have realized he was in trouble— at least that's what I told myself. I was pretty caught up in my own world."

"You were just a kid yourself."

"Of course. I know that, in my rational mind. But some things are beyond reason, right? Some things you just can't talk yourself out of. Can't rationalize away, like you." He smiles bitterly. "You're one of those things."

"Did you try to talk yourself out of it? Out of this?"

"Yeah, every day. But what about you? You have to tell me yours now."

"Hmm. I was hoping you'd forget." I sigh and shut my eyes, probing the damp caves of memory, searching the darkest corners for those moments that squirm from aware-ness, huddle in clusters like bats. I don't know how personal I want to get. I could tell him about the years in L.A., my "lost years" as Theresa refers to that desperate swath between eighteen and twenty-two—bad sex and panic attacks, dropping acid in a roach-infested duplex in Venice Beach....

"You don't have to tell me unless you want to," he says. "I don't need—"

"I killed my father," I hear myself say, and my eyes fly open.

"You *what?*"

"I killed my father," I repeat. "Though, I didn't really know it—until now."

"But your dad died in a car accident."

"Right," I tell him. "But I caused it." Now the trembling kicks up—a small, startling eruption near my kidneys, rippling up through muscle and tendon, ribs and throat. My fingers burning, heart suddenly hammering as if I've run a fifty-yard dash.

"How can that be, Sylvia?" His voice is so low, it's nearly underground.

"I told my mother to leave him—more than once. And I

provoked him, too, made him drink and lash out, made him crash—" I'm sitting hunched over, clutching the hard freckled knot of my knees, though I don't remember how I got this way.

"You don't really believe that?" He's smoothing his hand up my spine, taking a soft fistful of hair, tugging the roots the way he does.

"I think," I finally say, "that it's what I *have* believed. I've just never spoken it before."

"Tell me." He pulls me down beside him, cinches his arms around me. "I want to hear the whole story."

I have never told the whole story to anyone, but now I do. Wrapped in his ivory quilt while the light traverses us in panels, I start talking about Mr. Robert and the shoe-box letters, my dad's anger and drinking, the church and its threat of damnation. As the winter sun rides to the top of the sky, I talk about Wallowa and the Corvette, how Mom sought my advice and I gave it. How I chose her lover—cherished his letters, held his secrets. How I told her to leave because it seemed like the answer we needed. I confess about the night my father left—the violence, the phone call, his sobs, how I burned the letters in a Santa Ana, then walked until dawn. How his car flipped across the highway as a man crashed through my dreams. I pause, breathing fast. Tai takes my hands, pressing the pain from my palms. "Keep going," he says.

The words rush like water through a dam—the second marriage, my bungled baptism, how Alison found God as I was turning my back on all that, how she went after law and order while I embraced chaos, how she was born again as I sought annihilation, taking longer and longer walks, thinking if I went far enough, fast enough, deep enough into the night,

I could somehow walk clean out of my guilty skin and into another life—a happier life.

"And did you?" he asks me after many breaths. "Did you find that happier life?"

"I don't know—I might have," I say. "If so, I've been doing my best to screw it up."

I have no idea how much time we've spent, except that it's past noon now—clearly time for me to go. I am strangely still, hollowed out and clear as he strokes my damp face, outlining eyebrows, lips, fingers, throat, as if inventing me from scratch. His touch is so light, I almost don't realize we're making love again—softly now, this last time.

2005

DRIVING DOWN THE MOUNTAIN AT HALF PAST ONE, I'M tending an unaccustomed quiet, seeing the old landmarks as if for the first time: a narrow white house lists between frozen swells of farmland, clapboards peel from the north side of a barn, four Holsteins hover against the leafless foothills. In an empty field, that board still sits propped in a rusted truck bed, the words *All things pass* scrawled across it in blue paint.

Finally pulling into the parking lot at my studio, I'm surprised by a sudden urge to paint. I need the rigor of canvas to ground me, the consolation of oils and dirty brushes, the familiar sting of turpentine. Still spent and sad and swollen, I need the sharp, solitary focus of creation to fill this hollow place between my breasts. There's a load of work to do— Roz Benton was right about that—and as I bound up the stairs of my building, unlock the studio door, I'm wondering how much I can accomplish in the slim hour before school is out.

I slap my mail onto the worktable, hit the flashing play button on my answering machine. Interspersed between telemarketing calls, workshop inquiries and a brief, uninformative message from Hannah's school are three messages from Nathan.

"Sylvie, it's eleven-thirty Monday. We need to talk. Give a call the second you get this, okay?"

"Sylvie, Sylvie, Sylvie… Where are you, hon? I've tried your cell. And the line at the house." Pause. "It's urgent, okay? I've got some news, so call me."

"Goddamn it, Sylvie. I wish you'd pick up! I'm with Hannah—she came home from school today. Nobody's been able to reach you—can you please call or get your butt home?"

"Shit," I say aloud, pulling in a resigned breath. I pick up the phone, square my shoulders in preparation for this call.

"Sounds like you're in deep," a low voice behind me drawls, making me startle and drop the phone. Eli leans against the open door frame, clad in baggy camouflage pants, a torn brown sweatshirt, a black ski hat. His arms are locked over his chest, eyes piercing. "Sounds like your husband's having a hell of a time finding you."

"Eli! How are you? Can I do something for you?" I force a smile and shove my hand in my pocket, fishing for Tai's agate—a habitual nervous gesture now.

"Nah. I don't think so." An uncomfortable smirk inches over his face. "I'm just here to get my paintings."

"Okay. Well, you're welcome to them." I'm trying to appear casual, pretending my heart isn't thudding in alarm. "But class starts again next week, you know."

"Yeah, only—I'm not coming back." He moves to the

corner of the studio, starts rifling through a stack of half-finished canvases. "Maybe you should just call your husband."

"I'm sorry to hear it." I ignore his last comment. "You've got tremendous—"

"*Talent,*" he interjects. "I know. You told me already." He selects two acrylics from the stack. "And I believed you, by the way."

"Well, you *should*. I was—"

"Yeah, 'cause you know that night at my dad's? I actually thought you'd come up to talk about my artwork, Ms. Sandon." He chuckles. "I was so pumped, man. I guess I needed to believe it—pretty lame, huh?" He shoots these words like small, sharp darts and they find their mark; my head grows dizzy and the blood feels thick in my veins. "I didn't get it yet that you were a damn liar, just like my dad. I mean, it's not the first time—"

"Okay—please listen, Eli." I'm gripping the metal edge of the table. "The things I've said about your work are absolutely true." I hate how phony my voice must sound—despise how I've ravaged my credibility. "You must believe this, Eli. My relationship with your dad has nothing to do with—"

"Don't talk to me!" he blurts, tossing up one arm as if to shield himself. "I'm not a *complete* idiot."

"Then don't act like one," I snap. He lowers his arm, regards me. "Giving up the thing you love—just because someone else screwed up? Threatening to *enlist*—what the hell is that?" We glare at each other. I feel a sharp pain in my palm and realize I've sliced my hand on the table edge. Eli shakes his head, tucks the paintings under his arm. Outside, someone's engine is revving, tires spinning on the ice. I think about the first time I saw him—how he looked as raw and vulnerable as a picked scab. We've made so much progress since then.

"I'm outta here." He walks toward the door. "Have fun fucking my father."

"Just—wait." I reach for his arm; he yanks it away and I put my hands in the air, in surrender. "Okay, you've a right to be pissed." His nostrils flare; I catch the sweet residue of marijuana and my own pulse churns in my ears. "You feel betrayed, I *know* it—probably better than you think. But it's not a reason to toss your future away!"

"It's my life," he sulks.

"Right—your one and only, far as we know."

He stares at the battered floorboards, sucking his cheeks. "Why should I listen to you?"

"Because. I'm an artist, too. And a teacher—a good one. Regardless of how I mess up my personal life." He glances up dubiously. "Listen to me, Eli. Every few years someone comes along who's got something special, and you *have* it." He sighs, shoulders sagging now, defenses starting to slip. Then he snorts, turns away from me.

"See you around, Sylvia." I watch him disappear through the door, my heart dropping like a brick. I'm wondering where he'll go, what he'll do, who he'll tell. I follow into the hall.

"Eli, please wait—can you just tell me one thing?" He stares back silently. "I just— I'm wondering how you knew. Was it obvious, or did your father say something?"

He considers me for a moment, something like pity relaxing his features, then says, "Your daughter told me, Ms. Sandon."

"My *daughter?*"

He shrugs once, arches an eyebrow, then walks off. And now the phone is ringing again.

Years later, I'll remember every lurid moment of the next few hours and days, as if the whole thing were happening in digital freeze-frames, though at the time I feel etherized, remote. I'll remember the dark plumage of January storm clouds as I drive home from my studio that afternoon, Nathan's voice still rumbling in my head: *Hannah's been suspended from school. There were drugs. I'll tell you more when you get here.* I'll remember the homeless woman humping her cart up to the Laundromat, the number of Iraq War casualties reported on my radio, a red sweatshirt flapping from a wire.

They're all in the kitchen when I enter, my head spinning somewhere near the ceiling fan. The girls propped at the counter while Nathan peels apples for their afternoon snack, popcorn popping in the microwave, as if this were just a regular Monday after school. Except that when Hannah sees me, she immediately jumps from her stool, stalks toward the stairs.

"She's pretty upset," Nathan explains, slicing the apple into a bowl as well as he can with his bandaged wrist, squeezing in lemon the way they like it. "I'm sure she'll talk to you about everything, in time." He looks up, smiles despairingly. In that split second, I probe his eyes for information, but come up blank. I can't tell what he knows, which conversation we're having.

"Okay," I say, making my way around the counter to hug Emmie, who clings to my neck like a baby koala.

"I got to leave before rest time, Mommy! Daddy got me

early!" she says, as if this is all a big adventure—cause for celebration.

"Why is Hannah suspended?" It's the safest thing I can think to say.

"Oh, boy." He shakes his head, pulling the popcorn from the microwave. "Where do I start? She and Brooke Stevens were caught writing graffiti in the bathroom."

"That's not so horrible—"

"That's just for starters, hon. *Then,* she told Bruce Hoffman, the vice principal, to f— off." He steals a glance at Emmie. "Damn, I burned it again—this is the second bag."

"She swore at Hoffman?"

"Yep." He dumps the charred popcorn in the trash, filling the room with its acrid smell. "Which somehow prompted a locker search—don't ask me why—where they discovered a joint and *these.* He reaches into his pocket, tosses a pack of cigarettes onto the counter. They're unfiltered Camels—Tai's brand, and lately, my own. I'm wondering, in fact, if she swiped these from my dresser drawer. "So Han's out for the week," Nathan concludes. "And I've told her no friends for a month, nothing after school." I'm nodding idiotically, fingers running through Emmie's thin curls, stroking her velvet earlobes. "She says Izzy Fletcher gave her the joint."

"What did she write—in the bathroom?"

"It was pretty strange." He sticks a new bag of popcorn in the microwave. "I was thinking obscenities, right? Something sexual, maybe a rant at a teacher. But that wasn't it." I raise my eyebrows, though half of me doesn't want to hear.

"'I'm gonna kill you, Hannah Jones.' That's what she wrote."

"Wow." It's all I can manage.

"I know—the guidance counselor wanted to talk to us about therapists. Where *were* you, anyway?" Then he turns to load the dishwasher, as if he doesn't want to hear my answer.

"I went up to the house, remember? And I was visiting with Rosalyn for a while. We had quite a conversation— remind me to tell you later." I'm struggling to sound nonchalant, but my throat feels like I've gulped down pine shavings, and Eli's accusations echo in my head. Nathan doesn't comment, doesn't ask how I could have possibly spent three hours chatting with Roz Benton. Still, he seems oddly reserved as he turns to me, drying his hands.

"You should go up and talk to her. You're the one she trusts most," he says, seemingly without a trace of irony.

But Hannah won't talk to me, not even after I stand outside her locked door for fifteen minutes, pleading through the crack, "Please, Hannah—I just want to see you. I'm not angry with you, honey, just concerned. We need to talk!" I slump into the hallway, sitting on my hands, knocking my head against the wall. *I have failed them. I've failed them all.* Then, "Please, Han. You can't just pretend nothing's happened, sweetheart. Please open up." At one point, I hear her stir and think she's going to let me in; then something hard whams against the door—a shoe, most likely.

"Nothing doing, huh?" Nathan's standing in the hallway now, our preschooler straddling his long back. He sets Emmie down in her room, then comes to where I'm sprawled, puts his face close to the door. "Mama really wants to talk to you, Han—can you open up? Just for a minute, please?" Silence. "Baby, why are you taking this out on your mom?" he tries.

Nothing. He shakes his head, squeezes my shoulder, then retreats. After a few more attempts I give up and call the guidance counselor, who suspects that Hannah is "engaged in some dramatic internal struggle" (*no shit*) and gives me the names of three therapists—all highly recommended, though none are covered by our insurance. The first two can't see us until March, but the third has a cancellation this week. I take it.

By Wednesday, Hannah still hasn't spoken one word to me, despite all my pitiful attempts. I've tried cajoling and tearful pleas, sugarcoated bribery and empty threats. Now, in the car on the way to the therapist's office, there's nothing left but to hand over the naked truth. I veer left onto Main Street, fill my lungs to bursting, then blurt, "I know you know about Tai Rosen and me, Han. I know that's why you're acting this way."

She doesn't respond. I try again, tongue cleaving to my mouth. "Sometimes people make choices for strange reasons, honey."

Nothing. Though as we pull into the parking lot, she stares me down, a look of supreme repugnance on her face—as if she's gotten a whiff of rotting meat.

"You've read my e-mail, haven't you?" She turns her face away. I take this as confirmation, take another painful, fortifying breath. How could I have been so obtuse, I wonder. Why didn't I see it coming? "Look, I understand you're upset," I continue, chest constricting. "And I hope you'll at least be able to talk to this therapist about it, even if you're not ready to talk to me yet—"

"I'll talk to the dumb-ass therapist about whatever I want," she finally says, as I throw the car into Park. Hope swells at these words—the first I've heard from her since Monday morning. We sit silent as the engine sputters. Then, staring into her lap, voice barely audible, "Are you going to divorce Daddy?" I place my hand on her knee, which she moves away.

"I don't know, Han—I hope not." She nods, gnawing the inside of her cheek. "I just need to know," I add, unable to stop myself, "if you're planning to tell him."

She snorts, opens the car door and swings her long legs onto the asphalt. "I think that's your job, don't you?" Then slams the door in my face.

The therapist concurs. As I sit facing her after the session, Hannah now banished momentarily to the outer room, she concludes that she can't work with us as a family if there are secrets. It all has to come out, she says, right ankle propped against her left knee. Years later, I'll remember that taut ankle, that sharp knee. I'll remember the brutal haircut—black and too angled against a tanned face set off by designer glasses. I'll remember her fashionable but androgynous clothing.

I am not just noticing these things; I'm holding them against her, tallying up my resentments one by one. She's clearly younger than me, probably makes more money, maybe doesn't have children of her own. She has enough leisure to paint her nails and maintain a tan. She can love whomever she chooses, without consequence. I'm tearing at my own unpolished thumbnail as she talks about social-emotional issues, attention-getting behaviors, how when children feel a fissure in the family they're forced to take sides whether asked to or not. Hannah's dealing with a *family issue,* she keeps saying. And she needs us to manage it responsibly as a family. I can hear my mother's voice in my head—*we didn't have family therapists back then. We prayed together*—I stifle a laugh.

"You find something funny?" she asks.

"No—nothing at all. I was just thinking about how my own family dealt with crisis."

"Oh? How was that?"

"We watched movies," I say. "We went to church and watched a ton of movies."

"I would like very much to work with you as a family," she continues. "But I can't really do it unless I get you and your husband here together—and then all the cards are going to have to be on the table."

I nod, allowing myself full access to the ragged thumbnail now. I don't want to give this woman the credit she deserves. I don't think I'm ready to show my cards.

"How much did Hannah tell you?" I ask.

"Enough to know that she's managing a secret for you, and the pressure is too much for her. She has to let it out. She's even thought about cutting."

"Oh—God."

"It's serious, Sylvia. She needs some relief."

"And you can't help her unless we all come? Unless Nathan's involved?"

"It makes my job pretty difficult, otherwise."

"And, she really does need help, doesn't she?" It's as if I'm just now surrendering to this truth. The words, as they leave my body, seem to break something on their way—tears rush up hot and unbidden. I cry then, to my horror and relief, as the therapist watches, her young brow creased. I reach for the tissues and cry as if I've been saving it up for this poor woman—so many tears, they take up the remaining minutes of our session. Just as I've resolved to confess and renounce everything, she glances at the clock, sighs and announces time is up. I gather my things to leave.

"She's a good kid, Sylvia," the therapist says, ushering me out.

Later, I'll remember every detail of the silent drive home, Hannah picking at a scrape on her elbow, plugging into her iPod and turning her gaze away, our car doors slamming in unison. I'll remember my daughter bounding up the stairs two at a time, locking herself in her room all through the afternoon and dinner hours; Nathan taking up a grilled cheese sandwich and apple slices, then bringing down the crumb-strewn plate when she's done. I'll remember the ghostly aura of his long legs spread in the tub that night, Emmie's fifth poop accident in three days. Emmie refusing to get into her own bed and crying until Nathan carries her to the living room sofa, lets her curl up on his chest the way he used to when they were colicky babies, Coleman Hawkins lulling them to sleep. I watch them for a long time before attempting to sleep on the chilly expanse of our king-sized futon. Freezing rain spatters the panes in bursts, like bullets, and I finally give up, flip on the computer and discover Tai's latest installment—

I'm afraid of everything we can't hold on to, Sylvie. Even the echo of your voice has changed. I should know better, right? Should let it be enough, as it is—or was? Outside my window, just this expanse of frozen ground...

Of all the possible responses I might offer, there is only one urgent enough to break through my anesthetized fear.

Eli knows, Tai—please talk to him. Tell him not to do what he thinks he must do. Tell him it's pointless to punish himself for others' mistakes. Please just be there for *him* now.

I press Send, then delete both messages. I tiptoe downstairs, past my sleeping spouse and child to the kitchen, where I retrieve a bottle of cheap Merlot and a plastic cup, carry them out to the car in the rain.

For the better part of two hours I sit there, staring back at the outline of our tight little dwelling—apology of shutters, faint glow through the streaked kitchen windows, one vase of drooping coral roses backlit on the dining room table. I drink down the entire bottle, thinking about how I've failed—as mother, daughter, artist, wife—while the public radio station plays reruns of *A Prairie Home Companion* and *Jazz Safari* and it gets too cold, finally, to stay outside drunk. Too pathetic to sit nauseous and hiding in the empty van. Too nuts to attempt driving onto the highway, though I do think about it for a while. I think about skidding down I-91 in the black rain along the Connecticut River and bursting clean through the guardrails—purified by water, rather than fire. I picture it for a minute, two minutes, ten. Then force myself back inside, throw up in the downstairs toilet.

And then the call comes, a little after midnight—Alison's voice rasping through the phone: someone's died. I must be having a nightmare, or perhaps I've gone back in time. This is my father's death again, maybe, and I'll have to relive it over and over for the rest of my life. Only, there's no Santa Ana wind brewing. I'm in the kitchen of my grown-up charade, remembering that it's 2005, trying to clear my head enough to make out what my sister is saying over the line. "She's gone,

Sylvie, can you hear me? Gram's gone. It was a horrible few days but she passed an hour ago—she's peaceful now. Are you still there?"

"Yeah," I slur. "I think so."

"The burial's on Friday," my sister tells me. "I know you guys were just out here, but it would be great if you could make it."

"Of course I'll come," I say. "Course I'll be there."

There is just not enough money for all four of us to fly again. "Stop fretting about it, would you?" Nathan declares in the early gray light of our room, when I say for the fifth time that I don't want to leave them.

"What will you do with them?" I whisper now, rifling through my dresser drawers. "How will you handle them both?"

"I'll take a few days off. We'll manage—my mom can help." Nathan yawns, then grins wryly from the corner of our bed. "Uh, why are you packing shorts, Sylv?" I look down, realizing I've been reaching for all the wrong things—sundresses and blue jeans, my favorite khaki shorts, flip-flops, a black-and-white polka-dot bikini. "You're taking a bikini to your grandmother's burial?" He laughs, one eyebrow cocked high. "You're taking flip-flops?"

"I guess that's not really appropriate, is it?" I put my hands to my cheeks, smoothing the scorch of grief and fatigue. My head is still spinning from the wine, eyes hot; everything feels grainy and skinned, as if the world's been rubbed raw with sandpaper.

"Hon, it's January. It's northern Cal. It's a funeral." I nod, removing my summer things from the leather duffle, stacking them on the *boudoir* chair. "That's probably the stuff you always took to Orchard Hill as a kid," Nathan observes astutely. "It makes sense, in a way."

"I've only slept three hours," I explain, trying to remember when everything slipped from the realm of conscious choice. "I guess I need a black dress—do I even *have* a black dress?"

"What about that cute dress you wore to the Planning Department party last year? You know—silky, above the knee, scoopy neck?" He draws an imaginary scoop across his own chest, raises his brows.

"Can I wear that at a funeral?"

"Do you have a choice? It's better than the polka-dot bikini, at any rate." We both start to giggle, picturing the scene—me, standing graveside in my beachwear. We laugh much longer than the joke is funny, desperate for this meager reprieve. Then he sighs and says, "Try it on for me, Sylv— would you?"

"What?"

"I'd really like to see you in that dress."

I'm just shattered enough, just threadbare enough to acquiesce, taking off my sweatpants and bra—timidly at first— slipping the black silk over exhausted shoulders as he watches, legs stretched before him on the rough quilt, that guarded grin, depth of the brown eyes I know as well as my breath. His coltish hands reach out, patient—almost shy. This man I share dreams and daughters with, this man who still trusts me. I spin once in my funeral dress, then swallow hard, put my head down and walk smack into my resistance and terror— it's like cracking through a sheet of hard plastic—to join him on the bed.

"Take off your clothes," I say, voice buckling. "It's been too long."

We're horribly awkward at first, fumbling for some new purchase in dry lips and coffee tongues, pulling back, coming together in fits and starts like adolescents. Then, finally, striking a familiar groove. I have forgotten all this: the buttery skin of his back, small furry ass and long-muscled limbs, easy abdomen and comfortable hip bones, the painful-looking scar at the base of his throat. I forgot the slow fluency with which he enters from behind, this cock that put life in my belly, his tall body spooning mine, fingers cupping the breasts that fed our children, mattress sloping toward his side in the dawn.

"Just take it slow, Sylvie," he whispers. "There's no need to rush."

These are the very same words he once used to teach me to swim, our first summer, before we'd dreamed of home equity lines, adultery or second chances. I'd grown up in a pool, spent hours diving through the chlorinated water like an otter, suspended in sunlit blue, hair a bright tangle above me. But I didn't really learn to swim, never once had a lesson, couldn't have done a lap of the Australian crawl to save my life. So that first summer, Nathan showed me how to lift with my elbow and reach upward, forward and down, using my hand like a sleek fin, synchronizing my breathing. It wasn't long before we were swimming across the lake and back again, sometimes twice in an afternoon.

One cloudy Sunday, about midway back, I was seized with the startling realization of how deep and cold the water beneath us really was, how far we still had to swim to get to shore. Exhausted from too much partying the previous night, my feet cramping up like claws, I suddenly panicked. "Just take your time," Nathan had coached. "There's no need to rush; you know how to float." As if on cue, the overcast June

OUTSIDE THE ORDINARY WORLD

sky broke open, rain pelting our upturned faces. "I can't make it back," I told him. "I've gone too far."

"Of course you'll make it," he crooned, moving beside me stroke for stroke in the black water, breathing, talking me through. He promised that he was a strong enough swimmer for both of us, said he could easily pull me back in if necessary. Trusting him, I'd found my courage, made my way to shore, and it wasn't until we were panting on the damp sand that he admitted he'd been acting. "I was scared shitless and wiped out myself," he gasped. "I really didn't know if I'd be able to get us back."

But it was a good act, well intentioned. And by believing it, I had made it true.

2005

DO ALL THINGS PASS? I WONDER AS I MUSCLE MY RENTED
wagon off Interstate 280 toward downtown Lafayette. *Or do
they endure?* Still pulsing with worry and fatigue as I turn left
down Happy Valley Road, I'm thinking again about
Hannah—her haunted eyes when I forced my way in her
room this morning, to tell her about Gram's passing. She
looked so forlorn, scrunched on her bed amid the anarchic
mess of her bedroom; I almost couldn't bring myself to go. I
leaned my head against the door frame and whispered, "We're
going to sort all this out when I get back, honey—I promise."

Groaning up the familiar slope of Orchard Hill, I park near
my three favorite redwoods, step into the fragrant mist. No
one comes to greet me this time, so I make my way across
the driveway, through the kitchen slider. The house is silent,
though everything looks the same: same clutter of custard
cups on the yellow counter, same broken transistor radio
squatting by the sink, same Sierra Club calendar curling near
the phone.

Someone snorts from the great room. I go in to find Poppy, asleep on the couch as if he's taken up where she left off. I crouch down to watch. The tanned planes of his cheeks are finally slipping, a network of broken capillaries strung around his eyes. But the nose is still strong and fine, the jaw firm. His handsomeness has always reminded me of Nathan's, or vice versa. Staring at him, I can imagine how my husband will look as an old man. A chill enters me, and I stand. All around us, Gram's things are gathered on tabletops, collected in shoe boxes, spread out on scarves across the tile hearth. Clearly, Mom and Alison have been busy.

I discover them in the master bathroom, sorting toiletries into Tupperware containers, filling up trash bags.

"Isn't it a little early for all this?" I ask, running my fingers over a ragtag of ancient cosmetics on the counter, staring at the shoe-box lids full of odds and ends—a tiny wooden bird whistle from Japan, a carved elephant from their trip to India back in the sixties, a striped hatbox stuffed with threadbare underpants. "Isn't this a bit premature?" I ask after my mother and sister greet me, then continue their cleaning and collecting. It seems wrong to be going through her things so soon, with her soapy linen smell still floating through the hallways, her presence so tangible, I'm half expecting her to come shuffling around the corner.

"We can't afford to be sentimental right now, angel," Mom explains without looking up from her work. "There are people coming to see the house next week."

"Coming to see the house?"

"Yes. We've got it listed with Uncle Peter's agency."

"You're *selling* Orchard Hill?" The words feel punched out of me; apparently my rib cage is going to fold up now, my lungs collapse.

Mom stares at me, shadows of fatigue ringing her eyes. Her mouth wavers, then tightens. "Of course we're selling it. You didn't think Poppy would stay on here all alone, did you?"

"Can't someone take over the place? Doesn't anyone want to live here?"

"Are you volunteering, Sylvie?" Ali smirks, sweeping a gold leaf of bangs off her forehead.

For the briefest moment, I try to imagine it—selling our house, leaving our jobs, giving up my business, extracting the kids from schools and friends—the possibility is strangely exhilarating, though I'm not sure how we'd pull it off; we're so in debt, I doubt we could even pay the movers.

"This place is terribly run-down. It'll need at least a hundred grand in renovations," Mom pronounces, sealing the deal. "You couldn't even afford the property taxes."

"But, Gram would be heartbroken," I protest. The truth is, I've never even considered Orchard Hill as a commodity, a sketch filed in some probate office with frontage and zoning and taxes—a hunk of prime Bay Area real estate—but of course it is. I feel such a fool. "She's not even buried yet," I add in a watery voice. My mother and sister glance at each other, and Ali stands and stalks from the room.

"Ali's just exhausted, angel," Mom explains. "It's great that you're going to stick around for a few days and help out."

"I was going to, Mom. It's just that—"

"You've been caught up in your own drama, I know." My mother's voice sounds terse, but her face, when she stands to embrace me, is gathered with worry, unhinged by sorrow.

"How's your family?" she whispers into my hair. "Have you given him up yet?"

★ ★ ★

Do all things come to pass, or do they endure? I'm asking myself again in the second row next to Mom and Ali at Gram's funeral—or rather, her burial. We don't have funerals in this family. We don't mourn our dead in churches, or view their preserved bodies—God forbid—in open caskets beneath an altar, holy light shining through the stained glass. Gram's peach, gold-trimmed casket is sealed up tight. Our family has small, graveside ceremonies, or in the case of my father, none at all. As Ali grips my hand in the drizzle, as Uncle Peter reads from the Beatitudes—Gram's favorite—I'm remembering Mom's words, twenty-nine years ago: *Isn't it better just to get on with things?* she'd asked. *To remember the dead as they once were and not dwell on the gruesome parts?*

Now the preacher is saying the gruesome parts aren't real— that death is just going to sleep, more or less, while we wait for the Second Coming. On that day of deliverance, he explains, True Believers will rise from their graves, young again and fully fleshed, rubbing the dirt from their faces, stretching toward paradise. I picture them disoriented and a little grumpy, like Emmie waking from one of her afternoon naps. Glancing around at my family members, I wonder which of them find comfort in his explanation.

As Sheila stands to recite another Bible verse, I find myself thinking about the Wallace Stevens poem Nathan used to read me on the roof of our old house, or in the midst of my 3:00 a.m. insomnia:

What is divinity if it can come
Only in silent shadows and in dreams?
Shall she not find in comforts of the sun,

In pungent fruit and bright, green wings, or else
In any balm or beauty of the earth,
Things to be cherished like the thought of heaven?

Have I been looking for God in the wrong places—perhaps even Tai? Seeking my lost faith in his earthy spirituality, his Zen Buddhism, his belief in the power of labyrinths and landscapes and love? Have I been trying to resurrect magic? Maybe there's another way. I reach into the pocket of my raincoat, feel for the blue agate, its rough satisfaction against my palm.

We are all wet by now and chilled to the marrow, ready to return to warmth and food and the other comforts of the living. The pastor says we needn't grieve for our lost Gram, we needn't be sad, since we will surely see her again. I close my eyes, letting the words burble together in my mind, the cool California air sting my cheeks. Whatever the preacher says, whatever these cousins and aunts and uncles believe, I want to gnash my teeth now, to tear my dress and howl at the indifferent fog rolling from the bay.

Sandwiched into my narrow twin bed that night, Alison's familiar soft snores beside me, I know I won't sleep, despite the exhaustion thrumming in my bones, twitching my eyelids.

I long to try Nathan and the girls again, but it's much too late. So I creep down the hall to the den, where Mom is sleeping tonight—to keep an eye on Poppy, she said—only she's awake, too. The light's on and when I push through the door she's reading *National Geographic* on the edge of her makeshift bed.

"You, too, huh?" I say, coming in and sitting beside her.

"Oh, angel—" She drops the magazine to the coffee table. "Just can't stop thinking about it."

"Which part?"

She glances at the ceiling. "How scared she was at the end. How she clung to me." She shudders. "Even after all these years, she didn't want to let go."

"Does anyone?"

"Probably not." She laughs dourly, pressing her eyes with the heels of her hands. "But Gram was so sick, and had such faith—I thought she'd be more peaceful about it."

We're quiet, breathing side by side, the grandfather clock clicking toward dawn. Finally I say, "Maybe faith and fear aren't mutually exclusive, Mom. Maybe faith is just a decision you make, in spite of fear. It's easy to be swept up by emotion."

"Well, I know all about that, don't I?"

"Yeah, you do." I yawn. I'm so tired, my knees are quivering. "I forgot my sleeping pills—I was in such a rush."

"Poppy gave me some Valium—should we take one?" I nod. "They work better with a little Chardonnay."

"Mom! I thought you didn't drink."

"I don't. Just a little Chardonnay now and then." She grins and I understand that I've always adored and despised this in her—her hypocrisy, her inability to behave, despite her good-girl roots and first-rate intentions. She waits in her purple nightgown as I retrieve a bottle, pour our wine into Gram's petite crystal glasses.

"Bottoms up, I guess," she says, handing me a Valium.

"Actually, I don't know how you ever had the nerve to do what you did, coming from this place, these parents. I don't know how you managed it."

"What? What did I do?" she asks.

"Mr. Robert. It was pretty courageous, considering." It's not the first time I've thought this. She runs a finger over her chapped lips.

"Oh, Sylvie—Dad and I were doomed from the start."

I sit down in Poppy's leather chair, facing her. "Tell me," I say. "You said you would, when we had more time."

She nods. "Well, you know I never should have married him at nineteen, but we were so in love. We thought happiness was just a room you could waltz into." She smiles, forlorn. "We were stupid; we had no idea how hard it would be— children, poverty, his internship, me working nights…" Glancing at her watery reflection in the window, she smoothes the hair from her eyes. "Just kids ourselves, really, and your dad so *wounded,* so very…"

"What?"

"Very early on in our marriage, I had a miscarriage, Sylvie."

"Wow." I gulp my wine. "You never told me."

"I know. It didn't seem that important." She shrugs. "I still don't believe it was the *cause* of anything, really, but that's when I started noticing him pulling away. Sensing his distance, how—how unsettled he was. You know he lost both his parents. I think he was terrified he'd lose us, too, that the abandonments would continue."

"So, it was safer to just stay estranged?"

"I think that's right. He started working all the time, coming home later. There were a couple of women, too— nurses at the hospital. It wasn't all that serious, honey, but that wasn't much comfort at the time. I was furious, and I hadn't a clue how to bring him back. And then I met Robert at the office where I was doing secretarial work—long before you were born. He was married, too, of course; we were just friends. *Good* friends—" Here she smiles, rolling her eyes.

"He used to take me to lunch on the Santa Monica board-walk when I was pregnant with Alison, bought me Coke floats. He'd talk to me in a way Don couldn't—was afraid to. Funny, how we actualize our greatest fears, isn't it?"

I nod, gripping my own wrist.

"And marriage is the very hardest work—*you* know that now."

"Well, maybe not as hard as—mining rock quarries, or solving the hunger crisis."

"It didn't help matters that your Dad turned to the bottle." She ignores my sarcasm. "And I to another man." She sips her wine, grunts softly.

"And that your *daughter* kept telling you to leave," I add.

She peers at me. Then sets her glass on the table and leans forward, taking my chin in her hand. "Sylvia dear," she says, over-enunciating. "You were a child. You were not respon-sible for my choices. Or your father's. Do you understand that?"

"In my rational mind, I do." I turn my face away.

"Think about it, angel—would you hold Hannah account-able for yours?"

We're silent as I refill our glasses. "No," I finally concede, voice crumbling. "Of course I wouldn't."

"Well, then."

"I just— Sometimes I wonder why you gave me your secret, Mom. Why you made me choose."

She stares at me, her gray eyes withdrawing. There is some-thing like defiance in the upward tilt of her jaw. Then her features begin to collapse pitifully; she covers them with her hands. I wait, resisting my habitual urge to reach out, allevi-ate, snatch back the hurtful question. After a few interminable moments the hands drop; her face is composed again, though blotchy, and her voice wavers as she says, "I was afraid to make the choice all my own, I guess, angel. I felt so very alone. So scared." She leans back on the couch, shaking her head.

"I know," I say. "I always knew how you felt." I don't tell her that, until very recently, I sometimes wondered if we were the same person. Mom sighs and I realize I'm still waiting. I want her to apologize. To say *sorry* for all the haunted years. Instead she reaches out, strokes my cheek with the backs of her cool fingers. Maybe it's enough.

"What about you and Robert?" I ask. "Are you guys happy?"

"Oh, you know—happy enough. Considering the trail we blazed. I made a lot of wrong moves back then," she concludes, slouching into the cushions.

I want to tell her that there are no wrong turns, that there is only the next step. It sounds so lovely, but I don't really believe it. "Maybe you have to make a few wrong turns to find your way," I offer instead.

"Maybe so. But your story's different," she continues, yawning. "*You* still have time—a chance to make things right. And a sweet husband who's willing to work it out."

"Well," I say. "He might be."

"What *are* you going to do?" Curling her mottled arm round a pillow, she stares up at me. Though still striking, she looks her age just now. It won't be long before she's the one needing care.

"I'm going to sleep on it," I say, kissing her on the forehead, leaving her to her dreams.

I'm the first to wake the next morning. The drizzle has cleared. The thick, golden California light I love is blazing over the hilltops as I make my way to the kitchen phone, anxious to talk to Nathan and the girls.

"How you holding up?" Nathan asks when I find him at the new Ashfield line. "Did the black dress do its job?"

"Not as well as the other day."

"That was really nice," he says in a low drawl. "I'm wondering why the hell we waited."

"Well—I guess *that's* a conversation we need to have, isn't it? What are you doing at the site so early?"

"It's nearly nine here, remember? The girls are helping me with the flooring—well, in theory anyways."

"Can I talk to them, please?" He's silent for a long moment—hesitating? Or maybe saying something to them under his breath. I can hear Hannah's muffled inflection, more silence, then Emmie's tiny squeak.

"I did a headstand by the blue thing, Mommy. I was all upside down for a long time."

"That's wonderful, sweetie." I laugh. "Are you guys doing okay?"

"Daddy gave us ice cream for breakfast, but I lost Pink Bunny."

"Oh, dear. Well, she always turns up, doesn't she?"

"Hannah doesn't want to talk, Mommy. Bye." Then she hangs up on me. I stand there, squinting into the dawn, chuckling despite my bereavement. A moment later, Nathan calls back.

"Sorry," he says. "It's pretty chaotic here."

"Hannah still won't speak to me?"

"I can't figure out what's up with that," he whispers. "She seems to be holding it all together, otherwise." I press my eyes shut, suddenly struck with the terrible irony of this—the enormity of what she's holding for me. The anxious fatigue prickles over my scalp like a colony of red ants.

"Can you just give her a message for me?"

"What's that?"

"Just tell her, we'll take care of it," I say, making my voice bright. "Tell her I'm here when she's ready to talk. Please say those things." He's quiet for a while, breathing.

"It's just a passing thing, Sylvie," he tells me. "Just a blip on the wide water."

"Nathan, remember how you used to read me 'Sunday Morning' when I couldn't sleep?"

"'Death is the mother of beauty...'" he intones. "Of course I remember—'Within whose burning bosom we devise our earthly mothers'—Emmie, sweetie, put that down please. *Now!*" There's some terse scuffle in the background. "Look, Sylv, I gotta go—call me later."

After he's gone, I know what I need to do. I make two more calls—one to United, to see if I can change my return flight from Tuesday to first thing tomorrow morning. Then I call Judy Fulton—the family therapist—and leave a message: "I think I want to do the work, Judy," I rasp into her voice mail. "I want to make an appointment for Nathan and me."

I spend the next hour walking the property, bowing—as Tai taught me—to the orchard and kumquat tree, the bomb shelter and the oaks. I stand in the center of the lawn watching the turkey vultures circling the valley, dominated by Mount Diablo's scarred shoulders and kingly head. I'm wishing I'd brought my acrylics, or at least a sketchbook, so I could capture the view one last time for Hannah, who's always loved it. I imagine my brush weaving those tatters of fog through January branches, my palette knife cutting that gleaming ribbon of fire road.

"I hear you're deserting at the crack of dawn." Alison has crept up beside me and looped her arm through mine. She's clad in leggings and a Pebble Beach sweatshirt, hair disheveled, smelling like her girlhood self—soap and lilacs and morning breath.

"The poor people who buy this place will feel us haunting it," I say, imaging our child voices echoing beneath the covered porch, swinging from the rafters, floating down from redwoods. "Do you think people go on inhabiting the places they love?"

"We had good times here," she answers, holding my elbow.

"Yeah—maybe the only good times."

My sister squints up at me, shading her eyes. "No, Sylvie—not the *only* good times," she says. "Don't let the bad years eclipse everything else, okay?"

"Okay," I concede after a pause. "I'll try. You know, Ali—you were also right when you said I was good at running away."

"Sometimes I'm right," she smirks, leading me to the white plastic glider on the edge of the porch, where we sit rocking.

"But that's not what I'm doing this time, okay? That's *not* why I'm leaving early." She continues to stare at me, eyes narrowed, so I try again, wishing to alleviate some measure of my guilt. "I know you and Mom need my help here, but I've got a situation back home—"

"I know, Sylvie," she interrupts. "Mom told me all about it."

I stop rocking, sifting through the lineup of possible responses—betrayal, outrage, shame? Then I start to laugh. "Jesus Christ. Nothing is bloody sacred in this family."

"Yeah, well." She smiles. "Some things never change, weirdly."

★ ★ ★

Later, as Robert is cooking his infamous pancakes for brunch, I tell them I have an errand to run.

"Where on earth could you be going on your last day here?" Mom asks, walking me to my car. "Can't you at least wait until after brunch?"

"There's someone I've been meaning to visit."

"You're very mysterious." She grips my upper arm. "I hope you're not getting into more trouble, Sylvia?"

"Not today," I assure her. I don't want to reveal where I'm headed. I'm not sure she'd understand my need to make this visit alone.

She stares at me dubiously. Then, as I'm getting into the car she slips an ivory envelope into my hand.

"Don't open it here—open it later. It's from Gram—something she wanted you to have. To help you and Nathan finish the house."

"Oh—thank you," I say, tucking it into my bag, reaching for her hand.

"There's still time, Sylvie."

It's a shorter drive to the small cemetery in Berkeley than I remember, but it's been at least ten years since I visited. I make my way on crooked paths through the old but well-tended grave sites, past overgrown juniper bushes and magnolias. My father's grave lies in the shade of a middle-aged oak. I lean against its rough hide, push one of its thorny, curled leaves into my palm until it hurts. There's his mother—Virginia Jean—still resting enigmatically beside him. I wish again that I'd known her. Wish again I had the right words for the occasion, the perfect, consummate sentence—something that could mend the silence, heal the ache.

As always, I feel tongue-tied in my father's presence, clogged with emotion. Even now, he bullies my thoughts—the loss of him, the rage, the guilt—all of it circling my dreams like a bad joke, keeping me from my life.

"I'm sorry about all that, Dad." I try over the shameless drone of lawn mowers.

"I forgive you," I say. What else is there? After a while I get up to go, regretting that I didn't bring something to leave him—a bouquet, a rosebush, a shell. I rifle through my pockets, and my fingers find Tai's agate, still warm against my thigh. I take it out, watching it glitter in the light. Pressing it to my mouth, I breathe in its sharp, earthy smell. Then I bend down, place it in a small hollow near my father's headstone and, weeping, walk away.

2005

WHEN I ARRIVE HOME THAT AFTERNOON, THE HOUSE is empty and quiet. I lug my bag through the kitchen door and discover Nathan's scrawled note on the counter: *Took dinner up to the site—trying to finish the g-d floor. See you soon!* But I can't wait that long. I grab a bottle of water and climb back in my minivan to commence my journey up the mountain, rehearsing possible scripts. Judy Fulton's words reverberate from our conversation in the airport: "You don't have to reveal everything today if it's too hard, Sylvia. Sometimes these things are better discussed in the safety of the therapy office. The important thing is, you've made the decision...."

Still, my throat tightens painfully as I pass by the exit for Route 116, to Plainfield. Maybe it will always feel like this. Maybe I'll learn to live with it.

Nathan's truck tilts in the driveway at the Ashfield house, though I don't see the girls playing in the meadows or hear their voices coming from the newly Sheetrocked interior. As

I make my way inside, I notice the freshly sanded porch railings, the clapboards on the north side of the house almost done. They've built a lopsided snowman next to the barn. His Tupperware hat is slipping sideways, though the charcoal eyes and banana smile are bright and welcoming. A few of Nathan's tools are strewn about the porch floor and Emmie's Polly Pockets clutter the entryway. I walk through the silent house, taking in changes.

Nathan's voice finds me a minute before I see him. "I was hoping all the signs weren't really adding up to this, hon," he says.

"Nathan?" My eyes are still adjusting to the dim kitchen. He's scrunched against the Sheetrock in the corner, gangly legs bent in his carpenter pants, forearms resting on knees. White sheets of printer paper litter the half-finished oak floor around him.

"Where's Hannah? Where are the girls?" I ask.

"They're over at the sledding hill." His voice sounds trodden.

"What's all this stuff?" I ask, indicating the mess of papers.

"This," he notes as he nudges one of the sheets with the toe of his work boot, "is our daughter's latest act of rebellion—a real doozy. Apparently she's been waiting all day to deliver this."

"Oh, God—what's she done now?" I pick up one of the papers near my foot, peer at it in the fading light coming through the bay window. My arms and legs grow leaden as I make out the words at the top of the sheet—*I can't deny this longing any more than I can willingly lose a fist, an eye. There is just no way to rise gracefully into the next day…* Tai's words, Tai's messages. I bend down to gather the sheets—pages and pages of illicit e-mails sent and received over the last six months—

from the look of things, my daughter hasn't missed a single one, including one I haven't even seen yet, dated yesterday.

S—Been talking with Eli. Told him not even the gods expect perfection: they're sick of our striving… Whatever you do, darling—don't try too hard to change who you are, what you've done. And don't give up. When the crocuses break through this wretched ice, I hope you can come to see this as some sort of blessing, whatever the cost. —T

I finish reading, tuck this sheet in with the rest. My head is shuddering at the temples and I cannot look at my husband, though I feel his eyes waiting. Instead, I continue grasping and gathering. There are enough pages here for a short novella, certainly enough to end a marriage.

"I was sort of hoping that my suspicions were wrong," says Nathan brokenly.

I can't find one single word to say, after all Judy's coaching, all my beautiful, silent rehearsals in the car. Or maybe there's plenty to say—oceans of things to say—only I don't know where to begin, and my vocal cords are seared shut.

"It's not that I don't understand, Sylv." He sighs after a graceless silence. "You remember—there was that woman at the conference. It's not like I've been a saint. It was touchy for a while. But, nothing like—like *this*." He gestures toward the mess I'm trying to clean up—like a crazy maid whisking dog shit off the carpet—until the e-mails rest in a thick sheaf in my hand. I place them on the newly tiled peninsula, my blood scalding.

"Can we put on a light, Nathan?" Of course I remember his lovely young architect. How could I *not* remember the 11:30 p.m. arguments? The nights spent twisting on the futon couch, sleeping in the girls' rooms, pacing through the dawn? None of it matters one atom to me now. "Is there a light we can turn on?" I repeat.

He chuckles, shaking his head. "I thought you might prefer darkness. Isn't that your thing—all those late walks, out there smoking beneath the stars, talking on your cell? God, what an asshole I am. What a *fucking* stupid asshole."

"Does the electricity even work?" It's all I can manage right now. My tongue, teeth, throat—everything turned to hardened clay.

"Yes, the goddamn electricity works! It works, Sylv—isn't that great?" He springs up, plugs in a floodlight propped against the counter. "And look—I've been working my ass off laying the tile, and I might as well be married to the floors!" He flips on another light clipped to a nail against the wall. And then another hanging over the new stainless sink, and another, and another, until the kitchen is absurdly, glaringly bright. His movements sharp, manic as he jolts through the house switching on lights wherever he can find them— in the great room, the entryway, the study. Then he bounds up the stairs, where fixtures have already been installed. The house is blazing like a horror movie when he comes back, breathing sharply before me in the doorway, clutching his bandaged wrist and slick with sweat.

Strangely, I find myself wondering about the couple that once lived here, arguing in this very kitchen, their voices echoing against these walls. There surely would have been rugs and chairs, that horrible morning-glory wallpaper we spent such tedious hours peeling, the thick yellow paint we painstakingly stripped from the sills. Little Lucy plunking down the stairs at two or three or four, bringing them to their senses, calling them from their fight. Was it the same fight as ours? Did Jennie stand braced in this doorway, wearing the same ruined expression that Nathan has now?

"Is that enough light for you, darling?" he pants. He never calls me *darling*—this is Tai's name for me and now we both know it. "Maybe now we can really *see* each other, huh?"

"Nathan, I—I was going to tell you." My voice is shaking so badly, I can barely make out my own syllables. "I was on my way up here to tell you. It's why I came back."

"Oh, yeah?" He's nodding in an exaggerated, *Fuck You* way, chewing the inside of his cheek as if stifling a laugh.

"Look, this is not a good way to start this conversation—"

"Is there a good way?" He yelp-laughs like an insane person. "Is there a fucking *good* way?" He raises his hands in the air, looks around as if for confirmation.

"Nathan, please. Just hear me out for a minute. It's been such a crazy time."

"What I don't get is—what the hell are you doing here? Why don't you just go to *him?*"

"I don't want to go to him," I say, understanding that, for the first time, it's true.

"I guess I should have seen it coming, right? I know it's partly my fault, Sylv, how we were spiraling off in our separate asinine obsessions, never connecting. I knew we were in trouble. I *knew* I was being myopic about the house." He's still breathing hard, though his voice has softened a shade, hands now braced in the door frame, arms visibly shaking. "But it's what we *wanted* once, right? All this—" He gestures around at the spanking new cupboards, the stainless steel range, that magnificent view through the cedars we planted almost a decade ago. With a jolt of fear, I realize he's referring to us in the past tense—a story already spun to its conclusion. Outside, the day is slipping fast behind the mountains.

"Which sledding hill are the girls on? Is anyone with them?"

He sighs, pressing his hands along the side of his head as if trying to remove his face. "Hannah took them to the hill near the lake," he says. "The Kinsey girls came up to meet them—they promised to be back before dark."

"It's getting dark now."

"I know, I know. We should probably go find them."

"Were you planning to give them dinner up here?" This is where we will always wind up—our bottom line—the drop-offs and dinner prep, homework and hunger and getting them to bed by nine. It's comforting, in a surreal sort of way.

"I made chicken and coleslaw. There's a cooler in the van," he tells me in a shattered tone. "We brought sleeping bags, too; the girls were hoping we could camp out here tonight." He shakes his head at the naïveté of such plans. Then walks to the opposite side of the peninsula, leans his bandaged forearm on the blue ceramic tiles, head drooping dangerously. "I can't help going back over all our days, wondering which times you were—how often you—"

"I know, Nathan. I know, sweetheart." Despite the dread pounding through me, there is also a sudden giddy lightness, the fast sting of grief.

"Why *him?* Can you just tell me that? Was he *good?* Teach you some new tricks or—or what?" He rubs his hand roughly over his brow. "What did he have to offer you, Sylv?"

I shake my head, taking in the broken lines of his face. I want to give him something honest and real—one true thing that won't further the injury. "I just— I had to find a part of myself that somehow, he had access to. He saw something that—"

"No, don't tell me," he blurts. "I don't want any more goddamn details!"

We're quiet for a block of ugly moments, breathing in the smell of fresh plaster and wood glue, all this beautiful, artificial light. I'm wondering how people do this. How do they travel back from this chasm—in leaps or gasps or millimeters? Where do they go for healing? How do they find grace? No one has given me a map for this moment.

"Well, the tile looks great," I offer, my voice a sliver. It's a ludicrous statement, but it's true. The last time I saw this room, the counters were still plywood and you could look into the cellar between two-inch gaps in the subflooring. I never believed we would get this far. Certainly never thought it would come to this, our marriage dusted into this plaster, splintered helter-skelter through the floorboards. "You've done so much," I say.

"Pretty, isn't it? Did you see the mudroom?" He can't help himself. "There's still a shitload to do, though, and no more money."

I remember Gram's check in my van, nesting in the black belly of my pocketbook. "Maybe, if we could get out from under the weight of all this—" I start.

"At least we'll get *some* of our goddamn money out of the place," he interrupts, voice splintering like an adolescent boy's. Suddenly, he's jumping up, grasping for his tool box on the far end of the counter, his features distorted as he clutches a hammer, swings it up through the waiting air, then smashes it down hard onto one of the fresh tiles, which cracks in protest—a single, deep crevice cut diagonally through the center.

We stare at each other, wide-eyed and gasping.

"That was really great," he says before hoisting the hammer to demolish a second tile, and then another—*crack crack, boom*. His arm pummeling the new counter, jaw setting, shards of ceramic spinning into his hair. I'm worried about the skin of his face, the unprotected eyes.

"Don't, Nathan." I grab on to his wrist; he wrests it away, cracks the hammer down, and again down. I'm wrapping my arms around his biceps now, using the whole force of my body in vain to contain this frenzy. "Please, Nathan, stop! I'm so sorry. *Please, don't.*"

"No—no, really," he pants, flinging me off easily, then wiping the dust from his brow. A sliver of tile has pierced him; bright blood trickles down his right cheek, past his ear. I reach to blot it and he bats my hand away. "How do you like the tile *now?* Huh, Sylv? How about these asshole cabinets?" Lunging for a cabinet door below the sink, he tears it free in two determined yanks, then hurls it into fresh white plaster, where it leaves a horrible gash. "How do you like the fucking house this way, darling?" he yells, gesturing into the dust. "Or should I call you *Elaine?*" I'm frozen in the center of the tile-strewn room, clutching my own arms as he wrenches off a second door and flings it; the corner of this one smacks me in the ankle.

"Stop it!" I scream, then crumple to the floorboards, crying like a child.

A moment later, he's touching my shoulder, swiping softly at my tears. "I didn't mean to hurt you," he says, reaching for the cut on my leg. "Jesus. Jesus Christ." Then his arms are wrapped around my torso; my fingers grasp his hair. He's curling around my bones now, sobbing into my open lap, coming apart in my hands in such an un-Nathan-like way.

My own throat is raw with sorrow by the time he pulls away, shoves the heels of his palms into his eyes. He looks like a boy—a lovely, abandoned schoolboy, bloodied and cross-legged on the floor beside me, staring around at the devastation as if trying to work out how it came to this.

"I wasn't trying to hurt you, either," I whisper, knowing how asinine it sounds. "I really wasn't."

He starts chuckling—ironically at first. Still, the laughter seems to cleanse the air a bit; we both giggle in strangled, exhausted surges, like coughs.

"I don't know if I'll have the energy to fix this," he finally says, indicating the mess.

"It doesn't matter," I say, wiping a blotch of blood from his chin. "I don't give a shit."

"I thought the house was everything to you."

"No, Nathan. All I really wanted was for us to be happy." I pick up a piece of the shattered tile, weighing it in my palm.

"Huh." He shakes his head wearily. "Well, I don't know if we can be *happy* now, Sylv."

"We need time to—"

"I just—" He jerks his arm from my touch. "I think I need to get away."

"Of course." The anguish expands in my chest until my eyes smart. "But maybe," I begin as I gulp a breath, "maybe we could work through it, and—"

"Work *through* it?" He presses his hands over his face. "I don't know."

"The family therapist Han saw—I was thinking you could come with me."

"Oh. I'm not sure I'm ready for that."

I nod, hugging my elbows, holding tightly to the words welling inside me. Finally, inhaling, I let them go. "I want

you to stay, Nathan," I blurt. And then, more slowly, "I know
we can't go back to how things were. But maybe we can—
I hope we can find our way together. If you're willing to try."

He's silent, staring into his bloody palms as the dust continues to filter down like pollen, settling in our hair.

"If only—" he starts. But before he can finish, Hannah is
bursting through the doorway in her snowsuit, bits of ice
clinging to her long hair, eyes huge and frightened. At first,
I assume she's just startled by my presence, this unexpected
scene between her father and me—sprawled in the center of
the ruined kitchen, blotting at each other's heartbreak—this
moment she's risked everything to orchestrate.

Then she pants, "I can't find Emmie."

"You *what?*" I ask. Nathan is up in a heartbeat, helping me
to my feet.

"I've looked everywhere, all over!" She leans over and
grips her thighs, trying to catch her breath. "We were
sledding by the lake—Andrea and Maggie and me, and
Emmie didn't want to go anymore so she was just playing up
the hill in the snow, and then—I don't know."

"What do you *mean,* you don't know, Han?" I realize that
I'm talking too loudly, grasping her forearm too tight, but she
doesn't pull away from me now. We lock eyes for a moment
while the terror begins its sharp work on my vascular system,
while Nathan grabs his sweater and flashlight and tells us to
come on, now—just hurry up, leading us into the night.

I stumble through the woods behind Nathan and
Hannah—all of us calling, calling—my voice shredded with
fear. The January sky's a lavender bruise, the light failing sick-
eningly, and she's not in her usual hiding place behind the
barn, not in the hollow near the stream. She's not behind the

cedars, where she and Nathan have built ten tiny, elaborate fairy houses. Not by the rope swing or the leafless lilacs, not playing a hiding game in the truck bed. An icy wind grates over the south meadow, but I can't really feel it—I'm too numb with panic.

"I really screwed up, didn't I?" Hannah wails in the middle of the driveway.

"Mom and I should have been paying more attention," Nathan tells her.

"Maybe we should split up and look for her." I am trying to keep my voice even.

"Good idea," he says. "Han, why don't you and Mom go back down to the sledding spot and I'll scan the woods and the gardens. If anyone sees her, use the family whistle. We'll meet back here in twenty minutes or so and call the police if she hasn't turned up."

At this, a tiny moan escapes my lips.

"Don't push the panic button yet," states Nathan. "It's easy to get turned around in these woods. Let's try to keep our heads."

"Okay," says Hannah, grabbing my sleeve, and I realize how deeply I need my husband's steady grace right now.

We stagger down the hill, tripping on tree roots. It's not until we're halfway through the fourteen-acre wood that I notice Hannah and I are clasping hands, step for step in the semi-darkness. I don't know which of us initiated this gift, but there it is. Clutching her warm, sweaty fingers, I feel no pain in my own, for the first time in weeks.

"Emmie!" I try again in a hoarse scream. "Emmie Rose, where are you, honey?" Again, there's no response—no distant crying, no laughter as she jumps from the underbrush, ending this wretched game. There's not even the sweet reassurance of chickadees, squirrel scratching or nuthatches. It's as eerily silent as Los Angeles before an earthquake.

"I'm sorry, Mom," whispers Hannah as we wind down to the lake.

"I am sorry, too, Han. I'm sorry, too."

"I really didn't mean for everything to get so carried away."

"Neither did I, honey. Neither did I."

"I should have been watching Em better, too—I just never thought—"

"Shh—no more regrets now, okay, Han? Just show me where you guys were sledding today. Just show me where she disappeared."

We scan the border of woods, the east meadow and the sledding hill, tromping through awkward clumps of last week's snow. It's raw, agonizing work in my clogs and leather jacket, my fingers lifeless now and this poisonous tangle of fear working its way through my chest. Hannah heads back up toward the place where Emmie left her sled while I comb the shore, looking for breaks in the ice—calling until my voice is nothing but toast crumbs falling through cracks.

Retrieving a single pink mitten from the shore, a sob erupts from my belly like boiling oil. I swallow it down.

When I can't yell anymore, I start to pray—to whom or what I'm not quite certain, but praying nonetheless, shamelessly bargaining in the silent air. *Just bring her back to me,* I whisper. *Just bring them all back.* Then my knees give out and I'm slumped on the frozen sand, head in my hands. Though I know I can't afford this now, my mind won't stop playing all its last-ditch disasters and lake-bottom scenarios. Suddenly I'm remembering little Lucy Kauffman, the car filling with lake water. Lucy Kauffman galumphing down the stairs, playing in the south meadow, chasing the goats.

Of course.

"Hannah!" I scream up the hill, scrambling to my feet, slipping on ice. "I think I know where she is."

We tear back through the woods in minutes. Entering the warm stink of the goat barn, Hannah tripping on my heels, I hear their voices floating from the back—Rosalyn's throaty chuckle pierced by Emmie's pixie squeal as milk squirts into a metal pail. My legs feel boneless, my lips stinging, my mind aching as I work my way toward them through the riot of goats, finally spotting them in a corner stall.

"Eeeww, it's all hot!" Emmie pipes as Rosalyn bends down beside her, helping her grip the nanny goat's pale teat.

"Jesus, Emmie Rose, you scared the living—" Hannah begins, but I stop her, grasping her wrist. I am so dizzy to see this child alive, so grateful to have them both within my reach, I don't want to say a word, don't want to spook away this moment, don't want to scold or accuse or demand explanations. Instead, I just have to sit down on a plank, lungs contracting, toes still numb and soaking, hands suddenly burning in the blessed warmth of this little hut.

"Well of course the milk's hot, Lucy," Rosalyn scolds, starting on the other teat. "It's coming straight from her hot old hide, dear, what did you expect? You didn't think it'd come out refrigerated?"

At these words, Hannah raises an eyebrow and I just close my eyes and nod, the chills moving through me in waves.

"Mommy, come try it," Emmie commands, as if we've been sitting here the whole time, all of us gathered for a regular Saturday night outing to our neighbor's. "Bitsy's going to have baby goats and Auntie Roz said we could keep one!"

"So it's *Auntie Roz* now, is it?" I turn to see Nathan, winded and hollow-eyed, arms braced in the doorway. At the sight of him, I remember what's still lost, and a heaping portion of dread returns to me. His hair is electrified, cheeks vivid—he looks like a man who's just glimpsed his own death. He leans over for a moment, clutching his ribs, then comes toward us. "Did Auntie Roz bring you over for a milking lesson, Em, or did you find your way here alone?"

"She brought my Dalton back to me, the dear." Roz straightens up and cinches her apron around her. "Out wandering the back woods at sundown; so I took them in for warm goat milk and cookies—that's what's called for on a night like this."

"Yes, that's just about what's called for," echoes Nathan, shaking his head. "Though maybe with a few shots of whiskey to wash it down." Hannah rolls her eyes, but can't stop herself reaching to pat one of the goats nuzzling her snow pants.

"Say, Sylvia, did you ever burn that sage stick I gave you for energy cleansing?"

"No, but I think I'll do that." I glance up at Nathan. "I think I'll do that right away."

"May take a lot more than sage," Nathan mutters, returning my stare.

"Another storm's expected tonight," Roz announces distantly, as if to her goats.

"She calls me Lucy sometimes," Emmie says, yawning. Rubbing her eyes roughly, she comes over and plops her head right down in my lap. My tingling fingers work through the diaphanous curls. I press my nose against the base of her neck, breathing her soft scent of baby shampoo and milk and apricots, my tears disappearing in all that hair.

"Let's get the girls back for dinner," Nathan says after a few minutes. "It's getting late."

Walking back to the house behind Nathan and the girls, I'm thinking that endings don't necessarily arrive with trumpet song and angel fire, as my Sabbath School teacher used to predict. The world comes apart quietly, with the smallest, most ordinary gesture—a woman slipping into her car at dusk, a man coming unglued in his kitchen, a child disappearing beneath the ice. In the time it takes to heat the tea water, drive to the neighbor's, walk through woods on a moonless January night. Ahead, the familiar backs of my husband and daughters recede through the trees, and I can't help wondering if these are the last hours of our family. A deadly thorn of regret works its way toward my heart.

Then Emmie stubs her toe again and starts whining as I approach.

"I'm cold, Mommy," she complains.

"What happened to your new coat?" I ask, trying to sound sufficiently annoyed. "What happened to your hat? We just bought those last week."

"I bet she left them near the sledding hill," Hannah says. "She always takes them off."

"I'll go look tomorrow." Nathan removes his sweater and wraps it around our preschooler, crouching down to let her crawl onto his shoulders. Then he continues solemnly down the path, keeping a wide berth between us in which our eldest walks, sending me anxious glances. I know she's trying to determine how much damage she's caused by delivering the e-mails, and I think about the impulse that provoked such a risk: Was it purely anger? The desire to take charge? Alleviate or claim some piece of the trouble? A similar compulsion to the one that made me ignite letters in a Santa Ana wind, the night my father died?

"I think we took the wrong path there," Nathan says after a few minutes, halting in a small clearing and shaking his dimming flashlight. "We should be going north here, not east."

We cluster beside him, straining for a glimpse of sky.

"You guys see Orion?" I ask. A gust of glacial wind rattles the branches around us. "Gram used to say that was the entrance to heaven."

"I wonder if she's there already," Hannah murmurs, hugging her shoulders. "Maybe she's watching over us."

"I hate winter." Emmie starts to cry. "I'm hungry."

"There's gonna be a lot more winter before it's over, little dude," says Hannah.

"We're almost home, Em—just hang on," says Nathan. "The house will be nice and warm." He carries her through a close stand of pines, leading us on a different course.

"Daddy made his fried chicken and coleslaw," I announce through chattering teeth.

"I want a hot dog," whimpers Emmie. "I want Friendly's."

Hannah groans.

"Would you rather go hungry for a week," I try, "or eat nothing but Friendly's hot dogs?" I'm hoping that our old game will divert them from the stinging chill, the evening's discord, the startling fact that we seem to have wandered from our path.

"Friendly's, Friendly's," Emmie chants. Hannah opts for the hunger strike and Nathan is silent. His flashlight wavers again, then dies completely in a dense section of hickory and oak. The branches are so low, they keep threatening to smack Emmie in the forehead; Nathan places her on the ground, where she clings stubbornly to his leg.

"Brilliant," observes Hannah. "We could be out here all night at this rate."

"The woods aren't that deep," I assure her. Still, with no moon or flashlight, this part of the forest is inky and untenable—anyone's guess. We might be wandering in circles. I'm so exhausted from the last few days' events, I could weep, and I picture us finally collapsing in a heap for the night, huddling for warmth in some makeshift burrow.

"Let's just stay in a line," instructs Nathan. "Let's stay close."

Hannah, who has the supple gait of her eight years of dance and sees through night like a raccoon, goes first. Nathan keeps a hand on her shoulder and Emmie clutches his pant leg in her tiny fist. I touch the top of her curly head, to let her know I'm behind her.

And so we go, making our way slowly through the underbrush like some awkward, primordial life-form, grasping for each other in the pitch-dark. There's no sound but our breathing, the soft crunching of leaves and ice. At one point, Nathan's freezing fingers reach back and curl briefly through mine. I'm reminded of Poppy's war stories—soldiers stunned and blinded after a gas attack who had to feel their way toward safety, inch by tender inch. Despite the cold, I have a sudden, childlike wish to stay here, linked in this sylvan blackness—never to reach the glaring havoc that awaits us.

Finally, we come upon the bridge where Emmie had her accident—our first recognizable landmark. Hannah ends the silence with a sigh that expresses our collective relief and disappointment.

"Okay," she says, "here's one. Would you rather be stranded in the New England woods all night with your family, or safe at home all alone, wondering about the ones who are lost out there?"

"That's a tough one, Han," I say as we break from formation, winding toward our winter gardens. "Would you freeze in the woods with those people, or just have to camp for the night?"

"No. You wouldn't die, but you'd think you were going to."

I have to laugh, though my arms are shivering violently, knees buckling as we stomp through frozen shrubs.

"And the one waiting at home—does that person know the others will return?" asks Nathan. He hoists Emmie back onto his shoulders, refusing to meet my stare.

"I hadn't exactly worked it out that far."

"I wanna be standed inside the house with the lost people," squeaks Emmie from her wild, windy perch. "We could be standed in our sleeping bags!" She giggles, amazed by her genius.

"It's *stranded,* Em," corrects Hannah with a sigh, sweeping aside hemlock branches. "Anyway, I've told you—that's not how the game works!"

"She'll get it eventually," I say. "It takes time."

"You did promise we would stay in the house tonight, Dad," Hannah reminds as we stumble into the clear. We all stare up at the vast, jeweled sky above us—a stunning respite between weather events. "Do you guys think that plan could maybe still work?"

I glance at her angular profile in the starlight, knowing that this is her way of asking if we will be all right, if we're going to make it past tomorrow. "We'll have to see, honey," I start.

The thorn of regret works its way deeper toward my center. "The place is kind of a mess now, and—"

"Let's give it a try," says Nathan, coming up beside me. He places the familiar breadth of his hand between my shoulder blades, behind my heart, his other hand gripping Emmie's thigh. It's difficult to hold his gaze, so pierced through with sadness, but I do.

Finally emerging from the woods, we tromp single file and freezing across the south meadow, hunched into the wind. At the top of the hill, our house still blazes with the light of our argument, unexpectedly bright against the new storm rolling in from the west.

★ ★ ★ ★ ★

ACKNOWLEDGMENTS

Because no writing happens in a vacuum, and because I am lucky enough to live in a rich community of writers, I have many people to thank.

First, huge gratitude to my fantastic agent, Jessica Papin, who's had unwavering faith in this story. Also to my gifted editor, Ann Leslie Tuttle, and all the people at MIRA Books who have showered me with enthusiasm and goodwill.

Many thanks to the writers (I can't name them all) who, through various Writers in Progress workshops, have offered their insights.

For valuable feedback on drafts, I thank the members of the WIP Manuscript Series and the Tuesday night manuscript group (especially Elli Meeropol, Celia Jeffries, Rita Marks and Jacqueline Sheehan), as well as India Nolen, David Lovelace, Linda Seligman, Peter Levitt and the talented Diana Gordon.

Big appreciation to Sarah Browning for her support through the whole process and for permission to use her poem "Something They Never Tell You."

My friend Julia Mines has bolstered me in the ups and downs, and I couldn't have steered through revisions without the solidarity and sharp editorial insight of Dix McComas.

And to my family: my mother, who offers boundless and unconditional support; my father, who has always expected good things; and my sister Renee, who shared it all. My husband, David, for his patience, love and deep insights, and my beautiful daughters, Audrey and Amelie, who put up with all my forays into fictional worlds.

For reader discussion questions,
please visit Dori Ostermiller's website,
www.doriostermiller.com.